THE LADY OF RAPTURE

Also by Sarah Raughley

The Bones of Ruin Trilogy
The Bones of Ruin

The Song of Wrath

The Effigies Trilogy
Fate of Flames

Siege of Shadows

Legacy of Light

Sarah Raughley

The Lady of Rapture

MARGARET K. MCELDERRY BOOKS

NEW YORK LONDON TORONTO SYDNEY NEW DELHI

MARGARET K. McELDERRY BOOKS
An imprint of Simon & Schuster Children's Publishing Division
1230 Avenue of the Americas, New York, New York 10020
Text © 2024 by Sarah Raughley
Jacket illustration © 2024 by Khadijah Khatib
Jacket design by Rebecca Syracuse
MARGARET K. McELDERRY BOOKS is a trademark of Simon & Schuster, LLC.
Simon & Schuster: Celebrating 100 Years of Publishing in 2024
For information about special discounts for bulk purchases, please contact Simon & Schuster Special Sales at 1-866-506-1949 or business@simonandschuster.com.
The Simon & Schuster Speakers Bureau can bring authors to your live event. For more information or to book an event, contact the Simon & Schuster Speakers Bureau at 1-866-248-3049 or visit our website at www.simonspeakers.com.
Interior design by Rebecca Syracuse
The text for this book was set in Matrix II OT.
Manufactured in the United States of America
First Edition
10 9 8 7 6 5 4 3 2 1
CIP data for this book is available from the Library of Congress.
ISBN 9781534453623
ISBN 9781534453647 (ebook)

TO EVERYONE WHO DARES
TO IMAGINE SOMETHING BETTER

THE LADY OF RAPTURE

ON THE EVE OF RAPTURE

AM THE EARTH, AND THE EARTH is me.

I do not know when I came into existence.

When I was born, so too was the earth.

And I was given the power over life and death.

Three gifts guide the shape and structure of reality: The ability to act. The will to act.

And the greatest of all: imagination.

It is justice that must determine the fate of humanity.

But what is justice?

One must choose what is right and what is wrong. And in my heart I could not.

So I gave my heart to you.

And so you were born of it. You are Hiva. You are justice.

"Anne, is that you?"

That is not my name.

Open your eyes.

Iris did as she was commanded. She awoke in a field that defied logic and mocked wonder. And yet she remembered it. This glorious field of crystal flowers. Their radical colors: every shade of pink, blue, purple, each too sharp to be real. White vines twisted around red trees underneath an eternal sunset. She remembered it all.

This was the earth's core, where souls gathered.

This was her home.

Everyone had a start. The earth may have had its physical core, made of stone and molten lava, but there existed a different "core" beyond the realm of space and time: a liminal, metaphysical space between dimensions. It was here her soul was created and here her soul had returned to after her murder.

Iris lifted a hand and let a golden butterfly perch upon her finger. It was good to finally remember. Like an itch that needed scratching, the secret of her identity had become somewhat of an obsession to her. Her "human" life had been filled with so much chaos and misery.

Misery.

"Jinn . . . ," she whispered, and when she closed her eyes, she felt it again: the violent thrust of a jagged sword made of her own bones. The sharp pain slicing her spine and her heart.

Jinn's reflection in the glass. His cold eyes staring back at her. Her anger stirred in her once more from deep in her stomach, hot and furious as it rose to her head and stifled each breath. *Jinn* had murdered her. After everything they'd been through. He'd taken up the sword forged by her enemies and dealt the final blow.

How else could she be here in the earth's core? She had been killed.

Her hands began to shake. She bit down on her lip to quell the pain of her memories, but they taunted her with relentless fury.

Rest. Rest now.

"Anne's" voice. It offered her little comfort, but as the seconds and minutes passed, she began to notice the clean air in her lungs again. There was much to do. Plans to be made. She couldn't lose her head now.

Now that she was finally home, she might as well rest awhile.

Revenge would come later.

When was the last time she'd returned here?

Ah yes. After destroying the Naacal. After her body had returned to dust inside Heaven's Shrine, her soul had returned here.

Inside the earth's core, up there in the sunset sky, as always, she could see the other earths. Not all of them. Some of them were too far away, obscured behind planets like hidden moons. Each of those earths had its own Hiva. Each had its own civilization cooking up monstrosities and disasters that warranted their deaths.

"Do you know about the other earths?" Iris asked the One who created her.

Yes, she answered. *On one earth, humans have become enslaved by the machines they've built. On another earth, four warriors battle in an endless cycle against creatures of nightmare that move like phantoms across the lands. On one earth, the diseases of bigotry, capitalist greed, and political strife have brought the planet and its billions of inhabitants to the brink of collapse.*

And on another earth, they plot our destruction.

"Our destruction?"

Or rather, the destruction of humans. They've heard the distortions of space and time echoing from our earth. They lie in wait to strike and conquer. All they need is for someone to open a door.

"And you don't care?"

The godlike creature did not immediately answer.

No matter the circumstances, humanity always seems to come to an end. Whether by Hiva's hand or another. Humanity's folly always leads to its destruction. I watched it for many cycles before I brought you into existence, and then I watched it for many more cycles after. If there is another way, then I have not yet seen it. Perhaps I'm incapable of seeing it.

Another way. The words reminded her of someone—the Hiva who'd orchestrated her death. An alien prince searching across dimensions for an answer to that same question, craving friendship and camaraderie.

Hiva. She remembered his golden skin and earthy locks as he'd embraced the Naacal's children in a field of yellow flowers. Hiva. Unlike Iris, he had no other name. Nature loved him. It had sensed his kindness and his hope—the simplest of desires:

Rather, I was hoping for companionship. Is it all right, Hiva, if I call you sister?

But Hiva was justice. Why did he wish for what he did not need?

Recalling came at a cost. She could no longer run from those painful memories.

The golden butterfly fluttered off her finger, and Iris suddenly remembered a flock of golden birds taking off into the thundering sky, the rushing winds battering Hiva's long locks. The betrayal etched in his face. The fury.

Even the children? he'd cried after she'd burned down a barn filled with frightened families. *Even the children, sister?*

The Naacal had loved her once. The civilizations she'd murdered had always seemed to love her before their adoration rotted and only hatred remained. The Lemurians and the Atlanteans had worshipped her too. And each time, when she'd brought the apocalypse down upon their heads, they had cursed her, as if her cleansings were unjustified. They'd fought back. They'd used every means to destroy her, even if it meant sacrificing their own.

Like the Naacal. Like that abhorrent day.

Iris closed her eyes, the memory all too dreadfully clear. The civilization of the Naacal had been under siege. She'd already murdered half the world. Their desperation had reached its peak. And so they had called upon a weapon of nightmare to destroy her.

There was a mountain range at the northern tip of the central continent. From inside the tallest of the mountains had emerged the Titans: mechanical monsters that looked and moved like spiders. They were the size of little moons themselves. Bigger than the most fearsome structure she'd seen made by human hands. The Naacal reserved Titans for only their greatest foes, using them in their most fearsome wars. They were weapons to obliterate the Naacal's enemies and threaten their oppressed into obedience. They were bombs, ready to annihilate anything with the click of a mere device.

Nyeth had told Iris all about them in the days he'd worshipped her. He'd shown her scrolls on their design and instruction hidden in a secret underground facility. He'd shown her the device. The device that shut them on and off at a whim.

"They are energy weapons powered by nuclear fission," Nyeth had told her. "Their blasts are said to be more powerful than the strike of a god's hand. The Solar Titan and Shadow Titan together can destroy an entire continent within one week." Nyeth showed her the shimmering tablet, upon which the

Naacalian symbols of the sun and moon were etched. "With just one touch of a button, we can activate them. Then the Titans will crawl out of their mountain dwelling place, ready for war."

At the time, Iris had wondered why Nyeth had been so proud of these aberrations. She'd destroyed their civilization before he could ever use them on her.

The Titans wouldn't have killed her anyway. No mechanical device made by man could fell her. The worst those machines would have done was blow away her body, but as long as her crystal heart lived on, so would she.

The Naacal, however, did not live on.

Iris had taken so many lives across so many generations—eons. It was about time, she supposed, that someone put a stop to her. She just never expected that it would be Jinn.

Iris hung her head, her fingers digging into her palms, irritated rather than calmed when more golden butterflies landed upon her head.

Being murdered by someone she loved. Was this recompense for her own millennia of murder? But she'd never asked for this life. She'd never asked to be justice. And she'd never forced humanity to be so wicked that her judgment would be the same every time she was called to hand down her verdict.

"It's all your fault," Iris whispered, a single hot tear dripping from her eyelashes before she wiped it away in a fit of rage. "You . . . you *humans*. You always deserved to die each time."

If justice shaped the future of humanity, then why did so many humans care not one bit for it? Why was it an afterthought for kings and ministers? From generals to landlords, even the weakest of men found ways to stomp on those even more powerless. It was the same in every era of humanity. People could not think beyond themselves.

Henry Whittle had wished to protect his toymaker grandfather and his maid, Mary White, who'd loved them both.

The shape-shifter Lucille Bouffant, if that was even her true name, had wished to live life recklessly with whatever identity she pleased, enjoying life's pleasures.

Lawrence Hawkins and Jacob Josefiub had loved each other. They'd cared for Cherice Winterbottom, the little sister in their group of thieves. Also among them, Maximo Morales, whose desperation to protect his sister trumped everything—even his newfound friendship with Iris.

Iris smirked bitterly. Maybe she was the only one arrogant enough to think that the bonds they'd built in such a short period of time had meant something. That she'd found a new family to make up for the lack thereof in her life. But among the myopic desires of each person she'd come across, in their narrow fantasies of the ideal lives they wanted to lead, Iris counted for very little.

She'd hoped, at least, that Jinn would be different. The thought of his sturdy chest and hot lips. Those whispers of reassurance. What she thought was love. They'd fooled her so perfectly. She'd meant nothing to him. She'd meant nothing to any of them. She was nothing but an obstacle that had needed to be wiped from the earth. Jinn had proved that. They all had.

Iris opened her eyes and saw more butterflies hovering over her head. "Humans are such vicious creatures," she said. "Why can they never be better?"

Anne sat next to her on her little brown knees, weaving her hands around an orb of light hovering above Iris's chest.

Ah, no. Her name wasn't Anne. Iris kept forgetting.

Iris had always known this being as the One who had created her, but right now, as Iris rested in this crystal field, she couldn't quite remember the goddess's true name. "Anne" would do for now.

Anne seemed preoccupied with the orb in her hands, and Iris knew why: that was her crystal heart. Anne was remaking it for her.

After Jinn had murdered her, she remembered desperately wanting to live again. To live and bring destruction down upon mankind for what they had done to her. She had finally embraced her bloody destiny. She would destroy humanity. She would do so happily. And for that, she would need Anne to remake her immortal body once more.

"How long will it take?" Iris asked, impatient.

Time flows differently here. By the time you reawaken in your true form, weeks will have passed. Months. Perhaps even years.

No, that wouldn't do at all. She wanted to become Hiva now. It was the decision she'd made from the pits of despair.

Jinn had *murdered* her.

Her partner. Her friend. The man she loved, though her heart ached to admit it. Instead of believing in her, he'd decided to rid the world of her in order to save humanity.

It was only fitting that she destroy humanity instead.

Such vicious creatures, humans.

The other Hiva had been such a fool when she'd first met him. So desperate was he to save the flawed humans he so loved that he'd given up his own arm, just so they could use his bones to murder her—not realizing until it was too late that the only bones that could kill her were her own. He had still been pleading with her when she'd sent him hurtling through dimensions.

"Isn't there another way?" he'd asked her once. Before the destruction of the Naacal had broken him.

She knew the answer now, just as much as she had then. There was no other way. They *all* had to die.

After her death at Jinn's hands, her heart had been crashing against her ribs, each brutal beat reminding her of her agony. But as each minute passed while Anne remade her, she noted curiously that this same agony had begun to feel somehow far away. Soon she became oddly detached from her emotions. Memories of her past life began to clear; her love, her fear, her happiness, and her excitement—they all began to float away, carried into the eternal sunset sky.

Even her hatred was leaving her.

"No." Iris clenched her fists. "Don't take away my hatred. I *need* that." It was unorthodox, yes. In the olden days, as she'd decimated cultures, she'd done so without a shred of emotion. It was how Hiva had been created to be. But not this time. "Without it, I can't become the Hiva that *I* want to be. Please! Even a little would do."

And what kind of Hiva do you wish to show the world?

One who would murder her enemies ruthlessly, who could utterly crush those who'd turned their backs on her without hesitation, but still relish the taste of retribution. She didn't want to simply judge and incinerate humankind. She wanted to *enjoy* it.

She wanted only to complete the mission she had been given: to bask in the blood of civilizations.

There was no other way to define herself as Hiva, the cataclysm. The destroyer of worlds. No other way to conceive of herself or her future.

This was the limit of her imagination.

A Hiva capable of emotion. Anne studied her for a long while. Then came the goddess's reply: *I will give you all that you want.*

"You will?" As much as Iris wanted this, there was a tiny, hidden part of her that feared this answer as well.

I will. But to become Hiva again and yet retain some remnants of the pain that made you Iris, you must pay a price.

"Anything," Iris pleaded with her. "Tell me what you want me to give, and I'll give it."

I will give you a part of me each time I remake you. So give me a part of you in return. Of your body, what part do you deem most precious?

Iris thought for a moment. When she realized her decision, she couldn't help but notice the irony in speaking it. "My voice. I will give you my voice."

For a moment, Iris swore she saw pity in Anne's eyes. *Your voice is connected to your soul. Your soul is connected to your self.* Anne gave a soft nod. *Yes, that will do.*

What a small price to pay. "Iris" was a bumbling fool who couldn't even win the trust of the ones she'd loved most. She fought and failed. She cried, helpless, hopeless. "Iris" was a blight. "Iris" was a self she didn't need. *Hiva* would exist in her place.

And the rapture would begin.

Before I remake you once more, remember that this is your home. And you can come back to it. If ever you so desire, if ever you crave it with your whole being, I will bring you home.

Iris nodded. But she knew that she wouldn't come back, *couldn't* come back—not until her work was done. Not until her revenge was complete.

Anne's astute gaze sharpened. *And perhaps one more thing,* the great goddess said. *Your desires go against the reason for your very existence. Hiva is justice, not vengeance. So you must give me the life of the person you most want to see dead. That person cannot die by your hand.*

She wanted to argue as Anne plucked the name right out of her mind. But she couldn't speak. She'd already given up her voice. The decision had been made. The deal done.

And so the woman once known as "Iris" slept.

This was how humanity's final year began.

PART ONE
The Evacuated Body

If the body as evidence locates the proof of existence, thereby equating visibility with existence, what happens under, during, and through displacement in slavery, colonialism, and apartheid? What kind of subjectivity, reality is shaped under these circumstances?

If the body as presence is evidence, how does the absent body map and negotiate subjectivity?

"Julle Moet Nou Trek" is Afrikaans for the command "You must move."

The evacuated body is represented by the imprint it has left on the sand.

—PUMLA DINEO GQOLA,
"SHACKLED MEMORIES AND ELUSIVE DISCOURSES?,"
ON BERNI SEARLE'S "JULLE MOET NOU TREK"
FROM THE BLOEDLYN EXHIBITION (1999)

1

MAX'S HANDS SLIPPED OFF THE COOL, rough surface of Iris's bone—remnants of her forearm sharpened into a deadly blade. He stumbled back, his mouth parted, his heart pounding in his ears, as two corpses collapsed to the ground at the same time.

Jinn and Iris.

Partners.

Lovers.

Lovers. They were lovers, weren't they? They'd been lovers long before Max had met either of them. None of the childish stunts he'd pulled had managed to change that. Not even this final one.

It took Max's mind a moment to catch up to what he'd done. Hiva, the other god of death, had appeared with his friends in tow. He'd brought them a sword made of Iris's bones and given them all a choice: kill Iris here and now, or risk her turning against humanity.

For Max, the choice had been clear.

He'd taken the bone sword and run Iris through. But not before Jinn had leapt in front of her.

To protect her.

Now blood seeped from their bodies and pooled against the marble floor of the Coral Temple.

This was Maximo's crime.

"I had to do it," Max whispered to their dead bodies, and then again to his own wide-eyed, unfocused reflection in the cracked glass of Hiva's Tomb. Iris's last breath remained on the chilled cylinder.

Hiva's Tomb. The Naacal, an ancient civilization, had created this technological wonder. Whoever stepped inside the glass chamber would become "disassembled" down to their very atoms. Iris had refused to walk inside. She wouldn't sacrifice herself, even if it meant she would one day fulfill her biological purpose and burn down the world.

That's why Max had had to do it. In that one moment when he'd felt his hands grip the sword made from her bones, he'd made the decision to bear the responsibility of her death. It was his duty as her friend. It was what he'd *had* to do to save countless lives.

Max was too dazed to block Rin's sword bearing down upon his head. He looked up and saw the glint of its sharp edge.

"Max!"

Max barely registered the frantic cry of his childhood friend Lawrence Hawkins as the young man tackled him to the ground. Rin's sword crashed against the floor where he'd been standing.

Rin, the Dahomean warrior, who had followed Iris all the way here, to the ends of the earth.

Her attack thwarted, Rin's resultant cry of fury shuddered through Max's bones. As Hawkins held him in a vice grip on the floor, Max spied the tears streaming down Rin's round cheeks.

Max's body was numb. His fingers throbbed painfully. He was a hero. Why didn't she understand that?

While his childhood friends Cherice and Jacob watched, frozen, it was his sister Berta who lunged forward and grabbed Rin's sword-wielding arm.

"Stop!" Berta screamed, her dark curls spilling over her face. "Stop, damn it!"

Berta and Rin were both young, younger than he was, and yet both had been forced into a warrior's life through no fault of their own. He couldn't protect Berta when they'd been separated as children. He wanted to protect her now, but his mind was hollowed out, and once he stood, his legs couldn't support his weight. Only Hawkins kept him upright, pulling him away from the battle toward Cherice and Jacob.

"Berta! Keep that crazy *savage* away from us!" shouted a boy Max didn't know, a lanky bloke with tan skin and crooked teeth standing on the edge of the dais. Max hadn't caught his name, but he could tell how cowardly he was by the way the boy's knees knocked. The little girl next to him, Lulu, seemed far more composed. Though she gripped her dress tightly, she watched the scene carefully, silently, waiting to see who'd come out victorious.

Berta had to wrap her entire upper body around Rin's arm to keep it still. "It's done. She's gone. What did you expect him to do now? Just let it go!"

Rin was shouting something back, but Max couldn't understand her. He didn't speak Fon. He didn't need to. Her bloodlust and pain signaled her murderous desires. He could almost hear their echoes bouncing off the walls of the dark temple.

"It's done," Berta cried, shouting in pain when Rin pushed her down to the floor. "You're pissed, I get it! But what's the point of shedding any more blood now? Stop! I don't want to hurt you, but I will!"

She wasn't in any position to be making threats. Rin hissed something vicious and lifted her sword.

Time slowed.

It'd slowed for Max that day too: when he, as a child, had seen that carriage steal his little sister away. When he had been left stranded in London, alone and frightened.

Never again.

Max's body moved on its own. He held his breath. His senses heightened. Rin's sword whooshed through the air as her strike slowed to a crawl. Berta's cry began to spring off her lips as she raised her arm to block the blow. Bodies in slow motion. All were affected except him. For that short moment, Max was time's master.

And he would only need a moment.

He strode over to Rin and plucked her sword out of her hand.

No. She'll just be able to summon it again, he thought to himself.

THE LADY OF RAPTURE

That was Rin's power—summoning a sword from inside her chest. Iris was dead. Rin wouldn't stop. Not until she had sated her need for revenge.

Max needed to kill her. *Now.*

And why not? He'd killed before. On that pirate ship, he'd murdered whomever he'd needed to if it meant he'd survive, if it meant he'd find his family again. Hadn't he killed his way through those British soldiers too, to get to the mining site that had held everyone's fates? Rin was loyal to Iris and Jinn. He'd already killed the latter two. Kill the third and he'd be in the clear.

Since the moment he'd been bamboozled into coming to England as a child, since the moment he'd been left on the streets of London as an orphan, since the moment he'd lost his sister, Max had only ever done what he'd had to in order to survive.

I really am such an asshole, Max thought to himself with a wry smile as he flipped Rin's sword around and readied himself to stab the young girl.

But out of the corner of his eye, he saw him: a man whose existence shouldn't have been possible. A statuesque body crafted from bronze. Curling brown hair stretching down to his waist. A chiseled face cut from glass. Pupilless golden eyes watching him with interest, unaffected by space or time.

The other Hiva. Max had almost forgotten he was there, but at the sight of the other god, in the sudden realization of his presence, Max jolted in fear. His breath hitched. And the moment he breathed again, time began to flow.

The spell was broken. It took Rin seconds to realize what Max had done. She squeezed her empty hands into fists, furious. Swearing, Max tried to run her through but missed, as Rin dodged his strike and kicked him in the stomach.

The sword flew from his hands and landed upon the dais's marble floor, breaking into pieces, disappearing into dust. And just as Max had anticipated, Rin summoned it again, pulling it out from her chest.

Max didn't have time to think. He instinctively lunged for Berta, hooking her around the waist with his arm and pulling her back, away from Rin to where Cherice, Jacob, and Hawkins stood. He'd wasted his chance. Slowing down time always sapped his energy from his body, leaving his bones worn. There wasn't anything he could do now but distract her.

"Hiva!" Max grunted, pointing wildly behind Rin. "Hiva! *Hiva!*"

It was like, in the aftermath of Iris's death, they had all forgotten that there was another god of death who could burn them all to ashes. And *this* god had no reason not to.

That's right, Max thought as he saw Rin suddenly realize it too, her gaze following his finger to the false god calmly watching them. *Hiva is the real threat here.*

Just like that, their battle felt like a petty squabble. Like Iris, Hiva could burn people from the inside out. But this wasn't Iris. Max had no idea what to expect from this particular monster.

Rin lowered her arms. For a time nobody moved. Silence descended upon the group, because all had realized what Max had: that their lives were in another demon's hands now.

Suddenly Rin lunged for the god, her sword raised, ready to land a blow. The American boy—the one Lulu had called "Fables"—screamed and shrank away, but he needn't have worried. Hiva didn't even look at her as he dodged her sword and backhanded her in the face so hard, it broke her nose and split her lips. Max watched, horrified, as the young woman hit the floor hard, her head bouncing awkwardly against the marble. She was knocked unconscious.

It was strange. Rin had been his enemy a minute ago, but his heart now dropped as he saw the young girl's body twitching on the floor. She looked like a helpless child. She *was* a child. What had Hiva done to her? What had *he* done to her?

As he saw Rin bleeding, something in Max began to break, but he didn't want to admit it. He didn't want to notice the way Berta looked at the other girl—with anguish and pity. Instead he stood in front of Berta, lifting his chin in some desperate attempt to look in control.

"You're Hiva too, aren't you? Iris—" Her name caught in his throat almost as if it wanted to choke him. "Iris is dead. I . . . killed her."

"You did."

And then Hiva moved.

Hiva's lumbering steps toward Iris's corpse echoed across the walls. Rin backed away, her hands clenched as the monster pulled the bone sword out of Iris's and Jinn's bodies. Max flinched when Jinn's right arm twitched.

Jinn. You were always one step ahead of me when it came to her. Max gritted his teeth as he remembered Iris's circus partner throwing himself in front of Max's attack in a hopeless attempt to save Iris. What Max had felt for Iris had been nothing more than attraction and fascination. It couldn't compare to Jinn's feelings for her. He knew that now. Max had betrayed Iris twice. Jinn had died for her.

"H-Hiva!" The strange American boy scrambled to Hiva's side, throwing his arms around his chest and holding on to him for dear life. "Hiva, you did it! You killed that wretched witch!" He looked up at him with shimmering eyes of reverence. "It's what you wanted, right?"

Technically, he was correct. Hiva had set up this entire encounter to get rid of Iris.

So why didn't he look satisfied?

Why was his expression so confused, so hollow, as he stared down at Iris's body?

"Sister . . . ," Hiva whispered, turning the bone sword again in her hand. "My revenge is complete. The Naacal's revenge is complete."

His limp fingers just barely held on to Iris's bone.

"So . . . who're you gonna kill next?"

It wasn't Max or any of his friends who'd spoken. It was the child. It was Lulu.

The American girl trembled as she stared at Iris's body. Her wide doe eyes seemed to look past Iris, past the bloodied temple floor, at something Max couldn't see. She was a girl haunted by ghosts that never truly left her sight—because that's what tragedy was, and this girl had experienced it. She knew it when she saw it. But she'd also learned how to deal with it in her own unique way. Squeezing her eyes shut, she rubbed her little brown hands down her dress. Then, when she was ready, she tilted her head and addressed the god again.

"You've come to kill the wicked, haven't you?" she reminded him. "Then Miss Iris was . . ." She looked back at Berta as if waiting for some kind of validation for her wordless indictment.

Wicked. Then Iris was wicked too. Wasn't she?

While spending time with Lulu in the port city of Ajashe, Max had wondered so many things about her, and she'd straightforwardly answered every one of his questions.

Who are you? *Lulu.*

Where are you from? *Oklahoma.*

Where's your family? *Dead. They hung 'em in a tree.*

How did you meet Berta? *She saved me from being lynched by those white people.*

All with the innocence and clarity of one who had already made up her mind about what this world was like. That was why her cherubic brown face looked suddenly hopeful now. She waited for Hiva's answer as one did the judgment of a righteous angel.

But Hiva didn't seem to know himself. "Next . . ." It was the one word he seemed to have heard Lulu say. "Who do I kill next . . . ? What comes next . . . ?"

Who was he asking? *Iris?*

Hiva's eyes were fixed on the dead. Max followed the god's gaze. That was when he finally noticed.

Iris was decomposing.

With the weapon made from her own body finally extracted from her flesh, that flesh began to deteriorate, skin charring, organs smoking as if her body had been placed into a furnace. And as the smoke curled up into the air, Hiva began to twitch—slowly first, then more violently.

"The people's revenge." He sucked in a deep breath through his nose and exhaled years of pain, eons of the history between them. "The children's revenge. The children you killed, sister . . . I've given them your death as penance."

Lifting his head as if in pain or ecstasy, with his eyes round and bulging, Hiva began wheezing as if he'd run around the whole world, as if he were on the verge of laughter. Unhinged. The sight was shocking enough to freeze everyone in place.

"Praise me, my old friends," Hiva begged, to someone Max couldn't see. "Tell me that I did well, Nyeth. Tell me I avenged the children."

No one answered.

Hiva inhaled and exhaled in a frenzy, until there was nothing left of Iris's body but ash.

No. Not just ash.

Iris's crystal heart remained. The size of a real, beating human heart but round like an orb. By no means was it smooth. There were creases and crevices carved into the crystal, bloodless veins etched into the white surface.

Hiva went very still. "Sister. Why didn't you listen to me? You should have listened to me before you killed them all."

Hiva bent down, picked up Iris's crystal heart, and stared at it for some time.

And then he crushed it in his hand. White dust slipped through his fingers and collected in a pile on the floor.

"Maxey! Get a hold of yourself!"

As Max's knees buckled, someone caught him around the waist. Cherice. It was her voice that had called him, probably, but nobody could stop his stomach from heaving. Heat flushed from the skin of his cheeks up to his eyes, drawing tears as bile burned his throat. The contents of his stomach, pouring over his hands onto the floor, reminded him of Iris's blood, now mixed in her ashes.

Iris. He thought of her shy smile whenever he'd tease her in Club Uriel. Her delight in Whittle's toy shop. Making her laugh back then had felt like a triumph. A badge of boyish honor.

Hiva rolled Jinn's body away and dipped his fingers into Iris's remains. "You brought this on yourself, sister. The children needed revenge. Now they have it."

"I—I did that." Max was mumbling now, swaying on his feet, remembering with a tactile kind of disgust just what it had felt like to pulverize her heart. *What have I done?* "I killed her. I killed them both." *Iris, what have I done?*

"You had to." Berta moved quickly, curling her fingers around his shirt and pushing against his chest. "You didn't have a choice. She was going to kill us all."

She said it, but Max saw the way she turned and took in the sight of Rin, still unconscious on the floor. Max could hear his sister's voice wavering as she told him he didn't have a choice.

"She was going to kill us all," Max repeated to himself, a salve to his ever-crumbling resolve, though he no longer quite believed the words.

"And *he* still might. Hiva." Jacob stood in front of the group, lifting his arms, but the protective gesture was just that—a gesture. What could any of them do against Hiva?

Damn it. Clenching his teeth, Max gripped Berta's wrists and drew her in as he and his thieving childhood friends closed ranks. He'd been so fixated on what Iris might do, he hadn't even thought of dealing with the aftermath. As the adrenaline began to wear off, questions he should have considered the moment he arrived inside the Coral Temple began popping up one by one. "Why the hell are you working with Frankenstein in the first place? What happened?"

"We didn't exactly have a choice," Hawkins hissed. They were all so close, Max could feel Hawkins's arm stiffen against his side.

"You still don't."

Hiva had said this so simply, he almost sounded human. He stared at the bone sword in his hand, far more fascinated with it than he was with them.

And yet.

"I . . . need you," Hiva said, throwing the sword aside.

Max heard Cherice's sharp gasp behind him. She pressed her head against his back as she wrapped her arms around his stomach. He could feel her every tremble.

"What are you on about?" Jacob replied. His voice always deepened to a low rumble when he was frightened. "What could you possibly *need* us for?"

Hiva didn't answer immediately. He stared at Iris's ashes. Then he turned toward Lulu. The little girl gave a start, but Hiva didn't look particularly murderous.

He smiled at her.

"What comes next?" he said, repeating her question. "I am Hiva. I was created for a purpose. To judge the world and allow it to be born anew—even if that means destroying humanity in the process. That is what Hivas must do."

But Max had *killed* Iris for that very reason, hadn't he? Did Hiva not realize that? Max shook his head, his heart beating harder against his chest as the god began to repeat to himself: "It is what we Hivas do. We live in solitude

THE LADY OF RAPTURE

in the space between life and death. And when we are finished, we return, alone, to silence. There is no other way. There is no other way. . . . Is there, sister?"

Iris, of course, did not answer. She had already gone ahead into that silence.

"So you'll kill me?" Lulu asked bravely, though she clenched her hands together.

Her innocent question seemed to give Hiva a start. "No." He shook his head quickly. "I wouldn't kill you. Never you. Not the innocent children . . ."

He held out his hand for Lulu to take. She didn't.

"I need you all for my journey." Hiva turned and placed his golden hand upon the glass of Hiva's Tomb. "I'm curious about the world my sister had been so desperate to live in. The world that was built after she destroyed the Naacal."

Sister, sister. Hiva kept calling her that. But Max wasn't sure what exactly that meant—were they related by blood? What exactly *were* these death gods? Where had they come from? What history had led them down this bloody path?

He could have just asked Iris if he hadn't killed her.

"The life cycle of Hiva always begins and ends the same way. Should humanity truly die? Upon being brought back to life by the One who created us, we would travel the world to answer this question. Only after observing humankind would we start the calamity. There is no other way." He paused, staring at Iris's ashes. "There is . . . no other way . . ."

Hiva's golden fingers were sturdy and long as he curled them. "My sister used to observe humans without feeling and kill them without remorse. She killed them all. She hunted them all down and burned them to ash. Even the children."

His voice trailed off, as if he'd suddenly lost himself in his own memories. He looked toward Lulu, his lips curling as she scuttled away from him.

"But somehow, sister changed. She became . . . 'Iris.' A new being entirely. What is this world, then—this civilization that transformed my sister in such a drastic way? Should that same civilization be destroyed? I'll find out after I've completed my journey."

He faced them. "One year." Without a change in his expression, he held up a finger. "You will journey with me as my guides. It's as I've done in the past for eons." He lowered his hand and touched his chin thoughtfully. "Within one year, I will almost certainly destroy humanity."

Max's stomach dropped. He couldn't feel his hands.

"What the hell is that?" Berta pulled away from the group. "What's this 'one year' bullshit? Within one year, you'll kill us?" Max could hear her quick, haggard breaths as her chest rose and fell. "Sounds like you've already made up your damn mind, don't you think?"

"So you will kill me," Lulu said.

"I would never kill children," Hiva answered. "Never the children."

"But you'll destroy humanity," Jacob pressed.

"Yes."

"It's the same damn thing!" Berta screamed. "Do you even hear yourself?"

Hiva was unperturbed. "It's as I've always done. There is no other way."

It was as if he didn't register the contradiction. Whatever had happened between Hiva and Iris in the past had left him a confused god with the power of life and death in his hands.

"You're certifiably mad, is what you are," Hawkins scoffed, his voice high-pitched enough to betray his fear. "Judge us? Some judge. What's the point of observing humanity if you're just going to kill us anyway?"

"The One who created me calls me forth to complete one task. First I observe. Then I judge." Hiva's eyes flashed. "That the judgment is always the same is the fault of humans."

It was then that Max realized, as his mouth dried and his teeth chattered, that he had murdered the wrong Hiva.

He'd killed his friend.

A grievous crime committed for nothing.

"That sounds great," said the lanky American, who rubbed his hands together with a lovestruck grin. "What's another year?"

"Fables, you ragged dumbass, you shut your mouth!" Berta snapped. Breaking away from Max, she ran to Lulu, who'd been standing alone, and grabbed her hand. "No. No, I ain't gonna let you do it."

That git, Fables, scoffed. "Since when did *you* become a hero? I thought you didn't give a damn about anything or anyone." He shrugged. "Don't matter anyway. When Hiva says jump, you jump. Unless you want to end up as another pile of ashes."

"You damn suck-up!" Berta yelled, and dropping Lulu's hand, she launched herself at Fables. The boy shrieked as the weight of Max's sister fell on top of him. Like a clockwork automaton whose wheels needed greasing, Hiva shifted his head to stare at the ruckus.

That's when Rin struck. Max hadn't seen her wake up. He didn't know how long she'd been playing dead, waiting for her chance. It was while Berta and Fables squabbled that she launched up like a rocket.

"Cut off his head!" Max yelled. He needn't have. Rin was already going for a clean sweep across his neck.

Until Hiva's hand found hers.

What happened next, Max couldn't quite understand. Hiva lifted Rin off her feet. As her sword clattered to the ground, a bone-shuddering *crack* curdled Max's blood.

Rin's arm. Hiva had snapped it. But that was the least of it. Rin was a warrior. She could handle a broken arm. But *this* . . .

Hiva placed his finger upon Rin's right eyeball. Steam began to rise from her face.

Rin screamed as her eye sizzled and melted. Her limbs, head, torso—everything was twitching.

Hiva was burning her from the inside out.

As she burned away, so too did the last bit of resolve he clung to—the resolve that he'd somehow made the right decision in killing Iris. His resistance to the truth. His denial. All of it burned away until only self-loathing remained. Before he knew it, helpless, desperate words were spilling from Max's lips.

"We'll do it! We'll go with you! Please don't kill her! Don't kill her, *God!*"

Rin's body fell to the floor with a thump. The slight spasm of her lips told Max she was still alive but just barely.

The smell of burning flesh. Like rotten eggs. The *inhumanity.* Max unraveled.

Jacob ran to Rin, cradling her in his arms. The kind boy choked back his tears, stroking her face, chin, and neck and then whispering to her as she wheezed and coughed in pain.

"We'll do it," Max whispered again. "We'll do it. Right?" Max looked from Hawkins to Jacob. Then he pried Cherice's fingers off his stomach and turned around, bending until he was at her eye level. "Right?"

Cherice, usually all sass, looked drained of life. She could barely manage a squeak.

Hiva had already been traveling with his sister and the Americans. Why go so far as to collect more of them? Why did he need more humans by his side?

Max stared into Hiva's empty eyes, and something curious glimmered there. Nameless. There was a whole lot he didn't understand about this volatile creature, but as Hiva stretched out his hand to them almost hopefully, he wondered just how much Hiva understood about *himself.*

"Come, then," the death god said. "Come with me."

It wasn't quite a command. To Max's ears, it sounded almost like a request.

Prying herself off Fables, Berta ran to Lulu and gripped her tightly. Fables spat on the ground and dusted himself off.

"We will use the same power that brought us here," said Hiva.

Hawkins was up to bat.

"We will teleport to the destinations of my choosing," Hiva said, and then paused. "After I rid this world of humanity, I will then go to the next world and destroy it. It is as it should be."

Jacob began to lift Rin, his features twisted in hopeless terror, when Max, thinking quickly, put out a hand to stop him.

"Leave her; she's useless now," Max said, shooting a quick glance to Hiva, who didn't seem to object. "Unless . . ." And he looked deep into Jacob's dark eyes. "Unless you have something special you'd like to give her."

At first Jacob just stared at him, confused. But then it was as if the hint in Max's intense glare had finally struck him.

"As always, friend, I'm way ahead of you," Jacob responded very seriously.

So it was already done. Perhaps when he'd first held Rin. Good. Max knew he could count on Jacob out of everyone. After stroking Rin's face and neck one last time, Jacob stood and followed Hawkins and Cherice.

Max dragged himself forward. He slowed down to let Hawkins, Cherice, and Jacob go to Hiva first. And when he passed by Rin, he bent down to caress her head. Her braids shifted a little across her shoulder as she struggled to breathe.

Max knew Hiva was watching these curious displays of affection. But as far as he knew, Hiva didn't have enhanced hearing and knew nothing of Jacob's power. That was why Max kept his voice in a whisper when he lowered his lips to Rin's ears.

"Go to Uma and tell her everything. Warn everyone. We all have one year to live."

Max didn't know if Rin's flinch was confirmation that she understood his words or another attempt to kill him. He wouldn't have minded either. She had every right to hate him. She was a better person than he could ever be. That was why he trusted her with this mission.

Trusted her with his sister.

As Max and his childhood friends gathered around Hiva and Fables, as Hawkins used his power to open up his blue portal, Max pushed Berta, who was still holding Lulu tightly, out of the void. The two girls cried out and tripped, hitting the ground next to Jinn's dead body and Iris's pile of ashes.

And it was as Max stared at Iris's pile of ashes that Rin opened her mouth and whispered just his name again and again.

"Maximo . . ."

Just his name, as if to ask him why he'd left her behind.

Tears streamed down Max's cheeks. "I'm so sorry, Rin," he mouthed as he disappeared with Hiva.

2

R IN GRITTED HER TEETH AND BORE the pain when the villagers
snapped her arm back into place. Her nerves twinged and whined like
broken strings of a violin. Her tongue went numb. She tried to keep a
brave face. She was a warrior. It was what she was trained to do—

Until they began to cut out her half-melted eye.

"Hold her down!" a woman screamed.

"There's too much blood! We have to keep removing the dead tissue!" said
the doctor.

"What did you say?"

"I said, don't stop removing the dead eye tissue!"

The doctor's assistant couldn't hear him because Rin's shrieks of pain cut
through each word with shuddering ferocity, no doubt shaking the straw off
the thatched roof in this hut turned makeshift hospital. It was her damaged
eye anyway, the result of one of her earliest battles against the Egba clan. Her
right eye couldn't see, but she'd always felt a kind of comfort in being able to
feel it in its socket.

"Heat the metal," said the doctor to his assistants, his bare brown chest
glistening with sweat. A simple sheet of brown cloth covered his loins.

But sense and reason began to slip away when she felt the metal tools slip
into her eye socket and finally cut away the dead, rotting flesh Hiva had left

behind. He'd chosen only one eye to burn—not her head, not a limb, and not her whole body. Was it his show of mercy? Or the cruel game of a wicked god?

"We need to prepare for cauterization," said the doctor solemnly.

Rin wasn't sure what was more surprising—that they were able to find a doctor in this tiny village, or that she could actually understand what they were saying. After so many years with the Dahomey, she'd begun to think in Fon. So much of the intricacies of Yoruba, her native tongue, had begun to disappear from her memory. Then again, anyone could understand that look of sheer pity the doctor gave her before he handed a slender metal rod to his assistant to heat in the campfire just outside. Rin could see it through the open door of animal skins held up by string on either side. She could see the almost-dead bodies of two men by the fire.

John Temple and Jinn. Would they make it? Would she?

As the smoke of the fire rose, the villagers threw in palm nuts and animal bones to aid in their prayers. There were many ways to heal someone, after all. Science, medicine, and drugs were enough to heal Rin of her problems, but with those two near-corpses, the villagers had decided only the intervention of their gods could spark the dwindling life inside them.

Gods, huh? But not even the Moon Goddess could save Isoke . . .

Max's sister stood outside with them, nervously sneaking a peek inside the tent before reddening and turning back around. Rin guessed for all her bluster, she couldn't handle the bloodier mess in here. Amateur.

"Wait," Rin murmured, because in one corner of the hut, a villager was twisting an object around in his hand: a skeleton key as pure white as the mystical sword she called forth in battle. It caught the light, just as Isoke's own crystal heart had before it had disintegrated into dust.

The Moon Skeleton.

"Give that back . . . ," Rin murmured, trying pathetically to reach for it. "Don't touch that," she wanted to add, but her throat was closing.

"I've got you," said that little American girl, Lulu, who knelt next to her, almost obscuring Rin's vision of the fire outside. Her little hands grabbed Rin's reddening palm tightly, shaking with earnestness as tears filled her eyes. "I won't let you go."

Damn Jacob, that sentimental brat. It was his fault that Rin could now understand English.

It was his power, the same ability he'd displayed during the Tournament of Freaks: he could give or take away others' languages. Maybe he'd thought he was doing her a favor. But she didn't want to know what this little girl was saying. Rin didn't want to hear her pity.

When the doctor's assistant came back with a smoking rod, a whimper escaped Rin's lips. Two other men held her down so she wouldn't escape.

"I won't let you go!" cried Lulu, and the sound of the girl's voice grated Rin's ears and filled her with an inexplicable rage that made her want to throw Lulu out of the hut. But she was helpless. Helpless against these doctors. Helpless against the pain. Helpless against that traitor Max. Helpless against Hiva.

"Okay, let's begin," said the doctor.

Helpless.

Rin screamed until she passed out.

"Miss Rin? Miss Rin? Are you okay?"

Sunlight streamed through the hut's arched window. With a labored groan, Rin raised a stiff arm, her bare shoulder blades scraping the straw mat underneath her. Her hand found her long braids first, letting the hair weave through her fingers. Then she rested it against her chest, confirming that her heart was still working, mapping each hoarse, shallow breath of her lungs. Her body had been wrapped in the same brown clothes as the villagers—no traces of the earlier splashes of blood anywhere. They'd really worked hard for her.

Then her fingers tenderly reached for her right eye.

From what she traced, the white, square bandage was shaped almost like a pirate's eyepatch, held around her head with some kind of elastic band. She resisted the urge to press down on it. She knew she didn't need to. Her damaged eye was gone.

It was just another thing that she had lost in her sixteen years of life.

"Miss Rin, are you okay?"

Lulu again? The whimpering girl grabbed her other arm with trembling hands, peering over her with those huge brown inquisitive eyes that, for some reason, irritated her to no end. Rin flung her hands away.

"I can't understand English," Rin said in Fon. A lie—not that the girl would understand her either. Words were the most inefficient way to communicate, yet this girl had babbled and babbled to her throughout the procedure until Rin had passed out.

Rin shooed her away and turned, letting the sunlight warm her face.

"The man, Jinn—I think he might make it," Lulu said in a soft tone, as if knowing it would reassure her. It did. Rin's breath hitched in her throat. Then her chest swelled with relief.

Inside the hut, Rin glanced behind her. There they were on the floor just past that trembling child—her fellow patients, sleeping on the other side of the hut by the open door, covered by the drawn animal-skin curtains: Jinn and John Temple.

Jinn had been stripped down to his pants. The villagers had tied white bandages around his chest, but they were soaked with sweat. Both his and John Temple's chests barely moved—yet move they did. Rin supposed village remedies and Ifá charms had power in them still. There was a pouch of water left by John Temple's side, and his thin pink lips weren't so cracked. Clearly the villagers had been hydrating him. Regardless, they were both in worse shape than she was.

Everything was a blur. Berta and Lulu had helped her out of the Coral Temple. It was Maximo's sister who had rushed back to retrieve the blade made of Isoke's bones. The elevator had responded to the sword's smooth surface—Hiva's touch—just like Heaven's Shrine had. But Rin couldn't leave Jinn behind. Isoke wouldn't have wanted her to. So she'd lifted him out of his lover's ashes and helped bring him back through the ocean and into Heaven's Shrine.

Back in Heaven's Shrine, John Temple had still had a bit of breath in him when they'd found him lying like a lump of flesh in the Room of Murals. John Temple, as Rin understood it, was the explorer father of that ridiculous, obsessive white boy, Adam Temple. Both were members of the Enlightenment Committee, who had been preparing for their rule after the apocalypse. John Temple had been studying the cataclysm known as Hiva for many years. It was only through his meticulous documentation of his research and explorations that they had been able to find this Naacalian ruin in the first place.

Once they'd reached him, he'd begun mumbling furiously. Even though Rin should have been able to understand the man's English, it didn't matter; by the time they'd returned to the Room of Murals where they'd found him, her consciousness was only holding on by a thread. Rin couldn't decipher what he'd whispered to Berta, but she noted the shock on the American girl's face and Lulu's resolute nod, just before Rin lost consciousness.

She'd awoken in this hut.

Had they made some kind of deal? John Temple seemed to be the kind of greedy man who'd do whatever it took to hold on to his pathetic life for as long as he could. What had he promised Berta in return? But more importantly, how had they been able to traverse the labyrinthine Heaven's Shrine to find themselves aboveground? This village was close to the mining site where Heaven's Shrine was located. The villagers traveled quite a distance to get water and supplies from a nearby lagoon.

Iris was the one who'd been to Heaven's Shrine in another life. She was the one who had led them through the tricks and trials of the temple. Rin couldn't imagine they'd be able to do it again with three injured people and a clueless child.

What did that girl do? Rin closed her left eye, squeezing both eyelids shut again and again to get used to the empty right socket. Her body was still weary. She closed them tightly, peering into the darkness. . . .

Blood spurted from Iris's mouth onto the glass surface of Hiva's tomb.

Gasping, Rin opened her eyes, her chest heaving. It was just a memory. Just a memory . . .

She closed her eyes again and saw it: the bone sword piercing through Isoke's back, cracking the glass. But the scream that erupted from Isoke's lips wasn't hers.

It belonged to Rin's father. A short and slender man who'd been running after his tiny daughter when the blade of a Dahomean warrior's machete had slid through his spine.

Their village had been in chaos. On the behest of their king, the Dahomean woman warriors were cutting down men, subduing others to be sent away onto slave ships. But the young girls—the young girls were theirs. In her youth, Rin's family and friends had always praised her for her round eyes, big and bright and filled with starlight. And through those eyes, she saw them murdered and captured while a pair of strong, muscled arms dragged her away. The child was to begin her new life in service of a ruler she did not know.

A small child screaming. Screaming for family.

You can be my family too. . . .

The memory of Isoke's gentle voice arrested her.

Jinn is my family. My granny is my family. I have a goose named Egg. And you can be in my family too, if you want. I'll add you. Only if you want, but why not?

Rin grabbed her own shoulders and squeezed tightly. But it didn't help. Her breaths were coming more furiously than ever.

"Quiet," she whispered, just like she had then, when Isoke had made this promise in the Atakora Mountains. "You lied to me, Isoke. . . ."

No. *Iris.* She seemed to like being called Iris. Rin had always just stubbornly called her whatever she'd wanted. *Isoke. She Who Does Not Fall.* And Iris would just smile and accept it, even though she probably didn't like those names. Isoke wanted to be Iris. It was why she'd fought so hard to find a way to escape her destiny. She'd wanted to be "Iris," whatever that had meant.

Every time Rin had barked or sneered at her—*betrayed* her—Iris would accept it. Smile at her. Cry with her. Maybe that was what it had meant. Tears welled up in Rin's left eye.

We will love you and take care of you.

"You didn't." Rin's lips trembled. She didn't notice or care that Lulu was looking at her strangely.

"I didn't what?" Lulu said, but Rin ignored her.

I promise, said Iris's sweet voice again in her memories.

"You *lied*."

We can protect you. We will protect you.

Rin's laughter was harsh and bitter. "You're dead. How will you protect me now?"

You will always have a home with me as long as you want it.

"M-Miss Rin? Are you okay? Did I . . . did I do something?" Lulu asked, confused, because Rin's tears were now falling.

As Rin closed her eyes and watched Iris turn to dust, as she remembered Iris's body decomposing, as she remembered her father's blood spilled across the grass near the village well, those tears fell, and Rin trembled so violently that she thought she would break apart. What family? What protection? What love? Where was it? *Where was it?*

Little hands pulled her left arm off her shoulder with all their might. "Miss Rin!"

Lulu. Lulu again! She was staring at her, worried, with those brown eyes of hers.

But there was something else—something peeking out of the left sleeve of Lulu's dress. Its glitter caught her eye. Lulu noticed the direction of her gaze and pulled it out.

Rin gasped. The Moon Skeleton!

The key that powered the Helios. A key that could open many secrets. At least that was how John Temple had described it when he'd given it to Iris.

And before Iris had given it to her.

Can you keep this for me for now?

What? Why?

Because I trust you with it.

And in her secret memories, Iris smiled.

Rin snatched it from Lulu's hands, clenching it so hard, she thought it could break—but this ancient thing was made of sterner stuff. Not Lulu. The little girl looked taken aback.

She was probably just holding on to it for you, a calmer voice inside Rin pointed out, drowned out by a wave of sorrow welling up inside her.

As Rin shoved the key into her clothing wrap, Lulu opened her mouth, clearly ready to explain. An irrational hatred erupted within her.

"Quiet!" Rin barked in Fon, and this time threw Lulu off her with all her might. The girl tumbled across the floor. "Don't talk to me! Didn't I tell you I can't speak English? Why won't you listen to me? Just stop it!"

The animal-skin curtain whipped open. Maximo's sister flew into the room, the long brown sack tied to her back bobbing up and down as she stomped. When she saw Lulu crumpled on the ground, she ran to her immediately. After scooping the little girl into her arms, she glared at Rin, baring her teeth like a rabid animal. How like the sister of a duplicitous murderer.

"Rin! What the hell did you do to her?"

Rin hated English. She hated that damn language. And she hated Jacob for giving it to her. She refused to speak it. Rin covered her ears and shook her head. "I can't understand you," she lied in Fon, whispering.

But Berta wouldn't stop. Dropping her sack, she continued to curse and berate her.

"Damn it, I can't understand you! I can't understand anything!" Rin yelled.

And it was partly true. As Berta's sack dropped to the floor, as the tip of the bone sword that had killed Iris peeked out of the opening, dull and splintered, Rin realized she didn't understand anything anymore. She thought of Iris's blood dripping down Hiva's Tomb and just couldn't understand any of it.

Finally Rin snapped. "Keep that thing away from me," she barked in English.

As Rin pointed at the sword, Berta narrowed her eyes in confusion before she quickly gathered it up. She obviously hadn't meant to reveal it.

"You stay away from me," Rin said.

Berta and Lulu exchanged glances.

"You can speak English?" Berta frowned. "What the hell? Since when?"

But Lulu was far more excited. "We can understand each other now!" She clasped her hands together in delight. "That means—"

"And keep *her* away from me too," Rin added, pointing at Lulu, whose mouth snapped shut in a hurry. "She's stupid and weak. What does she think she's going to do, tag along like a lost little puppy while the world burns? She's an eyesore."

As Lulu's shoulders slumped a little, Berta clenched her fists in fury. "What the hell did you just say, you bitch?"

Stupid and weak. Like that little Yoruba girl whose family was newly dead, killed by a neighboring tribe. Trapped inside the enemy's camp with a machete in her hands. Training while her captors looked on. Practicing to kill. Terrified out of her mind.

An eyesore. Looking on while the world burned. Looking on. Watching them fall one by one. Her family. Her friends. Iris.

An eyesore.

"Just let it all burn, then," Rin whispered in Fon. Another language that wasn't hers. She bit her teeth into her bottom lip so hard, she could taste the tart blood on her tongue. "I don't care anymore. Let it burn!"

"What a sorry sight," said a familiar voice by the door, with a heavy sigh. "Natame, aren't you glad I convinced you to track down Olarinde? Look at her! She's falling apart."

Natame? Had she heard right? Rin uncovered her ears and sat up.

They stood in front of the door, their hands on their hips, their backs straight like the warriors they were. Natame and Aisosa, fellow *ahosi*, warriors of the Kingdom of Dahomey. Though they were younger than Rin, the proud lift of their chins had been earned through countless battles. Rin knew their irritated expressions well, for they stemmed from impatience—the kind a warrior felt when seeing their comrade flail about in shameless defeat.

"Pick yourself up, woman," said Natame, her hair divided into four long braids that grazed her shoulders. "At least wear your scars with pride." When Aisosa, her sister in battle, nodded in agreement, the thick buns on her head bobbed ever so slightly.

The idea of being chewed out by her juniors made her sick, but when she actually did try to pick herself up, she flopped back down again onto the straw mat. The sight of her floundering made the two warriors giggle. Still quite the irritating little duo, those two.

"What happened?" Aisosa asked.

A simple question. How could such a simple question draw tears from her eyes? Rin turned quickly and blinked them away. She would not cry in front of them. Never.

And yet an overwhelming wave of relief washed over her when she realized that she now had someone like herself she could speak to. Sucking in a deep breath and steeling her nerves, Rin told them everything. How she, with Iris and the others, had found an ancient shrine beneath the earth. How they'd adventured through the mysterious labyrinth until they'd found Hiva's Tomb in an underwater temple. How two Hivas had met and battled there . . .

"Wait, what is this 'Hiva' thing?" Natame nudged Aisosa in the ribs before glancing around the hut, her braids whipping around. "There's Isoke's servant-lover, but where's Isoke? And who's that smelly old man?"

Isoke is dead. Rin couldn't tell her that. The Dahomey only knew Iris as "Isoke," the name she'd been given during her past life as a fellow *mino* warrior. What would happen if Rin told Natame and Aisosa that the legendary Child of the Moon Goddess, She Who Does Not Fall, and the king's long-sought prized "possession" was, finally, well and truly dead?

King Glele had sent Rin to Europe to retrieve Iris. But rather than allow him to use her as his weapon, she'd tried to use Iris as her own. She'd been no better than any of them.

Rin pressed her lips together, her fingers curling around the edges of the brown cloth she wore. "Has the king said anything about me?" she whispered, though she wasn't sure she wanted to know the answer.

The two Dahomean women exchanged glances.

"We haven't been back to Abomey since we sent a message to your friends in Ajashe." Aisosa flicked her head toward Berta and Lulu. Yes, it had been Iris's idea to send them to that port city. If she hadn't, her murderer would still be languishing in that hospital.

Hospital.

"Aisosa. Natame. Check Jinn—Isoke's lover," she clarified with a blush, because she didn't think they'd ever learned his proper name.

The two warriors crouched down by Jinn and John Temple, lying on the floor by the mud wall. "He's been given some charms?" Natame said, prying apart his eyelids.

Even from where she sat, Rin could see his pupils were dilated. Behind

Berta and Lulu was a ledge of small silver instruments, now cleaned of Rin's blood, as well as some beads, herbs, and medicine bags, and a wand made of ivory with horsehair. All ritualistic.

While Aisosa checked Temple, Natame checked Jinn's body, lifting him with expert care.

"He was stabbed in the back. A few inches to the left and his spine would have been cleanly severed," she said, shaking her head in disbelief. "He's lucky. Very lucky. The gods must be protecting him. For what purpose, I don't know."

Rin shot a dark glare toward Berta. No one needed words to understand hatred.

"Where this wound punctured him . . . It was a miracle they were able to save his life, but he still needs better care, or—"

Rin shifted to her knees. "Or?"

Natame lowered her gaze. "I don't think he'll be able to move again. To be honest, even with the treatment, he may still end up . . ."

"Paralyzed." Rin squeezed her hands into fists, shutting her eyes as she felt the steady drumbeat of blood pump through her palms. That was his reward for trying to save the woman he loved. She'd seen everything with her own eyes—the way he'd leapt in front of Max's final blow. Would he even want to live, knowing that it had all been for nothing?

A mixture of sadness and rage shuddered through her. What would Iris have wanted?

"The best hospital I've seen in this area is the one in Ajashe," Rin said. "You've been there before. It's where Iris sent you to find those two." She flicked her head in Berta and Lulu's direction. "Take this man, Jinn, and make sure he gets the best of care."

Rin tried to lift herself off the straw mat, but her muscles twinged, and she collapsed again. Her right eye sizzled before she realized it was no longer there. A phantom pain. It felt so real. Her eye socket throbbed. She touched her bandage gingerly.

"You need just as much help as he does, I'd gather," said Natame. "If we're taking this man, we'll take you too. I spied a mule-drawn cart full of hay some-where in the village. We can take that, Aisosa."

Aisosa nodded and left to fetch it. *How like a Dahomean warrior to take without asking,* Rin wanted to sneer, but she supposed it didn't much matter. Jinn needed the help. That hospital was where they'd taken Max after he'd been shot on the high seas by a British captain. If they could patch him up well enough for him to murder again, maybe they could help Jinn too. She owed him that.

She also owed someone else.

"Natame, I also need you two to get a message to a woman named Uma Malakar," Rin continued. "She's currently in the Atakora Mountains where King Glele bartered with the arms dealer, Boris Bosch. She's his right hand: a scientific researcher who develops the weapons he sells. You can make up an excuse to see her again. Bring with you a translator, someone who can speak her language. You must tell her this."

Natame listened as Rin gave her a description: a brown-skinned woman who looked to be of Indian descent. Her clothes seemed a mixture of two cultures: her corset and blue sari, her bronze and silver headpieces, her silver nose ring a cluster of the gears she was obsessed with. She was a genius, and that made her Hiva's target.

Go to Uma and tell her everything. Warn everyone. We all have one year to live.

The memory of Max's warning chilled her blood. Hiva had promised to destroy humanity within only a year. The timetable was set. Surely there was something she could do.

But when she looked at her hands, she didn't see the battle scars. She didn't see the strength of her muscles earned from training.

She saw the useless hands of a little girl too weak to save anyone.

My family. My village. My friends. Isoke—Iris. Everything she had set out to achieve had failed. Everyone she cared for was dead.

What did it matter if the world ended? The world was a hellhole to begin with.

Still, Uma had helped them escape Bosch's facility in the Atakora Mountains. Iris would have wanted Rin to help the woman.

Of course, Iris would have also wanted to *live.*

"Tell Uma everything I've told you," Rin said finally. "Tell her that only one Hiva now stands, and within one year, all will end."

Natame shook her head. "I don't understand—who is this Hiva you keep talking about? One year? And where is Isoke?"

Tell her, Rin scolded herself. *Hiva aims to purge humanity from this world. The military deserves to mount a defense.*

The same military she'd tried to have Iris burn alive. Rin's lips quirked into a wry smile.

But then she lowered her head and shut her eyes. "Natame. Isoke is dead."

Silence. Rin didn't want to look at her. She could feel her shock, her blank horror.

"You . . . you're lying," Natame stuttered, and took a stumbling step back. "She Who Does Not Fall—"

"Finally fell before my eyes," Rin finished for her. "And I could do nothing to stop it."

Rin finally looked at the girl, at her clenched teeth and her round, terrified eyes.

"Hiva killed her," she said, because it was in part true. Hiva had orchestrated everything. Killing Iris was his goal, and he had achieved it. And now no one left alive could stop him. "Hiva is a god like Isoke. Another who cannot fall, yet more powerful and terrible. Hiva killed Isoke and has promised to destroy this world within one year," she said. "He can and will murder all of humanity. I don't care whether you believe me. What you, the king, and the rest of the military do with this information is up to you."

Natame's body tensed. Rin could tell from her rigid expression that the young woman somehow knew this wasn't a laughing matter, even if every instinct within Natame told her to dismiss it with a sarcastic grin. She also knew all too well that Rin was the last warrior among their ranks who would ever tell a joke.

Rin was serious, and she made sure Natame could tell.

It didn't matter to Rin. She just didn't care anymore. She would pay her debts and leave.

When Aisosa came back with the cart, Natame began carrying Jinn out of the hut in silence. Rin ignored the shooting pain in her back and finally forced herself to her feet. But Berta wouldn't let them go. Blocking the door with a stubborn scowl, she pointed to John Temple.

"John Temple," Berta said. "Pack up the old man too, because we're taking him."

"What is she babbling about?" Aisosa said as Natame buckled under Jinn's weight. "What is this girl saying?"

"She wants us to take the old man," said Rin as Lulu ran up to the explorer and grabbed his arm. Berta folded her arms, resolute.

So they really had struck a deal back there in Heaven's Shrine. What in the world had John Temple whispered to that murderer's sister before they all ended up here in this tiny little village by the lagoon?

Oh well. It didn't matter. They were all going to be dead in a year anyway.

Aisosa looked behind her and scrunched up her nose childishly. "Do we really need to take him? He's not as injured as Isoke's lover. He'll be all right with some food and water. Plus, he really does smell—wait." And Aisosa turned to Rin. "Olarinde . . . did you understand what that woman said? Can you understand English? Or . . ."

Shrugging her shoulders, Rin flicked her head toward Berta, giving her the go-ahead to take the old man. Lulu gave Rin a little smile before moving to help her friend. A smile that was not returned.

Just one more year of this nonsense, and it would all be over. Rin felt the Moon Skeleton cold against her skin.

What awaited them on the other side of death? Iris should know by now.

Peace. Rin hoped so badly it would be that, at the very least.

3

"JOHN TEMPLE. WHERE DID THAT BLASTED old man go?" Rin screamed as she burst through the doors of the Ajashe hospital. This port city that the Europeans called Porto-Novo was vast, with ships sailing in and out, and soldiers, missionaries, migrants, and every manner of merchant trying not to run afoul of any of the French colonial administrators sniffing about. It was all too easy for a recovering old man to get lost.

Or escape.

Rin slammed the door behind her, causing a sleeping Berta to wake with a start and jump from her seat—the same seat by the window she'd sat in while her brother had been recuperating a mere week ago. Now it was Jinn who'd taken his spot, mumbling, with his head pouring sweat. Unable to speak. Unable to move. And according to the Ajashe doctors, maybe permanently.

"We've done all we can for him. We're able to keep him alive, but his wounds are more than just physical . . . ," one doctor had told Rin when she'd asked for a prognosis. It wasn't just his body that had broken the moment Max had stabbed him. It was his mind. His heart . . .

"Where is John Temple?" Rin demanded again.

Berta scrunched up her nose. "What are you talking about?"

"Girls!" An angry nurse burst in from the neighboring room. "This is a hospital!"

Jinn was in a room filled with patients with all kinds of gruesome maladies. This was one of the fancier facilities in the city. All wood, underneath a long, red-tiled gable roof.

The moment the nurse retreated back to her room, Rin grabbed the collar of Berta's white blouse—seconds before Berta wrapped her hand around hers. The girl's sharp nails bit into Rin's skin. Good. She liked the pain. Rin could feel the white crystal of her sword stirring within her chest, like shards of ice in her veins.

Her sword. She'd once considered it the result of a heinous accident. Now, whenever she placed her hand on her chest, she knew beyond a shadow of a doubt that it was a gift from Iris. All the magic in this world was, as far as Rin was concerned: Jinn's fire-breathing, Maximo's time manipulation. These mysterious gifts were the ramifications of Iris's white crystal heart. Her very existence had brought the supernatural into the world. What better use of Rin's supernatural gift than to shove it right through the skull of that murdering jackal Maximo's baby sister?

Hearing a man moaning in pain next door snapped Rin out of her fury. *Calm down, Olarinde,* she told herself as she finally noticed the heat flushing her face. *What is any of this going to do? Iris is already dead.*

Rin let Berta go with a not-so-gentle shove. "I want to know where John Temple's gone."

"How the hell should I know?" Berta threw up her hands. "I just woke up, thanks to you."

"Then tell me what he whispered to you that day," Rin demanded, rounding on her. "When we were still in Heaven's Shrine. It's why you brought him here, isn't it?"

Berta averted her gaze, pursing her lips secretively. More than a week had passed since they'd escaped the Naacalian temple. There had been days of being carted around on a dirt road like a sack of yams, of convalescing here in this hospital. And during that time, neither girl had deigned to speak to the other. They'd just crossed over into the new calendar year.

"I'm . . ." Berta paused and gripped her palms on the long red skirt she'd "procured" the other day. Probably stolen. It didn't matter that her other clothes were in dirty tatters. She was a miscreant, like her brother. "To be per-fectly honest, I'm not sure I can fully explain it."

Rin raised an eyebrow. "You can't *explain* it?"

Berta leaned against the small table next to her, where she'd placed a cup of water and a few pieces of fried plantain to eat. "Well, it didn't exactly make any sense when he told me, did it?" She waved her hand in the air. "But sure enough, once I moved the altar, that symbol was there on the floor, and then we just—" When she started flapping her arms like a bird, Rin had the strang-est desire to punch her. "Then we were outside and—uh, well, you were out cold, so you didn't see it. If you'd seen it, then you'd get it."

"See what?" Rin shook her head. "What in the blazes are you talking about?"

"Look, all I care about right now is Hiva! We need to stop him. Maybe Old Man Temple can help."

Rin shifted her weight onto her left leg, placing her hands on her hips. "Well, I'm sure his research would come in handy."

"Exactly. He has the goods. Up here." Berta tapped her forehead with a fin-ger. "That's why we've got to—"

"Never mind, then. I thought you two had formed some kind of treacher-ous pact behind my back, but now that I know it's nothing important, I can rest easy." Adjusting the long wrap around her body just underneath her arms, Rin shrugged her shoulders and turned to the door.

"Excuse me?" said Berta behind her.

"What a relief." Rin reached to grab the door's metal handle, only to shift her head to the side with the quick reflexes trained into her when she heard a soft *whoosh*. A millisecond later, the clay cup of water Berta had been drinking from smashed to pieces against the door.

Rin turned back around slowly. A stray piece of clay had cut her cheek, just below her bandaged right eye socket. Not deep enough to make her bleed. But surely deep enough to piss her off.

"Hiva's still on the loose." Berta's fists shook with anger; she was clearly itching for a fight. "And you have the balls to say, 'What a relief'?"

"You have a problem with that?" *I already said I didn't care anymore,* Rin reminded herself when her own breath hitched at the thought of that automaton-like monster.

"My brother's with him now. He's basically a captive."

"Captivity is less than what a murderer deserves."

Berta stiffened. Her eyes darted to Jinn before she gritted her teeth. She'd been by Jinn's side since they'd arrived—the comical side effect of guilt, Rin guessed.

"You know he didn't have a choice." Berta spoke slowly, clearly choosing her words carefully. "There were two Hivas. My brother was trying to save us from one."

"And somehow killed the one who actually cared about this world, while leaving us helpless in the face of the other." Rin's lips quirked into a sarcastic smile. "What a hero."

Berta looked as if she'd been struck. "S-stop it!"

"Your brother is quite good at killing Hivas. He knows the method to permanently 'clip a god's wings,' doesn't he?"

By Berta's chair was her brown sack carrying the sword that had pierced through Iris's heart. Berta never let it out of her sight, especially when Rin was around. What was she so afraid of? If Rin wanted to kill Berta, she had her own sword, ready-made inside her own body. Not that she ever had the urge to summon it around the girl. "What makes you think he won't find a way to kill the one he's currently following around like a dog? It would be the end of all our problems," Rin said, folding her arms over her chest. "Or have you no faith in him?"

Seeing Berta lower her head, frowning in confusion, filled Rin with a sadistic kind of glee that somehow made up for the random stings of phantom pain in the empty socket where her right eye should have been.

"It's not surprising. You barely know him. You could hardly call a man you just met a couple of weeks ago 'family.'"

Berta's head snapped up, her eyes blazing. "You shut your mouth."

"Barely a family. Yet your brother was willing to betray and kill a friend for you. Then again, it wasn't his first betrayal, was it? Maybe *you* were just a convenient excuse, after all?" Rin stepped forward, the white crystal in her chest whispering for revenge. "Maybe your brother is just a violent sociopath!"

"Rin!" Berta began striding toward her.

Good. It had been several days of misery. Iris was dead, Rin's empty eye socket felt hot as if it were still burning, and they all had one year left to live. Rin could use a good fight.

Just then Lulu burst through the door excitedly. "Miss Berta! Miss Rin!"

Rin's hand froze over her chest. Irritated at the interruption, she looked down at the insufferable girl in her new, plain white dress, jumping about like a little lemur.

"I found him! John Temple!"

John Temple? Rin narrowed her eyes.

"I've been looking for him, you know! See, I can carry my weight around here!"

Lulu's accent was not something Rin was used to. She'd only heard it once or twice before, when she'd crossed paths with Black American missionaries who had repatriated to this part of the continent. They always seemed so content to see the "motherland." Rin didn't feel a kinship with them. She didn't feel a kinship with anyone anymore.

"Where did that old man run to?" Berta said.

Lulu nodded. "Follow me!"

She didn't leave Rin much of a choice, grabbing her rough hand and dragging her out of the hospital, with Berta trailing behind.

Rin always tried to avoid the market at the peak of the afternoon, when the sun was blazing and too many people were milling about. Vendors, at least, found shade under makeshift tents. Clothes swung on racks, and all manner of meats and fried stockfish were drying out on the counters.

Lulu was too excited. She almost tripped over a barrel of fruit while she ran through the crowded narrow path between the two rows of traders and merchants. Rin was surprised when Lulu apologized in Fon to a woman with a basket of yams on her head, for almost crashing into her. Just how long had it taken for this girl to learn some words? Had someone been teaching her?

Rin caught herself before she could become too impressed. She didn't care either way. Just where was this girl taking her?

It didn't take her long to find out. Lulu finally came to a crashing halt, the sand beneath her feet flying every which way, and pointed. "There!" she exclaimed, looking up to Rin and grinning, maybe wanting some kind of praise. "Look! There they are! Told you I found them!"

Rin gave her a sidelong look. "There *they* are?"

There *he* was. Just past a Quaker, arguing with some children with the Bible under his arm. A beige hat obscured Temple's sunken eyes. His body frame was so frail, he was practically disappearing inside the tweed explorer's jacket and trousers they'd found him in.

He was crouched in front of a stall where a man sold robes and wraps, jewels, and other accessories. But his skeletal hand shook precariously when he lifted it to scratch his graying facial hair. His body twitched every so often too, and when Rin and the others reached him, his eyes could not wholly focus on any one of them. He'd spent who knew how many days stranded in that ancient temple without food or water. It was a miracle he was walking. Rin wondered if this strange man would ever be okay again.

"John Temple," Rin said before Berta pushed past her, shoving her into the side of the stall.

"Hey, old man," she said with her usual gusto. Overcompensating, definitely. "You've kept your mouth shut until now, and I've been nice because you're injured and all. But the time for being gentle is over. Better make sure you've got the stamina, because we've got lots to talk about."

"I agree," said the figure next to him. "Lots to talk about."

Rin hadn't paid too much attention to the cloaked woman standing on Temple's other side—not until she lowered her hood.

Brass gears on brown skin. Uma Malakar smiled. "About our one year to live, that is."

4

A CLUSTER OF CHICKENS SCUTTLED PAST. UMA shooed them away with a kick of her feet and went back to the array of jewelry sprawled out on the vendor's counter.

"Ugh, I love everything," Uma said. "But where's the clockwork?"

The stall shaded them from the fury of the sun, but John Temple's skin still sweated as if he were sick with fever. His skin was paler than ever before. It wasn't fear. At least Rin didn't think it was. His expression seemed stuck in some kind of perpetual state of bewilderment. He looked as if he were going to collapse.

"If you're worried about him, you have good instincts," Uma told Rin as she wedged herself between them. "When I sent him a message to meet here, I wondered what kind of John Temple I would find, but it's worse than I imagined. According to what he's told me, and just from observing him with my own eyes, I think he's suffered a series of strokes and possibly has dysentery."

Strokes? Dysentery? Rin looked the old man up and down with the faintest pang of guilt. She hadn't really cared to learn his diagnosis from the Ajashe doctors. It was enough that he was alive. Dysentery was a disease of the stomach that made men leak blood, vomit, and other unsavory contents from more than one orifice. No wonder that despite all his treatment, he still looked as if death haunted him. And yet he was out here, meeting with Malakar. Whatever babble Berta had mentioned, it had to be important.

"You understood what I was saying just now, didn't you? Even though I'm speaking English."

Uma's sneaky glance made Rin's body clench. She pursed her lips. "How did you know I could?" Rin still couldn't get used to the way that language sounded in her mouth, the way the syllables curled off her tongue. It felt so insidious.

"A couple of little birdies may have told me, with the help of a translator. Still, not the most troubling of all the disturbing information they told me."

Natame and Aisosa. Rin cleared her throat. "You said the man has dysentery. Isn't that . . . ?" Rin looked at her nervously. "Isn't that infectious?"

"Yes!" Uma said cheerfully, clapping John Temple on the back, who murmured in response. "I certainly hope you haven't been sharing his food and water—or touching his fecal matter."

Rin made a disgusted face. Uma gave the two of them a suspicious look before shrugging. "The moment your two little *ahosi* friends told me your situation, I immediately made arrangements for him to travel back to England. We're on our way to the ports right now."

John Temple moved his ancient lips and muttered something. A name. Rin couldn't quite catch it. Apparently Uma did.

Uma nodded in agreement. "Don't worry, you'll have it soon. Just don't lose hope."

John Temple's slack jaw twitched into something that looked like a smile.

"He'll get some more of the antibiotics he needs on the ship," Uma continued. "I'll make sure you all get some too, just in case. As for the messengers, they're on their way back to Abomey to explain the situation to the Dahomean king. I can't imagine he won't launch some kind of defense."

King Glele. The man Rin had tried to murder not too long ago. She shivered at the thought of that imposing figure, sitting atop his throne of skulls as he sentenced her to death. It was only Iris who had saved her life. After everything Rin had done to betray her, Iris was the one who'd held her and cried with her that day. Wept as if she would die too.

Olarinde, don't you do it. Rin clenched her jaw and fists and willed her tears to stop welling up. *Don't you dare. Not here. Enough, you stupid, useless child.*

"Hello?" Uma bent over and waved a hand in front of Rin's face, causing her to start in embarrassment. "The end of the world? A wicked monster promising to end all of human civilization within a year? That's somewhat interesting to you, isn't it? It's interesting to *me*. What about you lot? Is it interesting to you?"

"And what does John Temple know about it?" Rin said, snatching a red beaded necklace out of Uma's hands and placing it back onto the counter. The vendor looked disappointed.

"Too much, it seems."

Uma reached into her dress and pulled out John Temple's journal. The man recognized it immediately. His deep, sunken eyes widened for a moment, but then they twitched at the sound of footsteps behind them. It wasn't just him. After Uma looked behind her, she quickly pulled on her hood, grabbed an orange shawl from the vendor counter, and threw it over John Temple's head so that his face couldn't be seen. With a hiss, she beckoned Rin to turn around.

Facing the vendor, Rin couldn't see the men behind them, but she could certainly hear their chatter in French.

"I thought I saw her come in this direction," said one man. Before Rin had turned around, she'd noticed they were dressed in a strange kind of uniform she'd seen before. Not quite a soldier, but some profession that was just as rigid.

"Why did she disappear in the first place? That troublesome woman is making our lives harder," said the other.

The group waited until they had passed. Then, from underneath her hood, Uma let out a sigh.

"I couldn't exactly leave Bosch's facility by myself, you know. But I managed to ditch my men once I got to town. This is a secret mission. I can't let anyone on the Enlightenment Committee know that John Temple's alive."

At the sound of the names of his old "friends," Temple shrank in fear.

"Don't worry," Uma assured him. "Come, everyone. I'm about to take him to the port, but first I need to explain how the Solar Jumps work."

The gaggle of chickens continued to waddle after them as if the feathered stalkers were secret spies. Well, if there were spies, they could have been hiding anywhere in the crowd as they made their way to the docks. The tart smell of spices and fried meat weighed down the already humid air, sticking to Rin's skin with her sweat. Berta kept John Temple, still hiding under a shawl, on his feet by holding on to the crook of his elbow. She'd sent Lulu home. This was a conversation for adults.

Rin didn't miss her one bit. Seeing the child day after day made her heart feel as if it were being wrung to death.

"You know, Lord Temple, translating your work wasn't easy." Uma reached into her cloak and pulled it out: John Temple's journal, that little book Iris had been obsessed with as she searched for clues about her own inhumane nature. "Using different ciphers for nonconsecutive chapters? Irksome but brilliant."

Uma passed it to the man over his shoulder. With hesitant hands, he took it.

"How did we escape Heaven's Shrine?" Rin demanded, turning to John Temple behind her. He recoiled at her fearsome glare.

"It was the Solar Jumps," Uma explained before bending down and swiping a fallen tree branch off the sand. "Try to follow along. The Naacal were a technologically advanced civilization. I've been studying their work personally, ever since the British crown lifted pieces of the Helios out of Lake Victoria on this very continent."

Rin had been there when Iris and Uma had discussed it, while the latter had been spiriting them away from London on some mad contraption that drove faster than a carriage. The Helios could open a door to other dimensions. And on the day the Crown had attempted to conduct some kind of research with it, Iris's crystal heart had reacted to it and caused an explosion that transformed humans at random into supernatural beasts.

"Of course, the Committee had been looking for the Moon Skeleton to power that machine and the Ark. It's a very important key, you know."

And was currently stuffed in the folds of the cloth wrapped around Rin's body.

"In lieu of finding it, they were going to try to use a more powerful source— Hiva's heart. And if the message your two Dahomean friends sent me is true, I'm assuming procuring that heart may be a little . . . difficult."

Uma's expression stiffened, her bottom lip curling as if she'd just tasted sour fruit. "'Only one Hiva now stands,'" she said, repeating the message Rin had given to Natame. "And am I to assume—?"

"It's him," Rin answered coldly. Though Rin didn't look at her, Uma's ensuing silence spoke volumes. Rin squared her shoulders and kept her head held high as a group of Portuguese traders passed by, clinking their beers and laughing loudly.

"I see," Uma whispered finally. "So there was indeed a way to kill a god."

Rin chanced a glimpse at the other woman, but by now Uma had turned her head and was looking straight ahead. She hadn't quite gotten a sense of where Uma's moral compass pointed. An employee of the Enlightenment Committee, but a friend to Iris when it suited her. In a way, she reminded Rin of herself. A kind of stubborn warrior, who fully understood that showing emotion was a sign of weakness that women like them couldn't afford.

"Well," Uma said. "What a waste of a good heart."

The group fell into silence again.

"We used her bones to get out of the shrine," Berta suddenly said behind them, dragging along the old man. It was clear she wanted to move the conversation along, though Rin wasn't sure that bringing up the weapon that had murdered Iris—which was once again sturdily strapped to Berta's back—was a great way to do it. Rin gave Berta the evil eye over her shoulder, but she had to admit, she was curious. "Lulu and I moved the altar in front of the mural. Underneath it, there was, like, this . . ." Berta searched for the right word. "Hatch. Like a manhole cover. It had this symbol scratched on it. A circle with four points."

A circle with four points . . . Rin frowned. Like what they had seen on Hiva's Tomb.

"The sun," Uma said. Yes, that was what it had looked like to Rin. And it had been littered throughout the scrolls she and Iris had stolen from the British Museum. A circle with four points—though, unlike on Hiva's tomb, without the cross to blot it out. "The Naacalians originally worshipped a sun god. They dedicated much of their technology to it."

Before Hiva had appeared and they had begun worshipping her. At least that was how Iris had told the story.

"The Naacalians were obsessed with distortions in space and time," Uma continued, and resumed drawing patterns in the air. "How to bend it. They never mastered time travel, but dimensional travel—moving from one space to another—they got pretty good at. They created the Helios to tear open a rift to new dimensions. But even that was reworked from technology they'd already created. Machines that could transport people to different areas within this world." Uma looked over her shoulder. "Right, Lord Temple?"

Temple dragged his boots along the sand, his shoulder blades protruding from inside his tweed jacket. "We discovered them in Bombay almost a decade ago." His words came slowly, his voice devoid of any of the gusto or confidence Rin would expect from an explorer. "An invention. An apparatus through which a man could be reduced to energy, transmitted to a new location, and reproduced in his form safely at the other end."

Rin furrowed her brows, trying to picture this nonsense; was that how they'd escaped Heaven's Shrine? She almost let out a derisive laugh. It felt impossible, but after everything she'd seen, accepting the ridiculous was, by now, a practice of simple common sense.

"Large metal discs hidden around the world." His thick, rough eyebrows furrowed as drops of sweat dripped down from his forehead. "Solar Jumps."

"The one underneath the altar led to another near the lagoon," Berta said.

The lagoon. She, Iris, and Jinn had passed it on their way to the mining site. It wasn't too far from the site, nor from the village where Rin's injuries had been taken care of.

"Yes . . . it disappears in a flash once it's no longer in use." John Temple paused. "From what I've gathered from my research, these Jumps were part of the Naacal's complex delivery system. They used them to transport any-thing from goods and technology to slaves—and even entire regiments—to factories and military posts. Each Jump has its pair, a twin somewhere in this world. The Naacalians designed them as such, based on the confluence of their religion and heliophysics. It's fitting, considering their fixation on the sun and its shadows."

Rin barely followed any of the slurred gibberish that came out of Temple's mouth, but "the sun and its shadow" was a phrase she recognized all too well. Like the conjoining rings of the Moon Skeleton. The sun and its shadow. Iris and her brother, Hiva . . .

And when Rin spoke aloud the word "Hiva," John Temple nodded. "Yes. Eventually the Naacal mistakenly blurred their religion with that of Hiva's existence. Hiva became their sun god. And so, even though the Naacal used special technology to operate the Solar Jumps, they were programmed to respond to Hiva's presence . . . body . . . touch."

"One thing I don't get, old man." Berta twisted a brown curl around her finger. "We found you in the Room of Murals in front of the altar. As in, right next to a Solar Jump. Why didn't you save yourself?"

At this, John Temple's wrinkles grew deeper, aging his sickly skin. "I was lost for days after trying to explore the temple in my hubris, thinking I could conquer it—the Naacal's past. Their legacy. By the time I'd managed to crawl back to the altar again, my body was bruised and beaten, but my mind was in far worse condition." He shook his head. Rin thought of the man lying there, defeated, with no energy to bat away the spiders crawling up his face. "I had the Moon Skeleton, made of Iris's crystal heart. Perhaps it would have reacted to the Jumps and saved me, but . . ." He sucked in a long inhale. "The family I'd left behind. In those days I was lost, they were all I could think about. And I started to wonder if I even deserved to be saved." He looked at Berta. "Or if I deserved death." Rubbing the creases in his forehead, he caught sight of the bag Berta carried on her back.

"It carries Iris's bones," she whispered, shifting uncomfortably as if she knew Rin's glare was upon her.

"Keep it," he said. "It may come in handy should you come across the Jumps."

A flock of birds took off overhead, singing through the humid sky. Crested terns. She could tell by their white plumage and the black markings on their head. Seeing them meant they were getting close to the ocean.

"Well, at any rate." Uma tossed her stick to the side, almost hitting a merchant in the head. "You've kept your discoveries quite hidden, Lord Temple, even from the Committee," she said while the man adjusted his turban, cursing as they passed. "Even from *me*." Uma sounded both impressed and irritated. "How revolutionary. I'm surprised you were able to discover so many around the world. The possibilities are immeasurable. I wonder if young Lord Adam knows your time away from home was spent toward such a noble cause."

John Temple stumbled over his own feet. It was Berta who kept him steady. At the mention of Adam, the man seemed to lose what little strength he had left.

"Oh, come now, stop getting so *sentimental*," Uma said quickly, her expression awkward as Berta tugged him along. "We can't dawdle for too long, you know, or you might get caught. The Committee commissioned your murder, from what I was told. They think you're dead. And you know, well, if at first you don't succeed . . ."

Berta got him walking again, one weary foot in front of the other, but John Temple didn't speak for a long time. "I've destroyed my family," he said finally, his voice barely a whisper. "Through my callous indifference. I destroyed my son, abandoning him when he needed me the most. . . . I'm sure he hates me. He has every right. I'm ashamed."

"You *should* be ashamed. Your son wishes to destroy the world," Rin said, feeling a sudden rush of indignation on Iris's behalf. She glared at the old man. "His cruel obsession with Hiva. His bloodthirsty nihilism. Where do you think he got it from? Why do you think he wishes to see humanity suffer?"

John Temple's cloudy eyes narrowed with the kind of self-pity that made Rin want to slap him in the face.

"And that's why I'll go back to England," Temple said, with a definitive nod. "To make things right before it's too late."

"Hmm. 'Before it's too late': a temporal phrase that implies we have time— which we do not." Uma used her elbows to help her squeeze through the crowds, which grew thicker as they approached the docks. "I agree with your son in one aspect, Lord Temple. This is a wretched world. But you see, I rather like it. There are too many treasures still left to discover and create. So we'll be needing a plan if we're going to stop Hiva."

"And what do you suggest?" Rin asked as a breath of salty air, carried by the ocean, caressed her face like the tide. When Uma gave her a sidelong look, Rin turned away. She supposed the woman had heard it: the complete lack of interest in her voice. Rin couldn't even be bothered to feign concern.

"Your Dahomean friends told me about Hiva's Tomb. From what they said, it seems the machine was built to break Iris down to her atoms and keep those atoms in some kind of suspended animation."

"It was only ever a temporary solution," said John Temple. "Eventually Hiva's atoms would overpower the energetic field and combine again. Hiva is immortal. It resists all methods of destruction created by man or nature. The Naacal knew that."

"Only Hiva's own body can take him down," said Berta, suddenly grasping the shoulder straps of the bag that carried Iris's bones. "But Hiva knows that."

"And Iris's bones?" asked Uma.

"May come in handy one day," Berta answered, or rather muttered, because she could see Rin glaring at her.

Uma scrunched her nose, batting away mosquitos. "Hiva will be on the defense. He can burn people alive with his mind. I don't suppose he'll just let us walk up to him and tear off an arm or two. No, we need every weapon we can get in our arsenal. We need to secure what's left of the Naacal's technology. And we can use the Committee for that."

"The Enlightenment Committee?" Rin exclaimed, a little too loudly. A few soldiers in uniform turned around and stared at her. Behind her, John Temple lowered his head. She dropped her voice. "You want to involve those disgusting death-mongers?"

"I'm already involved with them. I'm Bosch's weapons developer. I'm in charge of seeing their cheap imitation Noah's Ark to completion. Madame Bellerose in particular is knee-deep in the preparations, bothering me every day, making sure it's got properly furnished rooms for the elite guests she plans to bring and decks to marginalize the 'less important personnel.'" Uma scoffed. "Fussy idiot. It's the earth's first transdimensional exploratory vessel, not a luxury ocean liner."

Rin used to work for Madame Bellerose. She was all too familiar with that woman's ugly temperament, having had to play the part of her obedient servant during the Tournament of Freaks while she tracked down Iris in London. Boris Bosch was just as awful, dressed like he was always on the hunt for bigger prey, covered in the bones of his kills. Just the thought of having to be anywhere near either of them again made her want to swallow her own sword.

"Those people tried to kill Iris and me multiple times," Rin said.

"Yes, very sorry about that," answered Uma, with a dismissive wave. "But we'll need resources to secure the mining site and the entrance to Heaven's Shrine—the entrance to the Coral Temple, where Hiva's Tomb resides. That was the Crown's mining site, if you recall. I don't know how you got past those soldiers, but the Crown will be wanting to reestablish their possession of the land. If we're going to lure Hiva back to the Coral Temple and inside Hiva's Tomb, we can't let the British muck things up. The Committee can help us with that."

Rin remembered the mayhem of the mining site as they'd fought their way through. Berta must have been thinking about it too. She and her brother had killed quite a few people that day. When Rin turned around, Berta noticed and quickly looked away, her lips pursed.

"The Committee has the resources to establish control and keep the British out. I'm already in bed with them. Might as well use them. Or don't you want to save the world?"

Another sidelong look. Rin grimaced.

"And the Titans," John Temple said, his back suddenly straight as if retrieving a lost memory. "What about the Titans?"

With a nervous laugh, Uma shook her head, wagging her finger as if scolding a child. "Those particular trinkets are a tad extreme. Let's shelve that idea for now—unless the worst-case scenario happens."

Titans? The word was familiar to Rin. It reminded her of the time she'd spent in France with Iris, but the word was barely a shadow in her memory. How could it be anything more, when Rin had been, at the time, too busy plotting her revenge against the king of Dahomey? What did it mean? Had Iris known? As Rin struggled to remember, she caught Uma's gaze on her once more.

"What say you, young warrior?"

Rin let out an impatient huff. "If you want to go to Bosch and Madame Bellerose, then do it on your own. You don't need me for that. You don't need me for any of this."

"Actually, Madame Bellerose left for France a few days ago," said Uma, folding her arms and staring at the hot sand. "A political disturbance is brewing in Europe, or so I hear. She's gone to get her 'affairs in order,' whatever that means. Bosch is out in the Congo right now, conducting some trade in the rubber fields. He should be back in two months . . . and wait a minute—" Uma snapped her head up and gave Rin an incredulous look. "Did I hear you correctly? Did you say I didn't need you for this?" Uma scoffed. "Why wouldn't I need you? You were in the Coral Temple. You saw the tomb firsthand. Eyewitness accounts. That boy Jinn was there too, right? Where is he?"

Rin's stomach dropped as Uma looked around, like Jinn might pop up from behind a pack of goats and surprise them. "He's in the hospital with grievous injuries. It's . . ." Rin swallowed, banishing the torturous image of Jinn jumping in front of Max's sword. "It's bad."

"I see." Uma stroked her chin, her gaze soft and low. "Well, maybe I can do a little something about that," she said, with a secretive, mischievous grin. "But if he's out of commission for now, then I'll need you even more. I need both of you extraordinary women."

Rin and Berta exchanged hateful glances as the crowd dispersed. Ajashe was indeed a port city. The salty air was thicker here, filling Rin up as she stared out into the water. The ships perched at the docks were already busy with passengers filing aboard, looking to lead a new life. It wasn't too long ago that passengers of a different kind had been loaded onto these ships like luggage—in chains. The Dahomey military had fierce warriors who protected their people with pride. But they were also thieves and murderers who had contributed to so much of the pain that had taken place in this corner of the earth. This world indeed was haunted by a terrible history. And now, as that history threatened to come to an end, Rin found herself at an inflection point.

Join hands with Uma. Use Committee resources to lure in and stop Hiva, even if the Naacalian solution was a temporary one.

And then what?

Bide time until someone else came up with a better solution? Until it became another generation's problem?

Iris had told her that she only destroyed civilizations after finding them guilty of crimes that could not be undone. What made them deserve any better?

The fire that had once spurred Rin to make her decisions and act on her principles had long died out. At this point, she was a single boat drifting in the ocean to nowhere in particular.

"Fine," Rin said. "I'll do whatever I can, as long as there's something for me to do."

"Wow." Uma snorted. "Well, those are fighting words if I ever heard them."

"And what are you fighting for? The right to create more weapons of war?" Rin remembered those crates of weapons in the underground bunker where they kept the Ark. It was not a luxury liner, but it was not some exploratory vessel either. It was a warship, primed to do battle with whomever they found on the other side of the dimensional rift.

Uma responded with a defiant shrug. "I'm an inventor. You can't blame me for wanting a world to invent in."

"You just want the world to be kept alive so you can continue to wreck it with your needless gadgets," muttered Rin.

"The world owes me." Uma's expression darkened. "I can wreck it if I want."

A long series of coughs pierced through the ensuing silence. John Temple. An awkward interruption to a tense moment.

"At any rate, we have our plan," said Uma, straightening her back. "I'll take Jinn with me to see what I can do for him. And in two months we gather."

"Fine with me," Berta grumbled with a nonchalant shrug and a bratty rise of her chin. She lifted it still higher when she saw Rin shoot another glare at her.

John Temple reached inside his inner jacket pocket and pulled out a folded piece of parchment. A map of the world. Old and beige, as if written on an ancient scroll, it was torn in places. But Rin could still see the little Xs and other symbols drawn he'd drawn in ink. Temple shoved it into her hands.

"When you're ready, take it with you. You'll find them . . . ," he began to say, but then devolved into a series of ugly, full-throated coughs.

Uma grabbed his hand. "The ship I've arranged should be this way, Lord Temple. A few of my loyal men are there, waiting. Consider it a courtesy from one genius to another. But you must know—once you land in Europe, I can't protect you. Not from the rest of the Committee. Not from your own son. You're very brave, facing him."

"Whatever judgment my son passes upon me, I'll accept it. He's my son, after all."

John Temple walked forward just a few steps before turning, swiping the orange shawl from his face so they could see the dimmed light in his eyes.

"There is no action without consequence. What we decide to do now will determine the fate of humanity, but that has always been true. I've only just realized it." He let his withered hand fall to the side. It swung so dangerously, Rin thought it would break. "The choices we make will affect others. Perhaps for generations. Perhaps forever."

"Let us hope, then, dear Lord Temple, that we will all make the right ones in this coming year," Uma told him as the white sails of the port ships flapped gently in the wind.

Choose life. In the place of me, who chose this.

Those were the words he'd told Iris as he lay dying in the Room of Murals. But only one of them was still alive. Only one of them still had the ability to make choices.

Life wasn't fair. Anyone would be a fool to choose it.

5

HOT OFF THE PRESS! THE HEADLINES for today, January sixteenth: Civil War rages in the United States of Colombia! Read all about it in the *New York Times!*"

The newsboy, in his long black jacket, cap, and boots, grabbed Maximo's arm as he passed in the busy street. "A paper for you, sir? They say there's a war brewing over in Europe." He pulled a rolled-up newspaper out of his bag and waved it in Max's face. "Take a look-see—only a couple cents."

"No. Now, go on. Get away from here." With a nervous twinge, Max shooed him off. The child mumbled something rather rude about his British accent before turning to another pedestrian, hounding the foot traffic on Broad Street with the other newsboys.

Maximo's brow twitched as he looked up at the building looming before him. His breath scraped with each step he took up the marble staircase.

To his right, Cherice held on to his arm with both of hers, keeping her head down so that the chatty men in fine suits passing by wouldn't see the wild intensity brimming in her blue eyes. She nudged Max in the ribs. *Don't give up,* she seemed to tell him. He knew, because she'd told him too many times that week alone.

Yeah, I know. Max couldn't say it. Not with Hiva so near. But he hoped the expression he gave Cherice would do the talking for him. *It's now or never.*

At the corner of Broad Street, the white marble pediment perched atop a row of columns reminded Maximo of another grandiose building—the British Museum. He'd been at the museum once with Iris. If he closed his eyes, he'd be able to see her too, marveling at the triangular gable. Shrinking a little, but standing firm nonetheless, in the face of a structure clearly designed to intimidate her.

He hadn't paid too much attention to the precise carvings in the museum's pediment back then. One thing about important buildings in these parts of the world is that they would always make sure to include statues of near-naked white people engaged in bewildering acts, like Roman warriors spearing each other in the head. They were all the same.

But maybe Iris had realized something back then. Something Max saw now as he followed Hiva up the white staircase of the New York Stock Exchange Building, a place he'd only ever seen in newspapers.

The crushing weight of human history.

And of human arrogance.

Eleven limestone figures, crawling, working, writing, producing—and a robed woman in the center with a winged cap, her arms outstretched as if promising the greatest gift of the earth to those men willing to work for it: money.

"These men really did think of themselves as gods," Hiva had told them one night after days holed up in Chetham's Library in Manchester; he had been reading about the history of European civilization while Max and his childhood friends watched, terrified that at any moment the god could burn them to ashes out of boredom.

The constant threat of Hiva looming overhead wore down Max's soul, until all he could see were Iris's ashes, Jinn's corpse, and Rin's sizzling flesh. He couldn't rid himself of the smell of her eye burning. Even after he'd buried his face one day in the food they'd been allowed to eat, it remained. It was as if she'd cursed him.

And all the while, Hiva read about humanity.

"We can't give up," Cherice had whispered to Max as the four friends huddled, frightened, in the corner of the library. "We promise each other, here and now, that we won't give up." Even with sunken eyes and parched lips that had had all the vitality and grit of a wilted flower, she'd made them promise. And so Max had promised. He'd clumsily stitched together what remained of his soul. He'd done it for the ones he had left.

So far only that sniveling Tom Fables seemed to be enjoying himself accompanying Hiva on the god's educational journey, licking Hiva's spittle and wiping his every drop of sweat. That absolute *prat*.

Now, here in New York, Fables flanked Hiva on the right, his head held high like he was the butler of some important head of state, with Jacob and Hawkins on the tin man's other side.

Hiva was never far. His guard was never down. And he never let them run.

But the time for fear had passed. Those days in Manchester had been put to good use. Now they had a plan.

"Hey, Maxey—don't forget, yeah?" Cherice had whispered once in Max's ear, moments before Fables had finally found and brought to Hawkins a book with the picture of New York's infamous Financial District in black and white. That was all he needed nowadays to open up a portal to wherever in the world he wanted to go. A handy power for Hiva. "He's at his most vulnerable *only* after he's killed a bunch of folks. That's it. We got no other chances."

A handy power for them too.

It was macabre to talk about other people's deaths so casually, but they had no other choice. This was the end of days.

A wall of sound rammed into Max the moment he stepped onto the trading floor. In a vast hall that looked like the inside of a busy railroad station, droves of men in top hats and black coats screeched at each other as if they were going to war.

"We're going all in!"

"I want the whole lot! I said the *whole* lot."

"Because of the instability overseas—"

"War might be coming to our shores—"

"Let's take it to fifty—"

Words stumbling over each other in a jumbled mess. None of it made sense, even if he could hear full sentences. They waved their hands madly next to what looked like lampposts, with signs on them Maximo couldn't decipher. Underneath the vaulted ceilings, these men traded as if their lives depended on it, not knowing those lives would soon come to an end.

At the front of the room was a platform and gallery adorned with lamps. Max couldn't hear the ticking of the grandfather clock screwed into the wall behind it, not underneath all the bartering and bleating. Perhaps Hiva could. It might have been Max's imagination, but Hiva's steps against the wooden floor clicked in time with the movements of the second hand.

A man sitting in one of the chairs on the platform balked at the sight of Hiva, a copper-colored statue of a beast with flowers curling in his hair, long enough to sweep the floor. He and the guards rushed at the intruder—and he and the guards were promptly thrown over the platform's railing. Hiva had found his pulpit.

Chaos erupted on the trading floor when the men of commerce found a group of strangers, dressed like filthy-looking street orphans, standing among them. Well, they weren't too far off. But as Hiva burned a man alive to show his power and quiet the men into shock, Maximo suddenly longed for the days he and his friends had been pickpockets in the streets of London, nicking bread and fleeing constables. Those simpler days . . .

Next to him, Cherice gripped his hand. He hadn't even noticed it was trembling. He watched the god stare down the traders from atop his pulpit and waited for his chance.

"Who in the blazes are you?" screamed some old blond man in the crowd, his long, winding mustache twitching while he peered at them through a monocle. His fellow gentlemen of commerce shouted in agreement.

Hiva peered over the rabble. From east to west. His movements slow and subtle. Unimpressed. How like ants they all must have looked to him.

Iris's warm smile flashed in Max's thoughts, melting him on the inside. Tears began budding in the corners of his eyes, shocking even him. He blinked and gasped, taken aback at himself, turning to see Cherice gripping his trousers around the waist, staring up at him through the thick bangs of her apricot-colored bowl-cut hair.

Relax, Max told himself, shutting his eyes. *She's gone. She's in the past. Focus on the present.* He lifted his head. *On the future.*

Hiva began to speak.

"Men of all ages have had their vices . . . and their rituals," said Hiva, lifting his head to the arched rafters of the ceiling. "My first birth had been on the kingdom continent of Zeal, where the Enlightened Ones would sacrifice their children to their gods of culture and magic. Mankind here, too, has long given up human flesh to appease their gods. The Aztecs in the south. And in the central continent, the Dahomean people and the Efik."

A vendor on the streets of Manchester had told them of those "evil places" of so-called barbarians. It was related to the palm-oil soap he was trying to peddle. Palm oil was one of the treasures of Africa, a land too rich for the natives to know what to do with. While trying to sell a few bars, he'd told them tales of the atrocities of those dark, secret places. He'd said all this before offering Hiva, Maximo, and Jacob a discount on soap to wash the city filth from their skin. It wasn't an unusual experience for Max. But the questions Hiva had asked Max afterward had left him feeling unbalanced.

"Why does the man assume we are filthier than the others?"

It wasn't a question Max had wanted to answer, because when he did, he remembered watching his sister being carted off in a carriage without him. Off to be displayed in the next zoo. But he'd had no choice. And so Hiva had studied. Hiva had read.

"In just a few weeks, I've learned much about the world," Hiva said now to his crowd of stockbrokers, who were frozen in confusion and fear.

Things Max himself had never thought too much about. They'd passed by a charity office on Wood Street where volunteers were handing out leaflets decrying depravity around the world. Elsewhere in Manchester, several Methodists had gathered in the slums, publicizing their upcoming expedition to Hong Kong to spread civilization. "Be careful of the bread," he'd heard one say, because it wasn't more than thirty years ago that locals there had purportedly filled a bakery with arsenic to get rid of the colonial officials.

"I learned that human sacrifice comes in many forms," Hiva continued.

"But tell me, which is more evil? For even as you decry the barbarity in other nations, here you sacrifice human flesh on the altar of your own gods." And when Hiva swept his hands over the expanse of the trading floor, Max thought of the winged woman carved into the pediment.

"Gods of your own making," Hiva said. "Nameless and faceless gods with no language. Gods that can only be appeased by the destruction of lands and the slavery of peoples, all unseen to your eyes. How many have you sacrificed to enrich yourselves with their blessings?"

Hiva's riddles were beyond what Max could understand. But for some reason, he thought of his home. He thought of El Salvador and wondered if he'd ever again bask in its warm sun and see the sway of its palm leaves in the breeze.

While Fables grinned wickedly, rubbing his hands together in anticipation of what was to come, Max caught sight of Hawkins. Their eyes locked. It was almost time.

"Sacrifice without remorse. Without justification. Needless and cruel." Hiva's golden eyes glinted, awash with the light of the ledge lamps. "That is what I see when I look upon your kind. And that is why I have found you—"

"Yes." Fables's twig body was twitching in delight, his crooked teeth splitting his face from ear to ear. "Yes, say it. Please say it, master!"

"Guilty."

The gates of hell opened at once. Men were screaming as they burned to ash. Fables laughed fanatically with tears in his eyes as he bent over the ledge and watched Hiva deal justice.

And for a time Max was frozen. Even as Hawkins opened up one of his blue portals between Hiva and the grandfather clock behind him, Max couldn't move. He was supposed to move. He had to move.

But this.

Skin burning, flesh melting off the bone, until not even their skeletons were left. Max shook his head, his fingers entwined in his hair.

He'd heard Iris had murdered the British naval officers on her ship while en route to Ajashe. He'd been unconscious from a bullet to the back. Had it been like this? Life turned to dust with not even a drop of blood to commemorate it?

Wasn't this human sacrifice?

No one could murder so many at a moment's notice and still keep their humanity. It was impossible. Max should know. He was barely clinging to his own psyche.

Was this why Iris had fought so hard against her own destiny?

Was this scene of horror, of clothes without bodies to fill them lying upon the ground, the reason why Iris had moved heaven and earth to create a new reality for herself?

A new reality Max had ripped from her.

"Maxey!" Cherice's scream snapped him out of his spiral.

"Max!" Jacob.

"Max!" And Hawkins. He was ready. The blue portal swirled behind them.

Swallowing the bile rising in his throat, Max clenched his teeth and nodded. Then, without another moment of hesitation, he joined Hawkins in tackling Hiva through the portal.

The blue void slammed the breath from his lungs. He knew the feeling all too well from when he had fallen through this portal and into a grave. But now wasn't the time for memories.

While Hawkins gripped one of Hiva's arms, Max grabbed Hiva's slender body—sinking his fingers into his back—and slammed his head into Hiva's chest, as hard as the pediment's limestone. Wincing in pain, he braced for impact as the waters of the River Thames overwhelmed him.

He and Hawkins had gone swimming there once as a dare. That was the key to Hawkins's power: he couldn't teleport anywhere without first having seen it with his own eyes, whether in real life or in a photo. Then and now, the water of the Thames was a horror of filth and excrement. Here, as the ice-cold water beat against Max's body and chilled his veins, he could see nothing but darkness, even when he opened his eyes.

Don't breathe, Max reminded himself as he lifted his head and watched Hiva's blank eyes widen with bewilderment. Air bubbles burst from the god's mouth and nose. Yes, even a god needed to breathe. Even a god had weaknesses. If Hiva was at his weakest after murdering, then he wouldn't have the strength to avoid sinking to the bottom of the river.

The sharp pains stabbing his lungs told him they'd gone deep enough into the river. He glanced up at Hawkins, who nodded. They both released Hiva at the same time, letting him sink farther into the deep. The water shifted as a portal opened up in front of them.

Let's go, Hawkins seemed to say as he stretched out his hand.

And Max swam for it.

Until he felt a hand gripping his ankle.

He looked down. Hiva.

The god shouldn't have had the strength. Indeed, Hiva's grip felt weaker than it usually did, but it was still strong enough to hold a sinking Max in place.

Damn it! The constant, painful twinging of his lungs shot to his head, making his whole body quiver. Max shook his leg, his arms, his entire body, but Hiva wouldn't let go. In the darkness of the Thames, Hiva's pupilless eyes were the only source of light, wide and glimmering with an inhumane calm. Blank and devoid of life. Max felt as if he were being sucked into them—as if he'd drown in *them.*

That was when he realized he was drowning.

Hawkins grabbed Max's arm and tried to pull him up into the void, but Hiva wouldn't be left behind.

Let me go. Max tried to shake off Hawkins, but his friend wouldn't do it. *You bloody idiot. Let me go.* The fool shook his head and only held on to him more tightly.

One night in Chetham's Library, the others had fallen asleep, but Max remained at the table where Hiva read, at the god's request. His eyes bloodshot, Max had scratched his fingers back and forth against the wooden table, until Hiva shut his book and looked at him.

This is it, Max had thought, his fingers stopping immediately. *I've made too much noise. Now he'll really burn me alive.*

"Maximo," Hiva had begun before saying something truly baffling. "What did you think of my sister when she was alive?"

It was such an odd question; Max didn't know how to answer it. So, after a period of silence, Hiva asked an even stranger one.

"What do you think of *me?*"

Max was at his wits' end and barely holding on to hope. The constant images in his head of Iris decomposing threatened to drive him mad. He had no idea what to say. So he shrugged and gave him one of his crooked smiles.

"Not so bad, I guess. Oi, what am I saying?" And he laughed. "You're a great chap. Good company. The best!"

A joke. But in response, Hiva's eyes had softened.

Or had Max been imagining things? Was Max imagining things now? Hiva's desperation? The pain of betrayal in that not-so-empty tin-man gaze?

Max's body felt as if it would be crushed by the pressure of the current. Blood rushed to his head with majestic fury. If he could get rid of Hiva here, if only for a moment, it would be worth it, even if he had to forfeit his own life. It would be his penance.

Maximo's skull buzzed with pain. His sight dimmed.

And in the river, he heard his mother's voice calling to him. A familiar sound from deep within his memories.

"Maximo, I met a man today," she was telling him in breathless Spanish. "He said he has a work opportunity for us all—you, me, and even little Berta! God knows we need the money. This might be the break we've been looking for."

That short European man with his blond hair curling underneath his hunting hat. Poking his nose around El Salvador on the orders of his wicked master, Carl Hagenbeck.

No, Mama, it's a trap. Don't give us to him. Max couldn't differentiate between his tears and the cold river water. *Everything will go wrong if you do. Don't do it. Please!*

A hand on his wrist pulling him up. A hand on his ankle dragging him down. And the grip of death inhaling him whole. Max gave himself over to all.

"Oh, he's awake. That was fast. You're awake, aren't ya? You bastard!"

Fables's taunts came with a swift kick in the ribs that made Max retch upon the hard floor. He clutched his own throat, frantically coughing out the ashes that filled it, and pried open his stinging eyes. Standing inside the New York Stock Exchange Building was Hiva, his vest, blouse, and trousers water-logged. The flowers in his hair lay limp upon his head, dripping with dirty river water. A screaming newsboy struggled in vain to free his collar from Hiva's grip. He must have heard the commotion and come inside to investigate. The poor boy pled for his life as his legs and black boots thrashed against the floor.

Hiva kept silent. He didn't need to say a word, for his blank eyes blazed with fury.

"I'm sorry," Max began, lifting his hands up as if to stay a beast, his heart beating rapidly in his chest. "I'm sorry for what I did. I was wrong. But please don't—"

"You should be sorry!" Fables kicked Max's back with more strength than Max thought him capable of, knocking the wind out of his chest. Max coughed and grasped at the floor, his fingers sliding along the ashes that were once traders and men of industry. "Pulling a stunt like that!"

Cherice, Jacob, and Hawkins were already on the ground. Only Hawkins was conscious; they had probably left him that way to make use of his power. He'd been beaten: his face was flushing, red, and bruised; his right eye was half closed, and his cheeks were swelling. Had Fables done it? Had that bastard Fables, who borrowed his confidence from being a monster's lackey, dared lay a hand on his friend?

"You son of a—" Max started to yell, but his strength failed him. His powers too. Droplets of water and ash still tickled his throat. Each breath lacerated his lungs. Fables took advantage by kicking him in the face.

"The Naacal once worshipped my sister as their god," said Hiva as the newsboy twitched and wailed in his grasp. "Yet you fight against *me*."

"Don't you mention her," Max spat. In his mind's eye, the face of the woman he wished he could forget smiled shyly back at him. "You're nothing alike. I know that now." And his voice broke. He hung his head as shame and guilt overwhelmed him.

"But you killed her," Hiva said, cocking his head while Fables kicked Max again. "You chose to murder my sister. You chose to believe my words over hers. You saw her as an enemy."

"Yeah. Well, as it turns out, I'm a bloody idiot." His lips quirked into a smile as river water that could have been tears streamed down his thick brown hair and wetted his lips.

What Max saw next he couldn't quite describe. Hiva showed an emotion he'd never seen before on the god's face. As Hiva's jaw set and his eyebrows furrowed, Max could have sworn—

Could have sworn Hiva was . . . jealous?

Hiva's expression was slight but unmistakable. The god's hands curled into fists.

"For eons, my sister destroyed humans without emotion. Life meant nothing to her. When I gave her an opportunity for reflection, she rejected it. When I begged her to change, she rejected *me*."

Begged . . . ? What the hell is he talking about? Max's rib cage felt like it would crack from the rampage of his own heartbeat.

"My sister is dead. *I* am still here. The love that she has received from you all, she doesn't deserve it." Hiva's expression turned dark. "And during this time—humanity's final year—you will learn as she did not to reject me. This is your warning."

"Please!" the newsboy screamed. Probably an orphan like Max. A boy working as hard as he could anonymously in the streets, wishing he had a family and a home to shield him from the evils of the world. "Please!"

Max saw the boy, and he saw himself.

He saw the boy burn to ash and saw his own childhood burst into flames.

"Stop. Stop!" Max wailed until all fell to silence, even Fables's maniacal laughter. Max shook his head. "He was only a boy," he said. "A child. You killed a *child*."

Hiva's fingers twitched, his eyes widening, his lips opening and then shutting again. Whatever vicious, inhuman rage had possessed him in that moment had abruptly vanished.

"I killed . . ." The god's body trembled as he stared at his golden hands. "A child . . ."

Max broke down and screamed, his voice bouncing off the vaulted ceiling. He didn't notice that in the moment, Hiva had taken the boy's ashes and sprinkled them upon himself, tears trickling from his golden eyes. He didn't hear Hiva's whisper:

"Sister . . . is there really no other way?"

WHY BRITAIN MUST GO TO WAR

William Thomas Stead
The Pall Mall Gazette
25 February 1885

We stand on the eve of destiny. On the day that was supposed to mark the triumphant end of the Berlin Conference, securing peace and prosperity for Europe's greatest
nations, Britain will hold a conference of a different sort;
henceforth the twenty-sixth of February will forever be
known as the day the House of Commons hosted their
final debate on the greatest political issue of our times:
Should Britain declare war on Germany?

Alas, there is but one answer I can offer, and that
is yes.

On the thirtieth of last December, the ill-fated Berlin
Conference, sometimes called the Congo Conference by
those aware of the ambitions of Queen Victoria's cousin
King Leopold II of Belgium, ended in blood and infamy
as the European delegates, who had gathered to divide
Africa's territories among themselves, turned on each
other instead in a strange show of barbarity.

The mayhem began when respected Belgian military
general Gerolt Van der Ven, now an international fugitive, assassinated German chancellor Otto von Bismarck,
resulting in Germany invading Belgium one month after.
The instability of Germany, newly at war, soon inspired
acts of Serbian nationalism and terrorism backed by
Russia, a fellow Slavic nation, making both enemies of
Germany. When Germany declared war on Serbia and
Russia, France joined the Slavic countries. It was only a
matter of time before our great nation supported its allies.

The invasion has spurred endless days of political debates as members of Parliament from both sides of the aisle quarrel over Britain's future role in the conflict. But the complicated political fallout of the Berlin Conference has already assured Britain's intervention. First, Belgium is a country Britain has sworn to protect. France is an ally. But most importantly, the success of Germany will almost certainly lead to the country's terrifying growth as a European power; in their greed, a direct attack on Britain's empire would be all but imminent.

I have seen the tragedy of human death that results when a great nation fails to act, even as the circumstances call for a swift hand. War is already upon us. Soon it will land upon England's shores, as surely as the sun will rise. Languid leadership and half-hearted political posturing will end in disaster for the English people, who can only wait and hope for this already raging conflict to end. Our men are ready and able. Our women are moral and upright in their willingness to lend a hand.

Britain must go to war. It is the only path that lies ahead of us if this conflict is to cease.

And as Britain goes to war, so too must her people around the world support her efforts for the good of the empire.

War is, perhaps, a consequence of man's folly. Therefore it can only be man who rectifies it.

May God have mercy on our great country. And may God save the Queen.

6

"YOU'VE DONE YOUR PATRIOTIC DUTY, MR. Stead. Well done."
Inside the cold and lonely office, with the curtains half drawn against
the windows, Adam Temple grinned at the newly printed black ink in
the *Pall Mall Gazette*, at the words he knew would stir the populace. Such was
the formidable influence of the *Gazette's* editor. "Although I wonder if you
went ahead and published your first draft?" Adam continued, making a show
of turning the paper sidewise and squinting. "I don't see nearly enough of your
usual sensationalist flair."

"I've used the power of the pen to enflame the fires of war." The chubby-
cheeked man, sitting at his desk in his long black jacket and vest, rubbed his
dark beard. "Like a boy with a match," Stead said, shaking his head, obviously
disgusted with himself. "Someone like Buckle from the *Times* would have been
much better suited to the job. Why not blackmail *him*?"

"Because *he* wasn't a member of Club Uriel, which participated in the very
same human trafficking you are very publicly against." Adam lifted his chin
only slightly and ran his hands through his hair. Oh, how he relished the titil-
lating sensation that possessed him whenever he heard the whimpers of fearful men. "The Club no longer exists, but the same cannot be said of evidence
of its activities."

Stead straightened his black lapels nervously, then tugged on the too-tight knot of his tie.

Rolling his eyes, Adam set the newspaper down onto a pile of letters and loose sheets of paper on the desk and placed both hands on the smooth chestnut surface, leaning over. "Your articles are applying pressure on the government. I thought you prided yourself on your political reach?"

William Thomas Stead certainly didn't have a problem utilizing his powers of persuasion when he was scandalizing Britain with tales of immorality and sexual impropriety. But Adam knew as much as any prostitute walking the East End: all wealthy men were hypocrites. Especially his fellow evangelicals.

"Worry not. As long you keep to our agreement, no harm will come to your reputation or your career," Adam assured him with a dismissive wave of his hand. "You'll continue writing such articles for the next several months. You'll drum up public support and force the government's hand. It'll be your campaign even after Parliament votes to go to war."

Stead's trembling hand gripped his quill. "And what makes you so sure Parliament will vote the way you want it to? Gladstone won't let Britain go to war so willingly. Even after two months, his will is firm."

"His will is shaking," Adam said, straightening his back. "And it will soon break."

Adam knew because he'd sent Fool to monitor Gladstone day and night. Like any good spy, Fool saw Britain's prime minister in his secret moments, during those times when he wasn't posturing for his colleagues and the public. And like any good servant, Fool gave each report to Adam discreetly and in a timely manner. A furious campaign from the *Pall Mall Gazette*, of all newspapers—a publication accused of favoring him—now all but slandering him for his "languid leadership." It was only a matter of time before the man cracked.

"I remember several years ago when you sat in my Yorkshire parlor with my father and his friends. The group of you were enjoying a spot of tea, talking about politics and what was wrong with the country these days and the rest of it. I poured you a cup. Do you remember?"

Stead gave a silent nod, though Adam could tell from his downcast eyes that he didn't.

"That was when you said something I'll never forget. Something you said some friend of yours had once told you: 'The governments would have no difficulty keeping peace if only the journalists were all hanged.'"

Stead stiffened while Adam laughed, a hearty, youthful sound.

"As you implied, Mr. Stead: you are like a boy with a match." Adam's blue eyes flashed. "Journalism is a powerful tool. I *order* you to keep the fire burning."

Stead's breath hitched when Adam plucked a journal off his desk and flipped through the pages. Some reports on child prostitution. Looked like he was investigating. And what was this? Early notes on a manuscript he was planning to write next year: "How the Mail Steamer Went Down in Mid-Atlantic, by a Survivor." So Stead had plans for the future. How quaint.

Adam knew that many members of the ill-fated Club Uriel hadn't actually believed in the apocalypse. Stead certainly didn't: he was a man with ambition. For some, their membership was merely a matter of status. It had counted for something, being a member of one of Pall Mall's most illustrious gentlemen's clubs.

What's more, knowledge of the supernatural—of the secrets of the world— made those so-called gentlemen feel powerful. And when men felt powerful, they were willing to hang up their morals like a coat on a hook to revel with the false gods of Babylon.

Adam believed in no false god. His life's journey thus far as a schemer and a dreamer had taught him that only one god existed, created for the purest purpose of all: the genocide of mankind. He was a true believer. That was why he still stood, while many members of that ruinous club had already met their bloody end.

All men would fall when Hiva began her rapture.

Stead's thick Adam's apple bobbed carefully in his throat as the man gulped. *Yes, choose your words carefully, you fool,* Adam thought, grinning and throwing the journal back onto his desk.

"A-and how long do I have to keep these fires burning?" Stead asked.

A nonsensical question. But Adam was very calm when he answered, "When I find her again. Then the *true* fires of hell will burn."

Adam had clawed his way into the media. Now for just one more push.

Donning his top hat, Adam adjusted his long coat and walked out into the busy London streets, shielding himself with his hand from the early morning sun. The horses stamped their hooves impatiently as they waited in front of the building with his carriage in tow. The newsboys nearby were screaming about the war and the vote Parliament would soon hold. It was a pressing matter in Europe; Adam supposed the pedestrians who snatched newspapers left and right would be more worried about that than about what had just happened in New York. But it was precisely that news across the pond that bothered him now as he swiftly entered his carriage.

The murders at the New York Stock Exchange Building . . . Was it her doing?

The horses began trotting through London. Adam settled into his cushioned seat, his shoulders rubbing against the arm of a tall man's black cloak. The tickle caused a burst of laughter to erupt from the man's lips, but laughter wasn't at all foreign to a Fool.

"What news do you bring me?" Adam asked as beside him, the two halves of Fool's harlequin mask glimmered.

"Madame Bellerose is still in France with her sights set on populating the Ark. She's not only spearheading the creation of charity organizations—she's sent the Committee's Fools to the doorsteps of select people across the globe: Rockefeller and Vanderbilt in America. The Romanovs. Cecil Rhodes, and Viscount William Hesketh Lever and his brother James. A number of French nobles—"

Adam put up a gloved hand to silence him. "I get it," he said, and turned his head, smiling at his reflection in the window. "So she's already sending out her invitations."

The country going to war was the perfect bait for the wealthy and privileged hoping to escape its ravages, especially given whispers of the destructive potential of brand-new weapons of war being used on the battlefield that exceeded the imagination. The world had Bosch to thank for advancements in the machinery of death. If he hadn't made use of the white crystal in his technologies, the weapons being put to use surely would not have been invented for another thirty years. The coming war promised to be the greatest ever in the history of man—an apocalypse in its own right. This, at least, was the fear of most men.

"And with these invitations, Madame Bellerose hopes to ingratiate herself with the most powerful figures in the world," said Fool.

"She aims for power herself." Adam laughed. "As chaos reigns over Europe, her powerful friends will be indebted to her. And whenever the war comes to its inevitable end, her 'charity' organizations will secure lucrative donations to pick up the pieces of a ravaged continent. She'll enrich herself in wealth and prestige. If things go her way, she'll become a queen of two worlds."

But for things to go Adam's way, there was one piece of information he needed to know. Sucking in his breath, half fearing the answer, he turned to his Fool.

"Have you found her?" A simple question.

As Fool shook his head, Adam yelled in frustration, slapping his servant across the face. Fool's black-and-white mask didn't budge. It never budged—not for this Fool, nor for any of the Fools under the Committee's employ—for deep down, the man who'd spawned the Fools could not live with the regret of the evil he'd committed in his earlier years. That man, Dr. Heidegger, had been the serial killer once known as the Harlequin Slasher before the South Kensington fair explosion had breathed life into his conflicting emotions, turning them into flesh-and-blood Fools who served at the behest at the Enlighteners.

Well, not all the Fools. Adam was quite persuasive and, save for a few bursts of anger here and there, was far more pleasant an employer than the likes of Van der Ven or Bellerose.

"We need to find Iris," Adam said. "We need to find both Hivas."

Ever since the strange stories from New York had spread overseas—tales of Wall Street men disappearing overnight—Adam had picked up the pace of the search. Only one creature could turn men to dust.

But there were two Hivas. Which of them was active? He hadn't spent nearly enough time with this new Hiva to get a sense of where his loyalties lay. If he was as Iris had been in her past lives, it very well could have been him laying waste to men in America.

That won't do. It has to be Iris. Only my Iris. Adam bit his lip hard enough to draw blood. It was Iris whose crystal heart had dazzled him in his childhood. Iris whom he had brought back to life when her bones hung on display in the South Kensington fair ten years ago. Iris whose exquisite beauty and daring nature had set his body aflame. Only she had the right to end humanity. No imitations would suffice. It was why he had started this war in the first place.

Iris was their Hiva. The Hiva called to end *his* wicked world.

No other Hiva would do.

"Tell the other Fools on our side to be on the lookout for both," Adam ordered Fool.

Fool nodded obediently before cocking his head sideways at such an odd angle, it made Adam cringe. "And what of Van der Ven? He's still on the run."

Adam couldn't hold back his laughter. "Of course he is! With his home under Bellerose's constant surveillance, there's no way he'll be returning to Eight Grandage View anytime soon. From a powerful and feared major general to a vagabond. Serves him right. But watch his movements. Report back to me if you notice anything amiss." Adam grinned, wishing badly he'd seen the horrified look on that arrogant brute's face when he'd learned that *he* was the assassin who had begun the Great War. He'd escaped Berlin by the skin of his teeth. "With all of Europe chasing him, I don't suppose he'll be much of a threat to me. Still, you can never be too sure."

"I'll do all you say, my lord," Fool responded.

"Yes, you will. Very good, then."

Fool bowed his head slightly, the puckered golden lips of his mask glittering in the sun. "There's no loyal Fool such as I."

Adam gave him a sidelong look, surprised at the pinch of sadness he felt staring at the broken man. And he was indeed broken. But broken men were easy to manipulate.

There were many pieces to play in this deadly game of chess. But Adam himself had his limits. He just hoped he had enough wits to move them at the right time.

This is all for you, Iris, he thought, closing his eyes. *For us both.* Before her suicide, his mother had warned him about the end times to come. The ascent of false prophets who would show them great signs and wonders, but who would deceive and lead them into the desert.

"All have been led astray by false gods," she'd warned him, just hours before she'd hung herself in her bedroom. Adam remembered the crack of lightning in the night outside her window. Her hollow eyes and sallow skin. Her body, wasted away because she'd barely eaten in weeks. Her physical health, which had deteriorated along with her mind. "Little Adam. Don't be led astray like the rest of these wicked men. The murderers and the robbers. The wicked and the greedy. Remember what I taught you: 'For as the lightning cometh out of the east, and shineth even unto the west; so shall also the coming of the Son of man be.'"

Adam had been quite young when he'd seen his mother hanging in her bedroom that night. And he remembered thinking, as he gazed upon her limp body and the red silk bedsheet tied around her neck, that her death had been quite beautiful—far more so than that of his siblings, whose brains had had to be scrubbed from the streets of Yorkshire.

If he'd had the power to save his mother that night, he would have done so. If he'd had the power to erase those who'd threatened his family's happiness, he would have burned them to ashes in seconds. But he had been but a powerless boy.

At times he still felt powerless. Enragingly so.

His mother's murder by the cruelty of his world had not surprised him, nor had he been fazed by the men and women of wealth and status gossiping at her funeral. Those were but the dark days his mother had warned him of.

For wheresoever the carcass is, there will the eagles be gathered together. Such must be the fate of all born in a world built by men.

One more push.

7

LATER THAT NIGHT, ADAM HAILED A cab. But no matter how expensive the cab a man hailed, once he arrived at the West End, he would eventually have to endure the foot traffic of the bustling streets. Tonight added more visitors than usual to the thick crowds of Leicester Square: Vesta Tilley was debuting a new show.

It was obvious to Adam as he squeezed his way through the street hordes that this new set from the famous cross-dressing impersonator was highly anticipated by her fans—a delight to the working classes, no doubt, and though most of the middle and upper classes wouldn't dare be seen braving the chaos of a musical hall, he spotted a few among the already drunk men primed for a night of entertainment. Certainly a few gentlemen in fashionable high-buttoned frock coats wouldn't seem so out of place in a crowd of giggling women, rowdy sailors, and pickpockets stealing food from windows in the darkening evening—even if two of those men were members of Parliament.

Gladstone lowered his top hat. "On the eve of the vote, no less," he mumbled. "I don't know how I let you convince me to leave Downing Street."

"Oh, come now, William, you can't stay shut up in Number Ten forever. Might I remind you that you were the one who agreed to go with the boy?" John Poyntz Spencer clapped the prime minister's bad back a little too hard. A cough escaped Gladstone's lips as he buckled forward.

Yes, the old man had agreed. Being a Temple came with a number of useful connections that Adam had no qualms about manipulating. "It's not so bad, is it—seeing a show with the masses every once and again?"

"The very same masses who have followed you for years," Adam reminded him. Indeed, a portrait of Gladstone adorned the walls of many a working-class home in London.

John Spencer, the fifth Earl Spencer, was twenty-six years the prime minister's junior, but not a young man by any means. His great brown beard covered his chest like a rug, but what mattered more was his tongue: as sharp as the tips of his drooping mustache. Some of the prime minister's own party had had to be persuaded by more . . . creative means. Finding weak points and exploiting them was not so difficult for Adam. Affairs here, embezzlements there. Being a member of the Enlightenment Committee gave one ways to find information on politicians, which could be used to control and ruin them when the occasion called for it. Earl Spencer was one of the few refreshing Liberals who had quickly fallen in line with the changing public sentiment surrounding the war. As one of the prime minister's closest friends and allies, he was crucial for pushing the old curmudgeon.

"War. War?" Gladstone shook his head. "My government's already in a weaker position than it once was. Things haven't been right since Major-General Gordon left for Khartoum."

Adam nodded, because he had to make a show of commiserating. "Ah, yes. The situation in Northeast Africa has been shaky as of late, hasn't it? The Mahdists beating back the Egyptians. Major-General Gordon vowing to evacuate the Crown's troops. It was the talk of the country—why, before the Berlin Conference, that is."

"Gordon, that bloody stubborn foozler. He's fast becoming a celebrity for playing 'hero' in Sudan." Earl Spencer rubbed the thin sheet of hair covering his balding head. "You're generally liked, Gladstone, yes. But the people haven't forgotten that you abandoned the man in that godforsaken hellhole."

Earl Spencer would have continued, except he'd bumped into a pedestrian—or rather, the pedestrian had bumped into him deliberately. A pale, willowy young woman in a filthy blue dress stopped and apologized, her back so hunched over, they could barely see her face from behind the straight-cut bangs of her short black hair. In her arms, she held a bundle of dirty white towels. The quivering thing inside must have been a baby.

Surely that was what the earl and the prime minister would assume.

"I'm sorry, my lords," she apologized again in a rough voice—too rough. She must have been practicing. Good girl.

Gladstone eyed her hungrily for just a moment before he realized he was among fellow gentlemen. Straightening his shoulders, he let out a cough. For all this boasting of ethics, he could never quite control himself when it came to lowborn but pretty girls out in the evening.

But this one you won't be so interested in for much longer. Adam covered his lips with a white-gloved hand.

When the girl looked up, she caught and held Adam's blue eyes for only a moment before lurching off again. With a wicked grin, Adam straightened his coat and continued.

"Come now, Earl Spencer, the prime minister has sent troops." Adam noted the too-rough click of Gladstone's cane against the cobblestones. "The Egyptian garrison and the civilians *should* be able to hold on with what little food they're *salvaging* among themselves." Out of the corner of his eyes, Adam watched Gladstone lower his head ever so slightly.

"But was it too late?" continued Earl Spencer. "The troops haven't even arrived yet. My lord, I won't coddle you with sweet words. The hard truth is that public sentiment can change with frustrating speed. Even the Queen was on Gordon's side. We can't make the same mistake in this case, not when Europe stands on the brink of war. Military intervention is needed."

"Military intervention is *costly*—in lives and money." Gladstone couldn't hide his age—not with his conservative words and not with his physical features. His white hair peeked out from the back of his top hat. He frowned with the thin lips of a disapproving old man, the lines creasing his face in deep folds. His little sunken eyes narrowed. "Your father and grandfather were the adventurers, dear Adam. And though they were good friends, close friends indeed, I share little of their zeal for such things."

"A war isn't an adventure," Adam corrected him as he stared up at the teetering tenement buildings bordering the square—and then at the Alhambra Theatre, an intimidating building with twin spiraling white towers, a splendid dome, and fenestration in the style of the Spanish Renaissance. "It's an investment. One that can help distract from your scandal in Africa—and certain scandals at home."

When Gladstone crinkled his long, pointed nose, Adam knew he was thinking of the problem that people in London had increasingly begun whispering about. The supernatural. Those accidents of nature, touched by Satan. Rumors and eyewitness accounts were spreading—of giant nutcrackers fighting in the street, and men disappearing and reappearing into thin air, or else transforming into all manner of beast.

And then there was the Basement: the Crown's dungeon beneath the Crystal Palace, where all manner of experimentation had been conducted against those given powers as a result of the South Kensington fair explosion ten years ago. A place of misery and sickness that had ended in blood, death, and rebellion.

The place was empty now, cleared of the corpses the prisoners had made as they fled the facility. Unfortunately, the Basement escapees had not been entirely subtle as they'd ripped through England, causing situations one could only explain by blaming a lower power. Gladstone, as a top official in the know, had far too much on his hands.

"Yes." He lowered his voice. "I had hoped the situation at home would have been . . . contained by now. But starting a war would throw this country into greater turmoil."

"Or would it galvanize them?" Adam said. "Give them a normal conflict to concentrate on—one of mere flesh and blood that they can understand. You're still wondering yourself. That's why I asked you to come out with me, and that's why you agreed to come."

"I agreed to come as a favor to your late father, who once convinced me that you would one day make a particularly loyal member of my party."

Adam's shoulders rose quickly. He gritted his teeth. His father had always wanted him to go into politics. It was a strong front for what had been planned to be his real work, in continuing his family's legacy as members of the

Enlightenment Committee. Power and prestige. That was what mattered to his father—much more than the adventure. The excitement of *getting* more of what others didn't have.

Taking a deep breath, he slapped on his mask and grinned amicably nonetheless. "Prime Minister, I brought you here so that you would relax. But I also wanted you to be among the people. I want you to see this new show. See the support that the British people have for the war effort."

A noncommittal grunt was all Adam received in response, but even that was according to his plan. Here at the Alhambra, Gladstone would see a show he wouldn't soon forget.

Once they had entered the theater, the three gentlemen sat in a private box on the upper left of the auditorium's third circular floor. It was a grand theater indeed, opulent with a heavy velvet curtain separating the stage from the orchestra pit, but the intricate design of the maple floor and the ridge of their box couldn't compete with the musk of cigarette smoke and body odor, or with the bawdy laughter of the raffish crowd that packed the rows of scarlet floor seats.

Gladstone let out a frustrated sigh, wiping down his coat as if the stench of immorality was clinging to him. Indeed, the theater was an odd mixture of the grandiose and the slovenly. Music halls were never quite considered appropriate for respectable men and women and their families; Adam had very rarely seen so many young men scandalously associating with unaccompanied women, except in taverns on the East End. But this was where the people were.

Rowdy cheers filled the hall when the curtain parted and Vesta Tilley took the stage. Cheers were followed by gasps. The woman was one of the most famous entertainers in Britain. She'd made her bread impersonating men ever since she'd been a child. But how could the crowd not gape, seeing the tiny woman looking dapper in a brown, tightly buttoned British military uniform and trousers?

"Oh, is she supposed to be one of our soldiers?" Earl Spencer's laughter was deep and rolling as he slapped Adam on his left shoulder.

To Adam's right, Gladstone reached into his coat pocket, pulled out a gold-rimmed quizzing glass, and placed it up to his eye so he could see better.

With light steps, Tilley began dancing and singing to the jaunty tune of brass instruments.

"Here I am, here I am,
Patted and petted as though I were
A real live lord,
Better than the convalescent ward.
What a treat, lots to eat.
Who was it said we were short of meat?
I feel a bit queer,
But there's nothing to fear
With the Liberals here.
I might as well stay in bed.
'The war is too frightening,' the prime minister said."

And when a "frightened" Tilley knocked her knees together, the crowd burst out laughing. The three gentlemen exchanged glances as Gladstone sat up, his back pin straight.

"No complaints, no complaints.
The Liberals are satisfied, no complaints.
You could ask my French chums,
And if they were alive,
You'd hear them all say, 'Thumbs!'
But I left them to die on the front,
And bought some chocolates. Oh, I say!
Such lovely chocs!
The boys and I, we guzzle those sweets till our faces turn white,
While the continental boys fight,
While their wives cry all night,
Because 'the war is too frightening,' the prime minister said."

"What in the blazes is *this*?" Gladstone shouted, glaring at Adam and Earl Spencer, his cheeks bright red. "Is this a joke?"

He looked down at the jeering crowd and pressed his lips shut, just as an oafish-looking caricature of Gladstone himself stumbled onto the stage with a bottle of whiskey in one hand, swinging his cane in the other.

> *"Gordon cried. 'Help me,' he said.*
> *Well, I'd rather they lifted me in my little bed,*
> *To hell with England; let the countries go on ahead,*
> *I'd rather a saucy little nursie*
> *Tuck me in and call me Percy. . . ."*

As Tilley's British soldier and "Gladstone" clasped hands and began fighting over the bottle of whiskey, Gladstone shook with anger. And of course he did. What self-respecting man of status would enjoy seeing himself lampooned in front of his constituents? The stage hadn't taken so long to prepare, but Adam had paid extra to make sure the material would be particularly degrading. He did quite have a flair for the dramatic.

Tilley stopped and glanced up at their box. For Earl Spencer and Gladstone, they would likely think it was their imagination, an accident, or a bit of coincidence. But there was no such thing for Adam. Resisting the temptation to give her a little wink, Adam lifted his head and she continued.

"This is ridiculous," Gladstone said, finally shooting to his feet.

"This is reality." Adam shook his head sadly. "Look at the crowd. My God, man. This is what they truly think of you. It's in the papers. Right here in the theater."

Gladstone's hands trembled atop his cane. He sneered at Adam as if he wanted to accuse him of something but didn't know how to make it sound sane. Finally he pried open his liver-spotted lips. "You brought me here because you knew about this show. You wanted to see me humiliated."

"He wants you to see reason." Earl Spencer stood and grabbed his friend's arm. "You can't hide in your home, afraid to hear what the people are saying about you. Don't gamble away the goodwill you have left. Don't give the Tories any more ammunition against you."

> *"While the continental boys fight,*
> *While their wives cry all night—"*

"Enough!" With an angry wave of his hand, Gladstone turned and began to leave the box.

It was because they'd spent so much time bickering, perhaps, that they didn't notice a young woman rush onto the stage and collapse next to Tilley. The crowd's jeers and laughter had already turned into gasps and confused chatter.

Gladstone stopped when the black-haired woman screamed bloody murder.

The music died. Earl Spencer raised a monocle to his face and squinted as he peered through it. "What?" He leaned in. "Why, that's—"

"The woman from earlier." Adam stood against the ledge and stared over the box. "The one you bumped into."

Still dirty from head to toe. Still in her filthy blue dress, and with the stained white towels covering what looked like her little bundle of joy.

"Gladstone! Gladstone," she cried like a ghoul in the night. "My husband is dead because of you! Oh, the horrors of the siege! The plight of Khartoum! How many of them have been slaughtered because of the prime minister's inaction?"

The child was crying too, but only because the boy genius Henry Whittle, grandson of London's premier toymaker, had programmed it to. As it turned out Mary, his maid, was a delightful little actress. Not as good as the flamboyant Lucille, but the shape-shifter had her own mission to complete for Adam. They'd each had their marching orders—Adam had given it to them personally while he caged them inside a decrepit shack in Devil's Acre by Westminster. A dirtied face, a black wig, and a toy babe were more than enough of a disguise for the Whittles' mousy little servant girl. Mary White, Lucille Bouffant, and Henry Whittle—with Cortez dead, his old tournament team was now under Adam's employ.

Vesta gritted her teeth, maddened. Adam hadn't told her about this part of the plan, because while money could pay for certain things—like a brand-new show tearing the prime minister to shreds—it couldn't soften the ego of an interrupted entertainer.

But this part was crucial.

"You! Prime Minister Gladstone!" And Mary pointed at their box. The crowd gaped, shocked at the three gentlemen—two of them members of Parliament—standing around in the gallery like lost children. "Prime Minister Gladstone! Oh, Prime Minister! Why did you abandon my husband in Sudan? Why are you abandoning us again?"

"Wh-what?" Gladstone rubbed his sunken eyes in disbelief. "What are you—?"

"You abandoned our men. The Egyptians. The civilians. My husband. Now you'll abandon Europe? England? Your people?" The "baby's" cries pierced through her own sobbing shrieks. "For shame!"

Even if Gladstone had answered, Adam wouldn't have been able to hear it among the jeers. It was when people began throwing things that Earl Spencer grabbed Gladstone's arm.

"We need to go. Now," the earl hissed, dodging a mud-covered shoe.

"I've . . . I've never in my l-life . . ." the old man stuttered as if he were half-traumatized.

Good. The vote should go smoothly tomorrow.

A flair for the dramatic indeed. Adam tried not to pat himself on the back. He looked back at Mary, who continued to weep on the floor before letting herself be dragged behind the curtain by stagehands.

"Come quickly." Adam had just grabbed Gladstone and begun to help him hobble out of the box—

When the crowd's jeers turned to shrieks of agony.

Dropping Gladstone's arm, Adam whipped around. Tilley and her performers were running for their lives. The musicians were not so lucky.

One moment they were there. The next, the orchestra pit was filled with lonely instruments in piles of ashes.

Men and women of the crowd were scrambling on top of one another to escape, pulling on one another's vests, bowler hats flying.

So did heads, when bodies began to disintegrate.

"Wh-what is this?" What little lingering flush in Gladstone's face disappeared in an instant. "What's happening?"

"We're under attack!" Earl Spencer cried, gripping his head with both hands, his eyes bulging. "We're under attack!"

"We're under attack . . . ," Adam whispered. Unlike the other two men, he slowly moved closer to the wooden railing separating their box from the mayhem below. People were disappearing. No, they were being turned to dust. Burned from the inside out.

He recognized this method of murder.

"Iris?" A sudden flower of hope blossomed inside of him, and his heart beat against his rib cage. It couldn't be. But who else could end lives with such grace? With not a single drop of blood? He peered through the auditorium, which was growing increasingly dark due to the ashes rising into the air. But he couldn't see her. He couldn't see his Iris.

Iris. The goddess of death sent to earth to judge humanity guilty and lay waste to civilizations. Adam's goddess of justice. Hiva.

Sparking the fire that lit the matches of war at the Berlin Conference. Pushing England and its colonies to join the bloody fray. It had all been to draw her out—to convince her of mankind's true nature. To drive her to bring this corrupt and worthless civilization to an end.

Had he finally succeeded?

"Iris!" he cried, leaning over the ledge, gritting his teeth in anger as Earl Spencer tried to tug him away. "Iris?"

"What are you doing, boy? We need to get out of here!"

Just when Adam shrugged him off, he caught a glimpse of someone standing behind a gap in the stage curtains. He held his breath as beautiful scenarios of reunion and reconciliation captured him, freezing him to the spot.

Then his shoulders dropped. He slowly narrowed his eyes, peering through the thick fog of ashes. It couldn't be. The boy's curly brown hair fluttered out of sight just as Earl Spencer succeeded in dragging him away. Of course he did— Adam hadn't the strength to deny him.

The boy's face was a scourge. But it was unmistakable.

"Maximo . . . ?"

Maximo Morales. That couldn't be. That duplicitous guttersnipe was *dead*. He had fallen with Club Uriel the day the building had burned down and most of the club's members had been torn to shreds. Adam hadn't seen or heard of him since. But his brown face and stubby nose were unmistakable. Adam would remember the face of the young man he'd once blackmailed into his service. The difference was that back then, during the Tournament of Freaks that had pitted London's secret monsters against one another in battle, Maximo had always hidden his self-hatred and shame behind that ridiculous lopsided smile of his.

But this time, his mouth had been agape and his brown eyes wide in horror before he disappeared behind the smoke and curtains.

A torrent of questions colonized Adam's thoughts as Earl Spencer pulled him down the stairs and out into the streets. Adam's brilliant mind could usually handle many questions at once. But there was only one he desperately wanted an answer to. The one that had been haunting his dreams for months.

Where are you, Iris?

8

*I*F *I CAN'T KILL HIVA, WHAT if I can use Hiva? Get him to only kill the ones who deserve to be killed? Like that bastard Temple?*

That was what Max had thought as he'd returned, defeated, to London through Hawkins's portal. If they couldn't find a way to stop Hiva, then at least they could make use of him. It could be an opportunity. After all, from all Max had seen in his short life, only one thing was certain to him: that some people in this sick world shouldn't be alive.

It had been another plan cooked up out of desperation. But like his assassination attempt in New York, it had failed. Miserably.

The ones who *deserved* to be killed? And who had made him the arbiter of justice?

With a crack of thunder, the clouds showered the earth. In the dark alleyway where they'd planned to meet, Max rounded on the black-haired woman the moment she turned the bricked corner. The moment he gripped her slender shoulders, she gasped and dropped the baby in her arms. The toy was well made—of course it was. It was a Whittle creation. Its jaw flew open like a nutcracker's, and from the inside, the sounds of a baby's cry whined in the night fog, but there was no damage done to its sandy-brown wooden body. Henry was quite the toymaker.

"It didn't work," Max told the woman who'd cried bloody murder on Vesta Tilley's stage. "I saw that rat escape with his Parliament stooges."

"Well, that's not my fault, is it? I did as we agreed." Mary White whipped off her black wig to reveal her long strawberry-blond hair, done up today in a tight bun. "I told you where Adam would be and when. I thought you said Hiva would do it. You said you'd convince him to do it. I thought you'd finally get rid of that madman!"

Adam. As Mary gulped back tears, Max thought of their chance meeting in the Devil's Acre near Westminster Abbey. Hiva's anger from Max's assassination attempt in New York had curiously dissipated. Curiouser still, after they'd returned to England, he'd sent Max to the slums to find them a "home."

"We will become closer, you and I," Hiva had told him. "To erase all misconceptions."

Max couldn't fathom what Hiva was thinking. Sometimes Hiva reminded him of that Roman god Janus: the god with two faces, Chadwick had once told him. A god who didn't seem to know whether he was coming or going.

Max could only do as he was told. That was when he had found Mary, cold, alone, and crying. A fellow freak from the tournament who was being held captive with her teammates, given a sliver more freedom than the others for reasons even she couldn't fathom. How useful would their powers be in the fight against Hiva? He'd just needed to get them away from that prat Adam. . . .

Another crack of thunder. Rain drenched the alleyway.

"All those people in the music hall." Max had never seen so much ash in his life. "All dead."

"Because of Adam," Mary said. "Think about what he's done to us." As the downpour drenched her hair and clothes, Mary squeezed her wet wig in both hands, peering up at Max with pleading blue eyes. "Think about all the horrible things he's made us do. The war in Europe—"

"I know." Max gritted his teeth, relieving his grip a little. Adam had manipulated the three into kick-starting a continental war. And now with this stunt, he'd all but ensured that Britain would join the mayhem. Adam was insane. He needed to die. That was what Max had told Hiva last night in their new "home."

"Adam Temple is evil. If there's anyone who deserves judgment, it's him,"

Max had said, and shuddered a little when Hiva stared at him with a kind of earnest, hopeful gaze.

"You *seek* my judgment? You acknowledge my worth?"

"O-of course!" Max slapped on the fakest, cheesiest grin he could muster. "Didn't I tell you? You're not such a bad guy!"

"You tried to kill me."

"What's a little squabble between mates?"

After Max saw Hiva fall silent in contemplation, he decided then that he would lie as much as he needed to. Adam Temple was wicked. And Hiva was all about punishing the wicked.

Hiva had just laid waste to an entire music hall instead. More blood on Max's hands.

How much more could he stand before he broke?

Max hung his head, breathing heavily to calm himself, bits of rain slipping through his lips and into his nostrils. It wasn't supposed to be like this. Adam had been right there in the upper box. With one thought from Hiva's twisted mind, he could have been gone.

And it would have been one more devil done with.

Thunder rumbled beneath the dark clouds. In the alleyway, Max looked up at the London sky. It seemed to be weeping for the lives just lost—as well as the lives that would soon come to ruin.

"What do we do now?" Mary asked, her mousy voice breaking. "Adam has Van der Ven under constant watch from Fool. I can't even be sure he's not watching us now!"

And with jerky movements, she began whipping her head around, watching the rooftops for a top hat, a harlequin mask, or even the flit of a cape. Max understood too well. Hiva had a system. If any one of them was gone from his sight for more than thirty minutes, he would kill the rest. It was how he kept them by his side.

Both teams were hostages.

Mary shook her head. "There's no telling what Adam will have us do next. Starting a war. Causing people to die. All for what? To draw out Iris?"

"If that's what he wants, then he's in for a shock." Max flashed a wry, self-hating grin and let his arms drop to his sides. "Because she's dead. For good."

Taking a shaky step back, Mary clutched her hands to her chest, her brows furrowed in utter disbelief. "Wh . . . what?"

"She's dead. Completely dead." Saying the words hollowed out Max from the inside. His body felt heavy as rain soaked his vest and trousers. "She's dead and gone. I saw it with my own eyes. I—"

I killed her. Max swallowed the words, his gaze unable to meet Mary's.

Mary was silent for too long, shaking her head. "But then . . . but then Adam . . ."

"If Adam were to find out, he'd either put a stop to his rampage or go on an even bigger one," Max told her, his expression venomous as he thought about that rich prat's smug grin. He couldn't even take pleasure in shoving Iris's death in his face, because Adam was too much of a loose cannon to guarantee that whatever tantrum he'd throw in response could be contained.

Mary bit her lip, squeezing droplets of rainwater from her wig. "What . . . what do I do?"

"The question of the year, isn't it?" Humanity's last year, that was.

"At the very least, please promise you'll help us." Mary brushed water-logged blond strands from her face as she pleaded, as if to reveal the desperation in her eyes. "Get us away from Adam. We can't do anything to help if we're still trapped in that house like dogs."

Max watched the rain spattering the pavement. "I don't know if I can—"

"No, you must!" Mary pressed up against him so suddenly, he moved back. "You must help! Promise me!"

"And then what?" Max gave her a gentle shove to widen the gap between them. "What are you, the shape-shifter, and the toymaker going to do in all this?"

Mary didn't answer. But how could Max expect her to answer a question that eluded him as well? No matter how many days passed and how many plans formed and crumbled, he simply didn't know where to go next. Once again he was lost at sea, drifting and aimless.

The story of his life.

"Maybe we should all just let Hiva kill us."

Mary's deep frown creased her pretty, cherubic face. "Max . . . do you really think that?" And when Max didn't respond, she shook her head. "Henry—I mean, Mr. Whittle—is a cynical brat, really, just terrible. As rude as they come—"

She caught herself. The sight of her sheepish expression made Max genuinely laugh for the first time in what felt like forever.

"Don't let me stop you," he said, giving her a cheeky smile. "Don't worry, this stays between us."

Mary blushed. "Well, what I mean is . . . as bad as things are, even he won't give up. Same with Lucille. We're all . . ." She paused and looked up at the thundering night sky. "We're all trying to find a way to survive this."

"Well. You all have a lot more faith than I do." Scoffing, Max rubbed the back of his head before a sudden realization seized him. "It's almost been half an hour. I have to get back to the others. Take care of yourself, Mary. Give my regards to Henry and Lucille."

The rain was so heavy, he almost didn't hear Mary calling to him after he started down the alleyway. When he turned around, the soaked girl looked even smaller standing alone in the night. He could see she hadn't been eating. Her once rosy cheeks were dull and sunken. And the moment he wondered if she were sick, he thought of Berta, his little sister, still somewhere in West Africa with plans of her own, as the countdown toward humanity's end ticked.

"We can't give up," Mary told him in a weak voice as rain poured down her face. "We have to do something. Whether it's the war or Hiva. We have to do something. I . . ." She pursed her lips together, and even with the streams of water, Max could tell she was crying. "I don't want to die."

But do I? Max asked himself. Despite the cold, his hands still somehow felt warm. The wetness reminded him of Iris's blood.

No. He shook his head. Even though he so badly wanted to, he couldn't give up now. Not with Berta's life on the line.

There was one more card he could play. One card. It'd been on his mind since the day they had returned to England from New York. Since the day that at Hiva's command—at Hiva's *request*—they'd begun searching for their new "home."

Wandering through London's worst slums was part of Hiva's "journey of discovery." Part of the process of validating his own destruction of humanity. He'd read about it in *Household Words*, a weekly magazine slipped in between the pages of *Crime and Punishment*. Hiva wanted to learn everything about this world. He wanted to see with his own eyes how "the most lordly streets are frequently but a mask for the squalid districts which lie behind them."

"'There is no district in London more filthy and disgusting,'" Hiva had read by candlelight, "'more steeped in villainy and guilt, than that on which every morning's sun casts the somber shadows of the Abbey, mingled, as they soon will be, with those of the gorgeous towers of the new "Palace at Westminster."'"

Hiva had read the words many times before setting the magazine down on the wooden table and asking Max a simple, pointed question: "In every civilization, in every world I destroy, the poor live, suffer, and die in the shadows of the wealthy. It never changes. Why?"

Hiva didn't ask Cherice, Hawkins, or Jacob. Not even that twitchy oaf Fables. He often let them rest during the night but forced Max to stay awake as he read until morning. It was only Max whose opinions he sought. Was it because Max was the one who had finally put an end to his "sister"? Or because of his nice hair and pretty face? Max didn't want to know.

But Hiva asked *him* his questions nonetheless. Especially after New York, he'd asked him questions Max couldn't answer.

"My life has been one mess after another since I was a child. I haven't had any time to think about such things." It was all Max could seem to tell him at the time. Max, Cherice, Jacob, and Hawkins. Squalor and hardship had simply been the lives that they knew. The tournament was to have been their escape, and escape they had—into another nightmare.

"I'm sorry," Hiva had responded with a curious sincerity before going back to his reading.

Hiva's curiosity had forced Max to think about the complexities of life and death in ways he would rather not have to. Beating up a few drunken jerks in an underground ring for a bit of cash was easier than having to sit and think about why he'd had to in the first place. Max hated Hiva for that. But Max wasn't so much of a fool that he hadn't noticed Hiva's confusing behavior, and he wasn't so kind as to not use it against him.

"Mary . . . I need you, Henry, and Lucille to do something for me," Max had told her. "But it won't be easy. And it sure as hell won't be pretty. Even still . . . are you with me?"

As Mary had responded with a slow nod, Max had sucked in a steadying breath. Even in those old stories, the ancient myths, it wasn't as if gods and monsters were infallible. They all had weaknesses. Max was confident he already knew Hiva's.

He thought of the bone sword in Hiva's hand. The one made from Iris's body.

Hiva was on alert at all times around Max and the others, even more so now than ever, after their failed murder attempt in New York. He wasn't about to give them a limb, and Max doubted he had any skeletons conveniently lying around in a museum nearby, as Iris had had.

But there were some "Fanciful Freaks" Hiva didn't know about. That meant they had the element of surprise on their side.

It wouldn't be easy. They had one shot. They just had to take it.

9

IT WAS A LATE NIGHT IN London when Adam Temple clinked wine-glasses with Lord Salisbury inside a rumbling carriage. The member of Parliament wiped drips of liquid from his wild beard, an ironic echo to Adam's messy black mop, before throwing his head back and laughing.

The debate in the House of Commons had concluded by noon.

"And so Britain goes to war," the Marquess said, for though he had attended the Congo Conference hoping to avoid confrontation with other European powers, he knew all too well the importance of demonstrating England's imperial might. More delicious than their territorial gains in Africa would be his political gains earned by the bloodshed of soldiers on the battlefield.

"And so Britain goes to war," Adam echoed, raising his glass. And not just Britain. Her colonies. Soon the United States would follow. And the world.

The two men laughed as horses pulled their carriage across London Bridge.

Despite this victory, Adam's mind lingered on the Alhambra Theatre, his thoughts still straining to peer behind the stage curtains for the figure who had laid waste to Vesta Tilley's audience. Only a god could do such a thing. Or had the massacre been the result of some kind of weapon Adam didn't know about? Now that the war was in motion, never-before-seen weapons produced by Bosch Guns and Ammunitions were being distributed onto the battlefield.

The battlefield. Not a music hall, Adam admonished himself. No, Hiva had been the perpetrator. It had to have been Hiva.

But *which* Hiva?

In the nights following the deaths of his sister and brother, Adam had lain awake in his bed and imagined himself as the God of Israel. In his waking dreams, he would tell his siblings just as He had once told Joshua: "Be not afraid, neither be thou dismayed: for the Lord thy God is with thee whithersoever thou goest." He would tell them this before utterly smiting their murderers. If he had the power of gods, he would use it freely.

And yet, for all his wealth and genius, he was only human.

He needed her. He needed her to understand the gift she'd been born with. The gift she had the obligation to use, for the sake of that poor boy who deserved it.

A gift he himself would kill for.

Iris. His heart ached as his body cried out her name. *Where are you?*

Hell on earth. It was a tiny wish. Just *when* would it be granted?

A heavy thump atop the carriage roof spooked the horses into a frenzied swerve. As the driver yelled, trying to pull them back into order, the force tugged Adam back and forth inside the carriage. Another thump. Then another. Adam crashed against the left door and fell off his seat as the carriage came to a halt.

"Who the bloody hell are you cretins?" Adam heard Salisbury scream.

A crisp gunshot silenced him permanently.

With his heartbeat pounding in his ears, Adam slipped his hands against the door as he tried to regain his footing. Another gunshot and the cabby slumped to the ground.

Before Adam could scramble out, the door opened, and a gloved hand gripped his collar, tugged him outside, and threw him onto the bridge with needless cruelty. His shoulder hit the pavement hard, the force almost pulling it out of joint. He gasped for breath, and as the sting shuddered through his body, he looked up.

Fool.

No, two Fools. Two Fools in the moonlight.

Three.

No, they were *all* here. One stood tall upon the carriage roof, his back straight, his gloved hands behind his back. The Pompous Fool. Adam could tell because he'd studied each Fool carefully once they had come under the employ of the Committee—their mannerisms, their handwriting, even the inflections in their voices. The one crouched next to him was the Desperate Fool, his head tilted inhumanely to the side, swaying a little like an excited child as he watched him with interest, his cape billowing in the wind. The Impulsive Fool was murmuring to himself, his words muffled by the black-and-white harlequin mask that covered his face. Adam didn't need the mask removed to know that this Fool regretted killing the cabby. He'd dropped his smoking gun to the ground and was pulling the dead man off his seat, mumbling, "Oh dear, oh dear," as he laid the corpse upon the bridge.

"No sense in regretting it now, you fool," said the one who'd pulled Adam out of the carriage so roughly. The Spiteful Fool. Of course he was there. He was often sent by the Committee to complete their dirtiest jobs. Cracking his neck and then his knuckles, he kicked Adam for good measure. The Broken Fool stood behind the carriage and watched—frightened, perhaps, of making the wrong move in front of his Others. It was what Adam would expect. He was at his least confident when surrounded by the stronger emotions.

Were they emotions? Desires? Or defects? What were the ingredients of a murderer?

Adam dragged himself to his feet. "How unexpected, seeing all of you here at once," he said, dusting off his shoulders. Tears and skid marks on such an expensive jacket. What a waste. "Although you could afford to be a little gentler."

"We owe you nothing, Temple," the Spiteful Fool shot back, and if he could have spat on the floor from behind his mask, he would have. The Desperate Fool was laughing.

The Pompous Fool clicked his heels like a soldier in a muster. "The Committee sends for you," he said, his head held high.

"And who is the Committee, exactly?" Adam folded his arms. "Half are dead or on the run. Bosch is in Africa. Bellerose—"

"It is precisely Bellerose, my lord, who has called," the Pompous Fool replied. "She believed it prudent to send all of us in order to express the . . . gravity of this issue."

He pulled a letter from his jacket, and while he began to unfold it, the Desperate Fool beside him suddenly clung to Adam's leg, rubbing his cheek against his black breeches.

"I've done well in coming, haven't I? Even though Hiva—"

"And what does the letter say?" Adam said loudly, cutting him off in case he said anything unnecessary. Adam pulled his leg out of the Fool's grip. Though all the Fools worked for the Committee, it hadn't taken too much effort to twist two of them to his side. But while the Desperate Fool was as loyal as his broken twin, his reckless abandon and twisted need for validation were sometimes cause for concern. Adam had sent him overseas for a reason.

"It asks you to 'join her in her newly purchased home for a meeting with the newly re-formed Enlightenment Committee,'" he read as the Impulsive Fool began frantically apologizing to the corpse of the carriage driver. "The ones who will lead the future into the New World."

A new Enlightenment Committee? Adam quickly glanced at the Broken Fool, who, with a start, hid more thoroughly behind the carriage. *What is that woman up to?*

"Tomorrow night at precisely seven in the evening." The Spiteful Fool purposefully bumped into him as he walked past, shoving Adam against the carriage, before turning and looking over his shoulder. "At Eight Grandage View. Don't be late. Madame Bellerose and the new Committee trust you only as far as you prove yourself trustworthy."

"Eight Grandage View?" Adam repeated as each Fool jumped off the bridge and into the sky, disappearing into the night with their capes flapping behind them.

Gerolt Van der Ven's home?

"This feels familiar," Adam muttered as he stepped into Van der Ven's abandoned townhouse on Eight Grandage View. Except this time it was Pierre,

Madame Bellerose's dreary, balding puppet of a servant, standing hunched on the blue Persian rug, welcoming him into the drawing room.

"This way, Lord Temple," Pierre said, the gray-faced man always looking half-dead. He led Adam past the roaring fireplace and arched windows. The wall of swords kept noble and pristine behind a glass case made Adam chuckle, because he knew how much pride a military man like Van der Ven had for his toys. Only dire circumstances would have ripped him away from them.

That Adam was behind framing him as an assassin—he wondered if Van der Ven had figured it out by now.

Pierre opened the double doors to the dining hall, a grand offering fit for a military man of Van der Ven's standing.

But the men sitting at the grand table represented those of a much higher status.

Adam almost let out a laugh, his eyes wide as he stared at the congregation. He'd never seen so many businessmen, politicians, and representatives of monarchs gathered in one spot. From all over the world too: England, Romania, Spain, and Bulgaria. Germany, Sweden, Belgium, and even the Principality of Liechtenstein. Each sat behind a flickering candle, with one at the center of the table in a bronze candlestick—the candle towering like a white pillar over a man's cracked skull. The calling sign of the Enlightenment Committee. The dagger in the skull's mouth was just the same too. Their meetings on the sixth floor of Club Uriel had been similarly set up to look just as dramatic and morbid—fitting, Adam supposed, for a death cult.

One by one the men turned over their hands, each bearing the pink scars drawn as a sword through a skull: the Oath Maker. The symbol of one's membership in a once-exclusive Committee.

And at the head of the table, grinning with the pride of a serpent, was Madame Bellerose, decked in red from her crochet shawl to her bell-shaped skirt. Prestigious men and women of the most powerful standing in Europe had to go through terrible trials created by agreement of the Committee to earn a seat at their table. Adam himself, despite his family's founding status, had had to kill a family friend or two. What had these men done, Adam wondered,

THE LADY OF RAPTURE

to earn their seats here, at this new pathetic mockery of the Enlightenment Committee that Bellerose had made?

But Adam knew: it was more about what they could give one another.

"Why, there's the guest of honor." Madame Bellerose leaned forward with her elbows on the mahogany table. "Didn't I say he was punctual?" And while the others murmured, she gestured to the empty seat next to her. "Come sit, my boy."

The mounted heads of boars and tigers on the wall told him to run in a silent scream. With a sigh, Adam took his seat next to Bellerose.

"Prince Albert of Monaco. How very nice to see you again." Adam bowed his head to his father's old friend, who wrinkled his mustache. "I trust we'll be seeing more of your scientific collections at the next exhibition in Paris. And Stanley, why, what a surprise it is to see you in London. I thought King Leopold had you stationed by now in the Congo, ready to terrorize the local people for their rubber."

Henry Stanley, that toad-looking American, hid a snarl behind his pasty face.

Then Adam tipped his hat. "Gladstone."

England's prime minister, who had just very reluctantly agreed to send his country to war, acknowledged him with barely a nod, but he kept his thin lips shut. Bellerose was the leader of this gathering. It was she who spoke.

"You're all too casual, boy, with those who'll lead humanity in the New World," she said.

Adam tilted his head in amusement. "I thought that was supposed to be us?"

Bellerose matched his cordial defiance. "That the Enlightenment Committee will guide the world after its end has always been our creed."

"Yes, well, the Enlightenment Committee used to be a little more exclusive with who they gave membership to. No offense," Adam added to Stanley, who scoffed. "Tell me, Bellerose. Who gave you permission to create a Committee of your own making?"

"We did," said Cecil Rhodes, a British mining magnate that Adam's father had used to call a sore loser, whenever he would lose in a heated game of poker in their drawing room. The cleft-chinned, square-faced man straightened his jacket over his vest and folded his arms. "When we offered Bellerose our support and in turn gained a seat on this Ark you've built in Africa."

That Bellerose had indeed sold Committee secrets to become the queen of the New World was not surprising.

Adam grinned. "So you've all bought your tickets, then."

"A great war has begun across Europe," said Hiram Stevens Maxim, an inventor in competition with Bosch to create automatic guns and aircraft that would no doubt one day find themselves on the war front. "It's shaping up to be one the likes we've never seen."

"A business opportunity for you, then?" Adam rested his cheek upon his hand and gave him a sidelong look.

"Well, of course, boy." Maxim's great white beard trembled as he laughed. "But with the current turbulence of the global economy, we believe it's best to hurry up the exploration and conquest of the unknown territories—the New World. They'll come in handy in our postwar reconstruction efforts. Especially with the displaced populations and the ruined cities we anticipate."

Adam kept his smile congenial, but the longer he sat next to these immoral death-mongers, the more his irritation threatened to seep out. With all the trouble Adam had gone through in starting this war, he'd known how most of the elites would react, but it still irked him to no end. Death was meant to be a spiritual release. A purging of the soul. Not a moneymaking scheme.

"The Ark is yet still incomplete, is it not?" Adam asked. "Without the Moon Skeleton as a power source—"

"Bosch's leading weapons developer has been steadily working on creating a suitable power source in light of our inability to procure the necessary device," Bellerose said, cutting him off quickly. "We have plenty of options. It isn't a problem."

Other than the Moon Skeleton, only a Hiva's crystal heart could power a flying ship of the Ark's magnitude. Neither Hiva was in the Committee's possession, so no, Adam highly doubted they had *any* options at this point.

Bellerose was just bluffing to keep her illustrious financial and political backers from running.

"Right." Adam sighed. "If that isn't the problem, then what is?"

"The problem is Van der Ven." Madame Bellerose's burgundy hair fell down her chest in ringlets. As she stroked her porcelain white cheek with the back of her black-gloved hand, Adam remembered just how that cheek had tasted in the Atakora Mountains—not particularly sweet, with a sour aftertaste. "We all know he won't stay hidden for long. Van der Ven's pride won't allow it. He'll show up soon to prove his innocence—even if it means exposing the Committee's secrets to the public."

"And how are you so sure he's innocent?" Adam asked just as innocently.

Bellerose only looked at him with that knife-sharp red smile. "At any rate, we of the new Enlightenment Committee won't allow that paranoid, rabid dog to ruin things at such a crucial moment. We wish to draw him out."

Adam narrowed his eyes. "Draw him out where? When?"

"Right here, in his own abode. This Saturday. And the ball will start promptly at six, thank you very much."

When Bellerose snapped her fingers, Pierre came scuttling up to her. On her command, he handed Adam a golden invitation. He stared at it in disbelief.

"A *costume* ball?"

"Grander than even the one Alva Vanderbilt threw two years ago. I should know; I was there." When she giggled, some of the new Committee members followed suit. Lemmings. "I've already taken care of the champagne, costumes, and catering. Which leaves the murder of Gerolt Van der Ven to you, my dear Adam. Think of it as your test to see if you're fit for the revived and improved Enlightenment Committee, soon to reign in two worlds."

"And how are you so sure Gerolt will come?" Adam asked with a dark grin, but he already knew the answer. Pride. It was what defined the man. He was smart enough to know that only another Enlightener could have pulled off framing him for assassination. Bosch was too profit-focused and Benini too incompetent to pull it off. The only two culprits who made sense would be at the ball. Hearing of his home being taken over by one of his possible betrayers, and for a gaudy society ball, no less? He would come for certain. He'd confront them head-on.

"My spies have reason to believe he isn't far from London. Trap and catch Gerolt Van der Ven at the ball. Only then will we accept your loyalty," said Bellerose, curling a lock of hair around her finger as she sat back into her chair.

"And a seat on the Ark, I presume," Adam said.

"Why so skeptical?" Bellerose must have caught a hint of it in his voice, despite his best efforts to conceal it. "It is still the Committee's plan to use the Ark to conquer the New World, is it not? It's an inevitability."

His thoughts drifted to the Alhambra Theatre—to the men and women turned to ash right in front of his eyes. A tingle of excitement shuddered through him.

"An inevitability," Adam said with a cordial bow.

Adam hated having new guests in the basement of his London home. Firstly, it was starting to agitate the languid Dr. Heidegger, stricken nearly comatose the day of the South Kensington fair explosion. Adam kept that husk of a body fed and cleaned in his red blazer and yellow vest. But Adam suspected that with his new company, some part of the doctor was starting to awaken. At times, his beak-like nose would twitch and his thin brows would furrow while he mumbled; then Adam would assume he was simply doing what he always did: channeling one of his personas—one of the Fools. It was how Adam kept track of them.

But then the old Harlequin Slasher's dark beady eyes would twitch toward little Henry Whittle, fourteen or maybe fifteen now, shackled to the wall. Or Lucille, tied up on the other side of the grand portrait of Adam himself, painted after his graduation from Eton. She was asleep. These days, when she wasn't under his command, she'd taken to wearing the face of her favorite opera singer, the "Swedish Nightingale," Jenny Lind: all rosy cheeks, bright blue eyes, and supple lips, just as Lucille liked them on her women. Perhaps it comforted her. Adam smirked. The things you learned from the people you kidnapped and imprisoned.

Heidegger's eyes rested on Mary the most, curled up in the corner of the basement on a pile of hay—so sick, frail, and tiny, Adam hadn't the heart to be unnecessarily cruel to her. At least that was what he had thought. Perhaps it had been a mistake.

They'd done well helping him frame Van der Ven at the Berlin Conference to begin the war. They'd done a fine job too at the Alhambra Theatre. But there were a few questions Adam needed answered. The arrival of Hiva at that moment had been a little too perfectly timed.

"Stop that!" Henry still had a little life in him. The grandson of the great toymaker Mr. Whittle battled against his shackles as Adam yanked his maid up by her frilly white collar. Mary grunted in a voice that belied her inner strength.

It had certainly taken a kind of inner strength to betray him to Maximo.

"Did you think I wouldn't find out that you went to that street rat?" Adam raised his eyebrows in amusement as he gazed upon her frightened expression. She was the only one he didn't lock up like an animal. Her cherubic face, which he cradled now in his hand, reminded her too much of his sister, Eva's. Perhaps this was what Eva would have looked like too, had she not been murdered.

Mary had taken advantage of his kindness.

"What exactly was the plan? You tell him where I am, and he tries to kill me?" Adam smirked. "He can't still be holding a grudge, can he? That fool."

"It was me!" Henry's hair had grown even more unruly than Adam's own. He had to shake his brown locks out of his eyes to glare at him. "It was my plan. I had Mary do everything. Please don't—don't hurt her."

As he choked on those last few words, Adam loosened his grip around Mary's collar and looked upon the boy. His pained expression and watery eyes were more or less the look of a young boy in love. For a moment Adam thought of his Iris, and his chest swelled with an unbearable emotion that made him grit his teeth.

Bending down to grip both of Mary's shoulders, Adam pressed her against the cold stone wall and waited until her eyes locked with his.

"Maximo's assassination attempt ended in the poor, poor patrons of the musical hall being reduced to ashes. It wasn't my doing, Mary. It was yours."

Mary twitched and looked away, her lips pursed as she held back tears.

"The House of Commons concluded the massacre to be a result of German warfare. Spies had used some class of weaponry we've yet to hear of. You could say it helped speed up their decision to go to war. But you and I know better, Mary."

Adam drew his lips to her ear as he whispered, "It was Hiva."

"Stay away from her, you bloody bastard!" Henry growled, but Adam wasn't about to be frightened by a besotted boy.

He stood up, straightening his back before placing his hands behind them, like a gentleman. "Which Hiva? Which Hiva did Maximo use to try to have me killed?"

He hated that his voice twinged as he spoke, because it could have betrayed the desperation he felt squeezing his throat. He wanted it to be Iris. If it were Iris, then that would mean he could find her. Retrieve her. But if it were Iris, then that would mean she was working with Maximo to kill him. . . .

He shook his head. Even if that were the case, he'd just have to sway her back to his side.

"It wasn't *her*, if that's what you're thinking," Mary whispered. "It was the other one. The golden man."

Adam stared at her through slitted eyes. "And how can I be sure you're telling the truth?"

"I am!" Mary said desperately, clasping her hands while she scurried to her knees. "I am. It wasn't Iris. It wasn't."

"Iris . . . ," Dr. Heidegger whispered, and the sound of his delirious mumble strangely set Adam off. More irritating than her name being sullied by the lips of a serial killer was the prospect of Iris still being lost somewhere out there.

Clenching his fists, Adam took a letter opener he kept in his left breast pocket for situations such as these and promptly slashed Henry's left wrist.

"No!" Mary screamed as Henry gasped in pain. "Mr. Whittle! *Henry!*"

Mary jumped to her feet and ran to him, but Adam hooked her neck with his elbow and hugged her against his chest. "I won't let you heal him until you tell me the truth. And if you don't tell me the truth soon, your precious Henry will bleed out and die right here in my basement."

He wasn't a monster. The sound of Mary's whimpering moved him somewhat. Under normal circumstances, he wouldn't murder a child or force another to watch him die. But these were pressing times. The end times.

"I swear it wasn't Iris. Max, Cherice, Hawkins, and Jacob are being held captive by the other Hiva. I don't know why he won't let them go. But it's not Iris. Iris is—"

Her eyes widened suddenly, her lips snapping shut. Adam pressed his face against her cheek so closely, his nose nuzzled against her skin.

"Iris is what?" he asked in a whisper, trying to keep his voice calm, though his heart was beating harder inside his chest. "Iris is *what*, Miss White?"

"No . . . ," Henry mumbled, blood dripping from his lips. "Don't tell him. . . ."

"Don't tell me *what*?!" Adam yelled so ferociously, he wondered if the servants above had heard him. Mary yelped, her knees buckling. Only his grip held her up.

"Iris is dead."

Dr. Heidegger had whispered it. The cold basement fell silent.

Letting Mary drop to the floor, Adam carefully strode over to the doctor slumped on the ground and lifted his drooping head with both hands. Adam didn't care that Mary immediately ran to Henry, healing him with a soft glow. Only he had the key to the boy's metal binds, so she wouldn't be able to free him even if she tried. He focused on the doctor.

"What did you say, Arthur?" Adam asked, his voice hollow as he tried to get the doctor's directionless eyes to settle on him.

He must have heard wrong. Dr. Heidegger couldn't follow conversations. The only words that spilled from his lips were those of the Fools, his personas spread out across England and wherever else the Committee sent them. He was a glorified transmitter locking on to frequencies, sometimes with such precision that it would make Hertz give up on his research in jealousy.

"Iris is dead." The words, spoken again, made Adam's blood run cold. But this time it wasn't Heidegger who spoke.

Lucille's borrowed face, still drooping downward as her hands twitched above her in shackles, twisted into a fatigued but defiant grin. "Max told Mary. Iris is dead. She died in Africa."

"Iris is a goddess," Adam whispered after a time.

"Well," mocked Lucille, "looks like your little goddess wasn't infallible after all."

Stepping back quickly, Adam turned his back to them all.

Iris was *not* dead.

No. Iris was a god. Iris was a god, and he was a man. And so Iris wasn't dead.

Because if she were less than a god, then he was less than a man.

That he could not accept.

While his heartbeat sped up and his arms trembled, he swallowed carefully, trying to stay the rise and fall of his chest. "Either you are lying to me now," he said with measured breaths, "or he was lying to you then. Well, I suppose we'll find out soon enough, won't we?"

Bellerose's costume ball. A way to murder Van der Ven and find out the truth behind Iris's disappearance. Why not kill two birds with one particularly dull stone?

Adam looked at his three Fanciful Freaks. "I have a task for you, Mary. You'll go and meet Max again tomorrow night. You managed to escape once more without me knowing. A blind spot, taken advantage of, if you will."

She curled up closer to Henry as he approached like an animal stalking its prey.

"Tell him that if he wishes to get rid of me and free you all, his last opportunity will come this Saturday. Don't try to tell him anything off script this time. A Fool or two will be watching." He grinned. "Oh, and tell him to bring a costume."

10

EVERY GOD HAD A WEAKNESS. AN Achilles' heel. But why was it that this Hiva seemed to have two? And only one was physical.

Well, first things first: they needed to cut off his arm.

"It's easier than a leg," Max told Mary when they met in an alley in Southwark, where he was staying with Hiva. "He doesn't know about your team. If you keep to the shadows and Henry and Lucille use their powers—"

"It has to be this Saturday. Bellerose and Adam are throwing some kind of ball at that man Van der Ven's house. He's going to use us to kill him. It's the only time Adam will let us out of his basement. That's our only chance to be free."

Not to mention, that rat bastard would be too focused on killing Van der Ven to see him coming. If Max played his cards right, he could use the opportunity to get rid of every monster.

"Throwing a ball in times like these, eh?" Max had already started to see war bond posters popping up all over the city. News of the war brewing across the continent was always on every front page. But that Britain would join its ranks was a new development. Even without Hiva's help, the world was going to hell. "I guess the rich really do live in a different world."

"I have to go soon, or Adam will notice I'm missing. Here," Mary added, slipping a golden invitation out of her raggedy skirt pocket. "This will help you get in."

Raising an eyebrow, Max stared at the cursive writing on the back. "Medieval?"

"What people won't do to enjoy themselves during the end of days," Mary said with a weak smile and a hapless shrug.

"Thank you, Mary. And don't worry—I'll do everything I can to get you out of there."

But why did Mary's smile look so guilty? She trembled as if she were about to burst into tears. Then she disappeared out onto the streets as the cold wind rustled around his ears.

The sun rose over the graves of Abney Park the next morning, its warm rays washing over Max's heavy, weary body. As Hiva stood in front of the sturdy stones, his eyes closed and his head raised to the early morning sky, Max wondered if the dead spoke to him in this lush woodland, which was silent but for the birds chirping. Was that how a Hiva worked?

"Where should I go next?" Hiva whispered to them, and listened to the whistling wind, for he was always open to suggestions, and the thoughts of the dead were as good as any.

"My king," Fables said behind him, taking a hesitant step forward and bending over with clasped hands. His feet crunched on crisp leaves still dripping from last night's rain. "Might I suggest we return to America? If it's the truly wicked you wish to murder first, there's plenty we still haven't gotten rid of in that godforsaken country. Like . . . like Kansas—"

"I was asking Maximo." Hiva took in a deep breath that seemed to suck the air out of Fables's lungs. "Where should I go next?"

Max's heart fluttered when all eyes fell upon him. Fables's shocked and hateful gaze made him itch. "Let me think about that, mate," he said with a wave of his hand.

That alone seemed acceptable to Hiva. More confirmation that Max's suspicions were not just conjecture. The god did have a weakness that wasn't at all physical.

"Why *not* Kansas?" Sitting on a nearby log next to Jacob, who held his head in his hands, Hawkins folded his arms. "Didn't you say that was where your old man was from, Tom? What? He didn't give you enough hugs when you were a boy? So that's why you're so happy to play faithful dog to this psychopath."

"Shut up!" Fables whipped around, crooked teeth ready to bite. "What do you know about me? Quiet, you little—"

"Maxey." While the two continued to go back and forth, Cherice pinched Max's sleeve, pulled him aside, and lowered her voice. "We can't go on like this. I'm at my limit."

"Tell me about it. The life's gone out of you." Max cupped her round chin, much to her surprise. It made her cheeks flush a little, but her shoulders were still slumped, her neck barely holding up her head. "Where's that Winterbottom fire, huh? You're the girl who used to pummel Chadwick if he beat you at a game of cards. Who wouldn't leave Hawkins, Jacob, and me alone. Always had to tag along wherever we went. Wouldn't take no for an answer." It was how she'd ended up at the South Kensington fair, transformed like the rest of them.

Cherice's sad smile deflated him. But he wouldn't show it to her—not her. For her, he had to keep some kind of cheer on his face, or else she'd fall completely apart. Even if he wanted to do the same.

"I don't know how many more people I can see turn to dust." And then, with shaking fists, she took a furious step toward Hiva, her feet snapping fallen twigs. "Is it going to be like this until the end? Planning to force us to stay with you until we've seen all the world go up in flames, are you?"

She was yelling now, and she may not have even realized it. Her red, swollen eyes screamed her despair.

"Cherice!" Jacob hissed, jumping to his feet and putting a hand up to stop her while keeping a worried eye on Hiva.

Fables pointed at her. "How dare you speak to Hiva that way? Shut your filthy mouth!"

"Why us?" Cherice continued, her fists shaking. "What did we ever do to deserve this? Why can't you just find someone else?"

Her words echoed in the trees.

Hiva's silent prayer was over. He turned slowly. He cocked his head to the side, and for a moment, his expression remained as blank as his eyes.

But then Max saw it—the same spark he'd seen when he had challenged Hiva in New York.

That same emotion.

"Do you . . . not wish to be at my side?"

The slight waver in his voice. It was unmistakable.

He was hurt.

Hiva was *hurt*.

"Are you bloody insane? You got rocks in that block head of yours?" It seemed the old Cherice was returning with each stroke of rage. "You *kid-napped* us. You're holding us *hostage*. You're making us follow you around and watch you kill people. Why? *Why?*"

The weeds and flowers in Hiva's hair, newly watered by last night's rain, seemed to droop at once, even though his expression didn't change. As birds began to perch upon the god's head, his golden fingers quivered.

"She's lying! Don't listen to that stupid wench! Of course we want to be with you!" Fables wrapped himself around Hiva's arm and burrowed his cheek into his shoulder. "You don't know what you mean to me. How you saved me. Saved me from that hell."

Max had no idea what he was talking about. Fables didn't speak much about his life, but just looking at this awkward boy, it was clear that Fables's anger at the world had twisted him into something entirely disgusting.

"We need you. The world needs you. . . . *I* need you," Fables whispered, his voice muffled by Hiva's shoulder.

"See? What did I tell you?" Hawkins nudged Jacob. "The lad is certifiably bonkers. Daddy issues, I bet."

"I told you to shut your mouth!" Letting go of Hiva, Fables rounded on them. "I don't want to hear anything from either of you two deranged . . . p-perverts!"

"Perverts?" Hawkins frowned, confused, but once he understood the implications, he stood up, his lips sliding into a sly smile. "Oh, is that what your daddy taught you to call lads like me?" Gripping Jacob's shoulder, he pulled the boy closer to him, rubbing his arm tenderly. Fables's cheeks reddened, and his lips readied an insult, but he couldn't find one. "Or are you maybe jealous? Because no one has ever loved you. Not like this."

And Hawkins, sliding his finger under Jacob's chin, pulled Jacob's lips to his, sealing them ravenously with a kiss. Max blushed but didn't look away. It wasn't something Hawkins could advertise freely, not with people being the way they were, but here he entangled his fingers into Jacob's black hair and deepened the kiss. Barely able to catch his breath, Jacob returned it hungrily, pulling away only when Hawkins's tongue grew too wild.

Max smirked upon seeing Jacob's satisfied grin. *Good,* he thought. His friends could still be happy. A bright spot in the midst of all the horror.

But Fables glowered at them, his expression dark, and his own lips wobbling with unmistakable jealousy. "I don't need anyone else." His whisper was filled with hatred. "I have Hiva. And he's going to kill you and your whore, your friends, and everyone else who ever decided to say a word against him."

"You mean everyone who ever *hurt your feelings.*" Hawkins folded his arms. "Am I wrong?"

Not in the slightest. This boy was nothing more than another Adam Temple. The big bad world had hurt him, and because nobody could figure out how to force the world to stop making him sad, it had to go. The desperate, nihilistic wish of broken men.

"But it's not what you want that I'm curious about." Max stepped in, his voice steady. "It's what *you* want, Hiva."

He'd noticed it—the way Hiva gazed at the little blue sparrow hawks and woodpeckers that continued to gather upon his head and shoulder. The way he lifted up his arm so one could land upon his fingers. Max noticed the way Hiva looked at them with kindness.

With humanity.

"You said you've done this before—destroyed the world, I mean. That having guides follow you around is part of the process. But I think it's all bollocks."

Hiva jerked his head to the side. Their eyes met. Max's heart clenched, but now wasn't the time to back down.

"You've already made up your mind to destroy the world. You don't need us for anything. Well, maybe him." When Max flicked his head toward Hawkins, the boy grimaced.

"You idiot," he hissed. As if Hiva needed reminding that Hawkins was his personal human carriage.

"You won't let us out of your sight," Max said. "You won't even sleep. Why?" He took another step forward. "Why did you manipulate me to kill Iris? If you wanted to destroy the world, why not do it *with* her?"

As if feeling the rise in Hiva's temper, the birds took off to the morning sky. "Did you ask these questions of my sister when you gave her your love and company willingly?" Hiva asked.

The god's jaw clenched. It wasn't Max's first time seeing it. Max remembered his anger in New York before he'd killed that little boy. The tremor in his voice when he'd mentioned Iris.

Fables wasn't the only one who was jealous.

"Don't forget," Hiva said. "*You* were the one who killed my sister. *You*, Maximo. It was your judgment that ended her life." He paused. "Are you saying you regret it now? Did she mean that much to you?"

There was a slight tremble in his voice.

"Iris . . ." Max closed his eyes and remembered her. Those heart-shaped lips he'd once kissed as passionately as Hawkins had Jacob. Her slender body, tightrope-ready. Those delicate hands that had grasped the glass surface of Hiva's tomb before Max had run her through with her own bones. "Iris didn't even know who she was when I first met her. But even though she was lost, she never gave up. She had this drive, this will, to find her true self. And no matter how much she was hurt by others, it didn't stop her from trying to do the right thing. It didn't stop her from forgiving someone like me. From accepting my sister. From making peace with her enemies . . ."

Because unlike this Hiva, Iris had been overflowing with life, with the never-ending fire of hope. "She didn't stop trying to find a way to save us all— even from herself," he whispered, his tears stinging his eyes as he remembered her constant reassurances in Heaven's Shrine.

I don't care what he thinks, she'd told him when he'd warned her of Adam's plans. *I'm here to decide my own fate.*

Max stared Hiva in the eyes, unwavering, unapologetic. The smile he gave was not for him but for the woman he cared for, the woman who'd reunited him with his sister. The woman he owed everything to.

The woman he'd killed without giving a chance.

"It doesn't matter how many times she's destroyed the world," Maximo said. "And even if she destroys it again. I'll still always choose Iris over you."

Chirping. For a time that was all Max could hear, along with the rustling of the tree leaves. Hiva lowered his head.

The god's laughter first came light and quiet. Slow and steady. It was enough to surprise Max, but then it continued rolling and gaining strength like a snowball tumbling down a hill.

"My king!" Fables cried, because even he was disturbed upon seeing his master unravel, seeing his stone face crumble into something ugly and furious.

This was just another plan. Pick at Hiva's weakness like a scab. Manipulate and spoil him. Because if Iris's tragic death had taught him anything, it was that no god was infallible.

And Hiva's weakness was clear.

"You did not see my sister in her heyday of glory," Hiva said, lifting his head and looking down upon them as if they were ants at his feet. "Her disregard for life. Her merciless genocides. You weren't there when I begged her to spare humanity. When she rebuffed me and sent me spiraling through dimensions. The face of this 'Iris' you fell in love with is but a mask. If only you'd seen the true face of *this* earth's Hiva. You have never seen a greater monster."

Hiva closed his eyes as if picturing her. Max couldn't begin to comprehend those old days. The ancient life the two had shared together. But his heart was sure.

"Yeah, well. She couldn't have been worse than you. *Mate.*"

The god's eyes snapped open, blazing with hatred. It was his smirk, however, that rattled Max's nerves and made him take a hasty step back.

"Everything I am now is thanks to her. The life that *I* wanted. The mercy that *I* sought." Hiva trembled. He actually trembled as he recalled memories of the past. "She doesn't deserve it. Not from you. Not from anyone." He lifted his head. "I am still Hiva. I will complete my mission. I will destroy the people that my sister loved, just as she did to me. But I am nothing like her. I am *better*. And you will be by my side to see it all. To see the truth. Be thankful, human. Be thankful that you never had the misfortune of meeting the true Hiva of this world."

Every word he spoke contradicted the next. He spoke as if he were still battling Iris. As if their millennia-long duel had never ended. It should have been over. Max had killed Iris with his own hands. Hiva had no reason to beg for anyone's approval, least of all his.

But this wasn't a world of reason.

An emotional bastard, aren't you? Who would have thought. Maximo grinned, for he'd discovered Hiva's second weakness. "You want me to believe you're better than Iris? Then prove it to me. The perfect opportunity's just come up too." Maximo pulled the golden invitation Mary had given him out of his vest pocket and held it between two fingers. "Wouldn't you know? I've been invited to a ball."

Jacob scrunched his face in disbelief. "Invited to a *what*?"

He hadn't had the chance to show the others yet, but now was the perfect opportunity. "Come with me. And kill no one. Just for this one night, show me your humanity. And then I'll know without a shadow of a doubt that you were always better than Iris. That you're a better friend than she ever was."

Better than Iris. That was the trigger. Hiva's lips twisted. The bastard couldn't resist, could he? Hiva stiffened, his body back to its automaton-like poise, his expression a void, as if all the emotion had been a figment of Max's imagination.

"Wait a second!" Fables ran to Hiva and grabbed his hands a little too familiarly. He loosened his grip at the sight of Hiva's empty gaze. "My king, this is a trap. I know it is!"

Max laughed. "What trap? What can I possibly do to him? We already tried once, remember? And failed miserably. Hiva said he wants to learn about the world. I want him to see people up close. To talk to them. Dance with them. Hear their stories. It's a fair lot better than reading about them in books and killing them from afar." Max waved his invitation. "What do you think, Hiva? Are you willing to take the risk that maybe you're wrong about humanity?"

And when he nodded, once, Max sucked in a breath. Hiva would go. But it was with one caveat.

"You and I will go," Hiva said, and turned to Jacob and Hawkins. "We will return from this gathering at three past midnight. If you are not there when we do, I will, without hesitation, murder one hundred people."

Hawkins instinctively grabbed Jacob's wrist, but the young men returned Hiva's threat with their own steely gazes. A timetable. That was fine. If all went well with Max's plan, neither of them would have to look upon this codependent tyrant again.

"I'll have to take Cherice with me," Max added, raising his hands up to calm her when the pint-sized girl shot him a wide-eyed grimace. "We'll stick out less if we come with a woman. Come on, this is high society. They're not exactly progressive. Besides," he said to Cherice, "don't you want to dance with me?" He shot her one of his patented cheesy grins, hoping she'd fall for it, even though he didn't feel particularly charming in that moment. He hadn't for a long time.

"Then I'm coming too!" Fables piped up, rounding on Max.

"Sorry, you're not on the guest list," Max said, pushing him away with a dismissive shove. "I can explain bringing a plus one, maybe a plus two. But a whole gaggle of miscreants? That's a harder sell." He leaned down toward Cherice. "By 'miscreants,' I didn't mean you, of course."

"Of course." Cherice rolled her eyes.

"Are we agreed?" Max asked Hiva.

The god looked up at the sky, raising his arms toward the heavens. Birds flew to him once more, as if sensing his kindness toward them. He shut his golden eyes against the sun's rays. "We are agreed."

Max and his old friends exchanged glances. Few words were needed between them. Their lives spent stealing on the streets had made words unnecessary. That spark of electricity before a particularly difficult heist flickered between them. Max nodded to them.

This would be his next, and likely last, assassination attempt of a god— whichever way it went.

11

THE WORD "COTONOU" MEANT "BY THE river of death" in Fon. How apt, then, that this trading city would be the place where Uma Malakar had taken Jinn's corpse.

No, not a corpse. His body still held a spark of life in it.

Rin held her breath and walked down the creaky wooden steps of Uma's apartment, which housed one of the handful of secret laboratories she had scattered across the world. Uma couldn't return Jinn to the Atakora Mountains; he wouldn't have survived the trip. This, apparently, was the next best thing.

But could this be considered surviving?

Rin stepped through the threshold of the lab and immediately felt the chill of the air. Thick violet curtains hung down from the ceiling to the floor, all angles and lines. The glass cylinder in the center of the room resembled a closed casket—and perhaps it was. Jinn had been placed inside. He looked to be in some kind of suspended animation; his angled jaw and high cheekbones remained stiff, his eyelashes not so much fluttering from behind the glass, which was fogged with the chilly air pumped in from a folded tube that stretched behind the curtains.

Perfumed lamps scented the air with a mixture of fragrances. Uma listed off a number of strange chemicals she'd never heard of, but when Rin let herself breathe in deeply, she caught a hint of herbs that were familiar to her: yew, wolfsbane, and myrrh.

"Aminadab!" Uma shouted, calling for her assistant. "Go to the fuse box. Bring down the temperature a little more, will you?"

A short, bulky man with shaggy brown hair peeked his head through the curtains from the outside. Then, after a short nod, he limped over to the corner of the basement next to a black metal furnace—a large beast that smelled of coal—and fiddled with the buttons on some kind of wooden contraption attached to the wall.

Uma sighed. "I'd love another assistant here. Someone who can keep a secret. All my other ones are at Bosch's facility in the mountains. It isn't fun, by the way, having to split my time between there and here." For a moment Uma tapped her chin, and then she snapped her fingers with a wide smile. "Don't you have a little angel living with you over in Ajashe? What was her name? Tutu? Lilith?"

"Lulu," Rin muttered, rolling the one eye she had left. The little girl was learning Fon at an incredible speed, playing with the village children, making friends by the day. Even after having lost her parents in such a horrible manner, she'd adapted to this new environment with uncanny speed. Rin hated to admit it, but she was a strong girl.

Stronger than you were at that age, accused a nasty voice within her head. *Stronger than you are now.*

Rin bit her lip to push down her sudden flush of shame.

"Would you mind sending her over?" Uma asked her, clasping her ringed fingers together. "What a wonderful opportunity it would be to introduce a young woman to the sciences. How fun would it be to be a mentor to girls—especially girls of a certain hue."

"Like I care. Do what you want," Rin snapped, and looked over to her present assistant working the fuse box. His skin was sooty with the grime of scientific progress. And yet there was nothing exceptionally grimy about this room at all. Inside the curtains, especially, it felt almost serene, like a final resting place—a secret sanctuary cut off from the rest of the world. Jinn's body had been placed in a bed of flowers; echinacea and lavender hugged his skin like a blanket.

And—

"The white crystal?" Rin narrowed her eyes as she counted the shards strewn about the violet and magenta leaves. They sparkled and trembled a little as the cool air pumped in and out of the casket. It was as if he'd been laid to rest in a sparkling garden.

Well. At least he could be with his beloved Iris, in a way.

"He isn't dead, thanks to me." Uma folded her arms as Rin stepped closer to the cylinder and placed her hand on the cold glass. "He *should* be. The surgery wasn't enough to save him. It's his heart. It's too weak to sustain his brain function. It's just no good anymore. But I've been experimenting with all manner of chemicals to go along with the mysterious properties of the white crystal. This will keep him alive. This will make him even stronger, until . . ."

Rin turned to her. "Until?"

Uma looked all too proud of herself as she whipped open the curtains and beckoned for Rin to follow. The shelves lining the wall were filled with books and instruments. A large map of the world covered the space where a window could have gone. And underneath the dirty furnace was a cabinet. Using a skeleton key, Uma unlocked it and pulled out a chest.

"Open it," Uma egged her on.

Her smirk made Rin uncomfortable, but curiosity got the best of her. She did as she was told.

Bizarre how a brass monstrosity made of shifting gears and pulsating fuses could be shaped like a human heart, but it was indeed. Inside the mesh of metal and clockwork was a mineral mixture unmistakably born from the white crystal.

"I always thought we were at least twenty years away from the first successful heart transplant. But Iris's existence has made many impossible things possible. Hiva told me of a thing called anima. People's life force. He and Iris could use it to track people—to track each other. Iris could never die because of her crystal heart. Do you know what that means?" The shining white crystal reflected in Uma's wild, shimmering eyes. "It means the white crystal *is* life. *I* can make life with it."

The shudder that cascaded down Rin's back had nothing to do with the cold. Rin stepped away from the scientist almost instinctively.

"This is . . ." Rin shook her head, pushing the chest back into Uma's hands. "This is nothing but conjecture. Your science is more like wishful thinking. Making a life?" She scoffed, though her body stiffened with a mysterious kind of fear and dread. "What hubris. Do you think yourself a god, Malakar?"

"Who needs gods? Gods can die. Look at Iris."

Uma had said it so nonchalantly, so disrespectfully, that Rin's body flushed with heat. Her fingers clenched into fists as she glared at the woman.

"Oh, don't be so upset. Iris's death is a tragedy, yes—poor girl. But it's more confirmation that our world is governed by the rules of evolution: survival of the fittest. We humans must use whatever we can to evolve and live on into the future." Uma stared at the artificial heart in her hands. "Science is the way. Thanks to Iris's existence, technology has advanced much further than it should have. And with the war in Europe getting rowdier, I'm sure I'll have plenty of new subjects to test my theories on. Then one day, more people like Jinn will be saved. See? The world tends to move in the direction of progress. Always."

Rin grew cold as Uma stashed Jinn's replacement heart back in the drawer underneath the furnace. In Rin's experience, those who felt they had power over life or death were not to be trusted with power in any form. It was the folly of most humankind. Iris surely knew this. It was what she'd been fighting against since the moment she'd regained her memories.

But if it could help Jinn . . . if it would give Iris peace . . .

"So what's next?" Rin turned from the woman and her strange inventions, focusing instead on the map of the world on the wall. It was similar to the one Temple had handed to her the day Uma had put him on a ship bound for Europe and watched him set sail, guarded by her men. It was made on yellow parchment, with old partitions marking colonial borders. The *X* symbols scribbled on sites around the globe were difficult to miss.

Taking her favorite pipe off a counter, Uma began mixing in fluid to smoke. "Each *X* marks a Solar Jump, as we've discussed. Do you see the different colors?" Walking up to the map, Uma took a puff of smoke and tapped one section. "It corresponds to pairs—according to Temple's research, each Jump had a twin." She nodded to John Temple's journal, left on the counter, as Aminadab began burning a pastille in the corner. "You have a similar map. Study it. Memorize it. With these we'll be able to hunt down Hiva, wherever he is. We'll be able to lure him to Hiva's Tomb." Uma's eyes glinted. "And disassemble him."

"Do you think he already knows of the Jumps?"

Uma stroked her chin. "Well, it *is* Naacalian technology. He seemed particularly fond of the civilization, judging by the way he spoke to me about them. It was during that period of time he battled Iris. So we shouldn't assume that he doesn't. And even if he didn't—you said he'd left with that boy Lawrence Hawkins, didn't you? Then either way, he can travel wherever he pleases, as long as it's on this earth."

And when Hiva was done with this earth, he'd need a way to leave it to destroy another. That meant he'd make his way to Uma eventually.

"Goodness. I guess I'm in a bit of trouble," Uma said with a shrug, before taking a drag from her pipe. Rings made of the fumes rose from her lips with each puff.

"Stay on alert then," Rin ordered, turning to the wall of purple drapes hanging from the ceiling that was concealing Jinn's frail body from her. "If you're going to play the mad scientist, at least don't die before you bring this man back to life."

"You care a lot about this boy," said Uma, giving her a sidelong look.

Rin scoffed. The man she'd willingly drugged and manipulated to force Iris to do her bidding? No. She couldn't claim such a privilege. But Iris loved him. And in one corner of her heart, she hoped that if the world were to end, at least those two might survive.

Rin turned and strode toward the staircase. "Tell me when Bosch returns from the Congo. We'll set out immediately after that."

"Yes, General."

Rin didn't care if the salute Uma gave her was in jest. She'd been used to giving orders and feeling nothing when her subordinates pounded their chests and shouted in response. But this emptiness was of a different kind. It was lonely and spread within her like a cancer threatening to decay her from the inside.

Rin's body felt heavy, her footsteps like lead as she dragged herself up the steps, refusing to take even one last look at the half corpse trapped in a cage like an experiment.

This was a war. Any warrior knew that one could not win a war without heart or will.

The two things she didn't have.

12

SATURDAY EVENING DESCENDED UPON LONDON.

Adam could barely believe it when Fool had told him the ghoulish news earlier that day. He'd dropped his schemes, left his prisoners under lock and key in his basement, and on Saturday morning immediately left for the Royal London Hospital on Whitechapel Road. That was where he had found him.

His father. John Temple.

The man had been dropped off here by an anonymous source, the doctors told him. He was suffering from severe malnutrition and all manner of disease that one could only contract while traveling through the so-called jungles of Africa, or so they told him. The trip home had apparently been torturous. They had already started treatment for dysentery.

Adam walked into his hospital room—the best one in the hospital. It was John Temple, of course. The famous explorer and scientist. The baron, writer, scholar, and lecturer. He'd finally come home from his travels, and once he was better—if they could make him better—he'd surely speak at their universities and socialite gatherings of the wonders he'd discovered while exploring the world. Or so they believed.

It was good that the room was private. It would make it easier for Adam to kill him.

The doctor had already briefed him and left. Adam shut the door and closed the curtains of every window. He picked up a scalpel left on a tray and approached his father's bed.

John Temple was emaciated. Red marks lashed his now-yellow skin, likely from being bitten by all manner of insects. His once-robust face was gaunt and skeletal, his flattened lids revealing how sunken his eyes had become. His hair had grown out of control, from his beard to his shaggy hair that curled every which way. Adam could tell from the smell of fecal matter that his father could no longer control his bowel movements. If the nurses did not feed him, there was no way those frail, fleshless lips could eat.

The scalpel trembled in Adam's hand.

"Father," he whispered. "Did you know . . . ? Everything I've had to endure while you were sailing off to your adventures? All these years? While you were conducting your . . . your *research?*"

He thought of the lonely nights he'd spent afraid in his room. He thought of himself as a child, back home from Eton to visit his mother's and siblings' gravestones alone.

"Do you know what I've been through?" His voice began to crack. "Did you know just what you've done to me? *Do you?*" he shouted, but there was no response. His fingers squeezed around the scalpel.

The Moon Skeleton was gone. The doctor had showed him everything Temple had had with him when he was delivered to the hospital—nothing but his clothes and an empty water pouch.

"He was conscious for a few minutes," the doctor had told him. "But he said very little. Only that he wanted to speak to you about something of the most critical nature . . ."

Speak to him? If his father had only kept his mouth shut. If he hadn't run off with the device and his secrets, then so many wouldn't have had to die. Carl Anderson and Neville Bradford would still be alive. *They*, at least, had never treated Adam with the same callousness and disregard his father had. Eva, Abraham, and his mother were also dead.

But this man had gotten to live. Not for any longer.

Adam's lips spread into a crazed grin, his teeth sharp like an animal about to tear apart his prey. "You've caused me trouble for the last time, you old bastard. You piece of *filth*."

But the broken husk of John Temple's body did not respond.

"Do you hear me?" Adam's eyes flushed with heat. He clenched his jaw, readying the scalpel. "This is it for you, old man!"

Adam couldn't seem to move his arm. He just stood there, shaking, until finally the scalpel dropped from his hands and clattered to the floor. Adam fell to his knees along with it and cried.

What victory was there in this, taking the life of a man who'd once filled him with fear and awe? What victory could Adam wrest from his father's grasp, now that the man was too feeble to grasp at anything? Limp and decayed, worse than a corpse. Helplessly gasping for air. This was his father. *This* was the mighty John Temple, whose fame, power, and intellect had taken him from his family to seek out the secrets of the world.

Humans were fleeting things, wretched and weak. Those thought of as gods among their peers were fated to return to the earth as food for maggots, like all the others. There were no true gods among any of them. Only bags of worthless flesh. No wonder Adam had been powerless to save his own family.

No wonder Adam was alone.

Adam stared at his hands, his chest heaving as he realized it. The hatred he'd had for his father—it was . . . gone. It wasn't enough that his mother and siblings had died. This wicked world had stolen from Adam this one last thing.

He couldn't bear it. He stumbled out of the room and slammed the door behind him.

"Lord Temple?" said the doctor, who was waiting out in the hall with his clipboard filled with sheets of his father's measurements and vitals.

"Keep my father's stay here a secret," said Adam. "He's a proud man. He would not want the public or any in his circle to see him like this."

As the doctor nodded, Adam thought of the Enlighteners, old and new. They would not hesitate to torture this already broken man for all his secrets, if only they could get their hands on him. Without the Moon Skeleton, they still needed a power source for the Ark. But it was more than that. Their coming war to conquer the New World would require every bit of knowledge John

Temple had amassed during his life. They'd suck it out of him like marrow from the bone.

I'm actually protecting *my father.* Adam's lips quirked into a wry smile that could not help but echo the sheer hatred he felt for himself and his own weakness, as he wandered through the corridor. And it was in one cold, narrow, and empty hall that Adam's knees finally buckled. Laying his back flat against the wall, he sank to the floor, his long black jacket crumpled against the brick. And with his head in his hands, he cried and cried.

He was so small and lonely when he'd first read his father's research and learned that gods truly did exist in this world. When he learned that divine justice was more than just the desperate dream of a helpless child.

Why didn't Iris understand the depth of her wondrous power? Adam could only *dream* of his perfect world—a world where his mother and siblings could live in peace while the rest of worthless humanity suffered as they should. But Iris could make that world a reality. Only a god could make dreams come true. And try as he might, Adam was no god.

"Iris . . . ," he sobbed, rubbing his burning eyes. "Iris, where are you? I need you. . . ."

"And that has always been your weakness, boy. Your need for others."

When Adam wiped his face and looked up, he found himself staring into the clinical glare of Doctor Seymour Pratt. The old man whose torturous experimentation and dissection of Iris fifty years ago had yielded so much of the information Adam's father had come to know about her. Adam knew Iris hated this man with every fiber of her being. But if it wasn't for the relentless work of his scalpel, Adam never would have gotten to know Iris or come to be in possession of her crystal heart. He never would have brought her back to life at the South Kensington fair ten years ago, when he was a frightened boy with a hopeless dream.

Adam supposed, at the end of the day, that he should thank this man, who now straightened out his lab coat with a judgmental sneer. No, only a *hint* of judgment. This man was made of ice. He was as cold and unfeeling as the study of science itself. It was the kind of clinical strength Adam lacked. Adam envied him, this man of science.

"A strange coincidence that I would meet you here, Doctor. Did you come to quote Darwin again to me?" Adam pulled up a knee and leaned over it, letting one of his arms dangle in the air as it rested upon his leg. "Or do you have another scientist in mind?"

Doctor Seymour Pratt smirked and, rubbing his great white beard, turned his head. "That creature you call 'Iris.' Did you know that I first met her when she was but an animal in a zoo?"

Yes, Gorton Zoo. Iris and two others had been part of a human exhibition of Africans. It was not an uncommon practice in Europe. But Pratt had said the word "animal" in such a nonchalant way, it made Adam's fingers clench into fists almost instinctively.

"The children would watch her and throw rocks. They'd point and laugh at her. Day after day." His small black eyes barely blinked as he spoke. "But it wasn't out of cruelty, boy."

"Really? That sounds rather cruel." And from what Adam understood, it was exactly that cruelty that had caused Iris to murder the zoo visitors that day—including Pratt's own family.

"Is it cruel for a man to kill a fish to feed his family? In those moments, those children at the zoo knew something instinctively: that there was a fundamental difference between those who looked and those who were looked at. Between them, the true children of England, and the beasts captured and put on display for their entertainment. They didn't need the tomes of Darwin or Cuvier to teach them. They knew the truth."

Doctor Pratt kneeled until the two men faced each other at eye level. "There is a difference between us and them. The cultured and the savage. The strong and the weak. There are, among us, weeds that need to be pulled so that the flowers can grow uninhibited. Only then can this world move in the proper direction."

Adam couldn't say that he was entirely wrong. Because indeed, despite his indignation at the doctor's foul words toward Iris, Adam felt the same way. The weeds of the earth needed to be culled for something new and beautiful to arise. On that very fundamental concept they agreed. And though Adam's conception of who counted as the detritus of the earth was far more inclusive than

Pratt's, he wondered if he could ever achieve his dream of making a better world through annihilation, unless he possessed Pratt's cold, unrepentant cruelty.

"There he is, Faith!"

A child's voice jerked Adam from his terrible thoughts. The laughter of little girls wasn't at all what he'd expected in this dreary hospital that reeked of death. Adam looked to his left and saw them skipping down the hall: two girls, their round, rosy faces and billowing black curls as identical as the extravagant doll-like dresses they wore. One dress was a dark green and the other black, the skirts swishing around their ankles with frilly white fringes.

Adam knew them. "You . . . ," he whispered, getting to his feet. "Faith . . . and Virtue Sparrow . . . ?"

Cortez's twins. The would-be champions he'd pitted against Iris to test her before the Tournament of Freaks. Adam had thought he'd never see them again after Cortez had banished them to the Basement in the Crystal Palace for experimentation. But here they were, their brown eyes alive in a way Adam had never seen them before.

"We've found you, haven't we?" said the twin wearing the dark green dress, and she grabbed Adam's hands. Virtue. She was the one who'd spoken earlier. "Madame has given us orders to help you, Lord Temple."

"Yes! We're to escort you to the ball this evening!" Faith's nails were painted as black as her dress and sharp as the teeth she grinned with.

Adam had never heard them speak before. Cortez had never explained before how he'd forced them into their control. Only that he'd found them in an orphanage, dressed them, fed them. To be honest, at the time Adam had been too focused on Iris to ask any further questions. And he wasn't sure he needed the answers.

"You're my escorts to the ball, are you?" Adam furrowed his brows.

"From my understanding, along with the Helios, Madame Bellerose had a few human specimens rescued from the Basement before the massacre," said Pratt, who didn't seem moved at all to discuss the murders of his scientist peers. "We've been able to retrieve a few, but the rest seem lost to the wind for now. What a waste."

"Yes, what a waste!" Faith's voice was lower and dreamier than that of her twin sister. Her eyes were, at times, unfocused, but both held a wildness that Adam couldn't help but recognize. "But we were not wasted, were we, sister? Madame Bellerose has fed us and clothed us and given us dolls." Every word was drawn out like the lyrics of a song.

"Not like the mean old ma'am at the orphanage. Good thing we killed her." Virtue's laughter was as pointed and direct as her voice. She grabbed his hands too. "Oh, but Lord Temple, we won't kill you."

"He will, maybe," Faith said.

Faith turned, and behind her, another ghost appeared before Adam's eyes. Tall and thin, with a shaved head mostly covered in the blue newsboy cap he wore. His mangled body was missing an arm.

Barry Bately. Adam's mouth quirked into a grin. "Well, this is certainly an interesting reunion."

But Barry did not respond. How could he? His cracked, dead lips had clearly once been sewn shut with thread. Nothing but shallow gasps escaped them now. Adam remembered a time when Max's fellow street-rat-turned-nemesis couldn't keep his mouth closed. And it was precisely his mouth that people feared, for his power lay in his words.

What cruel irony. Adam approached them like a scarecrow, his eyes wide and unblinking.

"They sewed his mouth shut because he wouldn't stop screaming," Virtue said in a voice so pleasing to the ear, it made Adam shiver in fear. "He doesn't speak much now, but his power still works. On Madame Bellerose's command, he'll certainly use it, so please be careful, Lord Temple."

Adam smirked as a dribble of sweat formed around his hairline. "Is that the message Bellerose told you to give me when she appointed you to be my prison guards?"

The twins tilted their heads at the same angle and grinned. Bellerose had ordered him to attend her ball so he could "trap and catch" Van der Ven. He'd already created a plan that was to her liking: using Lucille's shape-shifter abilities to pretend to be Bellerose. The madame herself would never so openly put a target on her back, not with Van der Ven as the dangerous predator they were attempting to bait. This would keep Bellerose safe and Van der Ven's focus on the wrong woman.

He didn't need to be at the ball for the plan to work, but she'd insisted. She just wanted to test his loyalty. She had a bad habit of doing that. These were her little birdies to make sure that he cooperated. Her spies. But the ghouls who stood before him made his hair stand on end. What in the world had happened to them inside the Basement?

More worryingly, Adam had his own plans for Saturday's ball: to trap and catch *Maximo*. To interrogate him. He needed to know what had *truly* happened to Iris. Mary and her band of misfits would ensure his meeting with the street urchin. But being trailed by Bellerose's Basement goons was a complication he hadn't foreseen.

Pratt straightened his back. "I've done as I was asked. I've brought these creatures to you. Now I go to Africa."

"Africa?" Adam repeated as Pratt turned his back to him. "Why there?"

"I've been summoned by Boris Bosch. It seems my expertise is needed. The Helios already resides inside the Atakora Mountains. But what kind of effect will its chemical reaction have on the bodies of the patrons of the Ark? No one wants a repeat of South Kensington fair—unless Carnegie and his wife want to be transformed into several-limbed monstrosities."

Adam smirked. No, the rich and powerful would much rather exploit and control the Fanciful Freaks than become one themselves.

"What wonders lie beyond the New World too?" And for the first time, Pratt's black eyes seemed to glimmer. "I'm eager to discover it."

Adam shifted on his feet. "And you won't tell them about . . . about my . . ."

Father. He looked at the now-chatty twins, who waited for him to finish his words.

But Doctor Seymour Pratt shook his head. "I have no interest in dead men. But heed my words. Don't end up like he did. And do not wait for a slave to save you. You were born of kings, boy. Claim your birthright." And Seymour's beady eyes beamed hatred as he looked over his shoulder one last time. "*We are the gods.*"

We *are the gods?* Adam lowered his head as the doctor left the hall, leaving him with the three Fanciful Freaks. *We?*

This world was cruel and wicked. He did what he could to challenge it. But Pratt was wrong. Adam needed Iris to transform it into what *he* desired. Iris was not dead. All his best-laid plans would not fall to ruin; he wouldn't let it. She would return to him.

And when she did, this life would take nothing more from him. This horrible, broken world . . .

13

A S MAX APPROACHED VAN DER VEN'S brown-bricked London home on Grandage View, wearing an auburn cloak over a tight brown tunic, he smiled wistfully, remembering the first time Lily Giralt had dressed him up for an extravagant operation. Back then his old friend had dressed him up like a woman so he could infiltrate the brothel where she worked. This time, with her connections, she'd rustled up some robes to fit Bellerose's medieval theme.

"I don't have enough time to teach you how to dance a court quadrille, so simply do your best to follow along with the others," the red-haired girl had told him and Cherice before leaving their apartment in St Giles. "Just *please* don't mess things up by making fools of yourselves."

"Same to you," Max had told her, in a whisper only she could hear.

And she'd understood.

Lily was a longtime friend of theirs. She was no stranger to lending a hand whenever Max and his friends found themselves in rather hairy situations. A part of him had felt guilty bringing Lily into Hiva's orbit, exposing her to danger, but she was never one to shy away from it.

That day at the brothel Iris had been with him. Between the two of them, he hadn't been able to decide who had worn the lovelier dress.

His cheeks flushed as he remembered kissing her that night in that sensually lit room, both of them fighting with their crinolines.

"What's that smile for?" asked Cherice. The girl was, surprisingly to Max, a vision herself. Lily had done her makeup: blush on her chubby cheeks, soft black eye shadow. Her pumpkin-colored hair had been primped and adorned with marigolds.

Lily had given her a pink silk dress and a red cape made of fur, which was tied around her neck with a gold chain. Not real silk, or real fur, or real gold. But this was a costume party, after all, and according to Lily, Cherice was meant to be the Isolde to Max's Tristan—that is, if people bothered to guess. As for Hiva—

"He's a bard."

Max hid his smirk behind a hand as the doors to Van der Ven's home opened for them.

It was a costume party. Hiva had no need to hide the weeds in his hair. It made his violet robe and Tudor cap somehow more authentic. If it was not humanity's final year, it would certainly be its strangest.

A blue Persian rug welcomed their leather boots into the drawing room. The servant who would let them into the ballroom was too mesmerized by Hiva's beauty to even ask for his invitation. But he handed them their masks. That was what mattered most. Max had a solid plan to distract Adam when the time came, but before then, they needed to hide their faces from him.

A set of grand double doors opened into the ballroom, which was lit with beautiful electric lamps and chandeliers. Men and women were already swirling across the wooden dance floor in expensive robes and gold-embroidered cloaks. Real gold this time, by the looks of it. Off to the right, musicians kept to the medieval theme, playing sprightly music on the stage next to the Grecian columns. Two arched wooden doors stood at opposite ends of the room for servants to come in and out of with trays of wine. Red-and-gold drapes fell to the floor, though most of the walls were left bare of drapery, probably to show off the silver-plated tapestries and the Gothic ironwork, among other opulent furnishings. It was a colorful, decadent display of wealth that made Max feel as small as he had when he, Chadwick, and the others had waited outside gatherings like these in the winter cold, hoping for a pocket to pick.

"I feel ridiculous," Cherice hissed at Max, struggling with her black leggings. After leaning back to spy on Hiva—who stood on Max's other side, watching the revelry with disinterest—she nudged Max in the ribs. "And you're entirely sure this is going to work?"

Max nodded and pointed at the main attraction at the front of the ballroom.

How fitting that she would place herself on a throne. Bellerose. And, of course, in a rejection of her own theme, she'd made herself up to look wholly unique from the rest of her guests. Something about her reminded Max of a Venetian princess. Her dress was embroidered with gold, silver, and reds, with a peach satin train and an underskirt of a light yellow brocade. And Max only even knew these terms because of Lily, though even Lily would have found the emerald gems on her Venetian cap a touch too much. Unlike the other guests, Bellerose did not cover her face. She wanted the others to see her in her throne, her red curls spilling over her diamond-covered neck. Bellerose watched her guests dancing the quadrille as if she presided over their very lives. A queen in the making.

It was then that Bellerose's sharp eyes caught his. Max's breath hitched, his hand stiffly gripping his curved red mask, which only covered half his face. But when the madame's red lips curved into a smile, his body relaxed.

Good. This was good. This was *very* good.

As Madame Bellerose's gaze slid to the musicians, Max turned to Hiva next to him. "Have you ever been to a party before, in your millions of years alive?"

Hiva watched the festivities with an uninterested expression. "In every civilization and in every generation, the elites have always found nonsensical ways to amuse themselves."

"'Nonsensical' is the word," Cherice muttered under her breath, before coughing innocently into her white-gloved hand.

"What did you do for fun in those days, anyway?" Max was curious. "Did you ever *have* fun? You know—" And he waved his hands, as if painting some kind of picture in the air of what "fun" was supposed to look like.

Hiva looked away. He was silent for a time. "During the ancient days of the Naacal, I played with them in the flower fields," he finally told them. "I played with them when sister wasn't watching. They gave me . . . joy."

Max and Cherice exchanged glances as Hiva seemed to drift away right in front of them. His voice died in this throat. His golden eyes faded.

Max cleared his throat. "Well, anyway—like I said, *talk* to these people. Learn their stories. Their hopes. Their dreams. Who knows, you might find that this world isn't the den of sin you think it is. You might find some mercy in that crystal heart of yours. *Iris* did."

Hiva's body stiffened, and his lips stretched into a sneer. "The 'Iris' that *you* knew, perhaps," he said, but he walked into the dancing crowd nonetheless.

"I guess everyone has a trigger, huh?" Cherice put her hands on her hips. "So? What now? What about us?"

Max bowed to her and offered his hand. "Shall we dance?"

Cherice's whole face exploded into a kaleidoscope of red shades. Max laughed. Just like when they were kids. She shook her head ferociously but gave him her hand anyway. He took it and whisked her off her feet. Bellerose's signal had told him the plan was in motion. Now all they needed to do was wait for the changing of the guards. Might as well dance until then.

Lily should have taught them the quadrille. Neither he nor Cherice could keep up with the flow of upper-class guests, who seemed to seamlessly glide upon the floor. With Cherice's little hands clasped in his, they knocked knees and stepped on each other's toes. Cherice banged her head against his chest—which meant the heels Lily had given her had lifted her a couple of inches, because usually the crown of her head barely reached the top of his stomach.

"Hey, Maxey, do you really think Hiva's actually going to learn something profound at a stuck-up, hoity-toity event like this?" Cherice asked, watching her feet to make sure she didn't step on his boots again. "I mean, it *would* be nice and all if he had a change of heart about destroying humanity after having a nice dance with some philanthropically minded, orphan-rescuing nun, but I don't think you'll find that type here."

Max scoffed. "This place? Please—look at all the peacock feathers on their masks. They're clearly all assholes. Hiva won't change his mind. But that's not what this is about."

"Then this is another elaborately planned ambush?" Cherice narrowed her green eyes. "Because the first time worked so well. . . ."

Max lifted Cherice's chin so he could look in her eyes. "It'll work this time, Cherice. We've got Mary, Henry, and Lucille. We've got our friends. And we've got our little secret weapon, about to make her appearance." He looked up at Bellerose.

"But what if—"

"No what-ifs," Max whispered with a stern note of finality. "No going back. We do this here and now."

Cherice bit her lip and turned away from him, relenting with a little nod. "Here and now."

Damn it. Max hadn't meant to snap at her. To break the somber mood, he spun her around a few times, almost lifting her off her tiny feet. After she adjusted one of the marigolds that had fallen askew in her hair, she looked up at him and broke out into laughter.

"Good to see you beginning to enjoy yourself," Max said with a wry smile, gazing around him and winking at the few elites annoyed by their clumsy display. It was then that he realized that he was enjoying himself too. For the first time since he'd disappeared from Iris's side that dark day in Club Uriel, he was actually enjoying himself.

Perhaps Max had thought this too soon. His jaw clenched as he saw, out of the corner of his eye, Adam Temple speaking to a group of men by the grand piano, behind which a masked man played his own perfect accompaniment to the musicians. In his long black tuxedo, Adam was one of the few who hadn't dressed up according to the ball's ridiculous dress code. He spoke with a full glass of wine in his hand, his black hair as raggedy as Max remembered it, and for a moment, Max felt a wave of heat rush to his head.

That man. That bloody man had used his love for his sister against him and manipulated him into betraying his friends. That sick, death-obsessed monster.

"Maxey," Cherice whispered, but he barely heard it above the ringing in his ears.

What would have happened if Max had never fallen into Adam's trap? What new path would have opened up for him, if he had chosen Iris's side during the Tournament of Freaks instead of his? Since he'd taken Temple's bait, he'd made one mistake after another until he could no longer differentiate between right and wrong.

Closing his eyes, Max remembered the time he'd spent in that casket. The torture that had been inflicted on him on the pirate ship. The torture he'd inflicted upon others.

"Maxey!" Cherice hissed, and finally she pulled her right hand out of his. He hadn't even realized he'd been crushing it in anger. Biting her lip, she rubbed her delicate, tiny fingers.

"I-I'm so sorry," he apologized hurriedly, standing awkwardly in front of her.

"It's okay. I get it," she said before offering her hands again. "I see him too."

As tears budded in his eyes, he gripped Cherice and held her tightly against his chest. And strangely, she didn't protest. She didn't so much as draw a breath. She melted into his arms, her fingers in his.

"You know, I always wanted to do something like this." Cherice cuddled up against his chest like a puppy. "When we were kids, I mean. I kind of always wanted to have a real dance."

"Are you saying a drunken Irish jig isn't a 'real' dance?"

Cherice's angry pout was a little adorable. She narrowed her eyes and huffed. "A dance, you idiot. A real dance. A . . . a ballroom dance. A close dance, you know?"

"Yeah, yeah, I know."

"*Do* you?"

Max wasn't used to seeing vulnerability in her expression. Not in the fiery Cherice, who made a living cheating men twice her size and half her wits out of their ill-earned money. As if sensing his discomfort, she quickly lowered her gaze but tightened her grip on his hands.

"A lot has happened in the past few months. I feel like I can't even process everything." Cherice shook her head. "I thought you were dead, Maxey."

"And celebrated, did you?"

"Don't even joke about that!"

She had almost shouted it. A few men and women, dressed as if they'd walked out of an Arthurian tale, glared at her for a few seconds before realizing that staring was considered rude and going back to their quadrille.

"Sorry," Max muttered under his breath.

Cherice was silent for a moment. "I thought you were dead, and I wanted to die too." Her voice was ghost-quiet. "I hated everyone. Temple. That stupid Enlightenment Committee. *Iris.*"

Max's stomach flopped. He didn't say a word.

"Or maybe I hated her before then. Just a little. When I thought you were in love with her." The flowers trembled in Cherice's hair as she shook her head quickly. "I know, I know. It's pathetic, isn't it? You can go ahead and call me a jealous child."

"It's not pathetic. . . ." Max's hands loosened their grip around Cherice's. "I didn't love her, Cherice. And as for you . . ."

She waited expectantly, and the tiny light of hope in her expression broke his heart. It was rather easy playing stupid after you'd done it for several years. Cherice had been following him around since childhood, always struggling to keep up with the boys whenever they climbed up trees and ran from bakeries with stolen loaves of bread. She pushed herself until she could run faster than the lot of them, yet Max could still always feel her behind him somehow, watching silently—always a little late, always a beat behind. He'd know she was there. But he'd never look back. Those were the rules. It had become familiar and therefore comforting. He'd never wanted to think about how much her unrequited love had hurt her for all those years.

The rules tended to change when lives were at risk. Hearts tended to open at the brink of the world's end. But not for Max. Not after everything he'd done. The blood on his hands.

"I didn't deserve Iris, and I don't deserve you," he said, and with an awkward tremble of his lips, added, "Let's just dance."

He felt Cherice's shoulders droop.

"Meater," she said under her breath with a little laugh, before directing her gaze once more to the dance floor.

They danced in silence.

Until . . .

"Heads-up." Max flicked his head toward the front of the room. Bellerose had risen from her throne and, with a haughty expression of disdain toward her own guests, slinked off through the door on the left. By the time the musicians had started a new song, she'd returned with her face covered in a harlequin red-and-pink mask, bejeweled with diamonds only a touch smaller than the ones draped around her neck. As if she'd only stepped out to the powder room, she sat back down upon her extravagant seat, with few guests any wiser as to what had *truly* happened.

"It's done. Lucille's made the switch," Cherice whispered. "What now?"

If, according to Mary, Adam's big plan was to trick Van der Ven, then he was smart to use Lucille's shape-shifter abilities. She made a good Bellerose.

But that prat had no idea he was being double-crossed. Soon he'd learn what *Max* had in store for him.

"Now we wait. Lord Temple's about to become very distracted." Max smirked.

A few moments later, and it happened. The sound of glass crashing against the hardwood floor. Everyone turned toward the corner of the ballroom to Adam Temple, who looked like he'd seen a ghost.

"Excuse me," Adam said, and barely managed a gentlemanly bow before rushing out of the room. Several servants rushed to clean up the mess—

Including a tall, tan, brown-haired boy who looked like *Fables*.

No, it couldn't be. That git hadn't been invited. Max couldn't get a good look at the boy's face before he disappeared with the other servants through the door, but he was almost certain it couldn't have been him.

He didn't have time to dwell on it, for Hiva soon approached him, accompanied by an old man Max didn't recognize at first. The man was another one too proud to wear bedazzled tunics and robes. His gray hair, wispy at the crown of his head, pooled at the back of his neck, nearly covering his large ears. The creases in his skin deepened as he frowned, though he didn't look particularly angry. It was as if this man never smiled even during festivities, where smiling was a requirement. His white collar was up, revealing a simple black tie he didn't bother to adjust as he stepped out in front of Hiva, his arms folded behind his back.

It took Max a moment to realize.

No. It couldn't be. Max froze to the spot. His fingers clenched into fists.

The old man gazed at him through wizened eyes before introducing himself. "William Ewart Gladstone. "

Cherice let out a yelp before covering her mouth and looking up at Max for some kind of instruction on what to do. But Max's mind had gone blank. He'd told Hiva to mingle, and the god had come back with the leader of the bloody *country.* Just what the hell was going on?

"These are the friends I told you about," said Hiva, waving his hands toward Max and Cherice. "If I am to make a decision, it is best that you include them."

Max balked while Cherice scrunched up her nose. *Friends?*

"What decision?" Max demanded, still too dumbfounded to grasp what was happening.

"One fit for a man capable of laying waste to a music hall with a mere thought."

He knew. Max and Cherice exchanged glances.

"Come with me," said Gladstone. "Let us find a quiet place to talk. There I'll tell you what I told him." Flicking his head toward Hiva—carefully, of course, with the weak neck he had—he began making his way past the dancing crowds.

"Why?" Max demanded after him. "What could you possibly want from us?"

Gladstone looked over his shoulder. "I'm recruiting."

14

IT WAS THE SECOND TIME THAT night that Adam's eyes had been playing tricks on him.

The first was after Lucille, playing the part of Bellerose, had vacated her seat. When she'd returned, she'd seemed . . . different. Oh, the clothes were the same, the jewelry. But something was off about this new Bellerose, who sat on her throne, her face now covered with a mask. He knew Bellerose's body intimately enough. This wasn't the real Bellerose, but was it still Lucille?

"Are you sure you're not being paranoid, my lord?" asked Fool, his fingers lightly caressing the keys of the grand piano. A costume ball was the perfect place for him to hide.

Adam had every right to be paranoid. Max was already in the crowd, dancing with his orphan friend Cherice, both of them stupidly thinking Adam hadn't noticed them walk in with a weapon of mass destruction.

That Maximo had brought the other Hiva unfortunately proved which Hiva had been with the street thug that night at the music hall. But after so many minutes of dancing, the crowd had not been reduced to ash. The god was actually *dancing*. Max seemed to have him on a leash.

Well, Adam had his own dogs. Mary, Henry, and Lucille. That Mary had managed to bring Max here proved their loyalty to him—their *fear* of him.

As long as they continued to do what they were told, he'd be interrogating Maximo soon enough.

"Fool. You remember what to do if it seems my new servants have betrayed me?"

"The little Whittle is in our custody as I speak," Fool said, nodding. "He remains your card to play, my lord. Mary and Lucille are none the wiser."

Good. Well, "Bellerose" was still in her seat. Perhaps his eyes hadn't played tricks on him, then.

But this time . . .

This time the trick was so cruel, so tantalizing, it had frozen Adam's very blood in his veins. He saw *her* for only a moment, in a green velvet cloak fit for Queen Guinevere. The wide hood covered her black braids, her brown skin. But he would know that beautiful face anywhere. There was no mistaking it. Did he dare to dream?

". . . Iris?"

His wineglass dropped from his hand and shattered upon the floor as the figure disappeared through the door, her green cloak sweeping behind her.

"My lord," Fool whispered from his seat at the grand piano, for only he could jolt Adam out of his spell.

With a start, Adam stared out over the ballroom, only to realize that they were all gaping at him now. It didn't matter. If that really were Iris, then he couldn't let her get away.

"Excuse me," he said hastily at the crowd, and offered an apologetic bow before turning his back. "Stay there, Fool," he whispered in a command to his servant before rushing out of the room.

You couldn't get into the ballroom without passing through the drawing room, but it was empty. The cloaked woman had moved fast. Which meant he had to move faster.

But no sooner had Adam entered the drawing room did two little bodies tackle him from the front. Two pairs of pale noodle-arms.

"Where are you going, Lord Temple?" asked Faith Sparrow, her mask hitting the floor with her sister's as they dropped them. Or at least he thought

Faith was the one with the red ribbon tied around the bottom of her top hat. Virtue's was white. Otherwise their gothic black dresses, lined at the bottom with red tulle, were exactly the same.

"Madame Bellerose wouldn't want you to leave the ball so early," the other sister said. "Not until the plan is done. Or did you forget?"

"Damn it," Adam cursed underneath his breath as he pried the girls off him. "Did either of you see a woman in a green cloak?"

They both looked at each other.

Virtue tapped her chin. "I really don't think so—did you, Faith?"

"I peeked inside the ballroom. There were so many lavish outfits; it looked so fun! Madame Bellerose looks like a princess!"

Adam sighed heavily. Whatever had happened in the Basement had made these girls chattier, and he wasn't sure that was a good thing. He searched the drawing room. Not everyone was dancing. A few people in costumes mingled by the grand arched windows and whispered by the fireplace. A couple of men admired Van der Ven's glass case of swords, knives, and all other manner of blades. Van der Ven had always boasted that every weapon he put on display had been used to kill at least three men on the battlefield. He was covetous of his kills as much as he was of his property. He wouldn't like this rowdy scene.

"Oh, Lord Temple—I think I saw a green cloak disappear through there!" said Virtue, and pointed at the little door that led down the stairs to a labyrinth of cellars. She clung to his tuxedo vest. "Shall we go and look? It would be ever so much fun."

Adam narrowed his eyes. The girls grinned at him with bloodred smiles and mischievous brown eyes. Bellerose had instructed them to watch him. But what were children if they didn't play a few games?

"I don't have time for lies. If you didn't see her, then just say so."

Faith and Virtue Sparrow's expressions darkened.

"Did you say that we are liars?" Virtue said, her voice hollow as her arms dropped to their side. "Ma'am at the orphanage used to say we were liars. She was an awful woman. She would leave us outside in the cold to punish us."

The temperature of the room suddenly dropped. Adam's whole body shivered as he hugged himself. No one else in the room seemed bothered. No other mouth but his breathed out chilled mist. And when Faith and Virtue held hands, no one but Adam noticed the room shudder with a sudden blizzard. Snow collected atop the mounted animal heads on the walls, icicles beginning to form down the snouts of the bears, boars, and Siberian tigers. Their wooden frames rattled as the blizzard picked up, the animals howling in pain—or was it the wind?

No, this is their power, Adam reminded himself. Cortez had explained it before. Their snow games were nothing but tricks of the mind. But within their sphere of influence, it felt all too real. His knees began to buckle. His chest felt tight, stinging as if his lungs were being stabbed from the inside. So cold. Was this what Iris had come up against that night outside the British Museum? The magic of the Fanciful Freaks truly was a sight to behold.

Snapping out of his own thoughts, Adam grabbed each of the twins' bony wrists and separated their hands. The spell broke. Adam was once again in Van der Ven's home, surrounded by chatting strangers sipping wine who were none the wiser.

"I'm not calling you liars," Adam explained quickly. "I'm just in a hurry. I'm sorry."

The twins gave each other secretive looks, as if conversing telepathically about whether they should forgive him.

Adam didn't have time for this. "You said she went downstairs. Are you sure?"

At this, they looked at him and nodded with amicable grins.

"Fine, then. Shall we?" He bowed and gestured toward the door. As the two girls giggled and raced each other to it, Adam rubbed his brow. Van der Ven could show up at any minute, and when he did, he'd go straight for "Bellerose's"—Lucille's—head. Well, Adam didn't want to lose such a useful chess piece, but if it did come to that, there was nothing he would do to stop it.

It was Iris now who had his attention.

"I'm coming," he whispered, and followed the twins through the door.

—◇◇◇◇—

The cellar was labyrinthine indeed, and cold from a draft that trickled through the hallways.

"Over there, over there!" cried Virtue, pointing to her left a yard away. Adam had seen it too: the green velvet robes sweeping the stone floor as it turned a corner.

"After her!" Adam cried as he followed the trail. But Iris was fast. Just when he thought he'd had her, he found himself in another hallway surrounded by red brick. *What's this game you're playing, Iris? Why won't you see me?*

Or was she testing him?

Iris is dead. Mary's, Lucille's, and Henry's voices taunted him as he turned every corner, just barely missing the swish of her robes' hem. He wouldn't believe it. Iris was alive, and he would gladly punish anyone who tried to tell him otherwise.

Finally he came to a dead end, the twins rushing to catch up to him. Green robes flowed down across the stone floor; the woman's back was to him. Her head was covered by her shimmering hood, and a golden rope was tied around her waist, like those princesses of the medieval age.

A flush of excitement gripped Adam as he wondered if Iris were teasing him. His rational mind told him such a thing was beneath Iris—so uncharacteristic. But the feral side of him pulsed and stiffened at the thought. How badly he wanted to touch her body . . . the body of a goddess of death.

Do not wait for a slave to save you. You were born of kings, boy. Claim your birthright. We are the gods.

"Don't be foolish," Adam whispered, even as his blood stirred. The doctor was mired in the discourse of evolution. To him, even the supernatural was simply another avenue through which to advance human achievement. His desire was only for science. That was why he didn't understand this higher lust that Adam now felt screaming within his bones: a longing for the divine. For an unearthly justice. For godly retribution.

Adam stretched his hand out to her—and yes, she turned. Slowly. Enticingly. She lowered the hood of her green cloak.

And there she was. Her perfectly sculpted, heart-shaped lips and large eyes. Her round nose and fluttering lashes. More perfect than he could have ever remembered them. His princess of disaster.

She did not speak, not as his dry lips ached and parted, not as he took his first step toward her.

"Iris . . ." His eyes welled up with tears. "Iris, it's you. . . . I've been told such terrible things. . . ." Another trembling step forward. His heart pounded furiously against his chest. "I knew you wouldn't disappear. I knew you wouldn't disappoint me."

"I know that woman." Faith Sparrow's singing voice dragged Adam out of his delusions and back into reality. "Sister, I know that woman."

Virtue nodded. "A dark-skinned woman with two men at her side." She pressed a pale finger to her cheek, tilting her head. "We battled her that moonlit night, did we not? Master Cortez forced us to."

"Or else he wouldn't give us any treats."

"Or else he would lock us up inside the orphanage forever."

"But sister, we *were* locked up." Faith looked at her twin sadly. "In a place worse than the orphanage."

"After losing our battle to *her* . . ."

Adam watched as Virtue's gaze suddenly became as sharp as one of Van der Ven's coveted swords. Yes, it was Cortez who'd forced them into that battle outside the British Museum to test them as tournament candidates. But that was the past. This was the present. The future. Humanity's future depended on this moment. That was of far more importance than whatever grievance these two little devils still clung to. But how could children ever understand?

The moment the two took a step forward, Adam put out a hand to stop them. "Iris is *my* responsibility. Don't even think about approaching her."

Iris had turned to him fully now. Her arms were sheathed in white gloves. Her whole body was shielded inside the drapery of her green robes. He could only see her face, and her face was all he needed. Though he wished she'd speak with him. Even for just a moment. Even just a word . . .

"Iris was your champion," Virtue said, her fingers twitching, her head lowered. "You sent her to fight against us that night." A shadow passed over Virtue's delicate features. "And when she defeated us, we were sent to that very bad place."

Faith gripped her chest as her brown eyes lost focus. As if she remembered. The Basement. All the pain they'd endured. How many scientists had Faith and Virtue killed, Adam wondered, before being given their new position by Bellerose?

Faith shook her head with a sorrowful expression. "You and Cortez are both very bad."

"Iris, stand behind me." Adam gritted his teeth, preparing a fist. As uncouth as it was, he wasn't above knocking down a couple of little girls if it meant he could get away cleanly with Iris. These children couldn't possibly understand. Now that he had Iris, now that he *had* her—

"God, no wonder Iris couldn't stand you."

Adam's throat closed. His arms lost their strength and dropped to his sides. He'd seen Iris's lips move. But that wasn't Iris's voice. He'd memorized every note, every melody and idiosyncrasy. That wasn't Iris's voice at all.

It was—

"Iris" grinned. "Fooled you. *Wanker.*"

Adam's eyes widened as chaos threw his heartbeat into turmoil. "Lucille?"

He barely had a moment to process her wicked grin. Faith and Virtue aimed for his shins, ankles, and knees, forcing him to the ground with each kick. And once he was down, "Iris" joined them, kicking him in the face and chest, forcing bile from his stomach out of his mouth.

Lucille grabbed his hair and lifted his head up. Blood dripped from his lips as he struggled to breathe. If Lucille was here, then who was the Bellerose inside the ballroom? He *had* been tricked.

"You'll regret this," he coughed. He hadn't enough breath, or else he'd ask her if she'd seen Whittle lately.

"Oh no, dear, I'm very sure the only one who'll be regretting anything is *you*, especially once Maximo brings Hiva down here to burn you to ashes. I do wish I could watch, but I'm not one for gore. I am, however, always open to a bit of revenge."

And she kneed him in the face, breaking his nose.

The three women beat him unconscious.

15

GLADSTONE FELT ALL TOO COMFORTABLE SITTING in another man's office. The dead animals on the wall didn't seem to bother him either. They bothered Max. Max had been surrounded by enough death in his lifetime. At least Gladstone had chosen not to sit in the desk in front of the double windows. In this room, nestled on the first floor of Van der Ven's townhouse, he instead sat in the rocking chair in the corner, wedged between the desk and the cast-iron fireplace.

The room was busy, as were most of the upper-class London homes Max had snuck into and stolen from. Standing lamps guarded the long bookshelf filled to the brim with classics. The walls were covered in paintings and family portraits framed in gold. Gladstone could have chosen any one of the velvet chairs or sofas in the room, but he'd found solace in the creaky wooden rocking chair. Max wondered if this was a sign of humility or dementia.

No, this man was as sharp as a knife. His eyes were certainly so. They never left Hiva as the god gazed at the paintings at the wall.

Gladstone settled into his chair, clasping his hands together. "Is there anyone who takes your fancy, god of death?"

Max's lips parted in a silent gasp. "You know who he is—*what* he is?"

Gladstone only grinned. "I had wondered what kind of creature could decimate so many men in an instant. Parliament believed it to be some kind of special gas. Certain chemists in France have long been experimenting with sulfur components that will one day be used to fell men on the battlefield. But this was not that."

Hiva seemed unperturbed. Gladstone watched him take in each painting while moonlight streamed through the windows.

There was one in particular that made the god stop in his tracks. It was an oil painting of a group of children in dirty rags huddled inside some kind of wooden shack. Crouched on the ground, or sitting on little stools near cobwebs, they watched an injured old crone sitting in the corner. A little hole in the wall gave them their only glimpse of the sky.

Max didn't know much about paintings, but the kids reminded them of his youth: him, Chadwick, Hawkins, Jacob, and Cherice huddled together, trying to survive in some dirt-filled hole in the world. Hiva didn't take his eyes off the children either. What in the world could he be thinking?

"Hiva is the cataclysm," said Gladstone. "A being of unknown origin and untold power. With his crystal heart, he is immortal. And with his ability to sense the life within men, he can burn us all to ashes. This is according to the information I've been given by the others who, like myself, have recently joined the Enlightenment Committee at the behest of Madame Violet Bellerose."

A Committee member? Max had been right to have Cherice stay on her guard.

"Don't come to Van der Ven's office yet," he'd told her on the dance floor before he'd followed the old prime minister out of the ballroom. "Lucille's on the move, which means Adam should be in the cellar by now. Gather the others and watch for Mary's signal."

Max placed his hands on his hips, but though he tried to keep his cool, he could feel the hairs on his arms standing on end. "Didn't know the Enlighteners were recruiting. So? What now, old man? What do you want with Hiva? If you know how dangerous he is, shouldn't you be shaking in your boots right now instead of calling him out for a little midnight chat?"

Max never imagined he'd be trash-talking the prime minister to his face. He'd really moved up in the world. If he ever saw Berta again, he'd make sure to tell her.

"You said you were recruiting," Max continued, unrelenting. "For what?"

Gladstone shut his eyes, resting his elbow on his knobby knees. "The war, lad. The war."

Max's hands dropped from his hips. "What?"

"I want to recruit Hiva. This god of death. I want to use him as a weapon to end it."

The prime minister's words had stunned Max into silence. For a moment, Max couldn't even close his lips. Recruit . . . Hiva? For the war effort? Was this old man bonkers? But no, Gladstone was dead serious. He could see it in those dark, cloudy eyes of his that pierced through him like a spear.

"What are you . . . ?" Max shook his head in disbelief. "What are you on about?"

"I want Hiva to become a soldier for England."

A short stream of laughter erupted from Max's lips without him even realizing it. He looked behind him. Hiva had not moved from the oil painting of the huddled, frightened children. Was he even listening? Was Gladstone listening to himself?

"*Soldiers* fight in a war." Max said this as if explaining it to a little child, rather than the political leader of the country. But it somehow felt apt. "Trained soldiers. Warriors."

"Young man," Gladstone said, without moving an inch in his seat. "Thanks to the mayhem at the Berlin Conference, a dozen nations across Europe have declared war on one another, and more will follow. New weapons are being produced and shipped out to the war front, and each shows startling advancement in the technologies of destruction. New strategies of warfare are killing men by the dozens. One day, boy, history will see this as the war to end all wars—the greatest and most vicious among all we've fought. The Enlighteners want Hiva to travel to Africa, to power their expedition into another world. I want Hiva to travel to the front in Germany and use his skills in *this* world. The greatest war to ever begin needs the greatest soldier to end it."

And what better soldier than a god? Hiva could decimate enemy soldiers in seconds and force countries to their knees. But was that what Hiva wanted?

Was it possible to change the mind of a monster who could never see humanity along national lines?

"Hiva . . ."

Max's words died in his throat as he looked upon the god, still gazing at the children of Van der Ven's oil painting. And whatever Max was going to say next drowned underneath the trickle of tears that now slid down Hiva's golden cheeks.

Hiva was crying.

Children had once given him joy. Hadn't Hiva told them that himself?

Hey, Maxey, you really think Hiva's actually going to learn something profound at a stuck-up, hoity-toity event like this?

The memory of Cherice's words numbed Max's hands.

"Hiva . . . ," he whispered, while Gladstone looked on silently from his chair.

"She started with the children," Hiva said, and though his voice did not shake, Max could hear the pain in it, clear as a bell.

And when Hiva turned, Max saw both of his golden eyes. No longer empty voids, they shimmered, dripping with tears.

"The children I so loved. The children who played on the green hills over-looking the ocean. Who plucked the flowers from my hair and danced." Hiva's eyes lost focus as he remembered them. "I begged her. 'Even the children, sister?' I had asked her in anguish. 'Even the children?' And she told me this: 'You misunderstand everything. There is no love and no hate. Only what needs to be done.'" He looked down at his trembling hands. "The truth is as it shall always be."

Months ago, in the Basement, Max had seen parts of Iris's former lives as Hiva. He'd seen her fell nations. Even though they were only glimpses of the past, they'd shocked him to the core—enough for him to betray Iris's newly unearthed secret to the other Fanciful Freaks. Enough to turn her into an enemy.

The Iris that Hiva had described was cold and unfeeling. But the Iris that Max had known was anything but. Somehow, in the midst of their bloody struggles and painful history, the two gods had swapped places. It was as if

Hiva was slowly coming to terms with just what had been stolen from him. And that became clear as Hiva moved his stiff fingers, flexing and unflexing them, as if he'd just noticed them now for the first time.

"Is there another way? I don't know. Sister wouldn't tell me. . . . And now I am alone. All I loved, I loved alone. Because of the demon in my view . . ."

And Hiva fell to his knees.

"No one wants to be alone, Hiva." Gladstone. His eyes sparked with the opportunity wrapped up and dropped into his lap by the gods of fortune. He'd clearly realized what Max had much earlier: that a god could have weaknesses. "You can save many more children if you end the war. You will save them all through your service on the war front."

"Save them?" Hiva laid his head back and stared up at the dark oak ceiling. "It's something sister never would have done."

"Then be better than her," Gladstone said. "You don't have to be a god of death."

Max glared at him, a flush of heat rising through his body as he watched the man talk of a "sister" he knew nothing about. How like a politician.

But then . . .

But then if Gladstone succeeded . . .

"I had asked my sister once on those rolling hills," said Hiva. "Isn't there another way for us to live? Lifetimes of traveling. Lifetimes of killing. I just wanted another way. . . ."

"I'm giving you one now." Gladstone's stone face never moved. "It's your right to choose, Hiva. Choose life."

"Choose life . . . ," Max and Hiva whispered at the same time.

And then Max remembered Cherice's teasing grin on the ballroom floor.

I mean, it would *be nice and all if he had a change of heart . . .*

"Cherice." Max's heart began banging against his rib cage. If Gladstone succeeded, then Hiva could end two wars in an instant: the one made by men and the one of his own doing. Max had wondered, on the night of the music hall massacre, if he could direct Hiva's powers. Maybe this was the way to do it.

That bloody Gladstone . . . What if that old bag was the miracle Max had been praying for?

"What say you, Hiva?" the prime minister asked.

Hiva remained silent for so long, Max started to wonder. The god in front of him was transforming in front of his eyes.

Finally Hiva answered. "Yes. I will," Hiva said. "I'll do as you say. I'll see . . . if there's another way for humanity—for *me*—to live."

A wave of emotion battered Max from the inside, causing him to sway on his feet. Joy and relief. Apprehension. Confusion. Humanity's one year to live. Weeks of watching senseless destruction. Was it all over? Just like that?

Had humanity won?

But Hiva looked at Max. He looked at him with the innocence and sadness of a lost child.

"Come with me," he said, with a strange tenderness that made Max suddenly too aware of himself. "Come with me." He repeated it again. "I never wanted to be alone."

The door opened with a creak. A little pink marble rolled inside and then sparked with white smoke. The tiniest explosion. Mary's signal. That was when Max remembered the plan.

Oh no.

Gladstone stood up from his chair. "What is the meaning of this?"

If he had a change of heart . . .

Oh God, no.

"Wait!" Max cried, but his pleas were drowned underneath the sound of window glass shattering. Hawkins, Jacob, and Cherice came through the window, ready for battle.

Max ran now, but Jacob moved quickly. Using the blowgun Henry had made in preparation for the plan, he shot Hiva precisely with two darts: one in the forehead, the other in his neck.

"Now!" Cherice cried, wielding a sharp blade Henry had cobbled together. "Get that bastard!"

Hawkins and Jacob didn't need telling twice. Why would they? The Hiva they knew had forced them to be willing audiences to his murder spree. In the blink of an eye, they ambushed a stunned Hiva, now drugged with the poison Henry had placed in each needle.

The plan was supposed to take place in the cellar where Lucille would lure Adam to. Max would manipulate Hiva into burning Adam to ashes, and while he was distracted, they'd take his arm using the "toys" Henry had made. Adam would die, and they'd escape with the weapon to truly put an end to Hiva.

The location might have changed, thanks to Gladstone, but nonetheless everything was going according to plan—

Except Hiva himself.

Hawkins and Jacob pinned him against the oil painting, not noticing the tears he shed.

"No!" The door burst open once more. Fables. He was wearing a servant's outfit. So it *had* been him Max had noticed in the ballroom downstairs, cleaning up after Temple. How had he managed to sneak in? It didn't matter. Everything was happening so fast. Fables cried as he lunged toward Hiva's attackers with a kitchen knife in hand.

Unfortunately for Fables, Cherice had the bigger blade.

Max couldn't move, couldn't think. He could only watch helplessly, clenching his fists as the window of hope that had opened slammed shut just as suddenly.

"Wait!" And Max lifted his head to the sky. "I said wait, goddamn you!"

Cherice cut off Hiva's arm, blood spurting as far as the office desk. Hiva lost consciousness.

"No! *No!*" Fables grabbed Hiva just as he slid to the ground, howling as if his own limb had been cut. "My king!"

"What're you standing around for? Hurry and take his arm!" Cherice ordered Jacob, who nodded and picked up the bloody limb off the floor.

All the while, Gladstone stared at the bloody scene, his hand clutching his chest. "What is this barbarity?" His coarse voice breathed out uneven breaths.

"Who's this grandpa?" Hawkins said, scrunching up his face as he finally noticed the prime minister.

But Max didn't have time to answer. As Hawkins readied his blue vortex to escape, Fables dropped Hiva and rushed forward, his knife in hand.

A blue marble found Fables's stomach before his own knife could reach Hawkins's neck. The explosion opened up the American boy's flesh.

"Oh God!" Jacob nearly dropped Hiva's arm as Fables slumped to the ground, holding his insides. And as Hawkins backed closer toward his blue void, Jacob faced the open office door. "Mary! What did you do?"

Max hadn't noticed the mousy girl behind the door. In her hands was some kind of wooden box filled with marbles. Creating, in mere moments, toys that exceeded the imagination was Henry's power. Max had come up against it before. But never had he seen Henry's power used so ruthlessly. And by Mary, of all people. The girl whose powers were to heal.

She didn't bother healing Fables.

"Go now!" Mary barked at the others, for their plan was now complete. The only thing that could kill Hiva was Hiva's own self. If a sword made from Iris's bones could kill Iris, then they now had the means to get rid of Hiva. This was good. This is what they'd hoped for.

So why did the sight of Hiva gushing blood all over Van der Ven's floor disturb Max so? The tears on Hiva's face hadn't yet dried.

Hawkins tugged the back of Jacob's vest. "Let's go," he said. "Cherice!"

Cherice glanced at Max, parting her lips, but Max put up a hand to stop whatever words were about to slip from them. "You go ahead. I'll find you at the meeting place," he told them.

As Cherice reluctantly followed Hawkins and Jacob into the void, Maximo wasn't sure what he was doing. He wasn't sure why he turned to Gladstone while Mary stood awkwardly at the door.

"That servant over there. His name is Fables. He needs medical attention. Can you get it for him? I'll let you have Hiva in return."

Let him? What was he thinking?

"Can you do that, boy?" Gladstone's question echoed Max's own.

"Hiva doesn't need medical attention. He'll heal on his own. But in terms of your war—he'll only listen to me. So if you want to have him, you've got to try to save Fables first."

"I'll call my men to take them," Gladstone assured him while Max's mind spun in disarray. "For now, you should escape. I won't be able to explain your part in all this."

Max's thoughts were jumbled, his joints stiff, as he and Mary jumped out the window. As the two ran to the back of the building, he couldn't meet her eyes.

"I thought the plan after cutting off his arm was to take his body and bury him," Mary said as they stood behind the brown brick of Van der Ven's majestic townhouse. "We bury him until we can sharpen his bones and then kill him!"

A stake through the heart, like a vampire. Max really had read too many of those penny bloods in his youth, but it had been the best he could come up with at the time. But things had changed. What if their attack had rekindled Hiva's hatred against humanity—what would they do? Should he have left Hiva in Gladstone's care? All to save Fables?

What the hell was he bloody thinking?

"I'm sorry." Max shut his eyes and gripped both sides of his head. "I don't know. I just . . . it was all the blood. It was all the blood, I suppose."

Blood he hadn't expected. There was already too much of it on his hands. Maybe he just couldn't take it anymore.

"I'm sorry too," Mary whispered in that angelic, gentle voice of hers, and Max felt her soft hand upon his shoulder. "I know what it's like to be confused. To hate yourself. To not trust your own decisions."

For a moment she was quiet.

"I was going to take the money for myself, you know. The money from the Tournament of Freaks. If Henry, Lucille, and I had won, I was going to take the money and run away."

Max lowered his hands from his ears, fearing he'd heard wrong. "W-what?"

"Mr. Henry needed the money to get his family out of debt, and I said I would help. We would have split it with Lucille. He thanked me so much. He thanked me with tears in his eyes. Me. A servant."

She shook her head against the memories, her hands trembling as she gripped the wooden toy box before hiding it behind her back.

"I don't know what came over me, but that was when I decided that I was going to take all the money for myself and run. I'm horrid. I know." Mary shut her eyes and bit her lip, her hands still behind her back. "I didn't want to die a maid like my mother. Why should I? The Whittle family's been good to me, sure. They took me and my mum in, but that doesn't mean they own me."

Mary gazed at him with shimmering wet blue eyes, her lips curved into a smile of self-hatred Max knew all too well. He saw it every time he looked in the mirror.

"I know how you must feel, killing Iris. After everything Henry did for me, I was going to betray him like that. I was going to take everything away from him."

Max hung his head. "I thought it was fine to betray Iris because I was doing it for someone I loved. My sister, Berta."

Mary raised her eyebrows. "Sister?"

"We were separated in London when she was a child, and she was taken to America. She's in Africa now, in some port city—Ajashe. If anything ever happened to her . . ." Max shook his head. "At least that's how I justified it to myself."

"I'm sure if you could go back in time, you'd change things, right?" Mary asked.

Yes. Yes, he would. He would change everything. All his ridiculous assumptions. All his paranoid imaginings. All the lives he'd taken. Every terrible thought he'd ever had toward the few people who'd only ever trusted him. Max pressed his hands against his eyes, squeezing his face as the agony of his bad decisions tormented him.

"I thought about it," Mary said, "and I don't want to end up like you. I won't betray Henry. I'm sorry, Max. This plan's changed."

What?

Max lowered his hands from his face, his blood still pumping in his ears. That was likely why he didn't notice the poison dart Mary had taken out of the wooden box. It was already in his neck before he could blink.

"Just how many of those things did that strange lad make?" he wondered aloud, swaying on his feet until he collapsed, unconscious.

16

I GOT FOOL'S MESSAGE LOUD AND CLEAR. You have Max. Now give us Henry!"

"Who knew you had such viciousness in you, Ms. White?"

"Give me Henry!"

A medley of voices dragged Max awake. His head throbbed in pain as he picked himself off the cold stone floor of what looked like a cellar. It was a narrow space, though long. The wall in front of him was lined with rows of shelves that carried vintage bottles of wine. His ankles were burning.

When Max tried to move his legs, his feet hit another small collection of wine bottles on the floor. Two tumbled over and rolled down the slight slope of the basement, hitting Henry Whittle's thigh. Henry was chained up against the stone wall of the cellar. Fool held a knife to his throat. And at the threshold of the cellar door was Mary, her hands trembling around her little wooden box of doom.

Adam Temple stood in front of her, his face bruised and battered, his arms folded across his chest. "So you had Lucille pretend to be Iris to lure me here so that Max could have his Hiva dog murder me. But I don't see Hiva. All I see is a terrified and treacherous little maid."

Mary was terrified. She couldn't bear to look at Max.

THE LADY OF RAPTURE

"Fool told you that I had Whittle and that I would kill him if you betrayed me," Adam continued. "I still might."

"Fool told me when he saw Max and Hiva leave with Gladstone." Mary scowled at Fool, who held his pocketknife so taut against Henry's throat that it drew blood.

Adam smirked. "So, like a little coward, you told him everything."

"You have Max now. Hiva's gone—he can't do anything to you. Release Henry!" Mary commanded him, in a tone more frightening than her tiny frame seemed capable of. "Fool promised that if I gave you Max, you'd give me Henry!"

Max now realized why he couldn't move his legs all that well. His ankles were bound up in rope. So were his wrists. Tied up in some white man's stuffy room. Huh, like at the auction. Felt somewhat nostalgic.

But the cold expression on Mary's face was not familiar at all. He'd been double-crossed. Max didn't think she'd had it in her. He probably shouldn't have underestimated her. Then maybe he wouldn't be tied up in a cellar.

Henry was conscious but weak. He grunted as Adam nodded at Fool, who lowered his knife, unlocked his shackles, and let him go. Henry stumbled forward, sparing a quick, pitying glance at Max as he limped past him. Mary rushed up to him and grabbed him, dragging him back out of the room.

"I'm so sorry, Max," she said before escaping, pulling Henry with her.

"And Lucille?" Max asked Adam with a slight groan, managing to sit up, though his headache still hammered away at his skull.

"Oh, she's long gone, young Maximo." Adam laughed, though he really didn't have any right to. He looked worse than Maximo felt. The purple bruise around his left eye and his broken nose told Max that his schemes against Mary's team hadn't been without a cost. "She left the house with a new face and a couple of young ladies looking for their mistress. Well, it could have been worse. They could have killed me. Now I get to kill you."

He walked toward the shelves of wine on the opposite wall. Then, reaching behind a wineglass, he pulled out a revolver. "Ah, just where I left it." He turned to Fool. "Leave us."

With a swift bow, Fool did as he was told. Adam didn't seem to mind that all his servants were now gone. His focus was now entirely on Max.

"We meet again, Maximo Morales." Adam's bottom lip had been split. Whatever Lucille had done to him, she clearly hadn't held back. But it didn't stop Adam from flashing him an arrogant, evil smile.

"Lucky me." Max lay back against the stone wall. "So how'd you like my present? Pretty smart, right?"

"Oh, you mean the fake Iris?" Kneeling in front of him, Adam grabbed Maximo's curly brown hair and gripped it tightly. "I didn't much appreciate it, actually. I *am* a little curious as to who that fake Bellerose sitting up in the ballroom is if it's not Lucille, but I suppose that'll have to wait."

Searing pain shuddered down Maximo's head. The ropes around his arms and legs had been tied in haste. But even if he could slip out of the binds, would he be fast enough to escape Adam's bullet when the gun was cocked dangerously close to his forehead?

Maybe this was really it. Suited him right. Max chuckled.

"So?" Max gave him one of his lopsided grins. "You wanted to see me?"

Adam seemed almost amused at his show of nonchalance. Well, they were both wankers. And how like a pair of wankers to be amused with each other's wankerishness, if that was even a word. Was it a word?

An exasperated sigh escaped Adam's lips. "I just want to know where she is, that's all."

And he lifted the gun to his own head. Max's breath hitched and he watched, stunned, as Adam shut his eyes and raised his head toward the ceiling.

"If I live, you'll tell me, Max. Tell me where Iris is."

And he pulled the trigger.

"God!" Max screamed and shut his eyes, but no sound came from the gun except a flaccid click. When he pried them open again, Adam was staring at the barrel. "What the hell are you doing, you maddening fool?"

"So it's not time for me to die yet?" Adam turned the gun over, examining its metal surface. "Then Maximo, what about you?"

Max gulped, staring down the barrel of the gun.

"There are six chambers in the cylinder of this revolver. But only one bullet. The quicker you tell me the truth about Iris, the better your chances of survival."

"Russian roulette, eh?" Max laid his head back against the stone wall. "Feels like an apt metaphor for my life these days."

Max felt the cold mouth of the barrel against his forehead.

"The last time I saw Iris, she was in West Africa," Adam said. "I was informed she went down to Heaven's Shrine with you, your sister, that circus freak Jinn, and a few others. Now you're here, but she isn't."

"That is correct."

"You then appeared at the Alhambra Theatre with the *other* Hiva. Not Iris."

"Also correct."

Max could hear the rough edges of Adam's breath as it came up his throat. A pause. "Where is Iris?"

"She's dead."

Click.

Hmph. A lucky break. The second chamber didn't have a bullet in it either. Otherwise Max's brains would have been splattered across the wall. A quick, giddy laugh escaped Max's lips, but his body wouldn't stop trembling. Fear pounded in his chest, threatening to erupt. He wouldn't give Adam the satisfaction. No, not that rat bastard, with his wild, sunken eyes that looked at Max with disdain just as potent as the day they'd met and formed their devil's pact.

Adam seemed to be trying very hard to keep calm. It wasn't working. "What happened to her after she entered Heaven's Shrine?" he asked.

"We found your father and went through a trapdoor, a secret entrance that took us down to the Coral Temple underneath the sea," Max told him truthfully, because he had no reason to lie. "There we met Hiva." Max closed his eyes, remembering that terrible day. The look of despair on Iris's beautiful, sorrowful face. "The other Hiva. He was there waiting for us."

Adam had stiffened at the mention of his father, but he never relented. The gun felt like ice against Max's skin.

"And what happened after you met Hiva?"

"Iris died."

Click. Another lucky break. This time Max's laughter was relentless, pitched high with terror and derision. "She's dead, mate! You're just going to have to get over it."

"She *can't* die." Adam grabbed Max's collar. Max must have looked so ridiculous in his tunic, dressed as Tristan, some star-crossed medieval lover mourning his lost paramour. Playing dress-up had almost made Max forget his sins. Almost. "She's a god. Death has no power over her."

"What if the only thing that could kill a god was herself?" Maximo said, his throat dry as he swallowed. "Iris's bones from the museum. That was all it took."

"Bones?" In that moment, Adam looked suddenly lost, like a child stranded, searching for his parents. But he wasn't a child. He was a grown man who'd caused Max nothing but pain and suffering. He was also a killer. And the moment he'd recruited Max to watch and betray Iris in the hopes of getting his sister back, he'd turned Max into one too.

"Clip a god's wings," Adam whispered, his eyes unfocused as if recalling a memory. But soon he shook his head. "You're lying. You are *lying!*"

"Enough!" Max growled, because he couldn't stand to look upon the sorry sight of this mumbling madman any longer. "Hiva took the sword he made from Iris's bones. If you don't believe me, go visit that little shrine you made in the British Museum. Her left leg is missing. That was what Hiva used."

Adam's teeth chattered as he gasped in air, his face twisted in horror. "No . . . ," he whispered.

"He crafted a sword out of Iris's bones and threw it on the floor. The lot of us made a mad dash for it like a pack of hyenas."

Adam shook his head again and again. "No, no . . ."

"I took the sword—"

Adam covered his ears. "Stop!"

"I took it and stabbed her through the spine. Through the heart!" Max was screaming now. The words were flying off his tongue, each one causing more agony than a bullet ever could. "I killed Iris. I killed her and watched Hiva take her crystal heart and crush it in his hands. I watched her turn to dust!"

"No!" Adam shouted. *"No!"*

"I killed her! She's *dead!*"

THE LADY OF RAPTURE

"Shut your filthy mouth!"

Adam used the barrel of the gun to strike Max across the face so hard that Max's body crashed into the wine bottles lined up on the floor. Glass jabbed his back and his tied-up arms and legs. As wine drenched Max's clothes, Adam pushed his face upon the wet floor, the broken glass cutting his cheek. And with the revolver's barrel, Adam struck Max's head again and again until blood gushed out of Max's mouth.

"You liar! You animal! You *demon!*"

"*You* are the demon!" Max bit back, his left eye bruised shut. "You used my sister against me. You turned me against Iris. It's your fault I ended up on that ship in the middle of the ocean. It's your fault I became like you: a murderer! It's *your* fault Iris is dead!"

Max didn't know how true it all was, but it felt true. To the depths of his bitter bones, it felt so true that tears leaked from his eyes. He wished he'd never met Adam. He wished he'd never met any of them. Adam stumbled back, falling to the ground after slipping on a pool of wine.

Something dangerous inside him wished Adam would just kill him. But when he closed his eyes, he remembered Berta, still somewhere on another continent, and began shaking loose his binds. Adam stared at the ceiling, dazed and silent as if he'd been knocked into delirium.

"Iris's death is the fault of both of us," Max said decidedly as he felt the ropes around his ankles and wrists slip little by little. "Her blood is on both our hands. We're *both* demons."

"Then I guess we both deserve what we get." Adam's voice was devoid of anger, devoid of even a hint of life. With languid eyes, his body limp, he got to his feet.

Max held his breath as Adam pointed the barrel of the gun to his own head—

Before changing his mind and pointing it at Max instead.

"You first," Adam whispered, and the gun fired.

17

N O, NOT ADAM'S GUN. THE ROUND of gunshots Max heard were
from the floor above. *Bang, bang, bang.* Each rattled Max's bones.

The shots had Adam distracted. He lowered his arm, staring up at
the ceiling. Adam was right. They both deserved to die. Max knew that for certain. But he wasn't about to give up *his* life to satisfy this prat. Not him. Max
was done dancing for a Temple.

He held his breath.

Come on, he thought, struggling against his binds as Adam remained frozen. Max's time-bending abilities would buy him some seconds, but only so
long as he could hold his breath. With the injuries he'd just incurred, his lung
capacity wasn't exactly optimal at the moment. Blood dripped from his lips and
eyelashes. A shudder of pain tore through him, causing him to let out his breath.

Adam looked at him.

"You," Temple said, his gaze suddenly wild. "What are you—?"

Max held his breath again. These ropes really were sloppily tied. He managed to twist his hands out of the binds. But no sooner did he yank it out than
he let out his breath. And before he could take another, Adam's gun was lifted
and cocked, ready to shoot.

Damn it, he cursed internally, his already battered muscles sore from the
use of his powers. *I can do it. I can do this.*

As time slowed to a crawl, Max could see a mixture of emotions in Adam's blue eyes, not least among them hatred—but perhaps even more pronounced was sorrow.

Sorrow for what?

Max didn't believe for a second that Adam had ever loved Iris. No. The only one who'd loved Iris was Jinn. Max was sure of it. Neither he nor Adam had seen Iris for who she was struggling to be. Neither of them had looked upon who she was and accepted her unconditionally. Neither of them deserved to mourn her loss. Not the ones who had killed her.

Max gritted his teeth as he struggled with the ropes around his legs. He kept that puff of breath trapped in his throat, but his body was starting to buckle. It hurt. It hurt so incredibly, so awfully. The excruciating pain begged him to give in, to give it his complete surrender and accept his fate.

It would be a release.

No. His squeezed his eyes shut as his lungs started rattling. *I won't die. Not by his hands. I'll survive this. I'll survive.*

I always survive!

He let out his breath.

The doors burst open. A deck of playing cards flew toward Adam, splitting open his right cheek and cutting his gun-wielding hand. The revolver fell from his grip, clattering to the ground.

"Cherice!" Max cried, drinking in air as Cherice came flying at Adam in the peach-colored robes of Princess Isolde, kicking the gun across the room before punching Adam soundly in the face. While Max watched in awe, Cherice ran up to him and tore off the rest of the rope around his ankles.

"Come on, Maxey, get your arse up." With a little grin, she grabbed him by his forearms and yanked him to his feet. "We're getting out of here before Van der Ven can make a mess."

"Van der Ven?" both Adam and Max cried at the same time, but while Adam went for his gun, Cherice pulled Max out of the cellar.

"Why did you come back?" Max said as they ran through the halls. "Where are Hawkins and Jacob?"

"Still at the meeting place," Cherice said, continuing to drag him by the wrist. "But what was I supposed to do when you didn't show? I knew you'd screwed up somehow."

Cherice's older brother Chadwick had been a gambler and passed on his vice to his little sister. But after the South Kensington explosion, Cherice could use her will to sharpen a deck of cards almost to the point of knives and throw them with a precision that could only be described as supernatural. In a group full of street boys, Cherice had never wanted to be the one left behind, the little brat.

Even the chuckle he managed hurt his cut and bruised sides.

"I'll need a good patching-up once we get back," Max said with a smile. "You game to play nurse?"

"Oh, shut up and *run*."

Max summoned every bit of strength to run at full speed, yet he could barely keep up with Cherice. The marigolds bounced in her apricot hair. She really had become the fastest in the group. And the bravest.

The stairs took him to a chaotic drawing room. Guests were fleeing out the door.

"He's mad!" said a man, almost tripping over an expensive vase as he fled. "Call the police! Van der Ven is going to assassinate Violet Bellerose!"

Cherice and Max exchanged glances, and their faces paled at the same time. Adam's plan had been to replace Bellerose with Lucille. But *their* plan had been to replace Lucille with someone else entirely. They'd made the switch perfectly: Lucille, leaving her face bare to convince Adam. Then, after disappearing through a door, the second Bellerose, with her face covered.

And now she was in danger.

I don't have enough time to teach you how to dance a court quadrille, so simply do your best to follow along with the others. She'd told them this before they left for the ball that evening. *Just* please *don't mess things up by making fools of yourselves.*

And Max had smiled at her. *Same to you.*

"Lily!" Clenching his jaw from the pain, Max rushed through the dining hall and into the ballroom.

The room was still half filled with guests in their ridiculous costumes, perhaps too frightened to move. The musicians hadn't been able to leave their seats. All eyes were trained on the back of the room, at the burly man holding "Madame Bellerose" hostage: Van der Ven.

This was not the proud man Max remembered. Belgium's once-famed major general had become a disheveled mess of a man. It would have been better if he'd shaved his black beard rather than allow it to grow unchecked into the unruly mess it now was upon his chin. He'd traded his military uniform for a dirty white shirt and beige trousers, his military medallions for a filthy stench that dampened the air. Max could smell him even from where he was. This was a man on the run. A man, according to Mary, who'd been falsely accused of starting the greatest war Europe had ever seen. Well, Max had had his low points too, but what was lower than this?

Even still, despite it all, Van der Ven kept a sword by his side, tied to his waist with a rickety brown belt. Even in disgrace, he was a military man.

Van der Ven stood in front of the congregation, holding "Bellerose" by the neck with a gun pressed to her head.

"Oh no—*Lily*," Max heard Cherice whisper next to him as she wrung her hands.

Lily's hair was already an auburn color. Max knew it wouldn't take much to disguise her as Bellerose, so long as her mask was on. Everything had gone well after she and Lucille had made the switch. Damn it. If Gladstone hadn't distracted him with his recruiting nonsense, they would have been able to keep a better eye on her.

"Why aren't you saying anything, madame?" Major General Gerolt Van der Ven roared so loudly, the ballroom felt as if it were shaking. "I know that none other than you and that boy Adam could have orchestrated such a perfect plot at the Berlin Conference. Tell them!" He shook Lily by the neck. "I didn't shoot Chancellor von Bismarck. I murdered *no one* at the Conference." His nostrils were round and flaring. "I was framed," he cried, "by a shape-shifter!"

He must have figured out how Adam had pulled it off, but it didn't do much to sway his audience, to say the least. Hushed whispers erupted among the crowd, who collectively looked at him—now even more so than ever—as if he were insane.

"It's the truth!" The cords on the collar of Van der Ven's shirt dangled and swayed as he took a sharp step forward, dragging Lily with him. "You fools in your costumes, drinking your wine and dancing in my home, with no idea of the true monstrosities that exist in this terrifying world. Tell them, Violet! About the Enlightenment Committee. About the South Kensington explosion ten years ago that produced human beings with supernatural abilities! About the other world and our plans to conquer it."

But Lily could say nothing, not with Van der Ven squeezing her throat. Underneath her mask, her skin was turning red. This was bad.

"Do you have any more cards?" Max whispered to Cherice.

"You know me. Always keep a few of 'em on me—tucked underneath my boobs."

"I *do* know you. But now I think I want to know more," Max said, with a little smile that made Cherice blush.

After sharing a quick nod, the two began making their way through the crowd to Van der Ven and Lily. Max was still bloodied and out of breath, but he would use whatever power he could to close the distance between them.

But no. He couldn't call on his ability at the moment. He grabbed his chest in pain. The cuts on his arms, legs, and sides still bled. His head still felt as if it would shatter in two from Adam's beating. He needed his breath. As he closed in on the front of the congregation, he needed it now more than ever.

"I am a future ruler of this world!" Van der Ven's booming voice shook the rafters of the vaulted ceiling. "Only I know the way to save it from destruction. Only I can control the beasts that threaten your annihilation! And you dare call me a criminal? You dare treat me as a fugitive?" His laughter was wild and deep. He grunted and sneered like a boar. How fitting.

"You? But dear Van der Ven, you are nothing but a relic of the past. Obsolete."

Max turned along with the crowd to the ballroom entrance.

It was the real Madame Bellerose. She stood, as haughty and arrogant as ever in an outrageous silver dress that looked like something out of the eighteenth century. The pannier was the width of a chest of drawers, embellished with frills, bows, and flowers of every color. Her red hair was done up and hoisted to a height that would have put Marie Antoinette to shame, with white feathers and diamonds blooming down its length. She looked ridiculous. But she looked confident. With deep red lips, she grinned evilly at Van der Ven before hiding the bottom half of her face with a large silver-embroidered fan.

Van der Ven looked at the Bellerose at the entrance and the "Bellerose" in his grip. And in that moment of confusion, Max sucked in the deepest breath his lungs could handle and moved quickly. Van der Ven's face had already twisted into a sneer, his finger moving to pull the trigger of the gun pressed against Lily's temple. As fast as he could, he snatched Lily from Van der Ven's grasp, falling down onto the floor with her just as Van der Ven's gun fired.

As Max held a tearful Lily on the ground, Cherice took the few cards she had left inside her robes and slashed Van der Ven's hands and face, forcing him to drop the gun.

"Stop!" the real Bellerose shouted from the entrance, pointing her fan at them like a weapon just as Van der Ven reached for his sword. "Gerolt. When will you realize? Your time is over. I've created a new Enlightenment Committee," she told him. "One that will operate just fine without you. As soon as I retrieve Hiva's heart, the Ark will set sail from Africa. The progress of human civilization will be spurred forward once more. I will be at the fore-front of modernity. But you—" Madame Bellerose tilted her head, covering her smile once more with her fan. "You, my dear Van der Ven, will be left behind in the annals of history with the other brutes."

Madame Bellerose's insincere pitying expression only seemed to enrage him further. Van der Ven lifted his sword high above his head.

"Filthy *woman*," he cried.

The cry was his last. When Bellerose gave a signal with her fan, every member of the half-crowded ballroom pulled out a gun from inside their lav-ish costumes. The princesses and the thieves. The maids and the bards. Even the musicians, who dropped their lutes and oboes just as guns began erupting.

Van der Ven should have died then. He should have died with his right arm raised in the air, holding aloft his sword with the pride of the general he once was. But even though his chest was riddled with bullet holes and his lips were dripping with blood, he stayed on his feet. He would not die in disgrace. This was a man who had once commanded armies. Who was to have owned worlds. He wouldn't let the devil take him until he was good and ready.

But the devil came anyway. A man appeared next to Bellerose at the threshold of the ballroom entrance. A man in a pair of trousers and vest dirtier than Van der Ven's. He was emaciated, and bald underneath the newsboy cap he wore. Jaundiced skin, sunken eyes, and a pair of thin lips that looked embalmed. A one-armed man. Max could tell by the way one of his white sleeves fluttered in the air. He was almost completely unfamiliar. Almost.

"Bately?" Max's heart shuddered in his chest. "Bately?" He gripped Lily's arm so hard, she let out a little cry of pain. "It can't be. It can't be you—"

Bellerose leaned over and whispered to him from behind her frivolous fan. Then Bately, clearly with great difficulty, opened his mouth.

"Kill yourself, Major General Gerolt Van der Ven."

His voice had none of the arrogant swagger it used to. Barry Bately spoke as if he were a shadow in the night. But his power worked nonetheless.

With the last bit of strength and resolve he had, Van der Ven turned his sword upon himself and plunged it into his heart.

It was the end of the mighty boar.

"You can take this carriage, sir and madams," said the driver.

The driver didn't look at them. He kept his face hidden beneath his top hat and turned himself to the side. Max didn't blame him. The gunshots inside Eight Grandage View had brought people out into the street, gossiping behind gloved hands. The police would be here soon enough. And Max, Cherice, and Lily had just made it out of the townhouse. Bellerose's murderous guests, likely Committee spies, had already dispersed into the night, either on foot or in other carriages. This driver was clearly antsy from the situation but wanted his few shillings nonetheless.

"Get in first, Lily," Max said, helping her inside the carriage. It only seated two, but they'd have to squeeze in somehow.

"God, I can't believe I let you talk me into this madness," Lily said, huffing as she tried to fit her ridiculously ruffled skirt inside the tight space.

"Well, you made it out alive, didn't you?" Max turned to Cherice, but too quickly. Pain stabbed his side, causing him to buckle over and spit out blood.

"What are you doing?" Cherice grabbed him around the waist and held him upright. "You're still hurt! Go on. Go in next."

She helped him into the carriage.

"Thank you, Cherice," he whispered as he slid next to Lily, gasping.

Madame Bellerose was still inside the townhouse. When the bobbies arrived, he was sure she'd pull some strings and turn them into a cleanup crew instead of the actual police force they were supposed to be. He wondered just how many of them had been on the Enlightenment Committee's payroll this entire time.

Like Bately. Though Bellerose was still inside, Bately was not. After she'd ordered him to finish off Van der Ven, Max's old nemesis had collapsed and begun howling in pain. Bellerose had ordered men to whisk him off to some location. At least Max knew he wouldn't be seeing him again so soon. But the fact that Bately was still out there, ready to kill, filled him with dread.

As soon as I retrieve Hiva's heart, the Ark will set sail from Africa. The progress of human civilization will be spurred forward once more. I will be at the forefront of modernity.

Was that the Enlighteners' plan? Max had thought they'd needed the Moon Skeleton to power the Ark, but they didn't have that. Rin and Berta did. Would Hiva's heart do the trick?

But Hiva was with Gladstone now. At least Max thought he was. Max had made sure to check Van der Ven's office before fleeing the scene. No Hiva, no Gladstone, no Fables. Nothing to suggest they were even there but a pool of blood by an oil painting. Gladstone was an Enlightener, but he wasn't about to give up Hiva's heart to be used as some kind of ship engine. He wanted Hiva for his own ends—to end the Great War that Adam had started.

And perhaps Hiva would have done so if he hadn't been so horribly savaged by Max and his friends at the precise moment his humanity finally broke through his automaton's shell.

Max squeezed his forehead with a hand, the brown curls between his fingers soaked with sweat. This was a mess. How was he going to sort it all out? Should he meet Hawkins and Jacob at the rendezvous? Take his fallen arm and ready it as a murder weapon? Or should he go to Hiva first, wherever he was, and explain to him what had happened? Reawaken whatever sentimental kindness had sparked within him?

Kindness. Max coughed out blood with his little laugh. Murderers and monsters like them deserved nothing of the sort.

"Hurry and get in, Cherice," Lily called to Cherice, still on the sidewalk as people walked past her.

"Yeah, yeah, hold your damn horses," Cherice grunted and grabbed hold of the door. By the time Cherice had squeezed herself into the carriage, she was half on top of Max's right leg. Normally he wouldn't mind, but with his cuts and bruises, the extra weight was a little hard to bear.

"I'm not sure I'm comfortable with where your hand is . . . ," he complained.

"Shut up!" Cherice cried in response, but because of the tight space, she couldn't turn to him. She barely just managed to close the door.

"Driver, please take us out of the city," Lily said. They should go to the warehouse. Hawkins and Jacob were probably already there.

But the driver didn't move.

"Excuse me?" With what little room she had, Lily bent over in her seat. "Driver, we're asking you to leave."

That was when Cherice's door opened.

"Alas, fair Lily. He only takes orders from me," Adam Temple said before grabbing Cherice by the collar and dragging her forward.

Max heard her little gasp of shock. But he didn't see the knife in her heart until she was already falling forward into Adam's arms.

Max's mind went blank. He could no longer hear the beating of his own heart or feel his fingers. He couldn't tell what he was yelling or even that he was yelling. After Adam pulled the knife from Cherice's chest, he let her corpse fall onto the ground.

"You killed Iris. That's one for one," Adam whispered before shutting the door.

Max was still yelling. Fool began to laugh in the driver's seat before whisking them off, down the street into the moonlit night.

THE CATACLYSM KNOWN AS HIVA

S ECONDS TURNED TO WEEKS.

Hours to months.

As death brewed inside the planet's molten core . . .

She'd heard their screaming from inside the earth.

She'd seen their mayhem and witnessed their folly.

The man who'd murdered her was dead. The man she'd once loved. Hiva could not feel his anima. Ah, what a shame. Hiva would have wanted to murder him herself. But perhaps it would have been better to thank him for his betrayal instead. His betrayal . . . the betrayal that had sent her spiraling down the path of hell to her true calling.

Yes, she could feel the echoes of the past. Everyone she'd met in her lifetime. All those who still lived. Wherever they were, along this planet's forsaken surface. She felt their anima. She drank it in. She bathed in it, following their tendrils to every corner of the earth.

Somewhere in the world, a young man was crying. He'd been crying for days and cursing his existence. Against the wishes of his grieving friends, he ran to a god, pleading for mercy. The god of death must have also been a god of life. It was what the young man's feeble mind had suddenly decided on as he teetered on the brink of insanity. "Bring her back," he begged. "Bring her back to me." But the god could not answer, for he was but a corpse in an old man's house. He could not hear the young man's pleas and screams.

Retribution is the judgment of men.

Somewhere else, another man screamed in a graveyard—the one where his family had been buried. He screamed and tore his clothes. He fell to his knees and cried out a name until he collapsed upon his mother's gravestone. His schemes had come to naught. He'd lost hope for humanity's end. "To dream is folly," he lamented, and apologized to his fallen kin.

Schemes are the weakness of men.

Death was not a dream, nor was it a tragedy. It was the transformation of existence. Humanity's evolution.

And yet somewhere else, a young woman sat pondering death. The death of her family. The deaths she had caused with her own hands. The deaths she had witnessed. Deep within her broken heart, she hated mankind as much as Hiva did. And for that Hiva would spare her until the end.

It was Hiva's decision. The only one she was allowed to make, and the only mercy she intended to give. But in the end, all would disappear. Those who had abused her. Those who had manipulated her. Those who had betrayed her. All would die at her hand.

All but one. The one she wanted to kill the most.

That was the deal she'd made.

The preparations were complete.

She shed everything that was unnecessary. Every unimportant memory from her millions of lives. Every useless emotion. Whatever might stop her from completing her mission.

And so deep within the earth's core, a being of nightmare awoke.

For many days she crawled out from the earth's depths, her fingers and toes gripping sturdy rock, her mouth inhaling ash and the embers of molten flame.

She left her hopes and dreams behind in the layers of the earth; she let the planet's mantle keep her joys, fears, and desires. Even her pain she left to the crust, with the sediment and the clay.

Only a flicker of grievance remained. A silent wish for revenge.

She emerged a soulless vessel, a body evacuated.

She emerged *ready*.

———◇◇◇◇———

The second week of March had only just begun. In London, Adam Temple sat in his carriage, halted on the London streets, as screams pierced through his window. Men, women, and children were frozen in fear, some clinging to one another, some collapsing to the ground in shock. Soon even his carriage came to a halt. All were gazing at the sky, their jaws open, their hands shaking as they pointed at the sun.

The *sun.*

Where was the sun?

"My God!" cried a woman, dropping a basket of bread as Adam kicked open his carriage door.

He looked up before his feet even hit the ground, shielding his face as he peered up at the darkening sky. Soon there was no need. As the morning air chilled, Adam let his arm drop to his side. He stared at the pedestrians, at the crying children, at the shopkeepers barreling to the streets in terror. And when he looked up again, the sun was gone. They'd been plunged into darkness.

An eclipse.

"An eclipse?" Adam's quick mind was turning, flipping the pages of his father's old manuscripts and research, for a solar eclipse had suddenly come upon them, and there was a reason for it. There must have been.

What was it that old man had said? A solar eclipse . . .

His father's book: *A Family's Travels through West Africa.* What was it that John Temple had written?

> *Different cultures believed a solar eclipse to be an act of*
> *aggression, like the Vikings, who once believed that sky*
> *wolves were chasing the sun. But in the Americas, the*
> *Navajo believe eclipses to be a part of nature's order. What*
> *if it is both? A display of the earth's predilection toward*
> *order and balance, and also a sign of the divine?*

A sign of the divine. The global eclipse that had descended upon them decades ago.

With the awakening of Hiva.

Adam whipped off his top hat, scrunching it in his hands as he stared up at the sky.

No. Maximo hadn't lied that night. Adam could tell from the anguish in his voice, the guilt and self-loathing.

Iris is dead.

Max had believed it.

But . . . what if . . . ?

For the first time in a long while, hope flowered within him, warming his chest, leeching tears from his eyes.

Could it *be* . . . ?

In Ajashe, Rin ran out of the thatched house and into the chaotic streets. Women dropped the baskets from their heads. Children stopped playing with the goats and chickens and clung to one another. Some missionaries dropped their Bibles to run, while others clung to them tighter, praying in tears. Vendors hurled themselves out of their tents, toppling over their wares, because no one could believe their eyes. Rin certainly couldn't.

The sun had vanished. It was morning. Rin had found lodgings in her friend Abiade's humble home, a short walk away from Ajashe's busy commerce center. An old friend from Abeokuta and a graduate of the famed École Cambodgienne, Abiade had brought Rin, Iris, Jinn, and the others to Africa from France last year so they could search for a way to strip Iris of her death-dealing powers. Two months ago, when Rin, Berta, and Lulu had showed up on his front steps, Rin didn't elaborate on what had happened to the rest of the missing party.

Berta had reluctantly agreed to bring Lulu to Uma as her assistant, and Rin had thought she was finally rid of them both. Until Berta came back.

"We can't keep lying around. We gotta strategize. Something bad's going on in London, I can feel it," she'd said. "It's been weeks and no contact. Something's happened to my brother."

"Good," Rin had responded, hoping her cruelty would deter Berta. It didn't. Berta babbled on about how to defeat a god. Rin knew then that she'd never know peace.

Every day that Rin had spent in Abiade's lodgings since she'd parted from Uma had droned on with the monotony of a worthless, wasted life. Eating the same rice and stockfish. Reading John Temple's book. Ignoring Berta as she brainstormed plans for an assault against Hiva. Every day had passed by with the doldrums of a world slowly moving toward its end.

And then this.

"Rin!" Abiade burst out of the wooden door after her and clung to her. "Rin, what's going on? What—?"

His words died in his throat. The Ajashe streets had been plunged into darkness.

Off in the distance, she heard weeping. Elsewhere, praying. Elsewhere, dancing. Screaming. Running. It had all happened so suddenly that nobody knew what to do with their own bodies.

Rin's body trembled. She wrapped her arms around her stomach as a sudden chill seized her.

"It's a solar eclipse," Abiade finally whispered, flattening his cap against his skull with a hand. "The sun . . . the sun is gone."

"What does it mean?" Rin whispered, turning to Abiade for an answer, but his open mouth could only push out haggard, anxious breaths.

An eclipse. But this had happened once before.

The Day of Darkness. Fifty-six years ago, a global eclipse had plunged the world into night.

And mere weeks later, Iris had been discovered by Dahomey warriors.

It was why King Glele believed the eclipse was a sign of good, as if it foretold the coming of She Who Does Not Fall.

"But Iris is dead . . . ," Rin whispered, stepping out onto the street, gasping when a local man crashed into her while he was fleeing—fleeing what, she didn't know.

"I've heard whispers that the war raging in Europe is growing bigger," Abiade said, rubbing the sweat from his face with a shaky hand. "A war greater than they've ever seen, that will soon swallow the world whole . . ."

Abiade was a sensitive boy, studious and gentle. But as Rin looked at him, quivering and struggling to control his breaths, Rin wondered what to tell him. How much of the truth he could handle as the abyss of insanity taunted them.

"Hey, Rin!"

Down the street, Berta appeared under the sunless sky, pushing herself through a thick crowd of fearful onlookers to reach her. Emerging out of the crowd behind her were two white soldiers in beige uniforms. Their black belts held single-shot pistols, and in the middle of the chaos, their hands hovered over them, their fingers twitching as they stared at the missing sun.

"Hey!" While the two soldiers paused, whipping around and gabbling to each other fearfully in German, Berta bent over to catch her breath. "What the hell's going on? The sun was out and shining a damn minute ago!"

Normally Rin was perfectly fine to ignore whatever that murderer's sister said to her. But this time Rin truly wished she could answer.

"God, I hope Lulu's okay." Berta ran her hair through her brown curls, now grown past her chest.

Rin pursed her lips and shifted awkwardly on her feet, because she didn't want to think about that girl who would pass out in sheer bliss after one bowl of rice, stew, and beef at night, knocked out like a tired elephant. She didn't want to think of Lulu, much less worry about her.

"I just got a letter from Uma," Berta said. "Bosch is back from the Congo, and he's sent a cadre of soldiers over to the mining site. Like *these* coots. Hey!"

Berta's shout finally snatched the two soldiers' attention. Straightening their backs in an attempt to look somewhat authoritative, they marched up to Rin and Abiade, flanking Berta.

"You've been summoned by Boris Bosch and Uma Malakar to the mining site in the Oil Rivers region, recently purchased by Bosch Guns and Ammunitions," said the shorter one in English—and he was short, barely even matching Rin's eyeline. "Here is Mr. Bosch's signed commission. You are to travel there post-haste to aid in the removal of confidential materials."

Recently purchased? Rin raised an eyebrow as Berta pulled a letter out of the red blouse she'd been wearing and handed it to her. Bosch's signature and red stamp certainly looked official.

Use Committee resources to find, secure, and prepare the Naacal's ancient but powerful technology. Gather up an arsenal of weaponry already developed to destroy Hiva during the end times. Uma's plan was clearly in motion if Bosch had managed to purchase the site from the Crown.

But as darkness descended on the streets of Ajashe, a heavy sense of foreboding sank deep into the pit of her stomach. King Glele was wrong about this, just as he'd been wrong about many things. This was not a sign of good for Dahomey.

Not for anyone.

Fool hadn't taken Max and Lily far, and he'd disappeared into the night with wordless laughter. Lily had given them shelter in her mother's brothel, which doubled as a home. Here, inside this simple bedroom fit for a lady, Max had stupidly hoped he'd recover after breaking the lamps and the vases and the teacups sitting perfectly upon oak tables.

But Max felt nothing. His soul had left his body.

Adam hadn't pursued them. He must have wanted them to stew in their grief. And stew they did.

He looked out the window as Jacob cried and smashed the picture frame. As Hawkins lay upon Lily's bed, staring at the gray ceiling. Max looked out the window and watched the sun disappear and cast the world into darkness.

No. The last of the Winterbottoms was dead. The darkness had long since fallen. It was just that the sun was finally catching up.

Jacob fell to his knees, his hands bloodied from shattered glass. "If we never went with Hiva," he cried. "No—if we'd never entered that bloody tournament, Cherice would still be here! She'd still be alive! Oh God. What do we do?"

Jacob ran to the bed, took his lover by the collar, and shook him with every ounce of strength he had. "Lawrence. I said, what do we do? What do we do now?" He shook him again. "Tell me!"

But Hawkins didn't answer. With his eyes unfocused, he continued to stare at the ceiling in a daze.

With an exasperated moan, Jacob let go of Hawkins and turned to Max instead. "Max. Max, you have to tell me. You have to do something." He clasped his hands together like a beggar and approached him slowly. Max could hear his voice choke with tears. "Just tell me what to do. What do we do? Please, *what do we do?*"

His shouts may have been loud enough to echo, but to Max they were so far away. Neither Hawkins nor Jacob seemed to notice that the sun was gone.

It was a sign. Max was sure of it. A sign of what came next. A sign of what his life had finally amounted to.

He turned to Jacob and gave him the saddest of smiles. "I'm going with Hiva overseas, if he'll still have me," he told them. "I'm going to fight in the war."

And he was going to die there.

They had all sensed that death was coming. Whether they'd realized it or not.

The true Hiva was now walking among them. Through the forests and across the dirt trails, her bare feet and hands dirtied by soil from the earth's deepest depths.

Hiva was coming.

And on the other side of the world, as the women of London began screaming, as street urchins began crashing in and out of stores, looting what they could, as the sound of frenzied boots and horse hooves stampeding the ground filled the air with pandemonium, Adam opened his trembling lips.

"'Immediately after the tribulation of those days shall the sun be darkened, and the moon shall not give her light, and the stars shall fall from heaven.'" Adam shut his eyes. "'And the powers of the heavens shall be shaken.'"

The late baroness's son let his head roll back as he basked in the chaos to come.

18

R IN KNEW SHE'D MEET MORE OF Boris Bosch's private soldiers at the mining site, so she dressed in armor: the brown leather bandeau and skirt characteristic of the rifle regiment of the Dahomean military. It was the only *ahosi* garb she could procure in Ajashe, her own dress long discarded in the village that had carved out her useless right eye. She took no weapons. She needed none but the mystical sword she could call forth at a moment's notice, to cut down anyone who challenged her. But she didn't forget to strap a pouch around her waist. She'd shoved inside it the map John Temple had given her and one more item: the Moon Skeleton. Iris had instructed her to keep it safe. And so she'd carry it with her wherever she went.

A day of traveling by horse led them to the mining site. It wasn't so long ago that she, Jinn, and Rin had jumped into the fray of British soldiers there, with Berta and Maximo shooting their way to the underground scaffold. Now Bosch's men were everywhere, forcing sooty men with lightbulbs on their helmets into the descending elevator, down the chute, and into the darkness. They'd find Heaven's Shrine, but the true treasure was in the Coral Temple. Only Hiva's touch in the Room of Murals could take them there.

Rin gave Berta beside her a sidelong look. The girl still kept the bone sword that had killed Iris strapped to her back, covered in a blanket. As the soldiers lined the area, watching for any local "intruders" while miners conducted the exploration, Berta stood taut with her hand on the tip of the covered blade behind her. Nervous. Almost as if she were going to be attacked at any moment by one of these white men in uniform.

"You!" The green-eyed man grimaced at the two brown women as they jumped in surprise. "You're the ones Malakar told us about." He scrunched his pointed nose as he looked Rin up and down, his gaze lingering on her white eyepatch. "Which means you're supposed to help us secure the 'item' from underwater."

Rin could hear the disgust in his British accent.

"The 'item'?" Berta whispered to Rin, when the man turned his back to bark orders at some fellow soldiers. "This guy means Hiva's Tomb, right? If it is, then we're screwed. Getting to it is easier said than done. We *barely* survived the first trip through Heaven's Shrine. I couldn't describe that crazy hellhole if I tried." Shaking her head, Berta groaned, watching the miners continue to descend the shaft under the morning light. "There has to be an easier way. . . ."

Uma's smirking face appeared in Rin's thoughts. "What about those so-called Solar Jumps?" Rin recalled the story Berta had told her. "You said you rescued us from Heaven's Shrine by escaping from the Room of Murals. The Jump underneath the altar."

"Right . . . ," said Berta. "That one transported us somewhere by the lagoon."

"I guess we could go back," Rin said, though she didn't very much like the idea of having to trek all the way back west.

"That ain't the problem." Berta pointed at the sand. "It disappeared the second we were done using it. Saw it with my own eyes. It was in the ground by the trees—covered by dirt and grass, you know, this funny disc all glowing. And then it just—" She waved her hands wildly, like a floundering bird flapping its wings. Rin got the point.

There had to be another way to find this weapon against Hiva. But when she thought of the word "Hiva," Rin's thoughts slid back to the eclipse yesterday—the one that had lasted a full day. Just like the Day of Darkness decades ago.

The Day of Darkness. For Rin, that was the day Iris had been murdered. "Why am I even here?" Rin muttered, turning away from Berta.

As she'd waited to be summoned here, Rin had replayed that terrible moment again and again, trying to piece together how it all happened.

Was there anything she could have done to stop it?

But the other Hiva had appeared with his party prepared, as if he'd been planning Iris's downfall for millennia. That tall blond boy, Lawrence Hawkins, had waved that newspaper in the air so frantically, babbling madly to Maximo. Rin couldn't understand what he'd said, but she knew of his supernatural power. Those blue vortexes that swallowed people up alive. Hawkins must have brought them all here from England.

Still, from what Iris had told Rin about John Temple's murmuring in the Room of Murals, it seemed like Hiva and his party had arrived there before them. They'd found another way into Heaven's Shrine. A quicker way. Hawkins?

Or the Solar Jump?

What was it that John Temple told them in Ajashe? Rin lowered her head, covering her eyepatch with a hand as she shut her other eye.

Eventually the Naacal mistakenly blurred their religion with that of Hiva's existence. Hiva became their sun god. And so, even though the Naacal used special technology to operate the Solar Jumps, they were programmed to respond to Hiva's presence . . . body . . . touch . . .

Hiva's presence.

Her *body*.

"We're going to the lagoon," Rin told Berta. "Gather some men. Tell them that the Naacal left their delivery system behind, and we're going to use it."

From what Rin had heard from the soldiers, Bosch had spent millions of pounds buying the mining site from the Crown for this project. An untold amount of money, made possible with his ill-gotten riches selling weapons of war. And now Rin was helping him secure another.

It's to get rid of Hiva, Rin told herself as they traveled back to the lagoon with a dozen of Bosch's private soldiers and eight of his factory men from the Atakora Mountain facility. Getting rid of that beast wasn't something Rin cared much about, but she'd given her word.

Once they'd arrived at the site, the soldiers set out looking for the Solar Jump, but Rin didn't join them. With everything that she'd been through, she'd always felt some kind of fire burning within her, whether it was rage, or duty, or a desire for revenge. But she felt nothing today. Nothing at all underneath the afternoon sky. She'd become empty. It was as if only some twisted notion of duty propelled her forward, moving her lifeless limbs.

Duty. Not worry. Not fear.

Did Rin feel *anything* anymore?

Perhaps she did. Memories of the darkened sky and a missing sun almost filled her with dread, but it soon evaporated with her weary sigh.

She already knew the world was ending. She just couldn't bring herself to care.

This is my last mission, Iris, she decided, staring out across the still waters as Berta searched along the forest edge behind her. *I'm doing this to honor you. Your kindness. It's all I can do for you.* Rin touched her missing eye with solemnity. She'd been given so many "missions" in her short sixteen years of life. Missions that saw her kidnapping and murdering. So much blood on her hands, and for what? It'd all amounted to nothing. *Just this last mission, and then I'll leave the world to whatever fate it deserves.*

"I found it!" Berta screamed behind her.

Rin turned to find Berta by a sprawling bush, shaded by the leaves of one of the stumpy palm trees nearby. Squatting, she dug through the dirt and pulled out grass with her bare hands, eventually throwing off the bundle strapped to her back. The sword made from Iris's thigh bone rolled out of the cloth. And that was when Rin saw it: a hint of white light peeking out from the ground, illuminating Berta's small face.

Berta waved them over. "Come here," she cried, because the light was uncontainable now, bursting from the ground, mysterious and dazzling.

A plate made of metal, or maybe iron or copper—yes, it was the color of copper, and the shape and size of a manhole in London. With the grass and sand that had covered it cleared, its magnificence was out in the open, for all to see. Naacalian symbols were etched onto its surface, but the two rings interlocking in the center were unmistakable. The sun and its shadow. The shimmering glow beckoned them forth.

"It's reacting to Iris's body," said Berta, picking up the bone sword.

Hiva's presence. That was what had made it reappear again. Rin nodded. "The old man told us that each Jump has a pair—a twin. This one should take us straight to the Room of Murals. The Mural itself is the key. It'll react to the bone sword and open the gateway." And then the long voyage through the ocean to the Coral Temple.

A red-haired soldier with a wide, boxy face and robust beard stepped forward. He was decked out in his military medals for Britain, and she wondered if it made him keep some semblance of pride while he worked as a hired hand for an arms dealer. "Hand over the weapon," he ordered Berta. "Our men will check out the underground site. Once they've confirmed the presence of the temple and the item, we'll send for more."

Berta snatched up the sword. "Nuh-uh, no way, you little mutton-shunter, this is mine." And when she looked up at Rin, she stiffened immediately and corrected herself. "This is *ours*."

Funny of her to feel possessive over the weapon her brother had used to kill his friend. Was this the doing of her warped sense of guilt? Rin smirked.

"You called us here to lead you to Hiva's Tomb," Berta continued, standing up straight.

"And you've done that," said the red-haired soldier. "So we thank you."

He lifted his hand. Immediately his soldiers' guns shot up and pointed in their direction, cocked and ready.

"This site is the property of Boris Bosch. *We* will lead this expedition from here. You two, however, will stay right where you are until we've confirmed and secured the item."

Berta gritted her teeth as one of the soldiers ripped the sword from her hands.

"Johnatakis and Rockholt. You two will go back to the mining site and tell them of this discovery. We'll need more men to secure this site from locals, hunters, and merchants. Crosby and Gable, report back to me as soon as you've confirmed the item."

"Yes, Commander Randolph!" The greasy-faced soldiers lowered their guns and saluted the red-bearded man.

Rin and Berta were forced to move back as the men made their way to the

Jump, taking the bone sword with them. Nobody knew what to expect as the chosen soldiers stepped onto the plate. It was barely big enough to fit them. But once the bright light exploded from the surface, it whisked them away, frightened gasps and all.

They were gone.

"So this is how a Solar Jump works," Rin whispered as the other soldiers gawked in complete disbelief. Bosch's men were still for just a moment. Throwing suspicious glares to Rin and Berta, they formed a blockade, pushing them farther out toward the lagoon. Funny how they could be so possessive over a place they hadn't even found. Par for the course, she supposed.

"Now what?" Berta whispered to Rin as the other soldiers went about their duties. "How long are we supposed to stay here?"

"Until they've gotten what they've come for," Rin answered, and with a weary sigh, she sat down on the shores of the lagoon. She let the wind and the waves wash over her, savoring each breath of air, until she heard a thump next to her.

Berta had sat down on her right side, swearing under her breath.

Frowning, Rin gave her a sidelong look. "Can I help you?"

"What? Own the place, do ya?" Turning up her nose, Berta started to lie down on the ground, but Rin stuck out her leg at the last minute. Berta let out a painful grunt as her back crashed against it. "What the hell are you doing?"

"You asked if I own the place. What if I do?"

"Excuse me?"

"This is *my* land. Aren't you from America? Why don't you go back there? Believe me, you won't be missed." Rin flashed a cruel grin before her expression returned to stone.

Berta sat up, drawing her knees to her chest. "Did I say I was from America?"

"Oh right, I think Iris mentioned that you and your murderous, backstabbing brother were from El Salvador." Rin shrugged, using her hands to prop herself up. "Never heard of it before. Still, it sounds like a good enough place to piss off to."

"What's your problem, anyway?" yelled Berta. "I've stayed out of your way these past few weeks. Isn't that enough?"

"Staying out of my way won't bring Iris back now, will it?"

At the mention of Iris's name, Berta lost all her bluster. She pulled back, squeezing her hands together. "I suppose that's right."

Berta faced the lagoon as silence descended upon them. It was all well and good. Rin hated chirping back and forth in English with this brat.

Then again, once upon a time it had been Iris who translated the necessary words, making sure Rin was never left in the dark on the important things. Rin bent forward and rubbed her own face with both hands. Berta seemed to move as if to touch her shoulder but thought better of it.

"Rin." Berta traced circles in the dirt. "I . . ." She paused. Was Berta going to apologize? If she did, Rin would kill her. She would stab her without a moment's notice.

Berta squeezed her eyes shut and sucked in a breath. "I know you and Iris were close. What my brother did wasn't right. But he was just scared."

"Scared of the wrong god."

"What are any of us supposed to do?" Berta whipped around. "Has anyone ever faced something like this? Death gods, disappearing acts, and the end of the world?" Berta pointed to the soldiers facing outward from the Solar Jump, forming a strict line to block the platform from view. "We're all screwed. All we can do is make the best decisions we can in the moment."

"Even if it kills someone's family?"

Rin shut her lips immediately as her heart skipped a beat. But Berta was staring at her.

"Rin," Berta asked quietly. "Did you really consider Iris to be your family?"

Rin didn't answer. She supposed that would be answer enough. Berta buried her face in her knees.

The hours passed. Local men paddled across the waves in long wooden canoes, pulling out fish. Squawking seagulls snatched up the stragglers that the nets hadn't caught. Everyone was just trying to survive in this wicked world. But if they had a choice to end it, what would they choose?

What would Rin choose?

Behind her, as the afternoon sun blazed, Rin heard the soldiers begin to stir. The men they'd sent through the Jump hadn't returned yet.

"You lot!" Commander Randolph, or whatever that red-bearded man was called, beckoned them over. "How long is it supposed to take, this journey to the Coral Temple?"

"Not this long," Rin answered without looking back, as Berta stood. "Perhaps they've gotten lost?"

But as the afternoon sun began to descend, they did not return.

"Things don't seem to be going well for you," Rin said, finally getting to her feet as the day settled into evening. "Whatever will you tell your master Bosch?"

Commander Randolph, infuriated, stomped over and reached out to grab her. Rin caught his hand in the air.

"I wouldn't do that if I were you," she hissed through gritted teeth.

The sounds of guns cocking didn't deter her. Rin was annoyed enough as it was. Just how long was she supposed to stay here?

"Fine, then. You lot are going down there next," said Commander Randolph. "We'll be keeping an eye on you. You won't dare to do anything suspicious."

It was a threat. Not one Rin took seriously until she and Berta were being pushed toward the Jump by gunpoint. Randolph's men thrust the barrels of their guns into their backs. Between Rin, Berta, Commander Randolph, and two of his men, it was a tight squeeze on the Jump.

"We don't have Iris's sword, though," Berta hissed.

"No, we don't," Rin said. "But even if you told them, I doubt these idiots would listen."

But as Rin stepped onto the plate, the white light from the Solar Jump enveloped her. How?

The Moon Skeleton. Of course. It was made of Iris's body as well. It carried her presence.

Her presence.

The nerves in Rin's stomach twinged, making her face flush.

She was worried.

Why was she worried?

Coming back into Heaven's Shrine wasn't something she'd wished for. The Room of Murals was just the same as she'd remembered it: a long hall with standing torches covered in cobwebs. The mural on the front wall behind the altar still carried the Naacal's writings painted upon the surface. They reminded Rin of the symbols in the scrolls Iris had taken from the Library of Rule in the British Museum. While they'd stayed in that dirty tavern in France, Rin had asked Iris what they'd said. And amid the resulting gibberish about gods and Titans, somehow these were the words that had stuck out to her:

And in the same way, Hiva will rise again.

For it is Hiva's fate to destroy mankind forever and ever.

Misery unto eternity . . .

The words haunted Rin as Captain Randolph ran his hands along the mural, before he turned to them with the bluster of an overpaid blowhard.

"You said the gateway is here. Open it," he commanded.

Rin approached the mural, beckoning Berta to follow. Reaching into her pouch, she brought out and lifted up the white skeleton key. As the mural shuddered to the side, her heart gave a nervous thump.

Was it . . . *surprise* that she felt?

No.

She was afraid.

That fleeting sense of dread filled her up until she was silently buzzing with it. She didn't dare speak of it as the elevator took her through the Atlantic Ocean, withstanding the pressures of the deep. She lowered her head and tried to calm the beating of her heart, even as the soldiers cooed in awe at the sight of the whales, squid, and fish that passed them by. She clenched her hands against the brown leather bracket she wore and felt every painful thump of her heart, listening to it, for it was desperately trying to tell her something.

The round dome, glowing midnight blue in the dark expanse of the ocean. This was the Coral Temple: one of the underground facilities the Naacal had built in the ancient times. A technological wonder. The elevator brought them through the hatch in the roof and left them on the white marble dais. Everything was the same. Throughout the vast room, pillars stretched up to the domed ceiling. A pool of light rained down upon them from the hatch.

Behind them, a cube balanced on one of its tips, awash in golden light, towering over them and gripping the ground through some unseen force. It was all as Rin remembered. Hiva's Tomb stood on the dais with them.

But it was not Iris's blood painting its glass surface in sloppy red.

"What's . . . what's going on?" Berta said, her voice hollow.

One of Randolph's men lay dead against Hiva's Tomb, his corpse kneeling, his head bleeding just below the crack that Max's blow had made in the glass. Iris's bone sword lay at his feet.

His wasn't the only dead body in the Coral Temple. Both men Randolph had sent down to secure the tomb had met their end, their bodies torn and mangled across the dais or tossed in pieces upon the floor below.

As Berta rushed to grab one of the soldiers' discarded guns from the floor, Rin could feel her body trembling.

"What is this?" Berta said. "What's going on?"

"You! You there!"

Rin looked up in a daze, but Commander Randolph was not pointing at her. He was pointing past her—beyond the dais.

He was pointing behind her.

Rin didn't want to turn around, but her body moved in spite of her. The sounds of villagers screaming underneath a dead sun filled her memories. That eclipse. The Day of Darkness. The uneasiness that had settled deep inside her heart. She understood now what it had all meant.

Turning, Rin peered out into the dark hall beyond the pillars. Beyond the bodies.

And in the same way, Hiva will rise again.

For it is Hiva's fate to destroy mankind forever and ever.

Misery unto eternity . . .

"Misery unto eternity," Rin whispered, her hands and feet cold and numb.

The woman ascended the spiraling staircase to the dais with slow but deliberate steps. The two *shamshir* blades in her hands glinted under the skylight—her favorite weapon, even back during her days in the circus. Now they dripped blood. A terrified soldier shot her in the head with a primal, fearful yell. The bullet lodged in her skull, but it only stopped her momentarily. As she straightened her neck, her brown forehead spat the bullet out. It clattered onto the floor.

"No." Berta shook her head with wide eyes, stepping back, the gun faltering in her grip. "It can't be. It's not possible. . . ."

Rin couldn't even hear her. Berta's words had disappeared, along with every other sound in this godforsaken palace. Rin doubted the one eye she had left as the woman stepped onto the dais, her slender form tightly gripped in a fabric Rin couldn't name: something ethereal, sleek, and the color of sunset. The woman walked with the grace of a dancer.

And when she reached the soldier who'd attacked her, she immediately cut off his head.

Rin's throat closed; her body seized up in wonder, in confusion.

In terror.

It was only when she could finally draw a breath through her scratchy, clenched throat that Rin finally dared to speak. One word:

". . . Iris?"

Iris brought a blade up to her lips and tasted its blood.

No.

She was Hiva now.

Iris killed the other soldier just as fast. Meanwhile, Commander Randolph was screaming and shooting. He was clearly too frightened to steady his aim, but the few bullets that hit her limbs didn't stop her. Iris moved quickly, slicing his torso and cutting his neck.

Berta scuffled backward to the edge of the dais, her gun cocked. The girl had good aim. Rin had seen it before. But she didn't shoot. Maybe she couldn't, not as streams of blood streaked the air. But neither girl could move—not Berta, and not Rin, who had stood in the center of the dais and watched each soldier fall.

Iris faced Hiva's Tomb and stared at the crack. This was where she had died. But Rin studied Iris's reflection in the glass. Her expression was neutral—calm, even. She knelt down and grabbed the sword made from her own bones, the one Maximo had used to kill her. Tilting her head, she examined every kink in the rough surface. Then she burned it to ashes.

When Iris turned to face Rin, she gave her a little smile, as pleasantly as if she were greeting an old friend.

"I-Iris . . . ?" With great effort, Rin moved a leg forward.

Too many memories, too many questions, battered her with relentless fury. She felt as if her whole body were going to collapse upon itself. This blood-soaked woman. This woman who had died so many times, it'd become redundant—until she'd died and turned to dust before Rin's very eyes. Her friend. Her family.

Her sister.

Now a bloodthirsty demon.

Hiva.

"Iris!" Rin cried, bending over, because suddenly her back could no longer support her weight.

Iris opened her mouth and formed words, but no sound came out. Not even a puff of air. She did not seem to notice.

She lifted her *shamshir*, seemingly ready to take off Rin's head.

But then, curiously, Iris paused.

Berta didn't seem to notice her hesitation. "No!" she screamed and began shooting at Iris. Expert aim. Each shot landed, blowing Iris back. Stretching out her limbs, Iris shook the bullets off.

Rin could hear Berta yell. Berta shouldn't have paused, for it was enough time for Iris to counter her attacks by running to Rin, grabbing her neck, and throwing her toward Berta with an unnatural strength. Rin barreled into Berta, knocking them both off the dais. Berta's gun skidded against the ground, out of reach.

This is it, Rin thought as she heard Iris's footsteps grow near. *This is my punishment for everything I did to her. Dragging her back to the Dahomey. Scheming against her. Manipulating her. Then failing to even protect her.* As Berta flailed about, struggling to find her gun, Rin let her body relax upon the ground. *This is what I deserve.*

Iris jumped off the dais. A hush fell over the Coral Temple. Iris looked up at them with interest, and for a moment Rin's eyes locked with hers.

The eclipse. The Day of Darkness. Fifty-six years ago, it had been the sign of Hiva's arrival. A sign of the apocalypse. And so it was again. Iris had returned. She'd awakened to her true purpose. She was here to kill them all.

Iris turned her head ever so slightly. And without a word, without even the hitch of a breath, she reduced the corpses of Randolph and his men to dust.

They were next. Rin could hear Berta crying. Rin wanted to cry too. She closed her eyes.

But Iris walked away from them. Why, Rin couldn't fathom. Neither of them dared to call out to her to ask. They simply watched from the floor as Iris jumped back on the dais and called down the elevator from the ceiling by stretching out her arms. She never spoke. Not one sound escaped Iris's lips. She walked silently into the elevator and didn't look back as it took her up out of the Coral Temple.

The two young women sat up. After a few minutes of fearful panting, Berta grabbed Rin, pulling them both to their feet.

"How did Iris survive?" she demanded in a shaky voice. "How?"

But how was Rin to answer? They'd both seen her die. Max's sword piercing Iris's back. Her body returning to dust. Her crystal heart crumbling in Hiva's hand.

"Wait . . ." Berta narrowed her eyes as she suddenly realized something. "Where is she headed?"

Rin's blood drained from her face. As she looked at the ashes that were once men, her heart began to race. Where *was* she headed? Where else?

Rin grabbed Berta's collar. "We have to go," she snapped, and strode over to the spot where the elevator had been. The wait for the glass elevator was excruciating. They rushed inside once it arrived, staying silent as a grave as it took them back through the ocean and into the Room of Murals.

Rin and Berta stepped onto the Solar Jump, which whisked them back onto the shores of the lagoon. How much time had passed? What was Iris planning to do? Were they too late?

The ashes littered across the empty site were enough of an answer. Rifles littered the grass. Some shoes had been left behind. Rin could tell from the tracks that some of the men had tried to run.

This was Iris's doing.

How hard had Iris fought to avoid this fate? It had been the singular driving force that had brought her out of Europe to the shores of Africa. It had been her search for self. Her desperation to forge her own identity. And yet the woman who had so desperately wanted to find her own voice now could not speak a word, not even one, as she decimated and burned men alive. It was a cruel irony. A hopeless fate.

And it was all Rin's fault.

A wave of dizziness overwhelmed Rin. She struggled to stay on her feet. When she tipped to the side, Berta held her up, and it was only when she looked into the girl's eyes that she realized her anger had been misdirected. It wasn't Berta who she should have hated. Not even Maximo, who had murdered Iris in fear of this outcome.

It was herself. Her miserable, weak self. Just as she had when her family had been killed in front of her, she'd stood helpless as Iris had died, stood helpless as she was resurrected as a monster. Helpless. Hopeless. Useless.

"Useless!" she cried over and over again, beating her head with both hands until Berta pulled her arms away from her. "Useless . . ."

Her voice broke. The wind carried the ashes of Bosch's soldiers past their heads and up into the night sky.

"It really is the end of the world," Rin whispered before sinking to her knees.

PART TWO
Resurrected Monsters

The future is necessarily monstrous: the figure of the future, that is, that which can only be surprising, that for which we are not prepared . . . is heralded by species of monsters. A future that would not be monstrous would not be a future; it would already be a predictable, calculable, and programmable tomorrow.

—JACQUES DERRIDA

19

THIS CAN'T BE HAPPENING."

Rin wasn't sure how many times she repeated it as she and Berta began the long trudge back to Ajashe. Several days of travel on foot. Several days of seeing empty clothes on the dirt road and shoes at the edge of the forests where people had clearly tried to run. The wind carried thick, heavy black ashes.

They saw only one alive on their trek back. Deeper in the forest, Rin heard crying. After a quick search, Rin pulled the girl out of the pile of leaves she'd clearly hidden herself underneath.

"Are you okay?" Rin asked the girl in English without even thinking, not knowing what language she even communicated in.

The girl was of the Bariba people, for she spoke Baruba. Rin didn't know it. But it seemed that the girl did know one English word, as among the ones she stuttered out was "devil."

"Take her," Rin ordered, pushing the girl to Berta half in a stupor. "We'll find her some help in Ajashe."

That was what she had hoped.

That was what anyone would assume.

As they came to the threshold of the city, Rin's knees nearly buckled, taking her down to the ground. But her leaden feet somehow kept moving through

Ajashe, through the once-bustling port town. Her dilated pupils kept searching for a single merchant behind the vending tents, a soldier, or a missionary beating his Bible.

"Dear God . . ." Berta's long brown curls whipped across her face as her arms dangled at her sides. "There's no one. There's no one here. . . ."

Rin shook her head. She wouldn't accept it. She couldn't. So she ran through the city. She ran from the marketplace to the ships at the dock. She doubled back to the homes and hospitals. She stopped to catch her breath against a nearby palm tree.

This can't be happening, she thought for the thousandth time, touching her empty socket of a right eye from behind its eyepatch. *This isn't happening.*

Abiade. Her nails scratched the bark of the tree trunk as she thought of her friend. As her cheeks flushed and her chest heaved, she turned and flew to his home, the place he'd given her to stay in, despite knowing the dangers that seemed to haunt her every step. And when she burst open the door of that thatched-roof house, Berta was already there, kneeling by a pile of ashes next to a bookshelf. Rin hadn't been there when Abiade had bought it. But she had been present to hear him brag about it. All the money he'd saved to get it cheap from a merchant. All the books he'd be able to study before he started his career as a translator.

Abiade's clothes hung over an empty chair.

Rin dropped to her knees and finally began screaming.

"What?" Inside her secret laboratory, Uma dropped her pipe. "You saw *who* at the mining site?"

The curtains that kept Jinn's half-dead body—almost a corpse—hidden had been drawn closed in the center of the lab. Good. Rin couldn't bear to look at him, not now that this horror had been unleashed upon them. As Rin and Berta barreled down the staircase, Lulu, who'd been cleaning some empty conical flasks on the rightmost table, looked up at the filthy, terrorized women with her big doe eyes.

"Iris?" the little girl said, squeezing her white cloth. "You saw Miss Iris? So she really is alive?"

"Oh, thank God you're okay, kid," Berta said, running up to a confused Lulu and hugging her tightly.

But Rin went straight for Uma, grabbing her by the sari, nearly tripping over her pipe on the floor. "Iris is back." She could feel her teeth rattling. "I saw her with my own eyes. We both saw her. We both saw her *kill* Bosch's men inside the Coral Temple."

She looked back at Berta, who nodded in a daze.

"Well, that's..." Uma paused, glancing between the two of them nervously. "But she didn't kill you, clearly? We all know Iris is a creature who can't die. We know she doesn't particularly fancy the Committee either."

"You don't get it," Rin hissed. "She's killing. Right now she's killing indiscriminately. The whole city of Ajashe is . . . is gone. Everyone in it is *gone*."

She choked back a sob and turned away from them. Silence. Their sunken corpse-like expressions spoke volumes. Uma's shoulders fell, and that told Rin more than words ever could. Uma picked up her pipe and moved to the map of the world plastered on the wall, staring at it for too long. Each second that passed was a knife slicing away whatever sanity Rin had left, like carving meat off the bone.

"Then Hiva's Tomb is needed now more than ever," Uma said, with a dark solemnity that frightened Rin. "We'll need to go to Bosch. Ask him to send more troops to secure the area. Now that Iris is on the move, it should be safe."

"Should be," Berta scoffed, rubbing her dirty face with both hands. "*Should be*, she says. What is that? A guess? A wish?"

"That's all we have right now," Uma snapped.

Berta pounded the table with her fist, causing Lulu to jump in her seat and the glass flasks to rattle. "All we have isn't enough. We already had one Hiva to deal with. Now Iris has turned her coat. We don't know where she's headed or what she's planning."

"But we do know what she's planning," Lulu told her simply. "She's planning on punishing the wicked. . . ." She pressed an inquisitive finger to her full bottom lip. "I guess that means all of us."

Rin didn't know whether it was innocence or madness that had made Lulu so eerily calm—or both. Seeing the girl tilt her head and consider everything, as if calculating a math equation, made Rin furious as much as it made her jealous.

"Damn it," Uma cursed, muttering under her breath. "With the Solar Jumps around too, she may not even be on the same continent anymore."

Maneuvering around the curtains in the center of the room, Uma walked to a long wooden cupboard in the upper left corner. Opening the cupboard door, she pulled out a shawl and wrapped it around herself. "The nights here get chilly," she said. "Come with me, and quickly. We're going to see my employer."

Leaving Lulu with Berta and Aminadab, Rin and Uma traveled east to Lagos on foot. Because Iris could appear and strike at any moment, they stayed on alert, moving only at night and finding shelter among the trees during the day. Every time Rin saw another human being alive, she breathed a sigh of relief.

"But why did she leave us alive?" Rin asked one night as they trudged through a muddy path. "Or, more specifically, *me* alive? She looked right at me."

"Did she?" Uma hadn't taken her pipe with her and so sounded a little high-strung. The lack of nicotine probably didn't help her nerves. "Well, there's nothing to say that Iris wouldn't still have her memories."

"The other Hiva seemed to have his," Rin said, remembering the hatred seeping from him as he'd stared down Iris in the Coral Temple.

"It's her emotions that may be missing." Uma batted a fly away and gasped as she almost tripped over the thick, protruding root of a particularly tall kapok tree. "John Temple wrote of Iris when she was under the surveillance of Doctor Seymour Pratt's medical team in Cambridge. Though Pratt described her as a beast, Temple noted her frighteningly calm demeanor in between *procedures*." Uma said the word "procedures" with a shudder. "Well, Pratt's a racist sociopath who'd call anyone a 'beast' so long as they had a slightly darker hue than white porcelain, so that doesn't surprise me. But after everything that was done to that poor girl, even if everything we knew of 'Iris' is gone, I wouldn't be surprised if she did have one emotion left."

"Anger," Rin answered, staring up at the starless sky.

Boris Bosch owned a compound in Lagos, one of the major economic powers in the Yoruba territories colonized by Britain. The land he owned on the outskirts of the city could have rivaled that of any colonial administrator. White soldiers stood along the open arched entrances of his white mansion. When they saw Uma, they saluted, clicking their heels while keeping their rifles tightly bound to their sides. Uma nodded and gestured at Rin to follow her inside. Rin wondered if Uma quite liked it, being regarded so highly in this insular world of whites. Iris had told her once about Uma's history while they were traveling: Uma was the daughter of an Indian woman and an English military man, who had been cheated out of her inheritance by the British side of her family. She had competed against white men her entire scientific life. The military women of Dahomey were servants to their king, and they'd committed many atrocities against neighboring tribes. But they, at least, bowed to no white man.

Uma's jaw set once they walked into Bosch's dining room.

He was dressed as a hunter, just as he had been in his facility within the Atakora Mountains. Boris Bosch, the merchant of death, who sold weapons through his Guns and Ammunitions Company. The round white helmet of a hat and ivory tiger's teeth strung along his neck were just as she remembered it. The long slit that scarred his left cheek told the tale of his past hunts. But Rin couldn't concentrate on anything other than his thin fish lips, bobbing up and down disgustingly as he tore through the wild boar meat plated delicately on his long mahogany table.

Soldiers lined up against the floral-patterned walls, their guns at the ready. Though the table took up half of the extensive room, only the arms dealer was allowed to dine. No other plate was set.

"Uma," Bosch said, nodding his head but not looking up to acknowledge her. "I assume you're here for one of two reasons: to tell me that you've finished producing the energy source for the Ark, or to tell me the status of the project at the mining site."

Uma looked no less the proud genius, but Rin noticed that she seemed to stand a little straighter in this man's presence. She cleared her throat.

"My work on the energy source is coming along but is still, as of yet, incomplete. I'm here to report a problem with that mining project," she told him, folding her arms.

"I don't pay you to report problems." Bits of meat had gotten caught in his drooping mustache underneath that sharp, sloping nose. He brushed them aside and began carving into his food again with a fork and knife.

"And yet here I am." She shut her eyes. "Your men have been killed. By Hiva."

"Hiva? Nonsense. I thought he'd vanished from the mining site after promising to destroy the world within a year."

"I mean . . . the *other* Hiva, sir."

Bosch set his utensils down upon his messy plate with a careful clatter. The soldiers who stood just below the rows of framed elephant tusks and tiger hides straightened a little. Bosch's gaze finally lifted to meet Uma's but then shifted to Rin. Instinctively the girl lifted her chin with pride, before the crushing weight of her failure to stop Iris nearly broke her resolve. She clenched her fingers into fists as the foul man looked her up and down.

"Isn't this her?" he asked most ridiculously, though his tone was fully serious.

After a quick, awkward glance toward Rin, Uma cleared her throat. "This is her ally, Olarinde. A member of the Dahomey military."

"Ah. Well, such women look alike to me."

Uma and Rin were rigid as Bosch sat back in his grand chair. Rin could feel her indignation, her hatred, for this man stirring within her, burning her dark brown skin. The audacity of this fool, whose manhood had to be supplemented by such a gaudy display of dead animals. Rin's hands itched to pull out her sword, dormant and brewing inside her chest.

"Then the first Hiva is alive." Bosch clucked his tongue as he brushed off breadcrumbs that had stuck to his fingers. "Yes, I remember her. That day near the Ark, during my meeting with the king of Dahomey. But the Ark is yet incomplete, as you've so astutely reminded us. Two Hivas mean two power sources. Uma. It is your task to oversee the capture of both."

Rin clenched her teeth. "If it were so easy to capture Hiva, then we would have done so by now, you—"

Uma put up a hand to silence her. And though Rin bristled, she couldn't ignore the apology in her stern face.

"Since Iris—the first Hiva—is gone from the mining site, you can send your men to resecure it," Uma suggested. "If Iris appears there again, we can spring a trap."

"We cannot wait for that girl to suddenly appear," Bosch said, dismissing her with a wave of his hand. "We need to *make* her appear." He leaned against the table, the sudden weight of his elbows making his solid silver dinner plate rattle. "We will spring a trap. But not at the mining site."

The legs of his chair screeched against the tiled floor as he stood from the dining table and left through the arched doorway behind him, beckoning for them to follow. The narrow hallway was plastered in beige, with lamps hanging from the ceiling—each one lit so bright, it stung Rin's remaining eye.

"These are desperate times, Uma," Bosch said, with his hairy arms behind his back. "The invitations have already gone out to those who will patronize the Ark, and according to Madame Bellerose, many responses have returned favorable."

Rin wondered who in the Enlightenment Committee had thought it a good idea to allow Madame Bellerose to vet who was "worthy" enough to be a passenger on a transdimensional flight.

Bosch's thick leather boots pounded the wooden floors until he came to the end of the hall. After placing a hand on the golden doorknob, he turned to them, his bushy brows knitted together. "We cannot leave anything to chance."

The vast room Bosch had led them into reminded Rin of a grand exhibit at some world's fair. The ceiling was high enough for their footsteps to echo. Half the room was closed off by some thick metal meshwork that Rin couldn't see through.

What she could see were rows of connected parchment that covered the wall. Traced on them in thick black ink were drawings of two giant spiderlike machines, one short and squat, the other long and lithe. They looked like designs for a new weapon. A new type of armored vehicle, perhaps? She'd never seen an armored vehicle before, but her military superiors had told her once that somewhere in the world, scientists were developing such monstrosities in earnest.

Each machine had a circular glass plate in the center of their heads. Black scribbles of English and German writing surrounded the diagrams. Rin could make out the words "Solar" and "Shadow." And "Titans."

As Bosch walked up to the wall of diagrams, Rin whipped around, looking to Uma for some kind of explanation, but the woman remained silent, her expression grim.

"So then," she said. "You want us to activate the Titans."

Titans? Rin scoured her memories for the word. Thanks to Abiade's library, she'd managed to read John Temple's book, *A Family's Travels through West Africa*. But she remembered nothing about any Titans.

Wait. Iris. Iris had mentioned it in France while they'd stayed in that dusty tavern. It was among all the gibberish in the scrolls they'd stolen from the British Museum's Library of Rule. At the time Iris had furiously pored over them, searching desperately for some clue that would help her take away the curse of Hiva. The Titans . . . what were they?

Bosch walked up to the wall and touched the drawing of the shorter machine. "The Naacal had created so many advanced weapons during their time—like these. Their 'Titans.' John Temple was the one who discovered and deciphered the information they kept on the Titans. Such monstrous machines the Naacal built. They must have been desperate in their war against Hiva to go so far as to use them."

"The Titans," Uma said, and for some reason, Rin felt as though the woman were speaking directly to her—though she didn't so much as turn her head. "The Solar Titan and the Shadow Titan: twin mechanical beasts with the ability to release energy blasts that had an explosive power never before seen by humanity. From the information John Temple discovered, I was able to draw out what they might have looked like in those ancient days. But I've never actually seen them in person. I can't even be completely certain they still exist. The Naacal were a frightening people—to think they'd managed to create weapons that could erase cities in one fell swoop?" Uma suppressed a shudder.

Machines with the ability to erase cities? A chill sank through Rin, settling as an icy lump in the pit of her stomach. The hairs on her arms stood on end. Such a thing couldn't be possible. Such a thing *shouldn't* be possible.

"The Titans *do* still exist. John Temple was sure of it—so sure that he even managed to pinpoint the precise area where the Naacal had hidden them. The Atlas mountain range in the north." The wicked curve of Bosch's liver-pink lips made Rin's skin crawl. "We'll use them."

Uma took two careful steps toward her employer. "I would advise strongly against that. Even if we're able to trap Iris—Hiva—in the delegated site, using the Titans would certainly mean sacrificing tens of thousands of people. The cost is too high."

"Too high?" And at this, the man whom Rin had only ever heard speak in deadly, quiet tones let out a stream of awful, guttural laughter.

Each chuckle made Uma angrier, and she gripped her shawl more tightly. Then Bosch said something in German before gesturing toward the metal wall to their left.

"For you of all people to talk about the human cost in the pursuit of science is laughable. I haven't been told a funnier joke in recent memory."

"*Boris!*" Uma said, her nostrils flaring and her eyes blazing. "I'm serious about this. This is going too far."

"And what do you think you've been doing for me all these years, my dear?" Calmer now, Bosch slowly approached the metal wall, his hands once again placed behind his back. "All those weapons you've made. What do you think has been the result of your relentless desire for knowledge?"

Uma stiffened when Bosch slid open the metal door of a little window on the dark mesh wall. She didn't move when Bosch beckoned her forward, inviting her to look through the peephole.

But Rin did. She wanted to see.

"With the Great War now raging across Europe, Bosch Guns and Ammunitions is drawing in a higher profit than ever before," Bosch said as Rin approached him carefully, her heart thumping in her ears. "The weapons you've helped me develop, Uma, are being used on battlefields. And some of the research you've laid down has been used by my researchers to create untold wonders."

Bosch stepped aside. Rin looked through the glass.

Sealed inside a dark room behind the wall, African men, stripped of their clothes, each with one arm cut off, stood in a line as if in a firing range. The sight of their mutilated bodies infuriated Rin in ways she couldn't put into words. Some spat and cursed, their fury and their defiance crackling. Others held hands and prayed. All looked terrified. Each and every one of them. Looking at them rounded up like animals drew hot tears from her that threatened to fall, a rush of heat rising to her head. But she wasn't prepared for what happened next.

Inside with the men were soldiers whose faces were completely covered in strange-looking masks. They were like sacks wrapped firmly around the soldiers' heads, but with a bulbous filter over the mouth and a nosepiece through which each could breathe. All but two soldiers pointed their rifles at the African men.

Bosch knocked on the window with his knuckles. That was the signal. The two soldiers tinkered with some kind of metal barrel in the corner, and then—

Rin couldn't hear the sound, but she could see the steam rising from the barrel. It wasn't thick enough to obscure the African men, who quickly began to writhe and clutch at their throats.

"Presents from the Congo. King Leopold II's policies in the rubber fields are considered quite gruesome—but the men whose limbs had been cut for not collecting their daily quota eventually became of use to me."

Rin whipped around and grabbed Bosch's collar. "What are you doing to them, you devil?" she screamed, not so much as flinching when she heard the soldiers' guns cocking and then firing. But instead of bullets, the guns shot canisters that released plumes of noxious gas.

"I'm testing my wares. Poison gas made of sulfide components will revolutionize war in this decade, and for centuries to come," he said. "To ensure that those centuries do come, we must retrieve both Hivas' crystal hearts, no matter the cost." He glanced back at the window. "Ah, pity."

Rin followed his gaze. The Congolese men were clearly dying, clutching at their throats as they breathed in the gas—but they weren't the only ones. The soldiers' masks weren't working. Some threw them off to gulp in whatever air they could. Others were reaching for help—from Bosch, from the other soldiers, and even from the Congolese they were cruelly murdering. Eventually every mouth in the room began gushing blood, until there were none left alive.

"The gas is a success, but the masks are a failure. These aren't ready to ship to Europe."

Without so much as blinking an eye, Bosch turned and strode past a frozen Uma.

"According to Temple's research, the device to control the Titans is hidden somewhere else on this continent. A safety measure by the Naacal, I suppose. I order you to retrieve it. And use the Titans to take Hiva's heart. That is, if you don't want the world to end."

Uma's arms dangled listlessly at her sides as Bosch walked toward the exit. "What exciting technological treasures will the New World hold?" he said. "I'm sure you're also excited to find out, Uma Malakar. Escort them from the premises," he told the soldiers by the door.

Rin shut her eyes against the senseless death and pounded on the window glass in agony.

20

UMA BARRELED DOWN THE STAIRCASE INTO her secret lab so fast, Rin could barely keep up. "There isn't any time," Uma said, stopping in front of the map of the world. "I need you to memorize these Jump locations. You're going to get the Titan Control Device—and then destroy it."

"Wait, what happened?" Berta jumped up from her stool next to Lulu's. "What's going on?

"The Titan Control Device?" Rin asked, watching as Uma began mumbling to herself in front of the world map on the wall. With a finger, Uma traced a pattern in the air between the dark *X*s marked across the globe. As if she were connecting the dots.

"Sketches in John Temple's journal show a control device created by the Naacal that can operate the Titans," said Uma.

Berta balked. "The what?"

"The Titans—weapons of mass destruction of a kind humanity has never known."

Berta shook her head as if trying to shake cobwebs from her ears. *"What?"*

"Find the Titan Control Device and destroy it." Uma lowered her hand and turned to her. "Do it soon. Do it *now*. Eventually Bosch will send his own men to get it, when I don't give it to him. If Bosch has access to the Titans, it's only a matter of time before he uses them, and when he does, tens of thousands of people will die. Maybe hundreds." Uma turned back to face the map. "Maybe more."

As Berta exchanged clueless looks with Lulu, Rin grabbed Uma by the collar and pulled her around. "Bosch wouldn't know about these ancient weapons if it weren't for you, his star employee," Rin hissed. "A weapons developer. A genius of the highest intellect. Does it feel good being a puppet for that white man? Were the money and prestige worth it?"

Uma yanked Rin's hands off her and shoved Rin away. "You can waste your time working through your frustrations, or you can focus on the task at hand. Anything less, and whatever happens—whoever dies—their blood is on your hands too."

The audacity of this woman. She could still see those Congolese men dying as they drowned in poison gas, reaching out to her for help with the one arm they had. Gritting her teeth, Rin slapped Uma across the face, crisp, clean, and hard. Before she could do anything else, Berta rushed forward and separated them.

"Okay! I'm just catching up, but my understanding is that we have to stop some imminent disaster. Right?" Lowering her arms, she glanced at both seething women. "The Titan Control Device. Find it and destroy it. Save millions. Got it. So how do we do that?"

"We do that," Uma said, rubbing her cheek with a bitter scowl, "by getting here." She pointed to a region in southwest Africa. Rin recognized it. It was the land of the Herero. "You've been to Heaven's Shrine. You know that remnants of Naacal civilization still exist in this world. Temple always believed this to be the site of an ancient underground Naacalian factory, but he never confirmed it. And though he never deigned to tell me, I believe it was where he found all his information on the Titans in the first place."

"Probably should confirm it before we go barging in there," Berta said, placing her hands on her hips.

"John Temple's research isn't an exact science," Uma said. "We didn't learn much about the Naacal and couldn't corroborate everything he'd learned while traveling this continent. But he's the world's leading expert on this civilization and its trinkets. His work is trustworthy. And, well, we don't have another option, do we? During his travels, Temple bought the land where he thought the entrance was and stationed men to protect it. There's some kind of manor there, I believe. But as for what the entrance looks like or how to open it?" She shrugged and shook her head. "Temple kept certain details close to his chest."

Rin folded her arms and glared at the marks on the world map. "The last Jump we used took us into the Coral Temple."

"Yes, because they were twins. Each Jump has a pair. It's about finding the right one."

Wait. She had the same map. The one John Temple had given her! She reached inside the pouch she kept strapped to her waist and pulled it out, stretching out the parchment and holding it up in front of her.

"These symbols," Rin said, letting the light from the lamps illuminate the yellow paper.

Uma leaned over her shoulder. "Yes. Alpha. Beta. Gamma. John Temple used the Greek alphabet here to delineate the pairs."

She pulled a fountain pen out of a cupboard and began tracing a pattern across the map. Connecting dots. Drawing a route.

"You'll have to go from this city here in British North America and find your way to the nearest Jump, close to the border. That'll take you to Chinandega." She pointed to a region below Mexico. "And then maybe you can hitch a ride to El Salvador—"

"El . . . Salvador?" Berta's face paled as if she'd seen a ghost. She looked up at the map on the wall, her arms stiff at her sides.

Uma wasn't listening. "The Jump in El Salvador is the pair for the one in the southern area of Angola. And you'll need to get to that Jump, as it's closest to where the control device is." She circled the region that John Temple had purchased. "This is the fastest route I could think of, given what we've got to work with. Walking straight there on foot would simply take too long: six to seven weeks, to be exact. The Jumps will cut down that time considerably. Any amount of time won would be a boon to us."

Rin pressed a hand against her white eyepatch. Her socket was throbbing with phantom pains again. Everything was just so overwhelming. Her shoulders and neck burned with fatigue. How badly she wanted to sleep and forget it all.

"How do we get to that place?" Lulu set down the funny-looking metal instrument she'd been playing with and approached the women, pointing at the map. "The first place. You said every 'Jump' thing had a twin, so where's this one's?"

"Keen observation, young one. I was just getting to that."

Uma strode to the center of the lab, where four violet curtains flowed down from the ceiling to the wooden floor. Each curtain was wide enough to shield him from view—Jinn. When Uma pulled one aside, Rin could see him lying in his glass coffin, sealed up like a corpse, his life all but snuffed out—if not for the herbs and crystals keeping him hovering just beyond the grave. Aminadab was tending to him quietly.

Watching him like this always made Rin feel as if there were a cold, wrinkled hand squeezing her throat shut. Perhaps that was why she never noticed the floor hatch next to him, etched in the wood, veiled too by the curtains.

Uma knelt down beside it, grabbed the small metal handle in the wood, and pulled it open.

"You're joking," Berta said flatly.

Half buried in the dirt was a metal plate the color of copper. Round, like a manhole. Naacalian symbols were etched on its surface—including the sun and its shadow.

"What?" Uma looked up at them. "You thought I chose to build a lab here for the view?"

Dusting off her knees, she stood. The hole beneath the hatch was deep—nearly three times the length of the average man. But the width was another matter. Two of them would just barely be able to squeeze in at a time.

Rin reached into her pouch again and brought out the Moon Skeleton. The Jump began to shimmer and glow, agitated by the presence of Iris's body within the skeleton key.

"All right." Berta nodded and squeezed Lulu's shoulder. "Me and Rin'll do it."

"What about me?" Lulu asked.

"No," replied all three women so swiftly, it made Lulu blush. She folded her arms.

"So," Berta continued, ignoring the little girl's pout, "you said this control device is in some secret underground Naacal factory. Any idea of what we're up against here? Because the last time we were in one of those—"

Berta shuddered, and she had every right to. Rin remembered the monsters they'd faced in Heaven's Shrine. She wasn't too keen on facing them again.

"That I don't know," said Uma, and was silent for a beat too long as she stared down into the hatch. "You women are putting yourselves on the line here. I—" She paused, turning over her left hand to stare at her pink palm. "I probably should be the one to do it."

Rin smirked. "Feeling guilty, scientist?"

Squeezing her eyes shut for a moment, Uma walked over to the cupboard where she'd taken her shawl. This time she drew out a loaded rifle.

"That one's mine," said Berta, catching it when Uma tossed it to her.

Rin put out a hand before the woman could bring out another. "I've got my own," she said, tapping her chest.

"Remember," Uma said. "This is a search-and-destroy mission. We must keep this device out of everyone's hands. Especially the Committee's. And Bosch's."

Her jaw tightened as she spoke his name, but she didn't lose her composure. Neither would Rin.

I am a warrior, Rin reminded herself, squeezing her hands into fists. And Iris was alive. If she didn't do this, Bosch would find a way to use the Titans to annihilate her.

She wasn't going to allow that to happen.

Rin thought of Iris's expression, serene despite the blood of men dripping down her cheeks. This wasn't the kind of peace her sister had wanted. Iris had become Hiva, but she'd spared Rin's life. To Rin that could only mean one thing: Iris wasn't completely gone yet.

For so long after learning her true identity, Iris had believed in an impossible dream: that there was a way for her to transform herself. That somewhere out there, between the frightening arrogance of human ingenuity and the divine magic of secret gods, Iris could find the solution to the "problem" of her nature.

All she'd wanted was to create her own identity. To define herself.

Maybe it was still possible.

As Berta crossed the lab with her rifle, Rin sucked in a breath, dropping the Moon Skeleton into her pouch. Once Berta reached her, the two women exchanged determined glances.

They wouldn't let the Committee harm Iris anymore. This was their silent promise.

"Go," Uma said. "Go quickly. And be careful."

Rin jumped first, with Berta close behind. The shimmering light of the Solar Jump enveloped them. Wind rushed by Rin's ears, whistling so loudly that she could only just catch Uma shouting something behind her, until the woman's voice disappeared. Rin didn't have time to think. Gravity felt as if it were hooking her stomach from the inside.

And when Rin landed on the ground, her feet touched a sidewalk not unlike the ones she'd seen in London. The people in the crowd were dressed similarly too, in this busy street intersection. All newsboy caps and dull-colored trousers, suspenders, vests, and jackets. A couple of women, wearing white blouses tucked into their long brown skirts, saw Berta appear next to her, her knees buckling and the rifle strapped around her shoulder teetering dangerously. They blinked, rubbed their eyes, and shook their heads before speeding down the street, defiantly ignorant of what they'd just seen.

Rin looked up at the streetlamp next to her and stared down the red-bricked buildings sprawled down the street. More people were starting to notice them. Of course. Whether it was her Dahomey armor, her brown skin, or Berta's weapon, they stood out, to say the least.

"Let's find some shelter," Rin whispered to Berta. "Before—"

The pavement beneath their feet shimmered white. The Jump must have been underneath, its brilliant light peeking through the asphalt.

A third body bumped into Rin's back.

"Hey, y'all!" The little girl waved with one hand, showing a piece of white crystal she'd taken from Jinn's "casket." Clever girl. Tossing it aside, she rubbed the back of her head. "Wow, look at all those white folk. . . ."

Rin and Berta both cursed at the same time. "Lulu?"

WAR

TRUTHFULLY, SHE WANTED TO KILL HIM. But she couldn't. He was the only one she was not allowed to kill. So she went somewhere else instead.

Rows of men faced one another with guns and cannons. Hiva did not differentiate between the soldiers. Whatever the color of their uniforms, their anima was just the same.

She saw the explosions that darkened the sky. The dead ground trampled on by the dirtied boots of soldiers. The corpses floating in the crystal waters of the Marne river.

She met them on the battlefield with her *shamshir* blades strapped to her back: The men who hid behind tall grass or crawled through dug-out trenches. The men who rode through the battlefield on horses. The wagons transporting bombs and the taxis busing in reinforcements.

Their bullets were not meant for her—not until they realized no bullet could stop her.

Curses in German and French. Hiva understood all languages crafted by the human tongue, though no words were needed for her message.

Warriors existed in every era. For as long as Hiva had lived, she'd seen it: every civilization had felt as if they'd needed means to destroy human life en masse.

They were spurred on by the powerful, whose wealth and political muscle grew with each corpse that rotted on the ground.

An uncomfortable emotion sparked within Hiva as she watched them.

Soldiers. They fought for glory. They fought for freedom. They fought to civilize. All excuses.

Captain Slessor, the treacherous leader of the HMS *Diana*.

Major General Van der Ven, another murderer of the Enlightenment Committee.

Thomas Jones, captain of the slave ship *Marlow*. On that ship had been kidnapped children aching for home. He'd renamed them "Agnus" and "Anne" and sold them to an exhibition.

He hadn't known that he'd taken a goddess too. A goddess watching carefully how the evil of men unfolded.

With her body riddled with bullet holes, Hiva stared into the frightened eyes—blue, green, hazel—of the soldiers on the battlefield. The two armies had forgotten each other, each man scrambling to figure out just what had appeared in front of them.

Did demons truly exist?

For Hiva, they did. For Hiva, they stood before her with their weapons and helmets. Military men, whose uniforms and faces all blended into one. Bloodthirsty demons who could strip away flesh from bone if commanded. Who could kidnap and murder if lied to.

It was a mistake to believe that war progressed civilization. War drove only the empowerment of a few at the expense of others. Societies were destroyed. Lands taken. Bodies violated. Kingdoms conquered. An endless cycle of destruction that must be brought to an end.

Hiva lifted her head to the sky, stretched her arms out, and burned them all alive.

The strange emotion inside her disappeared. She felt nothing as their ashes drifted over the Marne.

This was but a test of her power. Soon all would meet the dismal fate humankind deserved. But for now there was much that Hiva needed to attend to. Some very important business.

There was more work to be done.

21

AS BERTA STRAPPED A BONNET OVER Lulu's head, Rin squirmed in her new yellow afternoon dress. The sleeves were too puffy and the bell-shaped skirt too long. She didn't know how Berta chose what to steal and where to steal it from. There weren't too many shops in this little town, and apparently all the women's clothes here had to be imported from bigger cities like "Montreal" and "Toronto." Or so Berta told her. It was useless information that Rin didn't care about, but Berta *insisted* on talking to her.

"If we're going to travel around, we gotta look like the locals. Rule number one of sneaking around," Berta had said, once she'd returned to the alley with an armful of these rags.

Rin sneered at the red flower patterns sewn into the fabric. Berta's dress, brown with gold highlights, didn't suit her skin tone. And Lulu—even in her white pants and long schoolgirl jacket, she stuck out like a sore thumb, gasping at everything she saw.

Lulu. Rin grunted as the little girl fixed her bonnet. It was too late to send her back to Uma's laboratory through the Jump. By the time they'd finished arguing, too many people were watching—including a police officer or two. How to explain three "colored" girls appearing out of thin air in the town streets? They quickly fled.

They didn't have time for any more detours or mishaps. Rin pulled her pouch out of the pocket of her skirt—the one good thing about the dress.

Berta leaned over. "Well, according to the map, it looks like we're in a town called Fort William," she said. "Wow—we're a hop, skip, and a jump away from Minnesota. Look at how close we are to the American border."

The sound of that country's name wiped the awed grin from Lulu's cherubic face. "America? We're not . . ." She clasped her hands together. "We're not going back there, are we?"

She looked truly terrified. Rin and Berta exchanged worried glances. Both girls reached for Lulu at the same time and were startled at the other's show of concern. Clearing her throat, Rin withdrew her hand.

"Don't worry." Berta nudged Lulu with her elbow. "See this symbol? The little oval with a line in the middle going across?"

Rin didn't know the Greek alphabet, and clearly neither did Berta, because she looked to her for help before grinning at Lulu. John Temple must have relished making things unnecessarily complicated.

"The same symbol's over here, where we were before." She pointed to Lagos in West Africa. "And now we gotta go west across to this whole other province. See the symbol that looks like a big Z, right by this narrow little lake?"

"'Lake Winnipeg'?" Lulu read.

"Yep. We gotta get there so we can head down to—"

The other Z was in Central America. A "hop, skip, and a jump" away from El Salvador—Berta's birthplace.

"What's wrong?" Rin goaded her, watching her stiffen with a little wicked grin. "Itching to run away?"

Rin felt strangely uncomfortable, even guilty, as the other girl shrank back. Soon Berta lifted her chin in defiance. "Hell no. I ain't no coward. *You're* the one we should be worried about. You haven't been yourself lately, oh great warrior."

As Rin silently seethed, she remembered Aisosa and Natame mocking her as she'd recuperated in the village, gazing at her with pitying eyes. *How far you've fallen,* they'd seemed to tell her.

"What if we run into a few nasty bad guys along the way?" Berta packed her rifle inside a leather briefcase. Where she'd stolen *that* item, Rin would never know. "You sure you can fend anyone off? Didn't do such a great job against Iris."

The memory of Iris's face flashed in her mind's eye. The heat rushing to her head, Rin grabbed Berta by the collar. The briefcase clattered against the ground.

"I'm still a pretty good killer," Rin told her in a quiet, deadly tone. "You want a demonstration?"

"Now, that's enough!" Lulu separated them, spreading her arms out to keep them apart. "No fighting! You're not supposed to fight on an adventure. Didn't y'all ever read *Treasure Island* and other stuff like that?"

Rin and Berta exchanged another glance—this time one of complete bewilderment.

"What?" Rin said.

"*Who?*" Berta spat out at the same time.

Their cluelessness only seemed to annoy Lulu. Rolling her eyes, she grabbed the map and inspected it. "The Jump's close to a place called Winnipeg. It says here that it's seven hundred kilometers away!"

"Seven hundred kilometers on foot. That's a five-day walk," Rin said.

"A five-day walk?" Berta bristled. "Damn it. Is this really the closest Uma can get us?"

Better than six to seven weeks, Rin thought.

Lulu shrugged. "No use complaining about it," she said, punching Berta in the arm.

"I guess not—wait a minute, who made you the leader here?" Berta tugged on Lulu's bonnet. "You shouldn't even be here, little lady."

Lulu shrugged, giving the two a sheepish grin.

Rin clucked her tongue in annoyance. She had better things to do than to babysit a child. Now it looked like she'd have to take care of two. Uma should have just sent her alone. As far as she was concerned, the others were dead weight.

This little town was still buzzing with life, and though they'd tried to fit in, their clothes weren't enough to hide them within the crowd. People still stared at Rin's and Lulu's dark skin wherever they went. Children still pointed at Rin's eyepatch, as though Rin needed to be further reminded of the violence that had taken her right eye.

"They must think you're a pirate," Berta said, before receiving Rin's death stare and immediately shutting her mouth.

Five days was too long to walk. But there were other options. According to the town chatter, this place, Fort William, had just gotten a new train station. And there were tracks heading west.

"You won't let us on?" Berta complained, after they'd reached a small wooden train station close to the Kaministiquia River on the southern edge of the town.

One of the officials that managed the station sneered at Rin and Lulu. "Here at the Canadian Pacific Railway, we serve . . ." He chose his words carefully. "Only a select clientele."

Rin stared at the growing crowds of white men and women in drab-colored suits, dresses, and bowler hats. It was clear what this man meant.

But Berta must have noticed that the man's expression seemed sterner looking at her two companions. Clearing her throat, she tried again.

"I'd like a ticket." She twirled her long brown curls with a finger. "These two are just . . . my maids. I'm visiting my mother in Winnipeg, you see."

Maids? Rin found it somewhat amusing that when she looked down at Lulu, the slight exasperation on her face matched Rin's own. Neither of them spoke, because in that moment, the same deep understanding connected the two of them, compelling them to play along despite their annoyance.

For a moment it seemed like the official was considering it. But though Berta's skin wasn't as dark as her brother's, Rin knew she wouldn't pass for a white woman. Perhaps if she'd come alone and used the right accent, she would have been able to role-play as a "regular" town girl who'd spent far too many days under the sun.

In the end, the official refused them a ticket. But there were other ways.

As the growing crowd waited for the train to come in the worsening heat, Rin spotted a gaggle of women on the outer fringe. Each wore black, wide-rimmed hats adorned with dark flowers and a veil. The veils would be useful.

"Ma'ams, you must come with me," Lulu told them, grabbing their hands, much to their shock. The women were scandalized. Scandalized but curious. "My mistress is hurt and looking for her mama! Please, you must come with me!"

It was strange how easily the women were separated from the crowd. Lulu had a special quality, Rin admitted, that made people trust her instinctively. Then again, perhaps these women didn't think the girl possessed the critical acuity to fool them. Either way, they ended up unconscious, bound, gagged, and propped up against some trees behind the train station, their hats stolen. The veils would help cover dark skin and a missing eye, so long as Rin kept her head down.

"That felt oddly satisfying," Berta said, emerging from behind the station with freshly pilfered tickets in hand. "Beating up the rich always does."

"How uncouth," Rin replied, though she didn't exactly disagree. The two girls exchanged devilish conspiratorial grins before snickering into their hands, just in time for the train to roll in.

Westward to Winnipeg. Each car, though a metal lump from the outside, was a veritable hotel on the inside. They were fit for sleeping, with beds and places to hang one's coat. There were dining cars and even cars to smoke in.

Lulu cooed, but Rin reminded her to keep her head down. The only people who looked like them were the porters who stowed baggage, shined shoes, and ushered passengers to their seats.

"Be careful with that," Berta said quickly to one of them, as the porter took her briefcase and showed them to where their tickets had seated them. Berta lowered her veil with a nervous laugh while Rin and Lulu kept their heads down. Something told Rin it wasn't enough. The porter's eyes lingered on the two of them, but he kept silent nonetheless, shutting the sliding door to their car behind him.

The berths were wide and covered in white cloth, but not in the least comfortable, not with the train rumbling along rickety tracks. Half a day. They had half a day to rest and prepare for what horrors faced them. Lulu spent far too long talking about all the books she'd read: *Treasure Island*. *The Mysterious*

Island. Around the World in Eighty Days. The Prince and the Pauper. She'd fight over them with her brother.

"I never knew adventures could be real, but now here I am, flying around the world." Lulu looked out the oval window. "Though I didn't think I'd ever have to leave home in the first place." Her brown doe eyes dimmed a little in the reflection of the glass.

Rin shifted awkwardly when the desire to comfort the child overwhelmed her. But with that compulsion came a bitterness she didn't quite understand.

She pictured herself, a kidnapped Yoruba girl training with other servants and slaves in the Abomey compound. Learning to kill with a spear in her hand. No one had been there to comfort her in those days. No one was here to comfort her now.

"Iris . . ." Rin was surprised with herself that she let that name slip from her lips. She covered her mouth and quickly looked up at the other two sitting across from her. She caught Berta's pitying, guilty glance, and her cheeks flushed with embarrassment.

"Miss Rin," Lulu said quietly from across the little square wooden table that separated them. "Is Miss Iris really an angel?"

Berta had her feet up on the seat and her arm cushioning her head against the wall. But she watched Rin, waiting for her answer.

"No," Rin finally said. "She's just a person."

Or at least she'd wanted to be.

Lulu nodded. "I thought so," she replied, and looked back out the window. "She was so nice when I first met her. So brave and strong. But my pastor taught me that angels were righteous. They always know what to do. Miss Iris wasn't like that. Always seemed to me like she was running from something." She glanced at Berta. "What do you think?"

"Me?" Berta stubbornly shut her eyes. "What do you want me to say? Not like I knew her. But . . ." She paused. "She reunited me with my brother. She couldn't have been that bad."

"And yet your brother killed her nonetheless," Rin snarled. Seeing the girl lounging around, speaking so comfortably about Iris, angered her in ways she couldn't express. She couldn't cause a scene here without drawing attention to the three of them, but she clenched her fists anyway, ready to fight.

A fight Berta didn't seem interested in. She took her feet off the seat and, after placing them firmly on the ground, leaned over the table. She shut her eyes for a time.

"He did," Berta said finally, in a solemn tone that surprised Rin. "And he was wrong to do it." Berta's eyes glistened a little when she opened them. "I'm sorry, Rin."

Rin blinked, sitting back in her seat. This wasn't what she'd been expecting.

"I've been thinking." Berta sat straight in her seat and leaned farther forward, her elbows on the table. "My brother was scared of what she could do. But he didn't even give her a chance. Maybe if he had, we all could have gotten rid of Hiva together, and Iris would be—" She shook her head with a little laugh. "I don't know. Somewhere, making babies with that handsome fellow. The one who almost died trying to save her. Max shouldn't have done it. I'm . . . I'm *so sorry*."

Rin deflated. But not because of the loss of a sister. In taking responsibility, in acknowledging her brother's crimes, Berta had taken something away from Rin—something she'd needed. Pressing her fingers against her eyepatch, Rin bit her lip and stared at the oak table, wanting to rage but having nothing to rage at.

"I asked my mom once what heaven was like," Lulu said after a while, breaking the silence. "And she said, 'Why, darling, it's probably like a perfect world. So what would a perfect world look like to you?' You know what I said?"

Berta shook her head. Rin didn't move.

"'A world where nobody hurts each other.'" Lulu gave a little resolute nod. "I thought about it and thought about it. Like, a world where you could be who you wanted, or a world where you could eat as much as you like, or a world where who had money and who didn't have money didn't matter. But in the end, it all came down to that: a world where nobody hurt each other."

"Sounds like a nice place," Berta whispered.

It did.

—◦◦◦◦◦—

The train journeyed on west. Soon the rolling countryside of evergreen trees turned into wide plains. The porter had come in a couple of times to check on them and serve them tea. It was strange. Their disguise wasn't exactly perfect. And yet the man never pried, never asked any questions or raised any concerns.

The last time he'd come into their car, he told them the train was half an hour from their destination. Before leaving, he gave Lulu a little smile.

"You remind me of my daughter," he told her before tipping his hat and leaving.

Surely there should be times when it doesn't matter who you are, Rin thought, sipping her tea. *Where we can all just be good to each other.*

"Ah, Mrs. Wesley!" When the door slid open again, it was by a large, drunk white man in a smoking jacket. The smell of nicotine wafted off him in plumes. "Why don't you and your sisters join us in the dining car for some biscuits and—wait a minute!"

And his brown eyes bulged at the sight of them. The "jig," as Berta would say, was up.

"Isn't this the Wesleys' car? Who the blast are you?"

"Oops! Time to go!" Berta grabbed her briefcase from the overhead rack and smashed it against the man's face.

"You broke my nose!" he cried.

"You broke his nose," Lulu repeated in awe.

"Better than killing him." She turned to Rin. "Let's go."

"Porters! Police!"

Rin, Berta, and Lulu ran past the man as he began screaming. People were poking their heads out of their cars to see the ruckus, gasping and crying out upon finding the three of them barreling down the narrow halls.

"Thieves!" and "Stowaways!" were among the kinder words they called them.

"There they go! Police! Police!" a redheaded child said, pointing at them before his mother pulled him back inside the car.

Two policemen moved to cut them off, their batons in hand.

"We don't have time for this!" Berta began reaching inside her briefcase, but Rin put up a hand.

"Watch over Lulu," she said. "I'll handle this."

It had been a while since she'd called her sword, and it felt good. The field of the crystal hilt erupting out of her chest. The smell of fear curling from the police and all who watched them as she pulled its long white crystal blade from her body, cutting through her blouse without a care.

The two policemen were clearly not heroes. When Rin rushed toward them and cut one of their hats in two, it sent them both fleeing in the other direction. But Rin, Berta, and Lulu didn't get far before more were summoned. The officers crowded around from the front and behind.

One clearly did fancy himself a hero. He ran for Rin with a revolver. "I've got you now, you—"

Berta bashed her body into the man's lifted arm, causing him to shoot one of the cabin walls. People screamed as Berta used her briefcase to knock him out.

"The door!" Berta exclaimed at a shocked Rin, pointing to its golden rim a few feet away at the end of the car.

Rin understood. "Carry Lulu!" she ordered, and while the train bustled onward, she flipped her sword around and rushed the officers, clearing a path. With one hand she pulled open the door to the outside, a gust of wind blowing off her stolen hat and veil. The rolling hills whipped past. It was now or never.

"Jump!" Rin cried. Trusting that the two were behind her, she jumped off the train and rolled down the hill below. A pile of bushes finally stopped her tumbling. She had barely managed to lift her head when Lulu and Berta crashed into her with pained groans.

As the train sped by, disappearing into the distance, Rin dusted off her dress and pulled herself to her feet, while Lulu hollered in excitement and Berta cursed, rubbing her back.

"I guess now we walk," Rin said, running her fingers through her braids.

Berta collapsed back onto the yellow grass with another groan.

22

PERISCOPE ON PORT BOW!"

"Throw out a smoke screen! Hide the ship from the enemy!"

There hadn't been this many men on deck the last time Max was on the high seas, but this British transport ship was different. Once an enemy ship had appeared, hundreds of sailors rushed to release the black smoke from the cannons that stretched over the water. Who was the enemy? Russian? German? Max couldn't bring himself to care. The smoke screen worked, at least. But a successful mission wasn't enough for these military rats.

"Hey, you!" One of the sailors grabbed Max by the collar. Thankfully Max wasn't in the same uniform. He'd lost a bit of his mind, yes, but not quite enough to wear the same silly hat upon his head.

Max stood out from them in his heavy brown jacket, vest, and turtleneck. Gladstone had given him permission to go to France's shore along with his own special rank. Everyone here knew it. But he wasn't one of them. He never would be.

"Where's your pet?" the sailor demanded. "We were promised an easy voyage to the war front! This look easy to you?"

This boy was his age, and he was new. Max could tell. Curled blond hair and piercing blue eyes that hadn't yet witnessed the horrors Max had in his lifetime. Well, he would soon enough. Nothing like a little bit of violence to shatter that alpha-male arrogance. Max would know.

"You don't really believe that shite the general said, do you?" said a dark-skinned boy, older and with ears bigger than his hands. "That 'top secret' bunk. Trust me, if the government has some kind of secret weapon, it's not going to be some gloomy bastard, I can tell you that."

"We'll see, won't we?" The blond sailor pushed Max so hard, Max almost stumbled over his feet. "Bring him up here, and bring him up here fast. Let's see if this so-called great destroyer can get rid of enemy ships."

There was a time Max would have killed any sailor who dared speak to him with anything less than fear and awe. But that *him* didn't exist anymore. Max nodded and went down to the lower decks. He didn't dare speak. He'd barely spoken in days. Not since abandoning Hawkins and Jacob, still paralyzed with grief. Not since meeting with Gladstone. Not since boarding the transport ship with Hiva in tow.

Not since Cherice's death.

"Go find Berta," Max had told Hawkins and Jacob before leaving Lily Giralt's London brothel. "She should still be in West Africa. Go to Ajashe—Porto-Novo—whatever you want to call the damn city. Make sure she's okay. Take care of her in my place."

It was all he could do for her. Time no longer mattered in Max's world. His decision had been made hastily in the moment, but it hadn't been made without purpose.

He wanted to die.

He was a murderer who'd killed friends, betrayed them, and failed them in equal measure. How long could he live with this putrid self-hatred pumping through his veins like a toxin? He didn't want to. But he didn't want his death to be meaningless either.

Max had thought Hiva would revert to being an emotionless murderer after the attack at the ball. But to his surprise, Hiva went along with Gladstone's wishes. He was here to fight in the war. To end it. To prove that he was better than his sister. None of that had changed. Hiva didn't even seem to care at all that Max had orchestrated his maiming.

Well, good. For Iris's and Cherice's sakes, Max would keep it that way. He'd use Hiva to put an end to this senseless war, before it grew big enough to envelop the whole world and the ones he loved. He trusted his friends to put an end to Hiva when it was all over.

"Whatever you do, make sure you forge that sword." It was the last thing Max had told Jacob and Hawkins before leaving the brothel. Lily had at least placed the arm they'd taken from Hiva on ice. It would take some work to carve flesh from bone. Nasty business. "If anything goes wrong, it'll be our only chance."

He trusted his friends to be the one to do it, because he didn't expect to return to England from the war front alive. He didn't want to.

The transport ship carried weapons Max had never seen before among the cargo. But each crate had something in common.

"'Bosch Guns and Ammunitions,'" Max whispered with a smirk, reading the big black letters on one wooden container. "No matter what I do, where I go, or who I kill, I just can't seem to escape the Enlighteners, can I?"

They had their tendrils in everything—even his attempt to die.

He wondered what kind of fate had befallen Mary, Henry, and Lucille after Bellerose's ball. The three had really pulled the rug out from under him. Traitors. He hoped they all died in bloody ways.

The only bit of hope Max could hold on to was the fact that his sister was still out there somewhere, alive. Rin may have hated him. She *should* hate him. But she wouldn't kill Berta out of revenge. Would she?

As frustration built up inside of him, Max slammed his foot against the floor. He felt so bloody helpless. It was more than he could stand.

In times like these, his mother would pray. But the years had not been kind to his faith. The only god Max believed in was the one he could see. And that god had to be dealt with very, *very* carefully.

Max tapped open the door to Hiva's room, specially prepared for him on Gladstone's orders. "Hiva?"

It was a simple room with a flat wooden bed and mattress, and a chair by the table against the far wall. Barely any room for a dance. Still, it was more than Hiva deserved. They were both reckless murderers. Perhaps their partnership made the most sense.

Hiva, his body fully healed and newly whole, had been given the uniform of a British soldier. Lucky for him, he also wore no ridiculous hat. His hair was free to spill over his body, the flowers twisting and shuddering, as Hiva turned to Max with a strangely focused expression that disturbed him.

"They're calling you," Max told him, shifting uncomfortably on his feet. "The navy men. They spotted some enemy ship. It's still far off, and they've cloaked the transport ship well enough, but they still want you to prove your worth."

Hiva did not move. The way he searched Max's face made his stomach curdle like he'd bitten into a rotten potato. When had Hiva become so familiar with him? So comfortable? So . . . so human? He almost missed the killer automaton.

It was just for a moment. Hiva turned and continued his thousand-yard stare, his gaze burrowing a hole in the wall.

"They want you up there, so . . ." Max waved his hands toward the outside of the door.

Silence. The automaton god did not move.

"Maximo," Hiva said after a time, startling him. "May I ask you a question?"

Max squirmed. *Here it comes.* "I thought it was weird you didn't ask earlier. Let me guess: you want to know why I helped hack off your arm a few days ago."

"No. It's of no matter to me."

Max blinked, shocked. "What?"

"You were frightened of me. You had tried to kill me once before. It's not surprising that you would try to do so again. You may still yet."

It was as if Hiva had made peace with it. Like he'd made peace with everything. Max didn't quite know how to take it.

"Then what do you want to ask me?"

And then Hiva posed a question that made Max's breath tight in his chest. "What is the meaning of life?" With all sincerity, and without a hint of jest or irony.

Silence. Max let the question hang in the air for just a moment.

Before bursting out laughing.

"What's the meaning of—what? *What* did you just ask?" Max held his stomach and laughed so hard, he could feel the muscles twinging in his back as he bent it. "Did you seriously just ask—what is this, a university lecture? I knew I shouldn't have let you read Marx."

But Max's laughter didn't seem to affect Hiva in any way. The god looked at his red palms with eyes as hollow as his voice.

"I am born to bring about death for the sake of life. Then why must I kill?"

Max's laughter died in his throat, and silence stretched between them. Looking at Hiva reminded Max of Iris struggling with the same questions. Desperate to find her own answer—dying before he'd given her a chance to.

"Funny. You looked like you knew it all when I first saw you in the Coral Temple," said Max, letting a bitter tinge slip into his voice as he leaned against the doorframe. "Now you're questioning everything."

"I have questioned before. For eons. I came to her for the answer." Hiva turned toward him. "To my sister. But her answer was as merciless as she was: humanity is evil and shall always be. And there will always come a day when they must be destroyed in order to start anew."

Death and rebirth. A cycle with no end. Max gave him a wry smile. "Well, what can I say? We're bastards. We take one another's lands and enslave one another. We conquer and kill. We wage war and pillage. We stuff our stomachs while others starve. It's just . . . how we are."

"Is it?" As Hiva pressed, the flowers in his hair trembled, almost as if mirroring Hiva's inner turmoil. "Can humanity ever change? Can we imagine another way to live in this world?"

Imagine another way to live? Well, Max supposed changing things would take a little bit of imagination—and daring. This world hadn't happened by accident. Hundreds of years ago, a bunch of mad folks somewhere had decided that societies should be structured this way. That some should have everything, while others had nothing. That power belonged only in the hands of the few. And over the decades and centuries, people just kept it up, following the same script until you had beggars on the street fighting for a piece of bread, mothers in zoos, slaves on cotton fields, and dead kids mauled in the mines. Max had always assumed that this was just how things were and had to be. In the end, they were all just living in someone's imagination. Definitely not his.

But could humanity ever change?

"Iris wanted to change, and I didn't give her a chance to," Max said, folding his arms over his chest and holding down the wave of despair suddenly threatening to drown him. When he thought of Iris, he thought of Cherice. And when he thought of Cherice, he thought of the cruelty of this world that wasted life so easily. Even if he hunted down Adam for revenge, it wouldn't change anything. It wouldn't give Cherice another chance. It wouldn't erase his sins. . . .

"I just want a chance. A chance to be reborn," Max whispered, his lips quivering as tears threatened to form. "To start everything anew . . ."

"As did I, once," said Hiva. "But sister would not allow me. She did not believe in change. Only justice—and the inevitable. I wonder . . ." Hiva gazed up thoughtfully at the ceiling. "What does she believe now? Sister. Have you changed?"

Now? Max frowned, studying Hiva carefully, not knowing whether the god was still speaking his usual nonsense or . . .

Or . . . ?

"What are you talking about?" Max asked slowly, boosting himself off the doorframe. "Iris is dead. What does it matter to you what she believed?"

Hiva didn't speak for a time; his silence leeched the warmth from Max's skin, as if he were naked and alone in the cold. Suddenly a wild thought gripped Max, but he shook his head—because Hiva couldn't have been implying what Max, in that mad second, had thought he was implying. No, it was impossible. What was done was done.

By Max's own hands.

Hiva didn't confirm his fleeting suspicions one way or another, but the curious expression on Hiva's face had Max worried, and he couldn't articulate why. Hiva raised his head and breathed in and out, in and out, in a calm, steady rhythm. As if he were waiting for something. Listening. Feeling.

Feeling what?

Feeling who?

What did Hiva know that Max didn't?

"Some fates are inevitable," Hiva said—certainly not to Max, because he couldn't understand a whit of what he meant. "This isn't my earth. Two Hivas do not belong in the same space. I transgressed in coming here. When the rules are broken, a correction must be made. Is that what you're trying to tell me?"

Max gave him an incredulous look. "Who are you talking to?"

"The One who created her," Hiva answered, with a serenity that spooked Max. "The One who decides whether she lives or dies."

"She?" The ghost flashing in Max's mind momentarily filled him with terror. But Max swallowed his fear, his wild speculations. He shook his head, because he knew what he'd done.

Finally Hiva turned to him. When he spoke, it was with a tinge of sadness. With the faint brush of regret. "If some fates are inevitable," he said, "then should I accept mine?"

Max didn't answer as Hiva walked out of the room.

FAMINE

TRUTHFULLY, SHE *STILL* WANTED TO KILL him. But she couldn't. He was the only one she was not allowed to kill. So she went somewhere else instead.

Hiva knew of the Solar Jumps. She'd memorized them in the days she'd watched the Naacal use them to transport goods and slaves—and then weapons to kill her. With them she could travel with ease. And with ease she chose her targets and destroyed her prey.

She traveled past the eastern border of Prussia, where a Polish-speaking congregation trudged across the fields of yellow wheat and dirt roads with what little possessions they couldn't sell. Men, women, and children, many starving and terrified as armed soldiers forced them onward. They'd been expelled from their homes by a ruthless government seeking to cleanse the land. She put them out of their misery. Ashes to ashes. Dust to dust.

All would one day meet their end. Even the children. Murder was Hiva's mercy, her divine strategy so that humanity could live again. But there were some, Hiva felt, who *deserved* to die. Some whose deaths she would relish. She would hunt them. This was her judgment.

Hiva traced one such anima into a grand manor in the countryside. There he stood at the center of a parlor, surrounded by the country's parliament members. Among them were many pristine jackets and military uniforms, but none more fanciful than the many-layered coat he wore to match his high red boots and bedazzled cane.

"Gentlemen," he said in perfect German. "Lend your support to me, not Bellerose. You can't tell me you trust a woman more than you trust me."

"Benini, even a woman is preferable to you," said one man smoking a cigar. His white mustache stretched and curled around his cheeks.

Swirling a glass of red wine, Riccardo Benini snarled. "Van der Ven is dead. Bellerose has been acting as if she's some sort of queen! If you lend me your support to help unseat that little wench, I'll make sure you get the best seats on the Ark. I—"

A wineglass smashed to the ground. "Who in the blazes is she?" cried a frightened man.

For Hiva had just made herself known to them, appearing without fanfare in the threshold of the parlor door.

"What—?" Benini looked at her, mouth agape as if he'd seen a ghost. Then his lips quivered into a nervous smile. "Why, Iris, my dear, how—how have you been? I heard you'd gone missing."

The men of empire gasped, some whispering in wonder. It did not matter to Hiva which seat they occupied. Their political affiliation was but a veil for the evil of their actions. Like Benini. Self-interest was their creed. Greed was the religion that tied them together. Certainly Hiva had noticed: their bellies were round and full, while the sorrowful procession marching east were gaunt and sick, wailing for home. From such wickedness, bitterness would sprout and more degeneration would take root until it had become a cancer spreading upon the earth.

"Who is this woman?"

Hiva heard shouts like these erupt around the parlor. Benini strode toward her, his arms outstretched.

"I really thought Bellerose had killed you—permanently this time. But you're as beautiful as the day I met you in that dingy underground club. Iris! This is the perfect timing. Gentlemen." He turned to the others. "This is Hiva. She'll do as I say. We've worked together before. With her on my side . . . with her on *our* side," he corrected himself, "we don't need Bellerose. We don't need *anyone* in the Committee. We can take the Ark for ourselves. We can choose how to use that technology."

Greed.

Benini turned to her with that oafish grin, cruel in its egotistical indifference to the suffering of others.

To *her* suffering.

Perhaps this is why he was not aware that he was part of her very important business.

"What say you, my dear Iris? Shall you once again be my obedient little clown?"

With a simple exhalation, she destroyed them all. It was a cleansing of a different sort. Ashes covered the furniture and the unfinished glasses of wine.

She was supposed to feel nothing. How curious, then, was the spark of sadistic pleasure that had flashed for just a moment within her.

More curious still was the regret that abruptly snatched the air from her lungs. A momentary anomaly.

But soon it was replaced with dissatisfaction. This wasn't enough. There was more to cleanse. More to make right.

More to kill before she could feel satisfied.

She was off to London.

23

RIN'S PARTY JUMPED ACROSS BORDERS TO the fertile flatlands of Chinandega, a town the locals called the City of Oranges. It was easier to blend in here among the crowds of all shades, though the girls discarded their veiled hats thanks to the hot, humid weather that reminded Rin of her tropical home.

Bartering their hats for a couple of horses, they traveled north—a journey of almost three days past palm trees, bean and avocado plants, golden trumpets, and bright red peppers. Lulu pointed each out as she rode behind them. Admittedly, it was nice having Lulu's commentary to listen to. Rin had gotten used to riding with limited vision; it meant she had to concentrate on the road ahead—not whatever wonders might be blooming around them.

If only humanity could be as beautiful and perfect as the plants and the trees, Rin thought to herself. Perhaps that was the world Hiva was aiming for. But after so many cataclysms, it still hadn't been achieved. It just wasn't possible, Rin supposed. Not for humans, with their greediness and hatred.

And sorrow. Rin saw it on Berta's face the moment they descended upon the soil of El Salvador. How cruel, this irony that had brought them to Berta's birthplace.

Lulu watered the horses as they rested by a tree, leaving Rin and Berta to eat fruit together in awkward silence.

"Here." Berta had sliced some ripe papaya with a pocketknife and handed some to Rin. "Gotta keep your strength up."

After a beat of hesitation, Rin took the slice from her. "Th-thank you . . . ," Rin whispered, and bit into it quietly.

The awkward silence continued. Rin didn't dare speak, especially after noticing that Berta was softly smiling—wistfully. The bitter nostalgia of happier days that could never again be retrieved: Rin knew that feeling all too well.

Soon they'd entered the city of San Salvador. That was when Berta found her voice.

"I grew up in Apopa, a small town not far from here," she said, hiking the leather strap of her briefcase over her shoulder. "But Mom took me and Maximo here a few times, to this cathedral. To pray for work."

Past the tramways and the busy shops was a majestic cathedral that seemed to have its own brilliance in this bustling city filled with life. A two-towered white building with a colorful façade painted red and blue, as if signaling a celebration.

"Do you . . ." Rin swallowed her next words, blushing before speaking again. "Do you want to go inside?"

Berta shook her head quickly. She stood at the black gate, in front of the maroon arched doorway, and simply stared at the religious shrine.

"My mother told me there used to be an old temple here, dedicated to a saint. Can't remember which one. My mom was the religious one. Whatever spirituality I had left me the minute we went to Europe and I lost my brother."

Lost families. Rin thought of her own being cut down by the Dahomey women during the raid. She'd become numb to pain since that day. Rin almost wanted to go back to those times. They were preferable to her present disarray.

"I'm sorry," Rin whispered.

"It was that blasted man who lied to us and lured us from home!" Berta said. "A headhunter from Norway who worked for some rich scumbag named Carl Hagenbeck. His name was Jacobsen. *Johan* Jacobsen. I can't forget that name."

Rin gripped the low black fence. "Where is he now?"

"Even if I knew, even if I killed him, then what?" Berta grimaced. "The bastard's *already* ruined my damn life. He put me in a zoo and paraded me around Europe. I was only a *kid*. If it weren't for that crazy woman stealing me away to America, I would have died there."

"Woman? You mean Madame Moustache?" said Lulu, who stood on Berta's left. Then, furrowing her brows, she put on her best cowgirl voice. "The shootin', lootin' gambler who shot her lover in the back for cheatin' on her."

"And ran to Europe," Berta said with a laugh. "She must have picked me up on a whim. Great impression, by the way."

"I've been working on it." Lulu lifted her head proudly.

Rin grinned at them secretly as they giggled like sisters, though not without a tinge of jealousy. She missed Iris. There was so much she wanted to do, so much she should have done while Iris had been alive and herself. But she'd let hatred steal every opportunity away.

Rin's breath caught in her throat as she felt Lulu's little hand tugging on her dress. "I can do a pretty good impression of you, too," she said with a mischievous smile. "Wanna see?"

"Yes!" Berta lifted her head.

"No," replied Rin flatly before turning around. "Let's not waste any more time. Remember what we came here for."

A disappointed Lulu puffed out her cheeks as Rin strode away from the church. Rin was doing it again. Pushing them away. What she did to everyone when her walls came dangerously low. The consequence was an acute loneliness that settled deep into her bones.

But that loneliness helped her stay focused.

Rin kept her expression cold and hard with a warrior's scowl, ready for the battle ahead. *We're almost there.*

The Jump took them right to the river's edge. That blasted dress. Her foot caught the hem of her bell-shaped skirt and slipped. Before she knew it, she was sliding down the muddy shore and then planting her cheek in the dirt. Berta and Lulu yelped and followed her into the water.

"The Kunene River," Berta coughed, gripping the mud with her hands and pulling herself up. "Just like the map said."

Rin pulled Lulu out of the water with one hand and hoisted them back up onto the shore. Nobody had drowned. Good. Neither had her pouch—it was still in Rin's pocket, carrying the Moon Skeleton and Temple's map. She sighed with relief and, slumping over, surveyed their surroundings. Far beyond the broken wood and fallen trees—felled perhaps by a recent storm—were little huts made of thatch and strung-together logs. Against the backdrop of green hills, a few villagers walked, some cooking meat over a fire. They were shielded by the fallen trees and sparse splintered trunks, so nobody had seen them appear. It made things a little easier.

Rin pulled Temple's map out of her pouch, soaked but still intact. The symbol that looked like a trident was in the southern region of Angola, just as Uma said it would be. But the area she circled—the land purchased by John Temple—was just outside a village called Opuwo.

"Let's go," she said, getting to her feet. "There's no time to waste."

They entered the village and traded their restrictive British-American clothes for more weather-appropriate light, colorful shirts with wrap skirts. But expensive Western clothes could be bartered for more than a few garments.

"A boat?" Berta spat, staring incredulously at the local men who were helping lug one down to the river. Lulu was busy packing some papayas, mangoes, and bananas she'd gotten from a particularly generous pregnant woman. "We're going river rafting this bright morning, are we?"

"The Kunene River will take us down to the town in no time." Rin grabbed a few double-sided paddles from the villagers. She wouldn't spend another few days trudging through the forest on foot while an instrument as destructive as the Titan Control Device lay ready for the taking. She launched a paddle at Berta, who caught it with ease.

"Don't slack off," Rin said before following the men down to the river.

The boat was thick and sturdy in the water. The locals used it to fish, from what Rin could understand. Lulu waved goodbye to the village children as they boosted off the shore and started down the river. The currents would take them south into the lands of the Herero. From there, it'd be a day's walk to John Temple's manor, according to his map.

"I wonder what that old man's doing right now?" Lulu said after a while, eating a ripe mango while she traced a line on the map spread out across the floor. With the other two paddling downstream, Lulu was in charge of directions. Berta's bright idea.

But to Rin's surprise, Lulu hadn't been perturbed at all by the rushing waters and the jutting rocks that they'd had to swerve to avoid. She kept her sharp eyes on the map, reading out landmarks to look out for. A little girl fit for an explorers' expedition.

"Who, John Temple?" Berta snorted. "Didn't that old grandpa have dysentery? He's probably dead by now." She shrugged before grunting from a splash of water.

If disease didn't take him, Adam Temple would. That is, if he ever found him.

Adam. Rin bit the inside of her cheek. What if that disgusting boy ran into Iris first? Iris giving in to her genocidal nature had been his plan from the beginning.

Find and destroy the Titan Control Device. Then get to Iris and . . .

And what? Iris had already made it clear. Once she became Hiva, there was no turning back.

"There has to be a way," Rin muttered, wincing as river water splashed into her face.

The current, though manageable, still battered the boat, tugging Rin's weary body back and forth, at times lifting her precariously—that terrible weightlessness that felt as if she'd be tossed off her feet any moment.

"You okay, warrior girl?" Berta looked at her over her shoulder and gave her a broad grin. "Don't get soft on me now!".

Rin smirked. "You wish." But the farther down the river they went, the more she turned inward, her thoughts becoming more turbulent than the river currents.

As evening fell, the river stilled. Berta breathed a sigh of relief and dropped her paddle into the boat.

"Where are we?" she asked, rubbing her arms for a minute before reaching for the wood again.

Lulu tapped the map. "Mr. Temple's handwriting's real bad, but it looks like we should be in the Kunene Region by now." She squinted as she tried to pronounce it.

Rin lowered her arms without dropping her paddle. "Are you sure about that?"

Lulu nodded, her eyes sparkling with pride. "You bet! I've been working real hard while y'all were paddling. Shouldn't be long now, Miss Rin!"

The little thing pumped her fists as if she were ready for a fight. After everything she'd been through, something told Rin she wouldn't lose in one.

"Is that a . . . smile?" As they began paddling near the shore, Berta gave Rin a ridiculous teasing expression. "Is the warrior princess *smiling*? Are we so lucky?"

She hadn't realized. Heat rushed to Rin's cheeks as she faced the front again, paddling through the calm current.

"Ha! Not so tough, eh?" Berta began, only to be shushed by Lulu.

So she'd seen it too.

Putting a finger to her lips, Rin pointed down the shore, where a crocodile had emerged from the trees and slid down the mud on his belly into the river.

Rin could tell from the number of mud slides along the shore that the area was inhabited by more crocodiles than she would have liked. But what mattered more was getting to Opuwo as quickly as possible, and these rushing white waters were the way to do it. As long as there were only a few crocodiles to deal with—

"And what's that?" Berta waved to Rin, nodding toward the trees on their left. A glinting piece of metal within the trees had caught the light of the dying sun. Then another one. Some to their right too, hidden between the thick branches and leaves.

Lulu tilted her head. "Those aren't crocodiles."

No.

They were guns.

Rin had just barely realized it before she heard one loud bang, followed by more as the guns began firing at them.

CONQUEST

THERE WERE NO FEWER THAN THREE pairs of aerialists flying through the amphitheater. Astley's setup hadn't changed since the days an African dancer and her sullen partner had dazzled audiences on a tightrope. This time trapeze artists had caught the crowd's attention, swinging and catching each other in death-defying tricks above the octagonal circus arena. The musicians plucked their strings and crashed the keys of the piano in the pit behind the circus ring. Audiences screeched in delight from the green-painted galleries as tigers roared on the circus ring, tamed by their master's whip. Each narrow miss of the aerialists brought gasps of fright and pleasure.

It was the promise of death that had lured the audience here to Astley's Amphitheatre. The promise of death that kept them seated and ravenous.

The gas jets set off a spring of smoke, and from behind the drawn red curtains, a man with a square, bald head appeared. In a sparkling red tailcoat and black top hat, he slapped his round belly with jolly laughter as he came to meet the crowds. *His* crowds.

"Ladies and gentlemen!" he cried, stretching out his arms and soaking in the cheers, for the circus proprietor loved attention even more than he loved money. "And even gentler women," he added with a wink, drawing laughter from whomever in the crowd could hear him above the ruckus. "Jugglers and clowns. Acrobats and ferocious animals!"

The tiger roared almost as if on cue, and shrieks from women and children erupted from the audience.

"Where else will you see such a spectacle? Such grandeur? Except here at the Coolie Company?"

The circus proprietor, George Coolie, rubbed the sweat off his bald head as the crowd roared with the tigers and clapped at the final leaps of the trapeze artists. Only after the artists had completed their sets and the stage had cleared did the audience quiet down.

Coolie waited until he had the crowd's attention before he spoke again. "Ladies and gentlemen, surely we are not the first circus to ever grace your eyes. Oh yes, there's Barnum & Bailey Circus, who claim to have The Greatest Show on Earth. There is Cirque Fernando, whose frivolities are considered the crème de la crème of La Belle Époque."

He spoke of his rivals with a wide grin. But Hiva knew of the jealousy seething underneath.

Hiva *knew* this man.

"But no circus has ever boasted the marvels the Coolie Company is about to show you. Marvels that will make you believe in gods and demons. Marvels that will change the face of the world as we know it!" Coolie straightened his bow tie and gazed over the crowds with the flare of a showman, a ringmaster. "And when you go home with tears in your eyes and shouts of joy on your lips, you just make sure to tell your friends: Come to George Coolie's circus, where there'll be no shortage of wonders you'll witness!"

He twirled out from behind the red curtain: the first clown, his face painted red like a demon. His wide, smoky black eyes seemed ready to suck in the crowd. His enormous white grin opened to reveal sharp teeth that seemed smeared with blood. All a painted trick. A mere illusion.

Not his magic. For when he flapped his arms like the wings of a crow, skeletons stumbled out from behind the curtains and onto the stage. No strings were attached as they danced upon the stage, much to the mesmerized horror of the audience.

There've been a lot of rumors lately moving around the country. Especially in the city. Strange rumors. Strange happenings, *as the papers say. Strange, even for me.*

This was what Coolie had once told her. And after witnessing those strange happenings with his own eyes, he'd decided on a new moneymaking scheme. He'd gathered the supernatural up and given them the opportunity to serve him. It wasn't a surprise that he'd put the unnatural on display. It was what everyone drunk on arrogance and avarice did.

Four blond women next appeared in airy white dresses, performing several pirouettes. They danced as beautifully as ballerinas, but nothing was as beautiful a sight as the strange white glow their slender bodies emitted. The crowd cooed—the women were shining bright as fairies, twinkling underneath the still trapezes dangling from the ceiling.

More Fanciful Freaks appeared, and Coolie named them all: Peaseblossom, Cobweb, Moth, and Mustardseed. Oleg the Necromancer. Euryale the Serpent Gorgon. Too many names. As they danced, their unnatural bodies twisted and terrified their audiences, and so too did their skeletons and snakes.

And inside Hiva, memories flashed:

A girl who can't die. An oddity stranger than anything Barnum can conjure up with his cheap parlor tricks. A true oddity confirmed in front of your very eyes. Confirmation that dark powers truly do exist.

Do you think that by being honest with me, it would change our relationship? On the contrary, my dear, I would be ridiculous if I didn't make you and you alone my star attraction: The Immortal Woman. The Daughter of Osiris. Princess of Death.

Ladies and gentlemen, I present to you our Nubian Princess Nefertiti, the Deathless.

Too many names.

Laughing, soaking in the voracious enjoyment of his spectators, Coolie raised his arms. "And now, ladies and gentlemen! The star attraction. The grand finale—"

Before he could finish, applause erupted from the crowd. They pointed above Coolie's head, drunk with the pleasure of spectacle.

Her leap was perfect. Her feet had touched the trapeze bar so lightly, the swings did not budge. Coolie's top hat fell from his head as he turned and saw her. He stumbled backward on the stage, his tailcoat crushed beneath his bottom. The skeletons stopped dancing. The snakes stopped hissing. The fairies stopped shining.

For Hiva had arrived.

"I-Iris!" Coolie peered up at her, his mouth agape and his fingers twitching. "You—You're here! What are you doing here?"

But Hiva did not speak. She pulled one of the *shamshir* blades off her back.

As Hiva took in the sight of the crowd, she remembered another life. A life in which spectators had clinically scrutinized her body, gaping with the hunger of hunters spotting their prey. A lustful kind of voyeurism from those who refused to acknowledge her humanity.

They were right, it seemed. For she was not human.

She was more.

"Iris!" Coolie got to his knees. "Iris! You're back! After that bastard Jinn threatened my life, I thought I'd never see you again. Does this mean you're not mad at me anymore? Can we finally bury the hatchet and put you back to work?"

And then he suddenly looked over his shoulder at the crowd. His eyes shifting nervously, he nodded at the performers, waving his hands, gesturing for them to keep the show going.

As his Fanciful Freaks danced, Coolie got up to his knees.

"And now for the grand finale! The return of the Coolie Company's greatest act. A woman for whom death is but a trinket of the gods, to be toyed with at her mercy." He spread out his arms once again, as if to hug the entire audience. "I give you the one, the only—"

Hiva jumped down from the trapeze and onto the stage.

Hiva could not speak. That was the pact she had made with the One who'd created her.

But she could be cruel. With the *shamshir* blade in her hand, she hacked off Coolie's left arm. And while he was screaming and crying, she hacked off the other.

The audience was in disarray. Blood pooled against her feet. And though she couldn't speak, when she pulled the circus proprietor off the floor and made him face her—when she remembered his cruel sneer, his depraved appetites, his lies, and his betrayal—one word somehow did slip from her ancient lips. She placed her hands upon Coolie's face so that she would no longer have to look upon his gaping, howling mouth. And out of the depths of her rusted throat, rotten air from deep within her escaped her lips. Had she the ability to talk, it would have carried out a single command. The word echoed in her mind instead:

Die.

Coolie's life force bubbled and burned. His anima ignited until the man's body incinerated from the inside.

Hiva spared no one. Not the performers. Not the crowd. Astley's Amphitheatre sang with their ashes.

And so she carried on backstage through the hallways. Every performer. Every clown. The stagehands carrying props. The passersby who stuck their heads out of their rooms to see what all the screaming was about. Hiva spared no one.

Until she came to a room. A little room in a lonely little corner of the hallway.

She opened the door. And inside that room, a goose with fire-blemished white feathers looked up at her and squawked.

"Is that Iris?" came the voice of an old woman.

Hiva . . . wasn't sure what had happened to her in that moment she'd pushed the door open. She didn't have a name for the confusing flicker of emotion that made her eyes hot when she saw the old woman's coiled gray hair. The woman sat in the rickety wooden chair placed in the white room's corner, piles of costumes upon her lap. Each dress fell upon the floor when she rose from her seat. Her aged knees buckling a little, she held on to the counter table beside her to keep herself steady. But neither her weak limbs nor her bad sight would keep her from stretching out her arms toward Hiva with tears in her eyes.

"Iris? Iris! *Ọkọ mi*, oh you've returned!"

The old woman who'd come to be called Granny Marlow by the circus seemed to grin with her whole body, her face crinkling, her coal-black eyes wet with joy. Hiva stood very still as the goose waddled in between them, pecking her feet lightly before nudging her legs.

"What happened to you? Where have you been? Oh my darling, you're wearing so little; you must be cold!"

Hiva was neither warm nor cold. But as the old woman hobbled toward her, she suddenly felt flushed and aware of her own body. They were not family. They were not even the same species. And yet Granny Marlow inspected her with the care and love of a mother.

"There's so much I've wanted to tell you, girl. I've kept your letter all this time."

Letter? Hiva struggled to remember. For the first time since awakening, she *struggled*.

From the top of her green dress, Granny Marlow pulled out a parchment. And Hiva's crystal heart shook as Granny held it up and began to read:

"Dear Agnus, I have a confession to make."

In her mind's eye, Hiva suddenly saw a brown girl at a splendid mahogany desk, crying as the ink spilled from her quill.

"You were right. I was once a military woman of the Dahomey. Decades ago, I tried to kidnap you and your sister, Anne, in the middle of a raid. It was what we did."

Yes. Back during the early days of her past life, she had fought under a powerful king. She'd obeyed his command as She Who Does Not Fall while wandering the world—all to experience the folly of mankind. To gauge them. To gather the information she needed to validate her judgment to kill them.

"But as fate would have it, the three of us had another foe. And after an unsuspecting attack, we all ended up being taken to England as Marlows. As entertainment for Europeans."

Granny Marlow shook her head, lowering the letter. "Oh dear, I remember. I remember now. I'm sorry I ever shouted at you when you tried to tell me. I just wasn't ready to hear it."

Shouted, yes. Hiva remembered that battle, like peering through a window veiled in fog and sheaths of ice. But now Hiva fought a battle of a different kind—the one within her. As the old woman gripped her bare arms, an urge rippled through her, surging up without remorse until she was prying her ancient lips open.

There, in the room filled with fabrics, needle, and thread, as a goose named Egg toddled around the room, Hiva tried to speak.

The sound was labored. Painful. The air lacerated her throat. Coughs, gurgles, and croaks. It was as if she were drowning.

"Oh, Iris!" Granny Marlow gripped her face in sorrow. "What has happened to you?"

Hiva gripped her throat and tried again, but to no avail. *Granny. Granny...* Words of another her buried deep inside, tortured and filled with regret. The "her" that should have no longer existed.

By the time saliva began dribbling down her lips, Hiva gave up.

"You were never satisfied with who you were," Granny Marlow said. "You had a fire in you, girl, a desire to know yourself. Your past. Your kin. You always looked to me as if you'd do anything to discover the truth. But this . . ."

Granny Marlow wiped the saliva from Hiva's lips. "Is this what you wanted, Iris?"

Hiva's hands shook. Judging mankind required no words. She'd had no desire to dialogue with the creatures she hunted. Pure will—the will to create a better world. It was all she needed. So why now? Why did the silent words, dead upon her tongue, hurt her so?

"I've known so many versions of you now. The military woman who tried to capture my sister and me. The caged specimen who shared our exhibit. The innocent tightrope dancer who called me 'Granny.'" The old woman's eyes sparkled. "And now this."

Hiva's fingers twitched as Granny Marlow stroked the side of her cheek.

"But no matter what, my dear." Tears glistened in her dark eyes. "No matter who you are or who you choose to be, I forgive you. And I will always, always love you."

And the old woman hugged her.

Everything was wrong. Such a weak embrace, and yet Hiva felt as if her body would break apart at the woman's touch. Hiva shouldn't have felt anything.

Something between a whine and a whimper escaped Hiva's lips. She still couldn't speak. She didn't want to desire freedom anymore. Her mission was just. Her mission was absolute.

The end of humanity.

Hiva's mind reached deep within the old woman. She felt Granny's anima flowing within her.

No. The voice of the troublesome "her" whispering from deep within the shadows of her heart pulled Hiva away from the woman. It wasn't the woman who burned, but Hiva's own chest from her raspy, frenzied gasps as she struggled for air again. Hiva stumbled back, afraid.

"Iris?" Granny Marlow called her again. The goose nuzzled up to the old woman's leg.

Hiva turned and ran out of the room. Away from the theater.

Hiva had awoken inside the core of the planet as a killing machine. Perfect. Complete. There should not have been another version of her alive in her heart.

She had to bury it. For good.

Her weakness had all begun when she'd met that girl again in the Coral Temple. It'd begun when she'd let her live. It would have to end with that girl.

Hiva knew where she was. She could feel her anima, taste it, and smell it. The girl was nearing *that* shrine—the base where the Naacal hid the key to their greatest weapon. Hiva did not know how she'd discovered its existence, and it didn't matter. The girl's presence there made her intentions clear.

What Hiva had to do next was also clear.

Hiva purged her mind of any doubt and fear. She calmed herself and once again became firm. One of the Solar Jumps that the Naacal had built lay up north. Hiva knew them all intricately, for the mightiest of the Naacal's generals and the most powerful among their priests had shown her in a former life— back when they had believed her to be their god. It would not take long for her to get to her destination.

But as she stepped onto the lonely London Bridge, one man stood in her path.

That man.

His black cape flowing, his dark hair fluttering upon his head with the heavy wind.

His face twisted into a crazed, gleeful smile.

"I knew it. Iris . . . it's you," the young man said, clutching his chest as if his heart might fall out of it. "It's you. . . . It's—"

He threw his head back and laughed, tears in his eyes, before he ran to her, enveloping her with slender arms. Hiva did not move.

"As soon as I saw the eclipse, I knew. You're alive!" The young man's blue eyes shimmered wetly with so much relief, it must have overwhelmed him. "And you . . . you're . . . ?"

The young man cupped her face with both hands and stared deep into her eyes. He waited for something. For what, Hiva did not know. A reaction? A word? She only stared blankly at him. But this seemed to please him so greatly, the tears finally began to fall.

"You've finally returned. The true Iris. The one I read about in my father's research. The one I've been dreaming about since my boyhood. Hiva . . ."

His tears dripped down his grinning lips. And in that moment, he was overcome with emotion—so much so that he grabbed the back of her head and forced those wet lips upon hers.

"You've done it. You've answered your call! You've become who you were always meant to be. My Hiva! Once I found out what that wretch Maximo had done to you, I had your exhibit inside the British Museum burned. Your bones are gone. Now nothing can be used to kill you. Now we are truly partners. Now we are truly one!"

But when he leaned in to kiss her again, Hiva placed her palm upon his face and pushed him away from her.

Truthfully, she *had* wanted to kill him. She couldn't. He was the only one she was not allowed to kill. It was the bargain she'd made with the One who'd created her. How unfair after everything he'd put her through. His crimes went without repeating. How unfair . . . or so she thought.

But now she saw the weakness and cowardice behind his ecclesiastical ecstasy, and her stomach lurched with disgust. Now she knew he was not worth murder.

Hiva did not know this man.

"Iris! Iris? What are you doing?"

She said nothing, her eyes blank, her expression hollow. He was a strange lump of human flesh blocking her path for reasons she couldn't fathom. She did not look at him. She looked *through* him.

The longer she stayed silent, the more irritated and impatient the man became, until his eyes were flaring with desperation.

"I'm talking to you, Iris!" He gripped her shoulders and violently tugged at her. "*Me!* What kind of game do you think you're playing?" And when she didn't respond, his anger finally burst. "Who do you think you are? Who do you think made you?" Silence. "*Answer me!*"

His violent shaking didn't faze her. Brushing him off with ease, she began on her way.

"Where are you going?" the man yelled frantically as she walked away. "Where are you going, now that you've come back to me? After everything I've done to get you to this point? Everything I've sacrificed. There's too much we've yet to do to see this world burn!" He ran after her. "Iris! Don't ignore me! *I* am the one who brought you back. I *demand* that you—"

The moment the young man touched her waist, Hiva broke his arm. She did not know him.

Even as he twitched upon the bridge in pain, the man howled that name into the night.

24

ERTA WAS AN EXPERT SHOT, BUT she'd only been able to pick off a few of the soldiers before the boat capsized. Rin pulled Lulu out of the crocodile-infested waters while dodging the bullets. Pulling her sword out of her chest, she threw it with precision at the gunman nearest her, stabbing him in the chest, sending his bullet ricocheting through the trees.

"Hold your breath!" Rin commanded Lulu and Berta, not waiting for a response before she plunged herself and Lulu into the waters. The current slowed down the bullets—enough to avoid them, but not by much. She saw one whiz down into the deep, inches away from Lulu's face.

They swam for safer waters, holding their breath for as long as they could. Rin's white crystal sword could appear and disappear at will. It was a tiny blessing, as she used it to stab a crocodile in the neck. Lulu, whose hands clung to her for dear life, began shaking her head.

Just hold on, you weakling, Rin commanded while she swam, Berta following close behind. Her eyepatch slipped from her face and sank through the water as Lulu began beating her chest. *Hold on!* Rin thought, panicking. *Aren't you made of tougher stuff?*

Rin had had no one to help her when she was an orphan child. No one to save her when guns and machetes were forced into her hands. It shouldn't be any different for this little girl. Why should it be any different?

Lulu snapped her eyes open. There in the Kunene River, though her pupils must have stung, she kept them open. Rin could see the desperation within them.

She wouldn't be able to make it. They had to come up for air.

What do I do? Rin thought frantically. They'd been lucky so far. But once they came up for air, she'd be shot. In the military, she'd been forced to face impossible situations, but with a half-drowned child clinging to her side, her mind went blank.

Blank but for the powerful resolve to protect her.

The three came up for air, and Rin and Berta grabbed onto a floating rock near the shore. It was Berta who put a hand up, blocking her face as if it would protect it from a bullet.

"We surrender!" Berta shouted immediately, waving her free hand. "We surrender!" Then she whispered to Rin, "Hurry, duck behind the rock as much as you can. I'll handle it."

Rin balked. She'd *handle it*? What if she got shot instead? Rin's mind blanked as Berta continued to scream out their surrender. She held her breath, terrified, as she saw one soldier lift his gun anyway.

A man's scream pierced the air. Rin recognized the fury within it.

It was a war cry.

The soldiers looked in the direction from where it had come, but it was too late. They were already being bludgeoned with flaming sticks and rocks, spears, and bullets. It was an ambush.

"What . . . what the hell is going on?" Berta said, lowering her hand.

An attack. As the sun set, men and women—some dressed in farmers' clothes, some in soldier uniforms, while others had only cloths wrapped around their waists—fought the soldiers. Rin didn't waste the opportunity.

"Take Lulu and get to land!" she told Berta, passing the child to her before swimming to shore on her own. No sooner had she crawled out of the Kunene River did she begin swinging her sword. The ambushers watched her in awe but didn't stop their assault. Rin made short work of the remaining soldiers, cutting the limbs from those who had dared raise their guns again. Before long, the rest of the soldiers had fled deep into the forest.

The ragtag group of fighters raised their weapons and cheered. But when they saw Rin's sword disappear into white crystal dust, a hush fell over them. Exchanging frantic glances, they stared at her as if she were a demon. Her lips quirked into a wry grin. As if the blood she'd just shed wasn't proof enough.

A tall, slender man emerged from within the group. He had a stern, proud look about him, one that Rin instantly respected, though she stayed on guard. His black, coiled beard, closely shaven, reached up to his ears.

"Samuel," she heard the others call him, though Rin couldn't understand their language. But from their look of defiance, she could tell she was in their lands. The Herero.

The man spoke to her, first in his native tongue, then in German, frustrated when Rin shook her head.

"I don't understand," she said in English, and almost laughed at the irony of trying to communicate in a language she used to hate.

"You," said someone from within the crowd. A man dressed as a German soldier with a rifle in hand. "Where from?"

Someone she could speak to. The small cross-shaped scar on his sunken cheek looked fresh. Rin began to answer, but Lulu's wail cut off her words. Relief turned to dread as she turned and saw the child crying on the shore, clutching her right arm. Rin could tell Lulu had been holding her tears in until now. She knew all too well what it looked like the moment pain broke one's will.

"She's been shot," Berta said, and the words fell upon Rin like boulders. "It's not serious, but we need to check it out!"

Rin rushed to them, supporting Lulu's other side as the little girl gasped through the agony.

"It—it's okay," Lulu said. "I can handle it."

Something about seeing a child cry and bleed seemed to soften Samuel's men. Samuel himself nodded and spoke to the man who'd spoken English.

"Come quickly," the man said. "And bring the girl."

Even during the onslaught from the soldiers, Lulu had managed to keep the pouch safe. It was smart thinking from the girl and allowed them to explain their journey to Samuel and his men—at least the parts of the journey that were explainable to the common man. As far as they needed to know, they were on their way to Opuwo to retrieve a sentimental item for a friend.

But Samuel still seemed suspicious. Rin could tell by how they'd built this camp of makeshift tents within a forest, away from any village and out of sight, that their well-oiled attack against the soldiers hadn't been by accident. They were planning a rebellion.

"The Germans. They take our land and cattle," said the English-speaking man, who hadn't trusted Rin with his name. "They harm and force us to work."

Inside this tent, Rin didn't need any more words to understand. This was a revolt. Luckily for them, they didn't look like settlers. Though some worried glances lingered on Berta, they didn't question her as she helped one of the men in farm clothes extract the bullet from Lulu's forearm. The girl bit on a stick of wood to keep from crying.

"Lulu! Hey, kid! You okay?" Berta squeezed her from behind as the man wrapped her arm in white cloth. Lulu could only whimper in response.

Rin turned from them. "Tell Samuel," she said to the English-speaking man with the cross-shaped scar, "that we're strangers here. We don't wish to interfere in your fight. We simply want to travel to Opuwo."

Rin showed them John Temple's map and the land Uma had circled. A few of the men nodded their heads as if they knew the place. But Samuel laughed. He said something to Cross-Scar before the man faced Rin once more, his eyes narrowed.

"He said the place is guarded by soldiers," the man interpreted. Rin already knew this. It was land John Temple had purchased, after all, most likely from the German colonial administrators. Land that didn't belong to any of them. "He does not believe you are there on behalf of a friend."

Samuel smirked. Rin stared him down, unmoved.

"However," said Cross-Scar with a wicked smile, "he cares not for the property of white men. As long as you don't interfere in our battle."

Rin nodded and bowed her head in gratitude. And when Samuel extended his hand, she shook it.

"Samuel Maharero," he said, lifting his chin—taking in the sight of a fellow warrior, no doubt.

"Olarinde of the Dahomey." She said it automatically. But now, as the words escaped her lips, they sounded strange. Like her parents, she did not have a last name. But she'd stopped introducing herself as their daughter the moment she had been kidnapped and forced to work in the *mino* regiment. These people had pride—pride enough to fight to take their lands back. It was a cultural pride Rin couldn't claim, because she was neither one thing nor the other.

But at least I was her friend.

Samuel let them stay in their camp for the night. And while Berta slept outside the tent, inside Lulu stayed awake, likely from the pain. There wasn't an antidote ready to take it away. No herbs to make her sleep. She would simply have to live with the agony.

"It's the burden every warrior must face," Rin told her, sitting down next to the girl. They'd been given fresh clothes for their journey: simple blouses and farmers' pants that were too big for them. Lulu's clothes swallowed her up as she tossed and turned and bit her lip to keep from crying. At least she didn't have a fever. Rin had checked.

Aside from that, they'd only given Rin the long wooden smoking pipe she had asked for. It was half the length of her forearm. That would do. Rin used a knife to whittle down the bowl so that only the shank remained.

"It really hurts," Lulu said in a squeaky voice before bursting into tears. "My arm hurts! I'm tired and my hair's a mess!"

Rin lowered her pipe and arched an eyebrow. "Your hair?"

"It's a mess! I haven't been able to wash it. And I don't have anyone to do it for me anymore!" Lulu lowered her head. "My mama used to, but . . ."

Lulu's hair did look dirtier and unrulier than ever. Rin watched her sob. Sometimes when one was in distress, every little inconvenience felt like the world's end. But this child had truly witnessed horrors no child ever should. It was only now, after everything, that Rin had seen her shed a single tear. Rin lowered her gaze. *You're much stronger than I was. . . .*

"I'll help you," Rin finally said, whittling the wood from her pipe again.

Lulu sucked in a ragged breath. "Huh? R-really?" she stuttered.

"Once I'm done here, I'll wash your hair and braid it."

"Thank you," Lulu replied in a weak voice. Lulu's last few teardrops fell upon her quivering smile, which collapsed as soon as it had formed. "Oh, Miss Rin. I'm sorry to bother you. I'm such a wimp. I wish I were stronger."

"Ain't nobody stronger than you, kid," said Berta, who had just slipped inside the tent.

"Berta," Lulu whined, though Rin could tell she was happy.

Berta tossed Rin a nectarine before sitting on Lulu's other side and feeding another to her. Rin watched Berta, touched and perplexed all at once. She remembered the first time someone had scarred her right eye. How she'd wanted to cry then. She hadn't, thinking that she'd have been punished if she did. But now, as Lulu's little body quivered while she swallowed the sweet nectarine juice, Rin realized it had only been her assumption. She had assumed she would have been punished. She had assumed there wasn't a single woman in the regiment who would have reached out to help her. What else had she assumed while working under the king? What other assumptions had kept her from making connections that could have saved her soul?

Setting down her knife, Rin touched her newly re-bandaged eye. "Your scars are a sign of your strength," she told Lulu before taking the little girl's hand in hers. "Wear them with pride."

Lulu's hands felt warm. So did her smile.

25

THE TWO PARTIES SEPARATED, EACH ON their own journey. Through the plains and forest, and along the lakes, they traveled, until they reached the land outside Opuwo. The site Lord Temple had purchased. There it was, his manor, surrounded by seven hired guards with rifles strapped to their backs.

Thanks to Rin, Lulu's hair had been braided in several cornrows that twisted up to the crown of her head. Rin had used a string to tie them all so that the braids could fall down her neck in a ponytail. Fixing hair was one thing she'd learned from both her mother and the military women in Dahomey. It was something that connected both of her worlds.

Even with her injured arm, Lulu walked more confidently with this new hairstyle, courtesy of Rin. But now, as she looked at Lord Temple's manor, she scrunched her nose as if she'd smelled something foul.

"Looks like a slave master's house," Lulu remarked in disgust.

Or the abode of a colonial administrator. Though small and rural, this home had pristine white pillars and many arched bay windows underneath a gabled roof. Bordered by perfectly carved balusters was a porch for sitting, though, judging from the fallen leaves and dirt gathered there, no one had sat upon it for some time. Purchasing the land here to protect his discovered treasures made John Temple no better than the rest of the men who laid claim to land that didn't belong to them. Whether he ended up dying of disease or being murdered by his own son in hatred, Rin couldn't be moved to care one way or another.

But she was here for a job. There was no time to indulge in her loathing.

Hiding behind some bushes, Rin nodded to Berta, and on cue the girl ran into the camp, crying and begging for help.

"Oh me, oh my, I am a woman in distress!" she said, falling on the grass, her long brown skirt strewn dramatically as if she were the heroine of a novel. "I've lost my husband! I've been attacked by savages! I need your help!"

The soldiers didn't know what to do at first, but seeing a woman in distress made them hesitate to reach for their guns. They shouted to each other in German, and a few ran to Berta to check on her.

That was when the first dart flew. It hit the neck of one man, taking him down easily. Rin didn't think it'd be so precise. She'd outdone herself.

Berta screamed, holding on to one soldier so that his arms were occupied. "Help! Oh, help me! I am just a beautiful and helpless *lady* who needs you so, so *terribly.*"

Another dart. Another. Three of them had fallen before any of them realized.

Bottle trees in this region were very useful. The poison they used to retain water in the desert regions was also a boon to hunters against their prey. On their way to the site, Rin had smeared the poisonous sap across broken twigs, which now flew out of the whittled smoking pipe she blew into from the bushes.

Three soldiers crept toward the bushes, their guns now in hand. Berta stayed clinging to one of the soldiers as Rin silently readied her sword.

"Whether you close your eyes or watch is up to you, child," Rin said to Lulu, gripping the handle of her sword. "But if you do decide to watch, then watch carefully: for this is how you slay a man."

Rin was lightning-quick. She slit one man's throat and stabbed another before the first bullet could fly. Berta, still wrapped up in her dramatics, tried to pull her soldier back, but he beat her down, rushing for Rin. Rin ducked the frantic bullet of a soldier whose arms shook as he held his gun. He pointed again just as a gunshot rang out.

Berta's soldier fell to the ground dead, with Berta holding the gun of one of his fallen comrades. One quick slice to the chest from Rin felled the last soldier.

"Lulu!" Berta called out to the bushes, relieved when the girl peeked her head up above the leaves. "You okay? You didn't see all that, did you?"

"I seen a whole lot worse," Lulu answered in a matter-of-fact tone.

Rin folded her arms over her chest, impressed at her toughness. Lulu pressed her lips together and walked past the dead men, sparing them a glance before sucking in a breath and following Rin and Berta into the manor.

John Temple's home was empty. Even Uma hadn't been sure how to reach the Naacal's underground facility from here. But as Rin stood in the foyer, she knew she would be damned if she'd traveled through half the world to sit around in a hollow house.

"Let's split up," Rin commanded. "Berta, take Lulu with you. Search for whatever clues you can."

They spread out. Rin shivered at the eerie silence inside this home. Though the house was pristine from the outside, dust covered the twisting staircase of the rotunda and the couches in the living room inside. A home that had never been lived in. Frozen in time.

"What a waste of someone else's land," Rin muttered to herself, grimacing in annoyance.

It was in the living room that Rin saw portraits framed in gold upon the fireplace mantel. A brown-haired woman sat in a luxurious chair next to her three children, who were dressed in the uptight clothes Rin imagined all upper-class British tykes would need to wear for picture day. One girl and two boys, one son an infant in the woman's arms. The painter had added blush to their rosy cheeks to lend them a touch more innocence, as subtle as a halo over the head.

And there was something familiar about the blue eyes of the middle child, who stood on his mother's right in a black cloak and tam cap. Innocent but deeply intelligent. He stared straight ahead as if looking through the painting itself, focused and yet somehow missing from the moment all the same, captured by his own thoughts.

And then she realized—the boy was a young Adam.

It unnerved her, seeing Adam's boyhood captured in this place—and knowing that such a small boy would grow up to become an agent of chaos. But wasn't this how so many of the world's monsters started? All vile men of history had begun as innocent children. She wondered if Adam himself knew that this place existed.

In the corner of the green-painted room, next to a grand mirror, was a bust of John Temple himself, curiously separated from the portrait of his family. Covered in dust, like everything in this stuffy room. Rin checked everything: the cupboards, the desks. She looked for secret hatches in the floorboards and threw the cushions off the chairs. Nothing.

"Lulu went upstairs. Ain't nothing in the dining room," Berta said, meeting her back in the rotunda. "Nothing to do with the Naacal, at least."

"Right . . ." Rin couldn't help but stare at the burlap sack in Berta's hand, the one not occupied with the soldier's rifle she'd stolen. It was curiously filled with clinking metal, which Rin could only assume was cutlery, antiques, and whatever else Berta thought she could sell.

"Oh, this?" Berta followed her gaze, shrugging with a devilish smile. "Found this in the kitchen. Doesn't look like anyone's been here in a while, so I figured they wouldn't really miss anything."

"Like brother, like sister," Rin muttered under her breath, though with a smile. Shaking her head, she ascended the winding steps.

On the second floor were four bedrooms: one master, and three that seemed made up for children who would never see the inside of this home. Had John Temple planned to one day bring his family here? Or had this been his way of commemorating what he'd lost? The room for the infant was the eeriest. Black curtains draped down from the ceiling, over a baby's crib with only empty-eyed porcelain dolls placed carefully inside. Dolls were everywhere in this room—on the bookshelves, on the bed coverings. Even on the windowsills. Lulu took one of them from the crib, tugging at the blue dress and sneezing from the resultant puff of dust.

"How's your arm?" Rin asked.

"Fine enough to take a swing if I need to." Lulu flexed it, wincing at a sudden twinge of pain and drawing a little laugh from Rin.

"Don't push yourself," Rin said as she began checking the room—the dressing table and wardrobe, and behind the mirrors—before letting out a frustrated sigh. She didn't even know what she was looking for.

"John Temple's family lived here?" Lulu asked, setting down the doll to join the others in the crib.

"Maybe. Maybe not." Rin rubbed her hands on her baggy brown pants. "Doesn't look like anyone's lived here in a long time, if ever."

"I think that old man was lonely traveling around." Lulu looked up at the dangling chandelier. "But he thought about his family a lot."

Rin surveyed the room, lit by a crack of sunlight streaming in between the heavy window curtains. For all the dolls in this room, her eyes almost missed the porcelain figurine on the small wooden dresser drawer next to the bed. It stood out among them. Tall, about the size of Rin's hand, shaded underneath the bed lamp. Two children with white wings hugging each other upon a cloud. Rin did not know what had happened to the Temple family. Adam seemed the only one still living, and he was a raving madman. Was this what John Temple thought of his other two children?

Rin picked the figurine up but paused when she heard something shifting within. She glanced at Lulu, who sidled up to her and then shook it again. It sounded like . . . paper?

"Something's inside," Lulu whispered conspiratorially. "Maybe you should—"

Rin smashed the figurine against the table, causing Lulu to jump. It was instinct. Quick and dirty. And she was right. Inside was a roll of paper. But there was something else: a small disc the size of a coin, shimmering with iron and bits of white—

Crystal.

The lamp wouldn't turn on, so Rin held the coin in the sunlight. Whether it was Naacalian or not, she couldn't tell—the markings didn't look like any she'd seen in the scrolls or inside the temple. Instead, there were four lines bent at ninety-degree angles. Four *L*s etched into the surface. The other side was blank.

"Look at this!" Lulu said from the bed, holding the slip of paper. The writing on it was definitely John Temple's; it had the same slants and slopes as his chicken scratches on the map.

Lulu read it carefully.

> "To ascend to heaven, the Lord first descended into hell and conquered death.
> To find you, I must do the same.
> Are you in heaven? Is the New World our heaven?
> Sacrifices must be made for us to learn the truth that lies beyond our eyes. Our bodies. Our souls. And at one point, I had even thought that I could sacrifice you....
> Will I see you again in this life? I will find the answer.
> No matter how high the toll I must pay."

Berta burst through the doors with bright, blazing eyes, her sack seemingly several pounds heavier. "Found it!" she proclaimed with a wide smile. "The cellar!"

Rin gripped the coin in her hand and rushed out the door behind Lulu and Berta, following them down two sets of stairs that led to a cold cellar. The brick room was filled with hay and barrels of coal. Rin could see a bit of gold peeking out through the hay. Berta set down her loot and gun and began sweeping the rest away with her hands. The other two helped.

"Another Jump," Rin said, because she could see it clearly once the floor was cleared.

"Not quite," Berta said, and she was right. This Jump was much bigger. The three of them could stand upon it and still have room to spare. While Berta picked her rifle back up, cocking it ready, Lulu bent down and traced her fingers along the Naacalian symbols.

"The pouch?" Berta turned to Rin, who lifted it out of her pants pocket. The Moon Skeleton had survived the journey across the world, which meant they had their ticket inside.

The Jump began to rumble. With a burst of dust and hay, it began to glow, enveloping them in light. Rin let out a gasp as gravity yanked her from the inside and sent her rushing weightless through time and space into a dark shrine.

Where had they gone? Rin wondered. To heaven? Or to hell?

They would find out soon enough.

26

THIS HAD TO HAVE BEEN A shrine. Kings in robes and gods crowned with the rays of the sun were carved into the dark orange stone like the Egyptian pharaohs of ancient times.

Beyond the columns reaching up to the low ceiling was an altar made of marble that reminded Rin of Heaven's Shrine. The mural, unspoiled by the ravages of time, was painted in yellows, reds, and deep oranges—the colors spiraling to form the figure of a man, crowned by the sun, pouring blood from a cup onto the twisting flowers sprouting from the earth. *What kind of flowers needed blood to sustain them?* Rin wondered. Or was bloodshed, to the Naacal, necessary for the continuance of life?

Two torches stood on either side of the altar. Rin couldn't believe their fires still burned, so many thousands of years later. As she approached the altar, as she walked up the stone steps, she thought of the Naacal, a civilization she could only imagine from what their ancient texts and shrines had told her, and from Iris's tales of a past life gone wrong. Rin's body clenched, fully on alert, as she remembered the technological weaponry in Heaven's Shrine that had been designed to murder Hiva.

Here in this underground haven was an altar with a flat, circular dish placed upon it. And in the center of the plate was a shallow groove with four *Ls* etched in a circle—a perfect twin to the coin Rin had clasped in her hand.

To ascend to heaven, the Lord first descended into hell and conquered death.

To find you, I must do the same.

John Temple's words rang through Rin's thoughts as she placed the coin on the plate, making sure the lines matched up to the grooves etched into the silver. The altar shuddered.

The dish rose from the center of the altar first. Then an hourglass appeared, no taller than the length of her neck. The sand in the top half of the glass had already begun to pour in silence.

No murderous automatons. No metal minotaurs. Just an hourglass whittling down the seconds. The altar was waiting for them.

"What the hell is this? What are we supposed to do?" Berta grabbed Rin's forearm and shook her. The girl had clearly become too familiar with her. "Hey, Rin?"

"I don't *know*," Rin snapped back, yanking her arm out of Berta's grip. It was a miracle they'd even come this far with Uma's scant instructions and John Temple's indecipherable coded symbols. If only they'd been able to interrogate the man further before Uma had sent him off to Europe, to be guillotined by his unhinged son.

"It wants something," Lulu said, just barely able to peer over the altar. She gripped the ledge and stood on her toes. "That kinda looks like the collection plate we had in church."

Rin and Berta turned to stare at the dish as the sand slowly filled the bottom glass. Rin shifted uncomfortably on her feet. Lulu was right. The dish gave her goosebumps as it waited for her. Her muscles tensed as the eerie silence settled into the chilled air—silence, that is, but for the light trickling of sand.

The altar wanted something from them. But it wouldn't wait forever.

"Damn it, I don't get it!" Berta slammed her fists upon the altar, but neither the hourglass nor the dish so much as clattered. "What's it want?"

"An offering," Rin whispered, gently touching her missing right eye.

Her thoughts roamed back to the slip of paper Lulu had read, hidden within that angelic figurine. Two cherubs embracing. Two dead children.

Sacrifices must be made for us to learn the truth that lies beyond our eyes. Our bodies. Our souls. And at one point, I had even thought that I could sacrifice you. . . .

Will I see you again in this life? I will find the answer.

No matter how high the toll I must pay.

"Sacrifice . . ." Rin stared at the expectant dish. "Is that what you want?" She spoke to it, drawing nearer, her gaze never leaving its glittering silver surface. "But what kind of sacrifice?"

"Clock is ticking." Berta pointed at the hourglass, its bottom now half filled. "And after what we went through in Heaven's Shrine, I'm not keen on finding out what goodies they have in store if time runs out and we haven't given it what it wants."

"What kind of sacrifice do you want from us?" Rin racked her brain, curling her fingers on the table as time slipped past.

Lulu spoke up. "When I was in church," the little girl said, looking up at the two, "we had to memorize this psalm. Psalm Fifty-One. You know it?"

Berta made a face. "What? Why the hell would I? Didn't I tell you two I wasn't the praying type?"

And when Rin shook her head, Lulu sighed. "My mom made me memorize it, but . . ." Lulu paused, pressing a hand against her forehead. "Let me think."

Berta let out an exasperated groan. "Now, what the hell do your church lessons have to do with anything, kid?"

"Wait, let me think!" Lulu stomped the ground and shut her eyes. Then she started whispering. "'Have mercy upon me, O God, according to thy kindness . . . blot out my transgressions . . . and cleanse me of my sin.' Right?"

A prayer for forgiveness. As Lulu bit her lip and continued to recite what she remembered, Rin thought of the Naacal. From what Iris had told her, technology and spirituality were intimately connected for the Naacal. They had worshipped a sun god before they'd worshipped Iris. They had mistaken Iris for their sun god before she'd begun laying waste to them. She wondered how many had thought of Iris's destruction as a judgment from heaven.

It wouldn't have been strange. Lulu had mistaken Iris for an angel as well. And Adam—well, Adam's thoughts were impossible to discern, but his worship of her was clear.

Gods required sacrifices to appease them. They were an act of contrition.

The control device could power the Titans. The Titans were weapons of mass destruction that would blot out countless lives. Lives the Naacal felt necessary to eradicate if it meant ridding themselves of the cataclysm.

"'Blot out all mine iniquities,'" Lulu continued, still squeezing her eyes shut. "Er . . . 'teach transgressors thy ways,' I think—"

"What about money?" Berta turned to Rin. "You got any more of those coins? Damn it, I think I left the stuff I stole back in the cellar. . . ."

"'And my mouth shall shew forth thy praise—'"

"Stay calm," Rin hissed at Berta, who was gripping her hair and yelling in frustration. "Losing control isn't going to help in this situation."

"So, what is?" Berta threw up her hands. "You confident we're gonna be able to face whatever's coming if we don't give up the goods?"

No. She wasn't. Rin placed her hand over her heart. *What is it that you want? What else do I need to give?* And she touched her eye. *Haven't I given enough?*

"'The sacrifices of God are a broken spirit,'" Lulu continued. "'A broken and a contrite heart, O God, thou wilt not despise.'"

"Oh, is that all?" Berta leaned over and clasped her hands together. "Oh, please, please forgive me," she said in an exaggerated tone. "I've shot and robbed a few folks, sure, but I didn't really mean it! No hard feelings?"

Sacrifice. A toll to pay. Rin looked up at the mural—at the sun god pouring out his blood over the budding flowers.

"Sacrifice," she said, as the last few trickles of sand emptied out of the hourglass. "Our bodies. Blood . . ."

"'Then shalt thou be pleased with the sacrifices of righteousness, with burnt offering and whole burnt offering.'" Lulu opened her eyes. "'Then shall they offer bulls upon thine altar.'"

Rin summoned her sword. The white crystal blade shimmered, ready for flesh.

But it was Berta who gave it that flesh. Rin watched, startled and too slow to move, as Berta grabbed the edge of the sword with her hand and slit her palm. Blood flowed out into the dish.

"Miss Berta!" Lulu shouted, covering her mouth while Rin watched Berta's blood pour out, silent and shocked. While Rin stood paralyzed, Lulu went to work, ripping her sleeve to make an impromptu bandage.

Droplets of Berta's blood trickled down Rin's sword and onto the floor. Rin lowered it as Berta, wincing in pain, squeezed the last out of her palm. The reckless girl struggled a little with Lulu before finally letting Lulu yank her arm down so she could start bandaging the wound.

To Rin, it felt slightly violating, having someone else grab her sword with such authority. But more powerful than any sort of indignation was the annoyance Rin felt, when she saw Maximo's sister give her the same lopsided smile that mirrored her brother's.

"What was that?" Rin banished her sword, letting her fingers curl into fists.

"I wasn't about to watch either of you two do it. No way," Berta said.

Rin tried to scoff, but the air was stuck in her throat. "Trying to be a hero, huh?"

"I figured it was my turn to give something up, one-eye." Berta smirked before letting out another pained grunt.

The girl was nothing more than a selfish bandit, and her brother a murderer. Both selfish and dangerous, with their unchecked victim complexes. Neither of them could be expected to do the right thing. This was what Rin had convinced herself. But . . .

"It was my turn," Berta said again, quietly this time. "You've given enough."

There's no point in holding a grudge, Rin thought. Except it was Iris's voice she heard, chastising her like a mother.

Rin's fingers uncurled as the dish and hourglass sank back into the altar. "Thank you," she told Berta, too embarrassed to look her in the eye, as the altar rumbled.

"Now don't sprain yourself," Berta teased, gripping her twitching hand.

The altar stilled. Rin placed both hands on the cool marble and leaned over. The three girls waited, sucking in their breaths.

Then out of the center rose a glass cylinder surrounded by a burst of mist, like the first breath of wind on a snowy day. The altar may have been cool, but the glass was frigid; Rin withdrew her fingers from the brutal cold. The glittering glass shook and shifted open without the aid of anyone's touch. Enveloped in a cloud of mist was a stone tablet, made of shimmering ore the color of iron. The size of an adult man's hand in length and width, it seemed to exude a special kind of magic.

"Wow, it's the control device!" Lulu cooed.

Rin reached through the fog and pulled it out of the cylinder. The back and front of the tablet had two Naacalian symbols etched into them. The spiral at the top was the same for both. But the symbol at the bottom differed depending on what side of the tablet Rin looked at.

One she could recognize: the sun. It had to have been. A circle with rays drawn as triangles around it. And the other: perhaps this was the moon? A circle with three extra curving lines drawn on the left—perhaps the moon's phases.

One side with the symbol of the sun, the other with the moon. These were the controls through which to operate the Titans. The device was in her hands at last.

Rin smashed the tablet upon the altar so quickly, it made the two other girls jump.

"Whoa, what are you doing?" Berta spat, pulling Lulu away and glaring at Rin as if she'd suddenly gone mad.

"We have the Titan Control Device," Rin said, inspecting the undamaged key. "We got to it before that ghoul Bosch could. Now we only need to find a way to destroy it."

Rin ran her hand along the stone. Not even a dent. Whatever it was made of, it was tough. The Naacal had probably used some kind of special technology. To destroy it, they'd need to melt it down somehow.

"Miss Rin." Lulu tugged on Rin's shirt, but instead of answering, Rin lightly swatted her hand away. She was too deep in thought.

Would fire do? Or would they need a more powerful energy source? If only they had Jinn. With his flame breath, surely they could incinerate it. Or a furnace. Yes, Uma had one in her lab. Rin remembered seeing it in a corner. Would its power be enough?

"Rin!" Berta this time. Rin shook her off in annoyance.

Furnace. The Dahomey had a machine called the very same. It was the experimental apparatus that had given Rin her powers. If Uma's furnace didn't work . . .

But that would mean handing over the weapon to King Glele, who had already been willing to do business with Bosch. Not to mention, King Glele would have her killed on sight for trying to assassinate him. Rin clenched her teeth.

"Rin!" both Lulu and Berta shouted at the same time, more frantically than before, jolting Rin from her thoughts.

"What?" Rin hissed before her bottom lip curled shut. Neither Lulu nor Berta was looking at her. They were gaping at something behind her, their eyes wide and their faces bloodless.

That was when Rin finally heard the footsteps.

Step. Step. Step. Light. Delicate.

She turned around.

Time slowed to a crawl.

And all sound fell away.

Iris emerged out of the shadows behind them.

N-no . . . Rin shook her head, stepping back and flinching when her back hit the ledge of the altar. *That can't . . . This can't . . .* Rin's knees nearly gave out.

Lulu covered a gasp with a clamped hand. Stumbling back, Berta let out a frightened grunt, cocked her gun, and aimed. With careful steps Iris approached them, and with a measured expression she gazed at them.

Not Iris. *Hiva.*

She pulled out the dual *shamshir* blades strapped to her back.

"No!" Rin grabbed the barrel of Berta's gun and yanked it down. "Don't shoot."

"Are you crazy?" Berta's eyes were blazing. "At least we can slow her down!"

But Rin couldn't understand it. What was Iris doing? Why was she here?

And why hadn't she killed them yet?

It was strange. Iris didn't need blades to harm them. She could just burn them alive right now, like she had so many others before her. It would take less than a second. In just the blink of an eye, Rin could be reduced to ashes before even realizing that death had come.

So why? Why were Iris's footsteps so slow? Why did her grip on her blades look so tenuous? Why had her lips curved into an almost imperceptible frown? Iris was hesitating.

"Iris?" Rin stepped forward carefully. "Iris . . . you're still you, aren't you?"

As she spoke, Rin realized she was speaking to Iris in this foreign language: English. It didn't feel natural. It didn't feel right. And so she spoke with the words that had connected them in the past.

"Iris. She Who Does Not Fall. Child of the Moon Goddess. My friend . . ." As Rin spoke in Fon, she gripped the tablet in her hand so tightly, it cut off the flow of blood in her palm. "Why do you hesitate? If you wish to kill me, then kill me!"

What a careless command. It was a good thing she was speaking in a language Lulu and Berta couldn't understand. Berta, especially, would have tried to shoot her for being so reckless.

Still, Rin's impulse wasn't wrong. She could *feel* it wasn't wrong. This Iris wasn't ready to kill her. Even though she lifted her *shamshir* blade. Even though her eyes had become frigid and narrow.

"S-stay away from us, you devil!" Berta cried, pulling Lulu behind her. The little girl climbed underneath the altar. And Iris's eyes followed her.

For a moment, Rin's heart skipped a beat. "Lulu," she whispered fearfully, sticking her hand out to try to shield the girl from view—except the rest of her body couldn't move. The crushing reality of their mortality had never been any clearer than during this moment, as Iris stared at the little girl, hiding in plain sight, with a gaze that had turned curious.

"Iris, you said that you had wanted to create your own identity," Rin told her, speaking too quickly in Fon. "To live your truth. If the truth is what you want, then there's something you need to know."

Just one second. That was all it would take for Iris to kill her.

"Don't look at Lulu—look at me!" Rin cried, running down the steps and grabbing Iris's arm. "Leave the child be; she's innocent!"

As innocent I was all those years ago . . .

But Iris didn't respond to her tug. Her gaze remained on Lulu. And curiously, her eyes began to soften. She opened her lips. Nothing but gurgling escaped from them, as if her throat were filled with liquid. There was a sound, though.

An unsteady vowel Iris uttered without confidence, despite her urgency.

"Aah . . . Aah . . . ?" Iris tried for a while, and then stopped.

Iris really was unable to speak.

"Iris?" Rin waited, watching saliva dribble from the woman's lips. The woman once famed among the Dahomey. The woman who had once promised to give her a family. Rin shook her head. "The truth is that this isn't you. The truth is that we did this to you. Losing your voice. Losing your very self. This affliction of pain and death. It's a result of your friends being unable to stand by you. Unable to protect you. The truth is—none of this is your fault, Iris. It's mine!"

Tears glimmered in Rin's eyes as she remembered the way Iris had looked at them as they'd dashed for the bone sword. Her hopelessness. Her devastation.

"Maximo may have dealt you the killing blow, but it was I who couldn't save you that day in the Coral Temple. If only I had gotten to the sword first. Then I could have stopped Hiva's selfish machinations. I could have stopped Max from killing you and Jinn! And then this affliction, this curse, never would have—"

The *shamshir* blades fell from Iris's hands. Rin narrowed her eyes in confusion, for Iris's expression had rapidly devolved into one so human, Rin wondered if she'd finally returned to herself. No. She still couldn't speak. But the doubt and uncertainty in her eyes reflected an inner turmoil that couldn't have belonged to some unfeeling god.

Rin looked over her shoulder to Berta, who'd lowered her gun, and Lulu, still underneath the altar. Neither knew what to make of this. They were as lost as she was.

A coarse breath escaped from Iris's throat. A gurgle and a gasp. And then, finally, a sound. A sound that was unmistakable.

A word.

A name.

"J . . . Ji . . . Jinn . . . ?"

A tear rolled down the goddess's cheek.

It took Rin a moment to realize what was happening. The shock heavy in her voice, even in that one attempt to speak. Did she not know what Jinn had done?

Iris pulled herself out of Rin's grip, sidestepping Rin when Rin tried again. She stumbled backward, almost tripping over her fallen blades.

"Iris," Rin said, too frightened to take a closer step. "Jinn's life . . ." How could she explain to her? That Jinn had died trying to shield her from Maximo? That he was being kept in a suspended state of existence, only barely alive thanks to Uma's scientific genius? Would she even be able to understand? "Iris, let me try to explain what happened."

But this Iris was not willing to listen. Picking her *shamshir* blades up off the floor, she turned from them and fled down the hall.

"Iris! Wait!" Rin called, but it was too late. Iris was gone. The only tear she'd shed remained on the stone floor.

27

IT TOOK THEM DAYS TO RETURN to Uma's Lagos apartment using John Temple's map. Days in which Rin could barely eat. Days of Berta berating her with questions, which Rin, in her stupefied state, could only answer with noncommittal grunts.

"Why didn't Iris kill you? What did you say to her? Where is she going now?"

Rin's muscles were tight and worn. Her right socket twinging with phantom pains. Her mind swirling, because it was anyone's guess why Iris had left her alive or what she would do next. What she did know, as she burst down the steps of Uma's basement, was that she needed his help. She needed this man, trapped in his eternal slumber in this chamber filled with flowers, crystals, and ice. If she was going to save Iris, she needed Jinn.

"You've got it!" Uma said when Lulu took Rin's pouch and pulled out the tablet: the Titan Control Device. Her brown eyes sparkled from the glint of its surface. "I can't believe you did it. Not that I thought you wouldn't, of course; I've always believed in you formidable ladies, but to pull this off—"

Uma reached toward the device, mesmerized, but Lulu snatched it away before she could touch it. The child had good instincts.

With an impatient huff, Uma turned to her assistant. "Aminadab! Stoke the furnace, would you?"

Her hunched, mute assistant nodded. The furnace, a black metal monstrosity, had a little cage that Aminadab opened so he could jostle the coal with a poker. The fire roared up into a pipe that stretched through the ceiling.

"Little girl," Uma said in all seriousness. And though it seemed to kill her to say it, she said it anyway: "Take the device and throw it inside the furnace."

With that one command, Rin could relax. She nodded to Lulu, who pursed her lips with determination. Walking over to the furnace, she threw the tablet inside. The fires enveloped it.

"That's that," Berta said, dusting her hands off with a few slaps.

But Uma sighed. "One of the greatest discoveries of the nineteenth century, and I'll never be able to study it. I guess this is what it feels like to be a good person."

Rin smirked. "Something you might get used to?"

"We'll see." Uma scoffed before turning to her assistant. "Aminadab, that child has a gunshot wound," she said, gesturing toward the bandage around Lulu's forearm. "Find something to help her treat it. It might be infected by now."

Aminadab motioned Lulu toward him. But Rin's attention had turned from them. Here, in this busy lab filled with Bunsen burners and flasks and all manner of wondrous devices, Rin's gaze was on him—the brown-skinned man living in stasis beyond the pulled violet curtains.

"Jinn," Rin whispered. "We need him. We need him to reach Iris." She shook her head. "It's the only way."

"What do you mean?" Uma said before deducing the truth. "You saw her, didn't you?" Her eyes narrowed, her fingers pinching her smoking pipe a little more tightly. "You made contact with Iris again."

"But she didn't attack us. It looked like she would, but . . ." Berta sat on a stool next to the central table. It was a mess. Clearly neither Uma nor Aminadab had bothered to clean it up.

Uma shot the three of them an incredulous look. "She didn't attack you?"

Berta shook her head. "Rin said something to her in some other language. I don't know what. To be honest, I was so terrified, I could barely hear a damn thing except a weird buzzing in my ears. Probably my blood pressure. But after

Rin talked to her, Iris skedaddled out of there like she'd seen the devil." Berta scoffed. "What other devil's out there but her?"

"The other Hiva." Rin placed her hand upon Jinn's glass coffin. "There're only two people in this world she'll go to next. The other Hiva, or—" Rin stopped and glanced quickly at Berta before pursing her lips shut. "Uma, you once said you could bring this man back to life."

Rin tapped the glass cage with her fingers, and the flowers quivered. Then again, the petals were always swaying, if only just a little. The cold air being pumped into the case chilled the glass, but Rin could still see Jinn's handsome features through the frost.

Uma took a puff of her pipe. "What makes you think I should? You seemed quite hostile to the idea before."

"Iris's demeanor changed the moment I mentioned Jinn's name," Rin told her. "When I told her Jinn had 'died.' Before I could explain what I'd meant, she ran off."

"Hmm." Ringlets of nicotine smoke rose from Uma's lips. "Hiva isn't supposed to have human feelings. Then again, there's little we know about what Hiva is supposed to be. The cataclysm. Destroyer of man. But what does that really mean? The other Hiva seemed almost affable the last time we had a conversation, in Van der Ven's home." Uma rubbed her chin. "Not at all like the devil I imagined him to be . . ."

"Are you saying Miss Iris is still the same Miss Iris?" Lulu asked from the corner as Aminadab unraveled her bandages carefully.

"No—God no." Uma laughed. "How could she be the same Iris after everything she'd been through? But then who was Iris originally? The girl I met spying in the train station wasn't the same girl who felled countless civilizations. But she also wasn't the same girl I spirited out of London. And she isn't the same girl now. Who is she? That's the question she seemed desperate to know that night in the Crystal Palace, when I showed her the Helios. But perhaps that was the wrong question." Facing the world map on the wall, Uma lowered her pipe. "Perhaps the right question was always: Who does she *want* to be?"

Rin bit her lip in frustration. There wasn't any time for Uma's useless musings. Whoever Iris was now, she was on the loose. Her distress and confusion only made matters worse.

"I believe Jinn is the only way we can reach her," Rin said. "Jinn can bring her back. He can get through to her. I know it. And so . . ." Rin paused.

"And so?" Uma repeated, arching an eyebrow. She waited.

The time had passed for hesitating. Rin nodded, strengthening her resolve, and looked up at Uma, resolute. "Jinn can bring Iris back. So you must bring him back. Do whatever you can to bring Jinn back to life. Whatever monstrous medicines, tools, and devices you have up your sleeve in this lab, use it. We need this man to live again."

Rin half expected Uma to smile or shout in triumph, but she did neither. Uma looked as serious as she did. Everyone knew the gravity of the situation. It wasn't time for laughter.

"Very well then," Uma said. "In the meantime, I would suggest you stay here. If Iris is unstable, there's no telling what she'll do when she sees you again. She could spare your life, or burn you alive where you stand in seconds. Better not risk it."

"No." Rin stepped forward. "I should go and try to find her!"

"Are you crazy?" Berta got up from her stool. "Didn't you hear the woman? Why would you want to track her down? You do that, you might not come back."

Berta sounded frightened of the thought. But if she knew what Rin did— that Rin had inadvertently told Iris the truth about her murder, and *who* had murdered her—then Berta wouldn't hesitate. She'd flee this basement in an instant, using the Jumps to hunt Iris down before anyone could stop her. She'd get herself killed trying to shoot Iris dead. Though not before turning her gun on Rin first.

"Damn it," Uma said, after rummaging through a cabinet. "I've run out of opiates. I'll need them for the surgery." She turned to them. "Could one of you venture out into town and see what you can find?"

"Will do." Rin knew by Berta's arched eyebrow that the girl was questioning just how quickly Rin had volunteered, and Rin wasn't surprised when Berta lifted her hand.

"I'll go too."

Rin grimaced. "I move more easily alone."

Berta wasn't backing down. "Never know when you'll need backup."

A stalemate. Neither girl would give in to the other.

"Both of you go! *Goodness.*" Rolling her eyes, Uma nodded to Aminadab, who began gathering tools for the surgery. "Just get back as quickly as you can."

With an annoying smirk, Berta started up the steps.

Their search of Lagos had yielded nothing. Uma needed a special kind of opiate—something similar, according to the scientist, to Ayer's Cherry Pectoral, which contained a mixture of alcohol and opium. A tincture of laudanum would be helpful too, she'd said. But none of the medicine men they visited had everything they needed.

Medicine . . . "What about the hospital in Ajashe?"

"Ajashe?" Berta repeated after leaving a shaman's tent. "Why go all the way there?"

It wasn't too long ago that she'd been there, painstakingly asking the doctor about the details of various drugs and medicines before choosing one in her scheme against the Dahomey. She recalled there had been quite a few types of opiates on the shelves.

"We're going back to check." Rin didn't accept any complaints. She was going with or without her.

Thinking back to the day she'd drugged Jinn filled her with shame and regret. She'd stabbed an innocent man in the back. Worse still, it had been the betrayal of a friend, one who'd never done wrong by her. If it weren't for Iris, he would have been executed. *She* would have been executed. And yet Iris had forgiven her. It was more than she'd deserved.

What can I do for you now, Iris? There must be something . . .

The last time they'd gone to Ajashe, the bustling city had been reduced to a wasteland of ashes. It was the curse of Hiva. But that had been days ago. News of the city's sudden decimation must have reached colonial administrators by now—she could see officials and soldiers stationed at certain intersections of dusty roads, looking out for intruders—French, by the sound of their chatter. Of course they would take political advantage of this situation.

Rin was surprised to hear some broken English among them. It'd come from an unlikely pair. One was a woman with blond hair pulled back into a proper bun. Her high, white-collared blouse and long black skirt looked foolish here, in hot and humid Ajashe. She certainly didn't look like she enjoyed being here either. She looked lost, as if she'd meant to go on vacation, but she'd been lied to about the destination.

Her husband, on the other hand, was all business. In his decorated military uniform, he sniffed the air with his long, pin-straight nose, his elaborately curled mustache twitching each time. "The stench of Africa. It sticks in my nose like flies to feces."

Rin bit her lip, enraged, but though her hands curled into fists, she didn't move. He sounded German by his accent.

"General Lothar von Trotha, I'd heard you were traveling to the continent," said one colonial administrator, much shorter and stouter than he. "But I heard you were headed to the southwest to quell the Herero rebellions."

Herero? Rin unconsciously gripped her shirt; she was still dressed in what the small group of rebels had given her after saving her from the soldiers.

"And so it would have been my honor to destroy the African tribes with streams of blood and streams of money," Trotha said, and nodded as if his own validation was all he needed. "Only following such a cleansing can something new emerge, something that will remain. But my wife Bertha and I are here on other business."

His wife moved to show the colonial administrator some kind of card in her hand. It was golden and folded with black cursive ink inside. "It is an invitation from—" she began to say, but her husband quickly smacked her mouth. Whatever he said to her in German made her lower her head in fear.

"I would like to arrange transport to the Atakora Mountains."

"We'll do so right away, good sir," said the colonial administrator, nodding at a few soldiers nearby, who saluted and began to move.

The Atakora Mountains. Rin remembered Boris Bosch's elaborate facility and began to wonder as the married couple followed the soldiers down the empty streets. Why there? Why now? An invitation … was it just a coincidence?

Rin shook her head. She couldn't forget what she was here for. "Let's keep moving," she told Berta.

More soldiers were stationed around the city. But not all of them were European.

"Hey!" Berta cried, just before Rin covered her mouth and pulled her in an alleyway between two wooden buildings.

The *ahosi* were here. Several of them stood in front of a vendor's tent, its pelts of animal skins still dangling from the roof, with no one to sell them. She recognized them. But the one whose eyes almost caught hers sent a spark of fright coursing through her: Izegbe. The Dahomean military's best riflewoman. She stood there speaking to a younger soldier with her head shaved, her chest covered in basket-weave brown leather, her wrapped skirt the same dark blue as the others' uniforms.

Izegbe had helped Rin escape Bosch's secret facility in the Atakora Mountains. But that didn't change the fact that Rin was still a fugitive. She didn't have time to deal with any complications here.

Berta yanked Rin's hand off her mouth. "Get off me, damn it," she said, thankfully in a quiet hiss—as a bandit herself, even she could gather the delicacy of the situation. "You don't need to be so damn rough all the time."

"I'm sorry." Rin muttered her apology but kept her expression stubbornly stern. "We'll go through the back streets to the hospital to get what we need."

But Berta had a bone to pick. And like a dog with one, she wouldn't let it go so easily. "You've been acting even grimmer than usual. Don't tell me you're still planning to go after Iris?" she demanded as they made their way through empty, dusty alleyways.

"You convinced me not to," said Rin, stepping quietly on the cool sand. "There's no issue."

"Nah, there's an issue. There's something you ain't telling me."

Rin's heart gave an awkward thump in her chest. After one awkward glance at Berta, she concentrated her gaze on the hospital at the opposite end of the street. There were a few Dahomey warriors several strides away. With their sharp senses, there was no way Rin and Berta would be able to sneak past them. The only option was to stay in the shaded path between these tall buildings and wait for them to leave.

They had to be extra quiet. What didn't help was Berta punching her in the back, between her shoulder blades.

Rin grimaced. "You fool—"

"Tell me the truth," Berta hissed. "What is it you really told Iris that made her run like the devil was after her?"

Rin's throat tightened. With a nervous clearing of her throat, she turned and continued watching the hospital. "Nothing much."

"Nothing much ain't nothing."

"Just keep quiet if you don't want to get caught."

Berta made an irritated noise and piped down.

If only she knew.

Rin had told Iris the truth about her final death.

Max had killed her.

No, not only that. Rin had let slip that Jinn had been "killed" as a result of the ambush. And so she knew better than anyone here that there were only two places in this world Iris could head to next.

To Hiva, who'd orchestrated her and her lover's murder.

Or to Maximo, who'd carried it out.

Rin stayed silent. Perhaps for revenge. Perhaps to save her own skin.

Or perhaps because the fact that she could no longer look Berta in the eye bothered her more than she'd thought it would.

Minutes passed. The Dahomey women began to move. Rin had been so focused on them that she barely registered the shift of wind behind her.

She should have.

Berta let out a gasp. That was what made Rin finally turn. And when Rin did, her knees nearly gave out underneath her.

The blue swirl vanished just as Rin stumbled back and collapsed in shock against the wooden building she'd been hiding behind.

"Good thing we found you," Lawrence Hawkins told a spooked Berta, his loose blond hair fluttering in the wind. "And look, she's with Rin."

Another of Max's friends, Jacob, stood behind him and nodded. Despite the casualness of their words, there was no levity to be found in any of their expressions. They both looked as if they'd witnessed hell.

"Good," Jacob said, his brows furrowed in all seriousness. "Because we'll need all the help we can get."

28

T HE GERMAN SHIP HAD SEEN THROUGH the black smoke screen of the British forces, but Hiva was ready for them. The sailors stared aghast as Hiva burned the enemy soldiers to dust. Still, as some dropped to their knees in fear and others began praising Gladstone's secret weapon, Max wondered what they'd say if they knew that Hiva didn't care a fig for political alliances or national rivalries. That before he'd "seen the light," he would have just as easily roasted them like potatoes. Yes, the Hiva that now walked with him off the boat and crossed the Belgium shoreline had changed. But how much? Max felt he'd find out soon enough.

Days later, in Belgium, Max saw things he'd never imagined. None of his adventures had prepared him for the sight of workers unloading horses onto the docks, making sure each animal and each man wore cloths to cover their faces. No, not cloths—gas masks. They were everywhere. Guns and bombs and cannons of every kind. This was the war Adam had started that fateful day in Berlin.

It was a war with casualties, and not just the dead. As the sun sank behind the hills, they walked deeper into the woods, where a campfire had been set up. There, nurses treated soldiers whose limbs had been blown off; others still had wounds of the mind. Leaning against a beech tree, one soldier smeared what looked like mud and smelled like feces all over his face, laughing hysterically as he spoke the same six names over and over again.

"Anderson. Johnson. Kelly. Jeffries. Madden. Jobs. . . ."

"They were his comrades," said one soldier, Carl, who was dropping wood into the fire. "He was the only man left."

He sounded American. So even the Yanks had gotten involved? This war really was swallowing up the whole world. . . .

"Survivor's guilt, then," Max said, sitting down in front of a tent. Hiva watched the man with a curious expression, unfazed by the insects buzzing around his face.

"More than that." Carl rubbed his bald head. "This is a kind of shock I've never seen before. I'll tell you, the horrors I've witnessed during this war are unlike anything. And I'm not a stranger to battle, believe you me. But the kind of weapons we're using, the gas . . . it all feels too advanced. Too soon." He stoked the fire with a fallen beech branch and sighed as another man howled in pain. "If everything had gone right at the Berlin Conference, something tells me this never would have happened."

Maybe not. But from what all the newspapers had said, that Conference had been a preparation for war in and of itself—war against people of a different continent, whose lands and resources these grand European powers had wanted for themselves. The evil they had been wholly prepared to inflict upon Africans—conquering and pillaging and enslaving across the continent with the stroke of a treaty—how was that any less of a crime than what they were now doing to one another?

It didn't seem as though Carl was ready for a debate. He was preoccupied with only the horrors he could see. "A war like this feels decades too early."

"And yet here we are," Max said, waving off a man who offered him a cigarette. He took the beer, though.

Carl watched the man rock back and forth. "And yet here we are."

So this really was hell. Well, Max had known it would be—otherwise he wouldn't have come here to die. How ironic. He was dead, while others here were still desperately clinging to their lives. Max stared into the crackling fire with a wry grin. He was an asshole. An asshole to the end. If Cherice were alive, she'd kick him in the 'nads.

Oh well. He didn't care whether it was childish or selfish. It was his choice.

But war—nobody chose that. Adam had chosen it for them with his endless scheming. With his dreams of death.

"Anderson. Johnson. Kelly. Jeffries. Madden. Jobs . . . !"

"Let's just hope that friend of yours is up to the task," Carl said, his eyes on Hiva, before leaving them to help one of the nurses.

"Kelly. Jeffries. Madden. Jobs . . ."

Max covered his ears. *Is this what you wanted, Adam, you prat?*

"Hiva," Max said to the golden god when the night grew still and quiet. "I thought about your question: what is the meaning of life. Right?"

Hiva kept his back to him, blocking the heat of the fire. "And?"

"It ain't this. I want something better."

The gentle sound Hiva made, his sigh of sadness, felt to Max as painful as mocking laughter. "So the world that men have created is a failure, once again."

To the side of the tent were rows of men on blankets, some dead, some maimed, some barely clinging to their miserable lives, all underneath a blinding moon and a pantheon of stars that couldn't care less about what humans did to each other. In a few hours the sun would rise; a few hours more and it would sink beneath the hills once more, and the stars would blanket the sky again. The world would keep turning. Men would still ruin each other.

"Instead of trying to drown and maim you, maybe I should have just let you kill us all." Max's wry smile disappeared as quickly as it had formed. He hesitated. "I'm . . . sorry, Hiva."

Max wasn't sure what he was apologizing for. Hiva was a god of death. But to this Hiva, who watched the dead in silence, Max felt compelled to apologize. In that confusing moment, in the midst of pain and suffering, he had to apologize for that which he'd inflicted with his own hands. Hiva seemed surprised to hear it. His golden eyes widened slightly before his shoulders relaxed. He looked, then, just like any man seeking peace.

"Being hurt by the world makes one want to hurt others in return," Hiva said, and for some reason the words—though spoken without malice—felt like an indictment. "Even if the vices of men were to vanish, this sorrowful truth alone would keep humanity spiraling in an endless cycle of pain and destruction. Perhaps that is the cataclysm."

Max stared at the palms of his hands. "What will it take for us to stop hurting one another?"

Hiva turned to him. "I've spent many lifetimes searching for the answer, but I could never find it. I came here hoping that would change. An impossible dream, perhaps."

Max shook his head. "I just can't imagine a world without suffering."

"Maybe that is the problem, Maximo." Hiva looked up at the moon. "We cannot imagine."

Max had no training. There was no time. But he'd been given a gun. It was more than enough for his role as the Hiva-wrangler. The other soldiers barely had time to spare him a glance. As they walked down a dirt road, away from the woods and into the countryside, Max heard explosions rumbling through the earth like thunder. Smoke shielded the sun on an already dreary day—a few villagers from some besieged nearby town fled past, carrying their possessions and trying to avoid being hit by shells. Some stumbled in puddles that had once been craters, which were now filled up with rain.

Wounded men were left by trees, crying for help. Other soldiers tugged on the reins of horses and mules carrying carts of artillery.

"Oh Lord, just take me!" one man wept as blood gushed from his missing leg. "Please just take me! Kill me, damn you!"

So this was war in the daytime.

A soldier grabbed Max's shoulder. "We're here to take you to the dugout," he said, looking beyond Max's shoulders to Hiva. "This is him? The secret weapon?"

Hiva hadn't tried to hide his hair or his pupilless golden eyes. Anyone could tell he was different. In normal times, a man would have scoffed at the idea of some wizard from another world, come to save the day. But these weren't normal times. The soldier looked as though he'd accept Oberon's help if the king of the fairies leaped out from the pages of Shakespeare in front of him. "Come now. Hurry!"

Bullets flew across them, narrowly missing Max's head, as they approached the entryway to a muddy dugout—no, a trench. That was what the men here called it. Deep in the earth—mud and bits of brick, sandbags, and wood to protect them from the bombs that exploded mercilessly wherever they landed. Max's heart leaped into his throat, and he dove for cover at the sound and impact of a nearby explosion. Debris rained upon his head.

"So where is it?" Shaking the dirt off his bald head, Carl grabbed Max's arm. "The miracle we were promised? General told us this one can kill fifty men without even moving an inch. Is that true?"

Max watched Hiva observe the mayhem around him, but the so-called god's eyes were unfocused. Almost as if the soldiers were the least of his concern. Indeed, he lowered his gaze, staring at the mud and debris from the bomb. Max could tell from his quickly shifting gaze that he was disturbed. By the front lines? Or by something else?

"It's true," Max answered, watching Hiva mouth something to himself. One word. He couldn't hear it. "It's true, but—"

"No buts. The soldiers here have been braving the Germans' onslaught for weeks. You step onto the field, and you'll get picked off by one of their guns. The enemy trench is hundreds of yards away, but that shouldn't matter to this 'secret weapon' of yours, now, should it?"

It didn't. Not quite. As long as Hiva was close enough, he'd feel their anima. As long as he could feel their anima, he could burn them alive.

"All right, tee him up," Carl said, pushing Max roughly toward Hiva. "Give him a command, knock him on the head, whatever you need to do to make Spot jump and wag his tail. Do it. Do it now!"

Max hadn't seen it last night, but now it was clear as day—the creases aging Carl's face. He was worn and his eyes bloodshot. And he wasn't the only one. While men ducked explosions, Max could feel their eyes on these two strangers who'd promised them a miracle.

Max gripped Hiva's wrist. "You said you couldn't save the children before," Max told him. "This is your chance. We'll start here. Get rid of the other side and—"

And what? Would killing a bunch of soldiers really bring peace? Wasn't that the lie everyone told to justify starting another war?

And what about Max? He was already a murderer. Was it okay to condemn more men to death? Would that wipe his slate clean?

Would death?

Max took his shaking hands and clasped his head. He had to keep Hiva in check. At least if he could convince Hiva that he was doing good, he could take away the god's murderous designs on humanity.

Take away his murderous designs . . . by making him murder?

Max shook his head. "I don't know," he said as explosions tore apart the land between trenches. "I don't know what I'm doing here. . . . I don't know what to do. . . ."

But soon it was Hiva's grip on his shoulder that jolted him from his internal crisis. Hiva's eyes had grown wide, the shape of glowing orbs, as intense as the sun. The flowers in his hair stood alert as his lips dried and cracked right in front of Max.

"The time has come," Hiva whispered. "As I knew it would."

"What are you talking about?" Max hissed, wearily eying Carl and the rest of the worn soldiers hiding behind the trench, waiting for their miracle. "What do you mean—?"

"She is here." And Hiva's voice became very quiet—more silent than a whisper. "Revived by the One who made her. She's arrived on the battlefield. She's come for us."

"What the hell is that?" cried some soldier from far off.

The soldier stood upon a ladder, his gun pointed over the trench wall. His mouth hung open, but he wasn't the only one. Other soldiers on their own ladders could see what he'd seen. They saw the land stretching beyond the trench, and their faces paled. Whatever they'd spied was worse than a bullet or a bomb.

"She's come," Hiva said again. He spoke as if he had no breath. As if the words had come in spite of him. He kept his face from Max, but his bottom lip was still visible, twitching like his golden fingers. He spoke with his limp arms resigned at his sides.

The fear that had seized Max on the ship returned with a vengeance; this time it'd burrowed under his skin like a tick. It wasn't going away. Max refused to believe it. Not because he didn't believe in miracles. Not because he didn't know the dead could come back to life.

But because he was afraid.

He was afraid for his own life.

His heart beat in his ears as soundly as the drumbeat of retribution. Max pulled down a soldier from a ladder and climbed it himself.

He refused to believe.

And yet there she was, walking across the dead flatlands. No bullet could stop her. And the blast of the bombs would not sway her.

Max felt his body numb as he said her name just once, a word as sharp on his tongue as the blade of a knife.

"Iris."

29

MAX HAD BEEN TAKEN FROM HIS home as a child. He'd lost his sister. He'd been chased by police, threatened, blackmailed, and almost killed. He'd been tortured. He'd faced horrors the common man would never know about. And yet as he stood upon that ladder, staring over the trench wall, Max had never been more terrified than in the moment when his eyes met hers.

Iris. She looked just as Max remembered her. Slender and beautiful, with just an ethereal slip the color of sunset covering her from chest to buttocks. When Max squinted, he could see something glinting behind her. He couldn't make out what it was, but it didn't matter. He could barely tear his eyes from her. Iris. Iris was alive. Iris was coming.

Coming for *him*.

She was more than a hundred yards away, and yet her gaze never left him.

Max's heart began thrashing against his chest as fractured memories rushed through his mind. Lunging for the bone sword. Feeling the rough surface against his skin. A snap decision drowned in his aching loneliness—in his desperation to never be alone again.

The sharp end of the bone messily burrowing into flesh.

"Hiva!" Blood rushed from Max's face as he turned behind him. With his eyes flashing, he stared down at the turncoat god. "You said the only thing that could kill Iris was her own bones!"

"Yes." A frustratingly short answer. This wasn't the same Hiva he'd seen in the Coral Temple facing Iris, his hatred shining through. This wasn't a god. It was barely a man.

"Then how is she bloody alive?"

"This was the decision made by the One who created her."

"What?" Max was screaming now. "What does that even mean?"

But Hiva, barely a god, barely a man, was more like a child resigned to his scolding. Perhaps he'd always been like this—limp and feeble in the presence of the *true* death god of this world. The grand villain who'd hunted down Iris was nothing more than a child throwing a tantrum, desperate to punish his sister for hurting his feelings but unready to deal with the blowback.

Blowback.

Max felt suddenly off-kilter on the ladder. Light-headed, he felt his body begin to sway. What was it that he'd seen in Iris's unmoving gaze? Was it . . . hatred?

She was too far away for him to see it for sure. Surely it hadn't been hatred.

But if it was—

No. Did she hate him? No, no. She understood. She knew why Max had done what he did. She understood the position he'd been forced into. To avoid a bloody future. To avoid her descent into the cataclysm she had been before, he'd had to kill her.

But it hadn't worked. She was here now. She was here, and she wasn't herself. He could tell. He could tell just by her steady stride across the dead grass.

Even if she could forgive him for killing her, could she forgive him for killing Jinn?

Jinn. Just thinking of his name, remembering the way his body had slumped on the floor, sent a shiver down his spine. No. No, how could she forgive him when he couldn't forgive himself?

The woman making her way through the flatlands. Who was she? Iris or Hiva?

It probably didn't matter anymore.

Oh God. Max grabbed a fistful of his curly brown hair and let his hand slip down his sweaty face. *Did I do this?*

"Wait—boys—you hear that?" Carl said to his fellow soldiers, because after a minute had passed, a strange silence had descended upon the battlefield. Where was the high-pitched screeching of the bombs whizzing by? Where were the explosions?

Max felt a hand unceremoniously tug him down from the ladder so another man could race up it. Other soldiers were doing the same, peering over the battlefields. No gunfire. Nothing.

"Who is that woman?" someone asked, but for most of the men who'd been besieged by enemy gunfire for weeks, a woman on the battlefield was the least of their concerns.

"Is it a cease-fire? I can't hear nothing."

"The bombs have stopped. The bombs have stopped!"

"What about the Germans?"

And next to Max, Hiva stirred. "She's killed them," Hiva answered with chilling calm.

Someone might have heard him. Or perhaps not. Perhaps, in this heightened state of battle where lives were on the line, they felt the sudden absence of human bodies as keenly as Hiva did. But this was the first lucky break the soldiers had had in weeks. So as Max stared at Hiva in frightful silence, the men began to stir and gather up their weapons.

Carl grabbed Hiva and pulled him into a bear hug that under normal circumstances would have embarrassed them all. Max was next. The man's vise grip choked the air out of his lungs.

"I don't know what you did, boy, but you sure did something." Carl clapped Max's back hard, drawing a hoarse cough out of his throat. With a naïve, all-encompassing relief, Carl stared between the two of them, man and god, and grinned as if on the brink of tears. "You both did it."

"Fire into the enemy camp! Full assault!"

Bombs flew from their side across the fields, exploding with no return fire. A boon. A miracle, as far as they were concerned.

Max covered his ears and crouched behind the trench wall, feeling the vibrations through his bones. A one-sided attack. An embarrassment of riches for Gladstone's men and their allies. Minutes had passed when the last bomb exploded and hissed into silence.

"Gather your guns! We're launching a full frontal assault, boys!" Max heard someone say. "Make sure you pick off anyone who survived the attack. We're going for victory!"

"Victory!" the men screamed, cocking their rifles, waving the weapons in the air.

And why wouldn't they? The longer time dragged on, the more courage they gained from the other side's silence. There was nothing to mind about the woman on the battlefield. She could be taken in for questioning—and then maybe comforting.

Hollering as if they'd already won the battle, the soldiers climbed over the trench walls and began their race toward the enemies. Very few stayed behind. Max hid in a corner, his breaths haggard, his heart beating in his ears, crouched with his hands still covering his ears.

"I'm seeing things, right?" he muttered to himself while filthy boots shuffled up the ladder next to him. "That wasn't her."

"It was."

Hiva.

"Sod off, will you?" Max spat while four men standing behind him pored over maps excitedly, discussing their plans after winning the battle. "If you're not going to talk any bloody sense—"

"Nothing about my existence here is rational. None of it, as you would say, makes any *sense*." Hiva looked up at the trench ledge, the battle cry of excited soldiers shaking the heavens. "Our creators are not the same. I was born on a different earth. When I first came to this earth, I came to my sister for help—a way out of this endless cycle. I voluntarily became her enemy only because I disagreed with her mission—the mission she was made to achieve by the One who created her. A mission she wouldn't abandon. I then chose to return out of vengeance. Each time, I made a decision. And each decision was made from emotion, not sense."

"I thought," Max said, sliding up the trench wall, "that you so-called Hivas were just unfeeling monsters. Killing machines."

"So too did I once, my friend."

Max's eyebrows arched up to his hairline. "What . . . did you just say?"

"Yes. I call you my friend, because there is no other entity, in any of the dimensions I've traveled to, with whom I have been able to express myself so freely. No one else on any earth. Not even sister. Especially not sister."

The soft smile upon Hiva's lips stopped Max's breath in his chest.

"I thank you," Hiva added, and Max could tell that he'd meant it.

When Hiva looked at him with such tenderness, Max's face flushed with confusion. Suddenly Max realized that the sounds of the soldiers aiming to ambush the Germans had disappeared. Their triumphant battle cries had vanished.

"I once thought I had been born only to complete my mission. But now I see," continued Hiva, "that I was wrong. Yes, the answer is so clear." Hiva looked up at a flock of white birds flying through the darkened skies as an arctic caress slid across Max's tight chest, paralyzing his lungs. "We are who we choose to be."

Iris jumped down into the trench, her feet landing with the grace of a dancer. When she shook her head, ashes fell out of her long braids.

Max couldn't breathe. The blades on her back, the ones she and Jinn had once used to twirl around in their circus act together, glinted against her back, begging for blood. He stumbled backward until he was pressed flat against the trench wall, while the four soldiers behind Hiva dropped their maps and their plans in surprise.

"Who's this woman?" said one soldier, picking up his rifle, which had been resting on a pile of dirty sandbags. He lifted it. "Stop right there, you—"

Iris's hand found his face, clamping his mouth shut. She burned him alive as he screamed in agony.

"What? *What?*"

"It's some kind of *devil!*"

More of the soldiers who had stayed behind began shooting. Barely able to catch his breath, Max squeezed himself into his corner, watching as Iris brushed off the bullets tearing through her flesh like mosquito bites. The last he'd seen her, it'd taken minutes, sometimes even hours, for her to revive after dying. Now her healing speed was nearly simultaneous with her injuries. Like her body, the slip she wore was of a material not of this world. Every tear mended itself. It was as if she were wrapped in the heavens. As if the very stars were on her side. Not even a bullet to the forehead stopped her as she burned several men alive with a twitch of her head.

In that moment, Max vividly remembered his mother. Her long brown hair, her hopeful brown eyes whenever she'd kneel down in their little hut, clasp her hands, and pray to a statue of Mary upon the wooden ledge in their kitchen. He couldn't remember when he'd stopped praying. It hadn't been after he went to Europe, nor had it been when Berta was taken from him. And now, as he curled up in this corner, he could not recall when his lips had begun muttering the Hail Mary prayer in the same Spanish his mother always had every morning before breakfast. Before he knew it, the words were flying out of his mouth, quiet but sure, each word a reflection of his guilt and his pure terror.

They only stopped when Iris's furious eyes met his.

Raising her arm, she reached for him as if to tear off his head. Max held his breath. Hiva gripped her wrist.

"Your quarrel is with me, sister."

Iris tore her arm out of his grip and lunged for Max again, only to be thwarted by Hiva a second time.

"It was I who set the stage for your betrayal and murder," said Hiva, his golden eyes flashing. "I who incited fear and hatred among your friends. It was only fitting. During the age of the Naacal, I had hoped so desperately to forge bonds, but you tore them from me. And so I would tear your bonds from you. That was what I set out to do when I reached this earth again."

Was Hiva . . . making *excuses* for him? No, Max could only think it because his fear had paralyzed him to such an extent that he could not move his lips to form words. *I was the one who killed you. No matter who set the stage, I made the decision to betray you for the second time. . . .*

Iris opened her mouth, and Max expected a tongue-lashing. But what he heard instead made his blood run cold. The sigh she'd exhaled from her lungs sounded like ghosts rustling within a dead graveyard at night. Like the dust of ancient bones. A dribble of saliva dripped down her bottom lip.

"I see. This is the sacrifice you made to return and exact your revenge," said Hiva, still struggling to hold her in place. "The 'Iris' that you once were told me her dreams in defiance; in defiance of all who sought to confine her, she asserted her 'self.' But you are but a shell of her. You cannot assert your dreams, your identity, your grievances. You can't even speak."

Iris backhanded Hiva so hard, he flew into the trench wall. Max flinched from the impact, biting his lip. He tasted the thick, tangy blood. Debris tumbled over Hiva's head, but he was unfazed. Slowly, Iris reached for the *shamshir* blades strapped to her back. She threw one upon the ground in front of Hiva and grabbed the handle of the other.

A duel to the death.

For a time Hiva looked at it. The two gods stood there, in the trench bred for war, the ashes of men speckling the earth between them. Silently, he took the handle of the *shamshir* and got to his feet, the weeds in his hair shivering.

"If I could have burned you alive, I would have done so a lifetime ago, when you sent me spiraling in misery through dimensions. The only weapon that can kill Hiva is the Hiva's own bones. It is the same for me. It doesn't make sense to battle in such a way."

Hiva stared at the handle with a solemn sense of the weight of whatever fate had brought them to this moment. Then, for one split second, Hiva looked over his shoulder to Max, cowering in his corner.

Looked over at him and smiled.

"Then again, decisions are often made from emotions, not sense."

The collision from their clashing blades sent shock waves through the trench, each so strong that Max felt as if his bones would shatter. They were so fast, his eyes could barely follow them. Slurping in breaths, he slid against the trench wall, but there was no direction he could slink off to in order to stay out of their way. Iris pushed Hiva down the long, narrow stretch and brought her blade upon his head, only for Hiva to block the blow and punch her in the stomach. Blood gushed from her mouth and from his eyes, where she'd bashed the handle of her *shamshir* against his temple.

Every blow was one that Hiva took in Max's place. Max couldn't bear the knowledge.

"I asked you once: Isn't there another way, sister? I asked you back then, and you wouldn't even listen to me. *The truth is as it shall always be.* But what is truth? What is justice?"

Iris's blade strike was quick. It slashed against Hiva's chest and would have severed him in half if Hiva had not jumped back.

"The truth before you is that you were betrayed," Hiva continued, spitting out blood. "And so you've given up. You've decided that all humanity must pay as recompense. But what if that isn't the answer? What if we've both failed in our true mission?"

He threw dirt in Iris's face, blinding her momentarily. But when he leaped upon her, Iris must have heard him, even though she couldn't see. She blocked the strike from his blade and kicked him up in the air over the trench wall. Hiva grabbed hold of that wall, lifting himself upon sticks and dirt. Iris followed, jumping into a high backflip that only a tightrope dancer could perform with such grace upon the opposite ledge.

The gathering dark clouds crackled with energy. There were no whizzing bombs, no gunfire. This was true thunder this time, as if the skies had cursed their battle. One raindrop. Another. Max felt the cool water plunk down upon the tip of his nose. Then the rain began to fall in a sudden, angry rush. If there were a real God out there, he must have meant to drown them all. Max's lips curved into a sarcastic grin before he thought of his mother and shivered in the cold.

Mom, I can't believe I'm rooting for Hiva, he thought to himself. And tears fell from his eyes, because he'd done this to her. He'd done this to Iris.

Blood and rainwater mixed down the edge of her blade as she stared across the gulf that separated her from her other half. The sun and its shadow—except Max could not tell which was which. All he could see was darkness and the promise of death.

"I chose revenge too, once," said Hiva, "because I still could not find another purpose—another reason for my existence. Now I've turned away from such things. I no longer wish to kill. That is why I now understand her. I now under-stand the 'Iris' that you once were."

Iris said nothing. But upon the wall of the trench, her grip on her blade trembled.

Hiva's grip, on the other hand, had never been stronger. His golden, pupil-less eyes stared across the chasm with the certainty and determination Max once saw in Iris.

"I no longer wish to kill"? It's the same for me. The salt trickling into Max's lips told him his tears had joined the rain droplets sliding down his cheeks. *I don't want to kill. I don't want to hurt anyone anymore.* Max squeezed his hands into fists.

"Sister," Hiva called over the crackling thunder. "I do not know who I am, nor who I should be. But what I do know is this: I cannot let you kill this boy."

I don't want to hurt anyone anymore.

Hiva and Iris bent their knees at the same time. Both prepared to end it.

I don't want to hurt anyone . . . and I don't want anyone hurt because of me. . . .

In his mind's eye, Cherice winked at him with that precocious smile.

No more!

The two Hivas leaped at each other, launching through the gray sky, their weapons drawn. And at the same time, Max threw himself to the ground and screamed so loudly, he could feel the flesh in his throat tearing.

"I'm sorry, Iris!" Kneeling, he shook his head, trench dirt gathering in his fingers as he gripped the earth. "I'm sorry I killed you. I was wrong. I'm sorry I killed Jinn. It was an accident! I'm sorry I betrayed you. I'm sorry for all of this! I'm so sorry! I'm *so sorry!*"

What was it that Max thought he would achieve? An armistice? A stand-still? In that moment, all he wanted was to stop feeling the toxic guilt and fear melting him from the inside. He wanted her forgiveness. He wanted absolution.

What he'd done instead was serve as a distraction. It hadn't been his intent. He didn't think that Hiva cared so much that he would look down in concern for his "friend." But that was the diversion Iris needed. Max heard his name from the god's lips: "Maximo."

When Max looked up again, Iris was already slicing off Hiva's head.

It landed with a thump next to him. Bile lurched from Max's stomach out of his mouth as he scurried away on his back, desperate to widen the distance between them. Hiva's body landed next, then Iris lightly upon her feet after it.

But what was this? Hiva wasn't dead. Of course he wasn't. Hiva couldn't die, not unless his own bones were used to kill him.

Was that why Hiva's lips still moved?

It was impossible. It must have been Max's imagination. Hiva had no throat. There was no air through which he could form words. But Hiva spoke nonetheless. In slow, steady words, he said only one thing:

"Sister, we are not gods. We are—"

Iris drove her sword through his skull. Hiva spoke no more.

Max gripped his own head, wanting to shriek but unable to summon the strength. Iris kicked over Hiva's body and drove her hand into his chest, ripping out his crystal heart. It was a different color than hers: an opaque pink. She used her own finger to crack a hole into the surface. Max couldn't work out why. All he knew was that he was next. He could tell by the way Iris turned and looked at him as if she had no soul.

Yes. Yes, this is why he had come to the battlefield: to die. Absolution.

He got to his knees and pressed his forehead against the earth. "Iris, I was the one who killed you," he whispered. "I took the sword made from your bones and stabbed you. I didn't stop, even after I'd realized Jinn had jumped in front of me to protect you. He died protecting you. And I killed you both."

Iris stepped toward him. It was fine like this. Fate. Retribution. He wouldn't complain. If he was to die by anyone's hand, it should be hers.

Cherice. I'm sorry. Wait for me. Max squeezed his eyes, surprised when he realized he had one last tear to shed.

And then the wind behind him shifted. A familiar whooshing sound battered his ears from behind. He looked up. His and Iris's eyes locked.

Those gorgeous brown eyes. They look so sad.

It was the last thought he had before he was pulled into a vortex of darkness.

30

LAWRENCE HAWKINS'S POWER MADE HIM UNIQUELY useful. He had been searching the Belgium war front since the moment Maximo had told him he was heading there.

"The bloody prat said he wants to die," Hawkins had told him while Rin had gathered up her medicine in the Ajashe hospital. "He told us to come here to take care of Berta. But I'm not giving up on him. We already lost one friend. We're not letting go of another."

Rin had said nothing. Hiva, the shadow to Iris's sun, was nowhere to be found. According to Hawkins and Jacob, Cherice, the woman who had been their comrade since childhood, had died in a battle against Adam Temple. The two had not given her any more details. But from the sound of things, she'd died a warrior's death. And so Rin would not cry for her.

"What do you want with us?" Rin had asked inside the hospital.

Jacob shook his head. "We can't discuss it now. Not until we find him."

Jacob. It was because of him that she could speak and comprehend English, such an accursed language. She didn't thank him.

Even after returning to Lagos together, Hawkins continued his search along the Belgium front for Max, until one day—

"Brother!"

Hawkins's blue portal had appeared once more inside Uma's apartment on the main floor, which was decorated with paintings hung upon the floral-patterned wall, several parlor chairs, and bookshelves carved with intricate woodwork. Berta had jumped off the red sofa and gasped the moment she saw her brother's body plop upon the wooden-paneled floor. Lulu followed her, hovering over them both while Berta covered her mouth with her hands.

Seeing him filthy and unconscious made Rin snarl in disgust. Such a weakling had killed Iris. He wasn't worth her notice. But she did notice. She noticed Berta grabbing her brother and checking his wounds, tears in her eyes.

Lowering her head slightly, Rin turned instead to the so-called étagère upon which Uma had placed various decorative pieces of jewelry: A pearl necklace. A ruby ring. A brooch that looked foreign—gold-set, with turquoise jewels and diamond gears strung together by gold. They were left out and placed carefully on the light hanging shelf as if they were mementos, important not for their monetary value but for their sentimental currency. In the corner was a painting of a fierce Indian warrior, cutting off the wing of a giant hawk with a sword. Against the backdrop of a desert sunset, he carried a frightened woman, her long, curly black hair flowing, averting her eyes from the violence with her jeweled hands. Did he aim to protect her or kidnap her?

It was a duel between gods. That was what was plain to Rin's eyes.

A different duel between two very different gods had taken place across the oceans, if Hawkins was to be believed.

"I couldn't see everything. But Iris was there in the trench with Max. And Hiva's—Hiva's head—" He shuddered, the words failing him.

Iris? Rin clenched her teeth. When she looked upon Max again, seeing Berta cry over his near-lifeless body, she realized that the disgust creeping up inside of her was not for Max—it was for herself. She'd known this would happen. She had sicced Iris upon him like a bloodhound. If he was dead, it was because of her careless tongue.

"Max!" Berta shook him with tears in her eyes, while Jacob rubbed her back reassuringly. "Brother!"

"Don't worry," Hawkins told her. "He's not dead. I could feel his heartbeat. Calm down and you'll feel it too."

She did. She pressed her ear against his chest and immediately let out a sigh of relief.

"Whatever had happened to him in Belgium must have been so bad, he passed out," Hawkins continued. "But he's not hurt. At least not on the outside."

Not on the outside. How scarred, then, was Maximo on the inside? That depended on what horrors Iris had inflected upon him. Though sometimes guilt was a horror in and of itself.

"Tell me, why did you seek us out?" Rin said, because she was growing impatient, and the longer she kept silent, the longer she concentrated on her own guilt nipping away at her.

"Just wait," Jacob said, and added darkly, "We'll talk when the whole group is here."

"Group?" Berta wiped away her tears. "What do you mean, group?"

The two men didn't speak. Hawkins disappeared back through his blue vortex without another word. Jacob's eyes were beset with dark shadows that aged him and made the kind boy seem somehow crueler. He wasn't going to tell her anything. Not until he was good and ready. Well, Rin had information too. And she would decide when the time came whether or not to share it with them.

And so Rin waited. Downstairs, Uma was in her increasingly-not-so-secret lab, doing things to Jinn that she didn't want to imagine. Lulu brought a cup of water to Berta, who fed it to Max while he lay sleeping on the floor. She stroked his forehead lovingly. Siblings reunited again.

There was something so mysterious about family, whether bound by blood or by feeling alone. Rin touched her missing eye behind its bandage and remembered Berta's downturned eyes in front of the church as they had neared her home of El Salvador.

Very quickly, Max became delirious with fever. He kept whispering secret things Rin couldn't understand. The only words clear on his lips were his apologies.

"I'm so sorry, Iris. God, I'm so sorry. . . ."

His apology was too late. Or was it? Was there ever a time when an apology no longer mattered? Rin didn't ask him. There was no point in asking a barely conscious man.

"Just keep him on the couch," Uma had told them on the first day. "He seems to be in some kind of shock, but he'll snap out of it eventually."

Rin noticed her bloody hands and curled fingers.

"What about Jinn's surgery?" Berta asked Uma. "Have you made any progress?"

Rin was glad one of them had had the courage to ask.

Uma's expression grew weary. "Just let me know when your brother wakes up."

That was the last time in several days that Rin saw Uma.

Days of silence passed before Max jolted awake, falling off the sofa onto the floor. Jacob, Berta, and Lulu jumped from their chairs and rushed over to him as he began coughing. Soon the coughs turned to frightened gasps. Then screams.

"Brother! Brother! You're okay!" Berta hugged him tightly as he thrashed on the wooden floor. "You're safe! You're safe!"

"Max!" Jacob grabbed his flailing arm and held it still so that Max wouldn't hurt himself or anyone else. Lulu kept her distance, clasping her hands together. "It's me. Jacob!"

"Brother!" Berta cried one more time, and the light seemed to return to his eyes.

He lurched over, his breathing rough enough to hear even from where Rin stood next to the bookshelf. It took a minute for it to even out, and when he was finally able to inhale fully, he squeezed his eyes shut and looked up.

"You're safe," said Berta again, with a smile so bright that Rin almost blushed, gazing at the pair in awe. She'd never seen the annoying thief look so vulnerable. This is what "family" was.

It was right at that moment that Maximo began to cry. "Berta. Berta . . . did you die too?"

"What?" Despair filled Berta's voice as her brother sobbed uncontrollably. "You're not dead. None of us are dead!"

"You're alive, Max." Jacob grabbed his shoulder and shook him. "You're alive." But Max's cries only grew louder.

The sight of Max wailing on floor disturbed Rin. It made it harder to hate him.

This was all his fault. That was what she wanted to tell him as he sat there blubbering in his sister's arms. But as his tears fell, as he covered his ears and shook his head, the hatred she held for him subsided. Something deep within Rin told her that he'd already paid his price. With whatever Iris had done to him, he'd paid.

"Hiva is dead," Max told them. "At least I think he is. I don't know. Iris murdered him and took his heart. She would have murdered me too, but Hiva saved my life."

"What?" Jacob grabbed Max's face and pulled it up. "Hiva did *what*? He *saved* you?"

"He died in my place," Max said with urgency. "He changed, Jacob. He somehow wasn't the same Hiva who kidnapped us. He fought to protect me from Iris. But Iris—"

But Iris. His words died in his throat, and his gaze became unfocused. It was the dazed look of a traumatized soldier. Rin had seen it many a time during her days as a warrior.

The air began to shift in the room. It didn't seem to bother Jacob. It couldn't tear him away from his shell-shocked friend.

"But Iris?" Jacob placed his hand softly upon Max's cheek. "But Iris what?"

"Iris is our new problem now," Hawkins said as he strode out of the blue vortex that had appeared, swirling with wind. "If what I saw in Belgium is any indication, we've exchanged one cataclysm for another. Which means we have to decide before it's too late."

Three pairs of feet followed Hawkins out of the blue vortex. They belonged to faces Rin knew too well, apparently.

Henry the toymaker. His maid, Mary, the healer. Then that meant the older woman next to her was Lucille, the shape-shifter.

"Ah, look at that!" said Lucille, in a voice she was clearly forcing to sound old. "We Fanciful Freaks are together again!"

Henry and Mary didn't seem to share her enthusiasm. As the portal disappeared behind them, Henry stepped in front of Mary protectively. To protect her from what, Rin didn't know. None of them were in the mood or shape for a fight.

Or maybe Rin was wrong about that.

For gentle Jacob glared at the three with the kind of hatred reserved only for the greatest of enemies. Berta, on the other hand, stared at the three, confused.

"Who the hell are they?" Berta held Max more tightly, not seeming to notice that Max's expression had also darkened. Lucille's expression had become strange too. She stared at Max's sister but said nothing. "And what's that?"

She was pointing at the bundle in Hawkins's hand. A long object wrapped in cloth. For one alarming moment, Rin was reminded of the Coral Temple—Hiva's sudden arrival. The fateful moment of his showdown with Iris.

Her instinct wasn't far off. Hawkins pulled off the cloth to reveal a smooth lance made of bone. "Another bone sword," she whispered, stepping away from Uma's bookshelf. "Where—?"

"This was made from Hiva's bones. The plan was to kill him with it, but thanks to Iris, there's been a change of plans. She's our *new* problem," Hawkins told them. "And this time we have no choice but to kill her for *good.*"

31

RIN HAD LEARNED ABOUT THE LAW of gravity from playing as a child in her old home, Abeokuta. Bread and Butter. That was the name she remembered. Two team leaders would choose to be either the bread or the butter. Then the other children would choose their teams.

> "Bread and butter,
> Gbaskelebe,
> Ma jo gbono,
> Gbaskelebe,
> Ma jo tutu,
> Gbaskelebe.
> Omodeyi ki lo mu?"

Lanky arms linked around torsos. Each team would form a giant link of bodies. And then the team leaders at the front would grip hands.

Pull! Usually whoever had more children on their side would win the tugging battle, but that wasn't always the case. Sometimes all it took to win was sheer will.

Regardless of who won, the result was always the same. One side tumbling to the ground. One child would fall and crash into another, who would fall and crash into another. A chain reaction that caused bodies to fall to the ground.

Like lining up little tiles in a sequence and knocking them down. Each would collapse into a heaping, giggling mess.

There was nothing to laugh about now.

Every chain reaction needed a trigger—the first body to fall. It was Mary's who fell, when Jacob of all people jumped to his feet in Uma's apartment and rushed at her, screaming.

"Jacob, stop!" Hawkins screamed, grabbing him and holding him back, but it wasn't an easy task. Jacob looked ready to commit murder. Henry's instincts were right after all—he'd held up his arms to shield her.

"You betrayed us!" Jacob growled, his voice sounding too vicious for his usual demeanor. "Because you betrayed us, Cherice is dead!"

Mary peered over Henry's shoulder. Her blue eyes immediately filled with tears of regret, but it didn't deter Jacob.

"Adam killed Cherice," he cried. "She's *dead*! What do you have to say for yourself?"

"Get a hold of yourself!" Henry yelled, sweat dripping from his forehead. "We didn't come here for this bunk!"

"Bunk? Oh, so what are you here for? To screw us over again?"

"Jacob!" Hawkins tried again, but the boy broke loose from him. He moved to tackle both Henry and Mary. But Lucille's hand caught his shirt collar instead. With one tug, she threw Jacob back, and he crashed into Max and Berta on the floor.

Hawkins's eyes were flaming with fury. "Bastard!" he cried, and dropping the bone lance, he punched Lucille in the face. "You have some bloody nerve—"

But Henry tackled him. The boy had grown taller and fiercer than Rin had remembered during the Tournament of Freaks.

The old woman, Lucille, opened her grinning mouth, surely ready to make an arrogant, unfunny quip. But the sounds that had come out of her mouth weren't anything Rin had ever heard before. The words seemed to surprise her too, because Lucille clutched her throat in shock. Then she glared at Jacob. He'd managed to brush her throat before she'd thrown him aside.

Strawberry-blond Mary cowered like a wilted flower, just like she always had during the tournament, but there was a terrible darkness weighing her down now. When Hawkins and Henry began to punch each other, when Jacob launched off the floor and grabbed Henry's hair, she backed up against the wall instead of joining the fray.

One body after another. A messy heap. Rin wished it were just a game.

"What the hell is going on here?" Berta cried, jumping to her feet and watching the boys fight with disgust. "Who the hell are you people? Max?"

She looked down at her brother, but Max didn't move an inch. His dead eyes stared at the floor. He bit his lip as if holding himself back. The way his fists shook told her he wanted to hit something—or someone—too.

"Miss Rin." Lulu ran up to Rin and tugged her sleeve. "They're gonna kill each other!"

Rin sucked her teeth. "I know."

It was time to end this mess. They didn't notice her come over. They didn't notice her pulling her sword from her chest. It was only when she pointed it at Jacob's forehead that the scuffling group seemed to snap back to reality.

"This fight is over. Any more nonsense and I will kill you all."

It was not an exaggeration. The group calmed. Straightening their vests, wiping their sweaty, bruised hands against their pants, and fixing their hair, they each cleared their throats and retreated into their respective corners. Rin stooped down and picked up the bone lance Hawkins had so carelessly let fall to the floor. Iris may have torn out Hiva's heart, but as long as that heart existed, Hiva could regrow his body. Rin would have to keep this just in case he did.

There, in Uma's apartment, they faced one another. Henry, Mary, and Lucille on one side. The rest on the other. Each sitting, in their chairs or on the sofa or on the floor, except Rin, who stood between them both. She kept her sword in one hand and the bone lance in the other.

"You said we need to kill Iris," Rin said to Hawkins, getting down to business. "What do you mean? When did you even see her?"

"I didn't see her. *They* did," he answered, and pointed to Henry's group.

"Rather, I saw the death she left behind," Mary whispered, her voice so low that Rin wondered if she were capable of sounding like anything other than a mouse. "In London a few days ago, I heard . . ."

Rin raised an eyebrow. "Heard what?"

"That an entire circus had been wiped out at Astley's Amphitheatre. Everyone was dead."

Wiped out? Frantically Rin searched her memories. Astley's Amphitheatre. Yes, Iris had mentioned it before, once or twice during their travels. It was where her circus performed.

"Correction," said Henry. "They weren't just wiped out. They'd been turned to ashes. That's the signature of Hiva, right? Just like at the music hall. Except we soon learned the other Hiva was already overseas in Europe, fighting on the war front. Unless there's a third Hiva we don't know about, who else could have done it but Iris?"

But her precious grandmother had worked at the circus too. Granny . . . Granny Marlow. Yes, Granny Marlow, the one who had doted on Iris like a mother.

Rin's stomach dropped. Iris had told her all about the old woman. Wasn't she like family? How could Iris have killed her? Rin wouldn't believe it.

"How did you find these three, Hawkins?" Max asked, still sitting on the floor with Berta at his side. Leaning over his knee, he seemed cooler-headed than the others, though Rin wondered if it was just a façade.

"Seems like this one has a special relationship with Lily." Hawkins flicked his head at Lucille. "She's a return customer. And return customers tend to be very chatty."

Rin wasn't sure what he'd meant, but the red patches on Lucille's old-woman face spoke volumes—volumes more than Lucille herself could, at any rate. When she tried to open her mouth to talk, only gibberish came out.

Henry gestured toward her. "When are you going to put her back to normal?"

"I don't know." Jacob shrugged, his tone as nasty as his scowl. "Maybe when you apologize for getting our friend killed."

Despite Henry's bravado, he seemed shaken by Jacob's words. He was not a soldier. He was a boy in way over his head, trying to prove himself yet deathly scared of failing. Rin had seen it before. She could tell now by the way he shifted from foot to foot.

Sitting next to him on the couch, Hawkins placed a gentle hand on Jacob's shoulder. "Before that, we need to talk about Iris's whereabouts."

Rin's heart leaped into her throat. She gripped her weapons more tightly. "Whereabouts?"

"She's in Europe," Max answered before Hawkins could. "She found Hiva and me in Belgium. She tried to kill me but ended up getting Hiva instead. He's gone now."

"But Iris isn't," said Hawkins, and after he gestured toward Mary, the girl pulled a newspaper leaflet out from underneath her apron. "It's all over the papers. Scores of people are disappearing across Europe. They think it's a plague making its way west through France, but nobody could tell where it'd come from."

"The Rapture, some claim." Mary waved the paper. "People are saying it's the end of days."

Berta scoffed. "We've known for weeks that it's the end of days, and we haven't been able to do a damn thing about it!"

"We thought it was Hiva we'd have to deal with. But this is *Iris*," Max whispered. "She was denied her complete revenge. She's just killing indiscriminately now."

"And whose fault is that?"

Rin hadn't meant to speak. Her only role in this détente was to menace and threaten them into order. But when she thought of Iris sweeping through foreign lands . . . when she listened to this group of fools speaking about her while knowing nothing about her at all, her blood boiled.

A plague. The Rapture. Rin wanted to strike at them. But her words moved before her body could.

"Iris knew she was a danger to humankind," Rin said, staring at the smooth bone lance in her hands. "And that's why she tried so hard to find a way to change herself. All you needed to do was to trust her. But you each refused. That night Club Uriel burned. Inside the Coral Temple with Hiva at your side. Each time you denied her humanity, you tore away a piece of her soul until she had nothing left. And now you act surprised?"

As her bottom lip trembled, Rin looked up from her sword and stared down every person in the room, her heart thumping hard against her chest as the blood rushed through her.

"What could you have done to stop her?" Rin felt her eyes prickle as she thought of Iris's determined face, which couldn't hide her fear of the unknown any more than it could banish her hope. "*Believe* in her. Why couldn't you believe in her just once?"

Her words dissipated in the air. Silence stretched across the room.

"You're right," said Max, running his hand through her hair. "You are bloody right. I was wrong. *We* were wrong." And he looked at Jacob and Hawkins. "We were wrong."

Hearing him say that softened the painful lump in Rin's chest, if only a little.

"We were," said Hawkins solemnly. "We did this to her. We're to blame."

Jacob and Mary lowered their heads. Henry and Lucille fidgeted with their clothes.

"Still," Hawkins continued, "it doesn't change the fact that hundreds of thousands of people are dying. Iris isn't stopping. There's no telling who's next. What Hiva promised to do in that Coral Temple, Iris is now the one carrying it out. We've got to stop her."

"That's why we're here," said Henry, rolling up his sleeves, either because he wasn't used to West African weather or because he was trying to show his determination. "Hawkins asked for our help, and, well . . ." He bit his lip. "We figured we owed him."

"Stop her with what?" Max stood, pulling himself away from Berta. "With *that*?" He pointed at the bone lance in Rin's hand. "You made that from Hiva's arm, right? In that case, it won't work. Only Iris's own bones can kill her."

"We went to the museum," Jacob said, gripping the fabric of his pants anxiously. "The exhibit where her skeleton was—it's been burned down. Not a shred remains."

Rin couldn't think of anyone other than Adam who would do such a thing. This one time, then, she had to thank him.

"Well, that's that, then," said Max with a shrug. "Only Iris's own bones can kill her for good. Some other bloke's bones won't work."

"You don't know that!" Hawkins stood too. "He's not just some other bloke—he's a Hiva, just like her! You don't know, maybe they share some spiritual or blood connection. It could work! We just have to find a way to trap her. We'll need all the manpower we can get."

"What if you try it and it doesn't work?" Henry asked. The boy had begun pacing.

"Then we'll try again."

"Be real, Lawrence. You can't make a shot like that twice. Come on, man, our families are at stake!" Henry shot a quick glance at Mary behind him before blushing.

"Look!" When Hawkins screamed, his blond hair flew about his face. "I'm not an expert at god-killing, but we've got to do something. We can't let Iris live!"

But Hawkins shut his mouth quickly once Rin pointed the bone lance at him. "Even if it did work, why should I stand here and let you kill her? Do you really think I will?"

Carefully, quietly, Hawkins sat back down.

"Iris isn't the same Iris. She's gone now," Henry said, and Lucille nodded in agreement. "Killing her may be our only choice to save the people we love."

"Bloody hell!" Max stomped his foot. "Don't you see, we're making the same mistakes over and over again? Rin is right. We have to believe in Iris."

"Believe in her? Max . . . I understand how you feel, but this isn't one of Chadwick's penny bloods," Jacob said, in a tone that seemed to better suit his gentle features than the rage he'd shown earlier. "The Fanciful Freaks could solve any problem with the power of their friendship. I want to believe that's true, but . . ."

Jacob went silent. Max didn't look at him. He was staring at the floor, gritting his teeth.

"But you don't understand how I feel, Jacob," he said. "None of you do." And he turned to his friends, resolute. "I've wasted enough time wallowing in misery. Now that I've seen Iris again . . . and like *that*." He shook his head. "I'm sorry. I won't betray Iris again. Never again."

Rin relaxed her shoulders. Finally somebody understood. Finally somebody cared about that poor girl, who was trapped and fighting a losing battle against a cruel destiny.

"I wonder how she feels," Mary said. Everyone turned, surprised, as if a mouse had suddenly scurried out of a crack in the wall. "I wonder if she's happy . . . or if she's sad."

"She's sad," Max and Rin said at the same time, and then exchanged meaningful glances.

"I know she is," Max told them without taking his gaze from Rin. "Just before Hawkins rescued me from Belgium, I looked in her eyes, and I just knew."

"It's the same for me," Rin said, remembering the teardrop on the floor of the Naacalian facility. "She's not gone. We can change her."

"How?" Hawkins scoffed. "Through kind words?"

Rin grunted. What was wrong with a kind word? But they had something stronger. "With Jinn," she said.

Max's arms fell to his sides. He stared at her, eyes wide as if he'd seen a ghost. "Wh-what did you say?"

Right, he doesn't know. Rin swallowed. "You didn't kill Jinn, Maximo," she said. "You almost did. But Uma managed to keep him just barely alive. This is her apartment. Now, as we speak, she's operating on him to try to bring him back to full health."

Rin could hear Max's heavy inhale from where he stood. As silence filled the room, he stared into the distance for a moment. Then he swiveled on his feet.

"You can't go!" Rin said, stopping him in his tracks just before he could spring to the basement. "The operation is delicate. One wrong move and we could lose him forever." She lowered her head, frowning. "Uma and her assistant are doing all they can, but in the end, it's difficult to bring a man back from the brink of death. We're not even sure if it'll work."

"Why should we hinge our plan on a miracle operation you're not sure will work?" Henry asked, shaking his head as if he'd heard pure nonsense.

Rin cursed underneath her breath. The rude little smartass. But it didn't matter. Iris could come back. She knew it in her heart. "We just need to believe in her!" she begged them.

"I'm sorry, I don't." Henry shook his head. Rubbing her throat, Lucille nodded in agreement.

"Neither do I." Hawkins crossed his arms over his chest. Rin scoffed. If he were so sure, then why couldn't he look anyone in the eye? "We have to find a way to get rid of her. If Hiva's bones won't work..."

"Then... then the Titans might."

It was Berta who'd spoken. Shocked, Rin held her breath. Berta hung her head and glanced up at Rin, an apology in her eyes, before she stood.

Next to his sister, Max raised an eyebrow. "Berta?"

"Berta!" Rin took an urgent step toward her, but the girl shook her head.

"I'm sorry, Rin, but we need to tell them," she whispered. "The stakes are too high."

Rin looked from a surprised Lulu to solemn Berta, panicked. But Berta had already begun.

"There are ancient weapons the Naacal made—the civilization Iris destroyed millions of years ago," Berta explained. "They've got more firepower than a thousand bombs. Maybe... maybe they can even vaporize a god."

"Berta," Rin pleaded, her emotions thrown into disarray.

"Rin, Lulu, and I found the device that works it. It's funny—looks like one of those stone tablets from an Egyptian pyramid or something. At any rate, if we use it—"

"We destroyed it," Rin growled.

"Maybe Uma can make another one. Isn't she a genius or something?"

"Even if she did and we used it, what would happen?" Rin shot Berta a furious look. "We'd end up killing hundreds of thousands of people while trying to 'vaporize' one god."

"I'm not saying I want to," Berta said. "I'm saying it's an option."

"We traveled the world to make sure it would *never* be an option."

"That's before you whispered something to Iris and sent her on a berserk killing spree."

"What I said to her wasn't all that complicated." Rin grinned. She felt spiteful now, and since her need for revenge trumped her senses, she let the words fly. "I told her your brother killed her and her lover, Jinn. I don't think she'd realized it. After all, her back had been to the murderer. But once she knew, I reckon she went straight to your murderous brother to gather his head."

Berta's breath hitched. Her face flushed hot with anger. "You said ... *what*?"

"You heard me. And I won't apologize. She deserved to know the truth." Rin shifted her challenging gaze to Max. "And he deserved to pay for what he did."

"You ... you *traitor*!"

Berta lunged for her, and with a blade in each hand, Rin was ready. Shockingly, it was Max who held Berta back, grabbing his sister's collar and pulling her to his side.

"Max!" Berta whined, looking up at him, confused.

"She's right," Max said. "She did deserve to know the truth. And I deserved her fury. There's nothing to fight about."

Berta struggled a little in her brother's grip before giving up with an angry groan and stomp of her foot. Lucille giggled. It was an odd moment, considering the tension. She didn't try to hide her youthful voice, either. Berta scrunched her face in disgust, looking back at the old woman.

"This is all messed up," Berta muttered, and for once Rin agreed. Everything was knotted and upside down. She couldn't make sense of anything except her own anger and the hint of fear growing inside of her.

Rin stared at the bone lance in her hand and felt like crying.

"At the end of the day," Jacob began, in as measured a tone as he could muster, "it all comes down to choice. Iris is killing, and she won't stop until all of humanity is gone. That's simply reality. We can try to change her back into who she used to be."

Rin's thoughts turned to Jinn, lying beneath their feet in Uma's underground lab.

"Or we can kill her, even if it means sacrificing others."

"S-sacrificing others?" Mary repeated.

"To save all of humanity for generations to come." Henry turned to her and placed a gentle hand on her shoulder. "To protect our futures."

"And what about Iris's future?" Rin whispered.

"Let's vote on it."

Lulu. She had been hiding by the bookshelf, watching all this unfold from the safety of her little corner. How foolish they all must have looked to a child's eyes. Rin felt embarrassed, but more so than that, she was surprised.

"Vote?" she asked Lulu.

"Yeah. You vote, and the majority wins. Not that I would know," she added with a shrug. "People like me aren't allowed to vote, where I'm from."

Mary, Lucille, Henry. Jacob, Hawkins, Max. Rin and Berta. They all exchanged glances, sizing each other up. Waiting for the first one to speak, to dismiss Lulu's suggestion as a childish waste of time. Except nobody did, because it wasn't. It was the only solution any of them could see. The clearer that became, the more Rin felt her stomach sink.

"It'll be an anonymous vote," Jacob said. "So nobody has to feel guilty."

Rin scoffed. "We all live with our sins."

He didn't answer. It took a few minutes of rummaging through Uma's cabinets to find what they needed. Some paper, which Lulu tore up. A fountain pen and inkwell. A jar of flowers on the windowsill, which they emptied to place the votes in.

"Adults only!" Hawkins said when Lulu reached out her little hand for a piece of torn paper in his hand.

"No," Rin said with a not-so-subtle threatening tone. "The girl votes. She's earned her right to have a say."

Lulu beamed at her.

Should we kill Iris for good? Yes or no?

That was the question for the vote.

So barbaric, Rin thought to herself as she wrote *no* in clear letters several times on her torn piece of paper. It felt like the kind of barbarity that had landed Iris in a zoo and then on an operating table. And then in a museum. *Hasn't she suffered enough?*

She'd often wondered while fighting with the Dahomey military women: How much suffering could one endure? When she thought about her family, when she'd killed and participated in raids, when her right eye had been cut and then burned out of its socket by Hiva: How much suffering could one human endure?

And what if humans didn't have to suffer? It was a question that reminded her of her conversation with Lulu and Berta on the train while they were searching for the Solar Jumps. What kind of a world would Rin have wanted to live in if she'd had her way? She remembered Lulu's answer as clearly as if it were yesterday: *A world where nobody hurts each other.* Alas, such a world didn't exist. Not for Rin.

Not for Iris, either.

"Five votes to four." Jacob laid them all out on the floor so everyone could see.

Five yeses. Their past mistakes didn't matter. Iris's pain didn't matter. They were going to kill Iris. No matter the cost.

"If saving the world requires sacrifices, then I'll gladly pay it," Hawkins whispered.

Dropping the bone lance, Rin stormed out of the apartment in anger and sorrow.

32

RIN NEVER THOUGHT SHE'D FIND HERSELF in the empty streets of Ajashe again. Being in the port city, especially under this eerie night sky, reminded her of Abiade, her friend—now dust, lost forever. She didn't blame Iris, no. She blamed herself. Iris had been lost and floundering in a void, hovering between existence and nonexistence. It was the fate she'd fought so hard against. To fight and to lose a battle of selfhood was more painful than anyone could imagine. Watching the people Iris had once fought alongside— had once fought for—choosing to deny that "self" one more time was the last straw.

This was the only solution Rin could come up with.

She didn't care that the Dahomey military troop had seen her. In fact, it was what she'd wanted.

"Olarinde!"

"It's Olarinde!"

The women called her name in shock, and as they rushed toward her through the dusty streets, Rin raised her hands in surrender. She wasn't there to fight.

Rough hands took her by the collar of her borrowed farmers' clothes and dragged her inside one of the round huts, away from the once-bustling trading area of the city. They threw her down upon the hard mud floor.

At General Sesinu's feet.

Yes, the general she'd tried to murder was alive and healed, though the scar in her torso where Rin had stabbed her was still very clearly visible. The older woman sat on an animal-skin mat, her arms crossed. Izegbe, the rifle-woman, stood beside her, gun cocked, ready to shoot should Sesinu give the order.

She didn't.

Rin was already pleading. "Forgive me for what I've done." She rubbed her hands together. "Forgive me. I was wrong."

The Fon language felt familiar against her tongue as she pleaded.

At the sight of her former pupil and attempted murderer begging in front of her, Sesinu grunted. Rin couldn't bear to look her in the eyes, not yet. There was enough disgust in that grunt that she could guess how the general felt.

"The fugitive has surrendered." Her words were as throaty and confident as ever. This was a woman who'd escaped death many times. Then again, betrayal was another matter entirely. "For what reason have we been given this sight of disgrace?"

Rin did not have the energy to flinch at her words. Her pride gone and her body hollowed out, she simply let her forehead rest upon the floor.

"I've come to give you a gift. I give it to you along with myself." Rin swallowed, her throat dry and hoarse. "I will surrender to King Glele. I will go back to the royal city of Abomey and accept whatever punishment he gives me for all I've done to betray him and you."

"What good is this when King Glele's hands are full with many concerns?" Sesinu asked.

Concerns. "The . . . the French?"

The *ahosi* laughed.

"The French soldiers in our land have all been recalled to their home country." Izegbe was the one who answered. "Almost every single one. What good are colonial interests when your homeland has been decimated?"

Iris. Hawkins had mentioned that she'd already destroyed much of France. Rin had thought it was strange that she hadn't seen any Western soldiers while rushing through Ajashe.

"It is Isoke's doing," said Rin. "As is the tragedy in Ajashe. She won't stop until she's destroyed all the world—"

"For she is Hiva. The Cataclysm."

Sesinu's words surprised Rin enough that she finally lifted her head. And when she did, she saw the calm dignity in the general's eyes. There was no hatred. Just a simmering sense of judgment and disappointment that made Rin squirm and look away.

"King Glele has been told everything by that man, Boris Bosch," Sesinu continued. "The Hiva, the Helios. The purpose of the Ark. All of it."

That was right. King Glele was doing business with Bosch. He had been there in the Atakora Mountains when she, Iris, and Jinn had launched their grand escape. He'd seen the Ark with his own eyes. But this was good. That meant it wouldn't take Rin too much time to explain her plan.

"With Bosch's own mouth, we were able to confirm Natame and Aisosa's warning." General Sesinu cracked her neck from side to side. "Isoke is She Who Does Not Fall. To protect our lands, we must make her do so."

"What if there was another way?" Rin said quickly, getting up to her knees. "Isoke cannot be stopped by human hands. This has already been proven time and time again. Sending military women to fight against her will only result in the loss of lives."

While the other women behind Rin grumbled and discussed quietly, Sesinu considered it.

"Then what do you propose?" she finally asked.

"We send her away." Rin pulled a tiny bottle out of her shirt. The opiate she'd retrieved from the Ajashe hospital to give to Jinn. She'd taken a little more than necessary—just in case—and she had two. Rin rolled one toward Sesinu. "We send her to another world. We send her on the Ark."

The chatter grew louder—no, it had exploded. *Use the Ark? Send her away from this earth?*

Yes. It was the only solution Rin's frenzied mind could come up with on short notice. If Hiva no longer existed on this planet, then fools would stop being so eager to kill her.

It was the only way she could save Iris.

322

"The woman named Bellerose will likely never accept it," Rin continued quickly, loud enough to break through the pandemonium. "She hates Isoke. She and Boris Bosch will not allow her entrance. But we can ambush Isoke. Drug her and stow her away on the Ark. She'll be taken away from this earth without ever knowing what happened to her."

Somewhat true. Somewhat a lie. If any Enlightener save Adam got their filthy hands on Iris, they would use her heart as a power source for the Ark. It was, in one sense, one way to "get rid of the problem." But Rin would never allow such a thing to happen to Iris.

In that case, the best option was to give them another power source.

"If we send Isoke away," Rin said, "then we'll make sure she's never again a threat to this earth. We'll be able to keep our lands safe."

"Our lands?" Izegbe gave her a sidelong look. "So you consider the Kingdom of Dahomey to be your land after all?"

Rin pursed her lips together. Izegbe did not say any of this with anger or judgment. She was a reasonable woman, though a strong soldier who wouldn't hesitate to shoot when ordered. It felt now as if she'd shot a bullet right into Rin's chest.

Rin made sure she didn't hesitate for long. She told them the truth. "You raid villages and recruit from your spoils of war. No matter how much training we go through, we cannot forget our homes. We cannot forget our families. To do so would be to throw away our very selves. That's what the military wants. Throwing away our 'selves' would make us better soldiers. However . . ." Rin paused, squeezing her fists against the dirt floor. "We are but human. I am but a human filled with faults and pride, but also love and memory. I cannot change that."

Her mother and father. The village children. Abiade. Iris. The women she'd fought alongside. The women who'd died fighting with her. Friends. Family. All tangled up in this complicated world of hope and misery.

"I've accepted my own fault in what I did to you, General Sesinu. Which is why, once we succeed in quelling the threat of Hiva, I offer myself to you and the king."

Sesinu looked up at Izegbe, then at the *ahosi* behind Rin, blocking any route to escape. She lowered her head and thought. Then, with a throaty sigh, she began to speak.

"This scheme will require that we find Isoke," she reminded Rin.

Rin nodded. "I will make sure you do. There's an apartment building in Lagos. It's where I'm currently residing. I'll bring her there in due time. For now, spy on the area secretly and wait until I return with her."

"And are you sure you will be able to corral this errant god?"

"I will, or I'll die trying."

Sesinu smirked. Perhaps she thought Rin sounded overconfident, but she'd meant every word. She would not have concocted this plan if she wasn't prepared to die.

"Okay, Olarinde. We will do as you ask," Sesinu finally decided. "Only if this plan is successful will we bring you back to Abomey. If it is not, then we are all doomed anyway."

"It will succeed," promised Rin, though the flutter of nerves told her it was more of a wish than a promise. "I will make sure of it. And you will too, when you give Madame Bellerose and Boris Bosch this."

Rin fetched the pouch from her pocket. The one that held John Temple's world map of Solar Jumps, still holding on despite wear and tear. She would need it soon, for there was another part to her plan that required she travel the world as quickly as possible. It would take days to reach that old woman, if she was indeed still alive—and Rin *had* to believe that no matter what version of Iris her friend was, she would never have killed Granny Marlow.

But right now, the second item in her pouch was more important.

She pulled it out, and immediately Sesinu's and Izegbe's eyes grew large.

"What is this thing?" Sesinu asked, staring at the skeleton key's linked rings and smooth surface, its shine not dulled by time.

Rin's left eye shimmered as well. "It's the Moon Skeleton. And when you give it to Bellerose and Bosch, they will use it to power the Ark and begin their expedition to the New World."

33

Yorkshire, 1874

D O NOT THINK THAT A YOUNG boy cannot go mad. Bourgeois perceptions of childhood innocence frequently interfere with the harshness of reality.

The boy was already a genius of ill temperament—a very different breed from the other boys his age, whose thoughts and ambitions were of a far less dangerous nature. Everyone who knew him regarded him as strange and kept their distance. A dark-minded youth who struggled to find a balance between the expectations of moral society and his own transgressive imaginations. *A gothic double of his brighter-dispositioned grandfather*, his mother would say with a smile upon her face.

Alas, that smile had become a rather rare sight after the murder of his siblings. His mother had then hanged herself quite efficiently.

The boy had nothing but stories. Stories of fire and brimstone and the wrath of an angry god. Stories of an absentee father, whose travels mattered more to him than his family. As the boy aged, his imagination grew more evil and more desperate.

Out of pure boredom, he began to pore over his father's research. The work that had become more important to his father than his own dead family and his one living son, practically now orphaned. Soon this research, the source of his misfortune, had become the single preoccupation of the boy's greatest fantasies and nightmares.

Maybe it was not madness at all but an obsession. Yes, an obsession. Locking himself in his room, refusing the company of boys his own age, his singular purpose was to learn the terrible secrets his father had discovered during his travels. His father had hidden his greatest secrets inside that blasted journal of his, which he always kept on his person. But the research locked in his safe was a good start. Deducing his father's codes had taken many months; his father and grandfather, both great minds, tended to use different ciphers for different research works. But with tenacity the boy managed to interpret portions, cross-referencing his own translations against his father's notes. There was one word, however, that gripped his imagination.

Hiva.

It seemed to be the only word that was not some kind of code, nor some other earthly language. Next to the first appearance of the word, his father had drawn a symbol the boy recognized: the Ouroboros. The chaos serpent, whose breadth stretched so long, it could embrace the earth and still swallow its own tail. And swallow the earth too, perhaps.

Swallow the earth. Yes, the earth was at stake in this great and dangerous game. The earth itself was at the center of this mystery, the boy was sure of it. And this Hiva was the key to everything. After learning what he could from the writing he'd deciphered, the boy could feel that one single truth in his bones.

Now the true test of his theory would be the broken white crystal in his red-flushed hand.

It was a heart. That was what the research had said. A heart ripped from the body of a goddess. Broken. Mending.

It was 1874. Dark clouds howled behind the high windows of his father's study. The moonlight, slipping between the drawn ivory curtains, pooled over the grand chestnut desk behind him. The clear crystal stone, no bigger than his fist, emitted a soft aquamarine glow, indents carved around its length like deep trenches. That old man had been in Paris for the year, coming back home so irregularly that he had no idea his son had already discovered the combination to his safe. There the boy found other treasures, but none like this crystal heart.

And so one cloudy day, the boy put on his frock jacket, slipping the crystal into one of its hidden underside pockets, and went out of his manor to central London.

It was the last day of the international fair, you see.

The crystal heart *was* the key. The boy's hypothesis was correct. His father's writings had already made clear the existence of the supernatural. But not even his father could have predicted what would come next. Here, inside the exhibit, a miracle would soon take place.

He'd needed her skeleton. The crystal heart had been dormant for so long. Even now that it seemed whole again, healed from its damages, it needed a spark—a push. Perhaps she needed her bones to build her flesh again. It was a wild guess, born from desperation.

This gallery, one of several in the colonial exhibition hall, was filled with clothing, raw materials, machinery, and fine art from Calabar and other surrounding regions in West Africa. They were in display cases lined around the room beneath a vaulted wooden ceiling; a stream of midday light leaked through the window. Flora and fauna surrounded maps and pictures of the region and its peoples, frozen in time for the education of South Kensington's spectators.

But even the boy had found it gaudy that they had included a human skeleton among the animal bones, front and center in a glass case as if in competition with that macabre display of human organs in Paris's Museum of Man.

The boy's father had once told him that international expositions were nothing more than a spectacle showcasing a country's power: scientific invention and machinery, art, commercial goods, and treasures stolen from the colonies. The annual show in South Kensington, inspired by the universal expositions in Paris, was meant to display English material culture to the world, their art and industry. But with its paltry exhibits—pottery and jewelry; instruments and machinery both ancient and new; textiles and ivory taken from India; plants and flowers from Australia; paintings from France—the boy had regarded each of the galleries in disdain because he knew the truth: it was not industry, its new discoveries and inventions that would advance civilization.

It was this girl. This *golem*. She was the discovery that would bring about revolution.

With tiny, shaking hands, the boy brought the crystal up to the girl's skeleton. His plan was to place it within the rib cage.

But wondrous fate would have other plans. For elsewhere on the exhibition grounds, a secret experiment was brewing. He was right. The crystal heart needed a push. It would only be years later that the boy would learn the push's name: the Helios.

Before he could get near the skeleton, a wave of energy blasted him back, knocking him down to the floor. The crystal heart flew out of his hands. The earth rumbled. It seemed like the ground would shatter. An earthquake? An explosion? The boy shut his eyes and covered his ears, waiting for the worst of the tremors to subside.

And when it did, when he dared to look again, he saw something wondrous. The girl had been reborn in front of him.

Not a girl. A goddess. A *Titan*. That was what the boy remarked to himself as he stared upon the sight of her resurrection, both horrid and wondrous. In front of her skeleton, still hanging inside a shattered cage, she looked at her own hands and body, almost fearful.

It was as his father had feared from his research.

Once her small mouth had finished taking shape, harsh-sounding breaths shuddered up her newly formed throat, escaping from the tips of her raw, bloody, heart-shaped lips, but she didn't scream. Her wordless gasp may have been more of a test—a test of her lungs ballooning in her ribs for the first time, perhaps, in decades. Air passing through her small, rounded nose, released in slower and slower intervals. One test, one breath after another, after another.

She was Galatea, stunning in beauty. A doll come to life.

She sat naked and shaking on the ground. The boy stared, his face flushed, having never seen a young woman in such a state. His scientific mind was already drawing conclusions and writing out his next steps from the perfect results of his experiment. But this was soon drowned out by the cooing captivation of the weaker, mortal part of his brain.

This woman. She was of average height, but not nearly so mundane. Dark brown eyes, wide and round like a deer's, swallowed him up.

The boy stared up at her, not with fear, but with adoration.

The forbidden knowledge of eternal life was the bane of alchemists of the previous centuries. His grandfather had written in one of his published works that the pursuit of the secrets of the world was nothing more and nothing less than a celebration of a scientist's unquestioning trust in the exactness of his theories. Like Frankenstein and Coppelius from his favorite childhood stories—each possessed a kind of arrogance that flew in the face of society's moral laws and even the very will of the heavens.

But the boy no longer believed in that will. Now it was this demon he believed in.

"Are you a goddess?"

Had she heard him? Or had he only asked the question in his own mind? There were so many things he wished to tell this girl. First, his name: Adam Temple. Second, the misfortune of his life: that he had no one. That he believed their meeting was fate.

But beyond his name, how should he introduce himself to her? As her master? Her creator? Her savior? Her partner? Her friend? Her servant?

Confusing feelings mixed as he stared at this woman newly born into the world, innocent as a babe. Feelings that had never quite sorted themselves out, even as she disappeared from his presence. Even as he'd aged and began to search for her. Even as he'd joined the Enlightenment Committee with the intention of returning her to her true purpose.

It wasn't until he saw her on the London Bridge eleven years later. Finally, her true self. Finally, the goddess she was meant to be, her body wrapped in the sunset sky, her hands freshly stained with the ashes from her kills. It wasn't until she left him broken and screaming for her in the night that he realized what he would have told her in the exhibit that day.

"My name is Adam Temple. And I need you. Please . . . need me too. . . ."

Some might accuse him of being in love with death, and they would be correct. But death and Hiva were synonymous. Iris and Hiva were one. He loved Iris. He needed her as much as he needed this wicked world that had taken his family from him to end in a bloody haze of fire.

It was all one and the same.

This fact became clear when he ordered his carriage driver to take him to Westminster Hospital to see a boy he'd only glimpsed for a short time months ago. A boy who had arrived in London inside Van der Ven's home along with the other Hiva. His utter devotion and concern for Hiva: Adam had never forgotten it. He thought about it during quiet nights, and each time it disturbed him. The fanatical glee and torment warring in the boy's eyes. It haunted him at strange moments.

He'd learned what had happened to the boy after Bellerose's gruesome costume ball. And so he went to him in the dead of night. No visitors were allowed, but he was Lord Adam Temple. He was allowed anywhere. The doctor opened the door to his room.

The boy, Tom Fables, was paralyzed. He would never be able to walk again, the doctors told him. It mattered not to Fables. All that mattered was that his Hiva would soon come for him.

"He can't do anything without me," Fables told him, once the door was closed and he and Adam were alone. "He's mine, and I'm his. We were born to be together, Hiva and me."

The American's smile drooped to the side. Saliva began to drip from his lips. Adam recoiled. His right arm still pained him from when Iris had broken it. It was in a sling strapped to his chest. Fables looked at the bandage for a while until his eyes became unfocused.

"Where is he?" Fables asked, like a child at Christmastime asking for his presents. "Where's my Hiva? He hasn't left me. I know he hasn't. He'll come for me!"

"Why do you love him so?" Adam asked quietly, his hands clenched around his bowler hat. When the American's eyes widened with frenzy, he dreaded the answer.

"Why do I love him? He's the answer to all my dreams. He's going to save me from my terrible life. He's going to punish all my enemies. He's proof that there's a God out there who cares. Proof that I'm not alone. I love him. I love him. I love him. . . ."

He repeated it again and again, each time a hammer against Adam's skull, until Adam couldn't take it anymore.

He and I are not the same. Adam turned from him and rushed out the door, clenching his teeth as Fables's mad cries echoed through the hospital hallways. *I am not him. My love is different.*

Yes. He loved Iris. Her tenacity. Her courage. Her beauty. The curve of her body. The mischievous glint in her big brown eyes when she was about to do something daring. None of these things he loved remained, not in this Hiva who'd returned so suddenly with the trumpet wail of an eclipse.

But Iris was Hiva. Hiva was Iris. He needed her to remember her power. To respond to his wishes. To love him so that they could burn down this world together.

Every Adam needed his Eve. Under his direction, she would destroy the world and rebuild it in the image *he* desired.

His love was not madness, and he would soon prove it.

34

FRANTIC NEWS REPORTS FROM DIFFERENT PAPERS across the country all said the same thing. The Great War that had swallowed up Europe had seemed to come to a halt, but not because some armistice had been achieved between national leaders. Soldiers were disappearing across the continent.

No, not just soldiers. Villagers. Men, women, and children. Vanished from their homes.

"The British papers are only paying attention to the happenings in Europe, but similar tragedies are befalling different parts of the world, my lord," said Fool, who sat next to Adam in the carriage, his top hat lowered to cover his harlequin mask. "Two other Fools have been tracking her on Bellerose's orders. North and South America. Asia. All over the world, the same strange disappearances."

"Then Iris must have found a way to travel quickly across great distances." Adam pulled up his black gloves. "My father mentioned it once in one of his papers. That ancient civilizations devised methods to bend the rules of space and time. It's possible. Anything's possible when Iris is involved."

"Do you wish to ask your John Temple, my lord?"

Adam considered it. But the thought of seeing his father an emaciated

THE LADY OF RAPTURE

corpse, barely animated in his bed, made him shudder. "No. Just tell me where she is now."

"The South of France, the last I tracked."

The South of France it was. "Get my travel accommodations ready."

But Fool was silent. "Millions have died thus far, my lord," he said. "Even Bellerose has noticed. She's using it as a way to stir her guests to begin traveling to Africa. The Fools have sent out word that the end is near."

"So the Ark should be full. Iris's return to form certainly benefits Bellerose."

"Iris is now Hiva. She can no longer be swayed or controlled. If you see her, my lord, she may kill you—"

A backhand sent Fool's head twisting in the opposite direction so fast and so hard, Adam thought he'd heard his neck crack. Perhaps he'd hit him too hard. It didn't matter. The Fools couldn't die, not as long as their primary body, Dr. Heidegger, still lived.

Fool adjusted his neck. His mask did not budge one inch. It couldn't.

"Iris will respond to me. She is mine, after all."

"You're right," said Fool. "I'm sorry, my lord."

He's mine, and I'm his, came Tom Fables's voice, followed by his frantic giggles echoing in Adam's mind. No. They were not the same.

Adam *loved* Iris. And indeed, Iris would reciprocate. Now that she was truly who she was always meant to be: at his prodding, she would come to see that they were meant to be together. It was fate, the same that had brought them together in that exhibit more than ten years ago.

And so Adam traveled to the South of France.

Fool had tracked the trail of death across the winding medieval streets of Montpellier, the ancient castles on the French Riviera, the estate and gardens of Gourdon, and the villages above the rocky hills.

"She's up there, my lord," Fool told him as they stood upon a green hilltop. He pointed to a quiet hamlet strung together by white, rocky roads. "I saw her enter the home next to the tavern. She has not, as far as my eyes can see, left."

"Very good, Fool. I'll find her from here."

The roads were empty as the sun sank beyond the hills. Each click of his boot heel upon the asphalt drew eerie echoes that joined with the hooting of owls in the evergreen trees. Every once in a while, Adam would spy a pair of shoes by a potted plant, a skirt fluttering across the street like tumbleweed, a jacket hanging on a street sign. A children's toy or two.

Adam closed his eyes and soaked it in. The death. Only with cleansing could something new emerge. He'd dreamed of this. Wished for this. Started a war for this. And now his work had finally yielded fruit.

No, not yet. First he had to see her.

There could be only one end to this story.

Wind battered the tavern sign against the filthy window: LE FAUCON ET LE CORBEAU. "The Hawk and the Raven." The home next to it was run-down and yet still somehow quaint, with its tiny little chimney, rustic white brick, and black sloped roof. A light was on in one of the square bedroom windows. One flickering light in a dark void under the stars.

Iris. He followed her there.

Carefully, he closed the door behind him. There was only one gray room with no lighting. A pail of water had been knocked over. Streams of water wound around rickety chair legs. Small pots of soup—still hot, judging from the smoke—had been placed upon the table. Adam picked up one of the used spoons. The pants and undergarments slumped across the seats belonged to one adult and two children.

Adam thought of his mother, the Baroness, and his siblings, Abraham and Eva. What they could have been had they lived in a better world. Now there was a chance. A chance to build up what must first be torn down.

His heart thumped as he gazed up the staircase. Sucking in his breath, he ascended them quietly so as not to scare her.

But when he opened the door to the room, he knew there was nothing that could scare this woman, this creature of magic and wonder.

Iris. She sat upon a hard bed with white sheets. She sat with her back straight and her eyes unblinking. With her arms placed gingerly upon her knees, she stared at the full-length mirror against the wall directly opposite herself. She gazed into it without emotion, with nothing to even prove she was sentient but for the steady rise and fall of her chest.

She did not stir when Adam closed the door behind him.

"You ran so quickly from me, my love. I wonder, what was the cause?"

He said it gently, but he couldn't hide the accusation in his voice. His right arm still throbbed. She'd broken it. But it must have been in a fit of confusion. The Iris who didn't accept herself despised him. He wasn't a fool; he knew that much. But the Iris that was Hiva, the Iris that accepted her reason for existence, would not—*could not*—refuse him. He knew that as surely as he could feel the excited blood pumping through his veins.

"How does it feel?" he asked her. "To accept the necessity of death without fear? To stare into the void and let it overtake you? Does it stir you as it does me?"

He took a cautious step toward her before silently admonishing himself. What reason did he have to be cautious? Iris wasn't a stranger. She was not even apart from him. She was *of* him. It was he who had carried her crystal heart to her skeleton and given her life. It was his face that had been the first she'd looked upon in fifty years while her heart mended itself from the brutality of Seymour Pratt's experiments. No words could ever be sufficient to describe the closeness of their relationship, except that they were fated.

Adam took two more steps toward her, quick and brazen, before he noticed something next to her on the bed. Furrowing his eyebrows, he inspected it before the realization flooded over him. A crystal heart. Not white crystal. It was a pale peach color, but it looked the same as the one kept in his father's safe for so many years.

A crystal heart. Hers? No. It must have been the other Hiva's. There was a great crack in the surface. Adam suspected it was this damage that kept that Hiva's body from reforming once again. Of course—just like her heart so many years ago. Had Iris done it herself? If so, then she was knowingly keeping it dormant, knowingly keeping the other Hiva at bay. She would only do so if she had no other means to kill him for good.

Did that mean Iris wished to be the only Hiva to lay waste to this world?

The thought sent Adam down a spiral of speculation. But he kept himself calm. He wouldn't embarrass himself in front of her.

"Iris, speak to me." This time he closed the distance between them. Taking off his black jacket and throwing it to the ground, he touched her cheek. "Did you battle the other Hiva? Did he try to harm you?"

She did not respond. No. She did not even look at him. It was if he were part of the scenery. The air one never noticed. As useless as the broken lamp upon the clothing cabinet.

He pursed his lips and waited for an answer, the heat rising from his head. And then, when the answer did not come, he forced her head around roughly and made her look at him.

She didn't look at him. She looked through him.

And then she turned back to the mirror as casually as if she had brushed off a mosquito.

"Why?" Clenching his teeth, Adam stood up straight, his eyes taking in the dirty floral carpet underneath the bed, spread haphazardly over the wooden floor. "Why do you ignore me?" He thought back to that night. Her utter lack of interest. "Do you not see me as important?"

No answer. His fists began to shake.

"My name is Adam Temple. I lost my family, but I gained you instead. I gained a guardian angel. Proof of God's existence. I gained a purpose. And in turn I gave you your life again." He could feel his fingernails digging into his hot palms. "Iris, what do you call the one who gives you life? Your mother? Your father? Your maker? Your master? Aren't there many words for it? They're all just words, but in the end, there is a connection between you and me, no? One impossible to ignore, because without me, you would not be here. Without me, you would be rotting away inside a safe or on a cold experiment table for scientific study. Or maybe in a museum. An exhibit for all to see."

Iris's eyelashes fluttered with disinterest. It infuriated him.

"Do you hear me, Iris?"

Silence. Adam let the silence roll into minutes. How many had passed? He couldn't tell. It felt like he stood for an hour without uttering a word, without drawing Iris's attention. If it were out of malice, then Adam would understand. Indeed, he'd relished the hatred Iris would point in his direction in the old days, her sharp tongue like a bloody knife ready to strike. He would be just fine with her malice. Her desperation. Her anger and pain.

No, it was not out of malice that she ignored him. It was not some game she was playing to rile him up and drive him mad.

She simply did not care.

That. *That* was what drove him mad.

As easily as she batted a firefly away, Iris stood from the bed and turned to leave.

That was his breaking point.

He tackled her to the bed, the other Hiva's crystal heart flying off the sheets and crashing against the ground. As it rolled on the wooden planks, Adam pinned Iris down with one arm, the other one screaming in pain, but he ignored it. He brought his face close to hers. He forced her to look into his eyes and to see his love. To accept it. To accept his presence. To accept him.

My name is Adam Temple. And I need you. Please . . . need me too. . . .

He kissed her. He felt her soft lips against his, then ran his across her cheek and down her neck. He kissed her protruding collarbone. Then he kissed her stomach. Whatever cloth she was wearing tasted and felt like the air.

"You really are wrapped in the heavens, Iris," he whispered as his heart pounded, as the blood rushed down to his legs and he felt his pants tighten. "You are mine. I am yours."

He kissed a line from her stomach up to her chest, then to her cheek, but just before he kissed her lips once again, he chanced a look. He didn't want to. *It is a risk,* something from within him screamed. *Don't do it.*

He did it. He looked.

Iris's expression had not changed. She was not looking at him but at the ceiling.

She didn't care.

He had spent his childhood thinking of her. He'd killed for her. Started a war for her.

And she just didn't care.

He was nothing to her. Not an object of hatred or revenge. Not a partner. Not even a human to incinerate.

He was nothing.

Adam's hand found her throat. And he was squeezing so hard, saliva began to drip from his mouth.

"You are mine. I own you. I created you. You dare, you *dare*, treat me like this? *You?* You, who were once put on display like a filthy animal?"

And he cursed at her. He cursed at himself.

"I come from a line of knights and lords. My power can shake mountains and move the nations of this earth. I gave you your life. And yet you . . ."

And yet she was the god, not him. She was the one with the power he'd desired since childhood. The power to punish his enemy: *humanity.*

His power could shake mountains and move the nations of this earth, and yet it still paled in comparison to hers. It was only in this moment he realized just how *infuriated* this made him.

He envied her.

Finally her lips began to move. Adam held his breath, blinking back tears. She was forming a word. She was speaking to him. The word was coming. With an exhale of breath, it would soon be here. What would she say to him? *Thank you? I see you? I love you?*

"Ji . . . nn . . ."

Adam's left hand went numb. Iris pushed him off her, not with annoyance, but with a polite expelling of breath. She brushed herself off. And without a word, she left the house on the green hill next to the tavern.

What happened to him next, Adam wasn't sure he could describe it. He lay down upon the bed for hours. He stared at the ceiling and thought of Tom Fables paralyzed in a hospital, abandoned and yet still crazed with devotion over a god who'd left him behind. He listened all through the night to his own heartbeat and to the owls and crickets, his eyes open, until the sounds together drove him mad.

Adam's world turned a harrowing white.

35

T HE BASEMENT OF ADAM'S LONDON HOME felt bare without his abductees. They'd escaped after Bellerose's ball. Yet another mistake he'd made because of his hyperfocus on Iris.

There were to be no more mistakes.

For two days he'd sat in front of the rotting and helpless Dr. Heidegger until Adam's clothes were as filthy as his. He did not eat, nor did he feed the former serial killer as the man mumbled feverishly. Sitting with his legs crossed and his back hunched, Adam listened to each detached sentence, using what he knew of the Fools to discern which persona the doctor was channeling at each moment.

"Yes, Madame, I agree. If Malakar is not able to produce a power source in time, we would have to make our guests wait in such uncomfortable tropical lodgings while we procure Hiva's heart. . . . Oh yes, Alva Vanderbilt looks quite beautiful—many would say so—but she pales in comparison to Madame's beauty. Indeed, the African sun has been shown to be a horror for Alva's already patchy skin. . . ."

The Pompous Fool. No doubt he was buttering Madame Bellerose up. But if the Vanderbilts were already in Africa, that meant Adam's Fool was correct: the invitees of the Ark had begun to gather in the Atakora Mountains. Their interdimensional voyage, exclusive only to the rich and powerful, would soon set sail—that is, if all the pieces were in place.

The Fools were the Enlightenment Committee's greatest source of intelligence. Right now they were Adam's best bet to gather the information that he needed.

"You blasted twins! I swear to God, I'll tear you limb from limb!"

Adam flinched. Heidegger's yellow teeth gnashed at the air, his lips curved into a snarl for a moment, before:

"Oh, I'm sorry. I'm sorry, my sweets, I would never . . ."

And Heidegger's body went languid. The Impulsive Fool, then. Without context, the threat was meaningless. Yet he listened for hours more, waiting for information he could glean. And when he was done, he put each fragmented line in logical order, like pieces to a puzzle.

"That bastard Bosch has secured the mining site. But so far none have dared venture into the Coral Temple, not after what happened to the last soldiers that went inside. They're scared, the little cowardly shits."

"Bellerose's new toy, Bately, will force them to go inside. Don't worry, Doctor Pratt's going with him. He'll be able to bring Bately back to life if he croaks."

The Spiteful Fool was the gabbiest, it seemed. It went along with his crankiness.

"A Fanciful Freak? Where? Why is that boy in Lagos? Shall I follow him?"

As Heidegger's lips trembled shut, Adam frowned. A Fanciful Freak in Lagos? A male . . . surely he didn't mean Maximo or his friends.

Unless, Adam thought darkly, *he means* him.

He pushed the thought of that circus clown out of his mind. No more of that. With his new purpose, he was through with such petty emotions as jealousy. He'd promised himself.

"Hiva's Tomb! I want to see Hiva's Tomb inside the Coral Temple!" Heidegger cooed like the Desperate Fool Adam knew him to be, probably on his back, begging to be petted like a dog. "I wonder, how shall I go? Through the wicked labyrinth of Heaven's Shrine? Or shall I *jump* there from the lagoon? Jump! Jump! Jump!" He began giggling. "Yes, I want to disappear and reappear again. How exciting. . . . Please take me with you. . . . Lads, don't leave me behind. . . ."

Out of hundreds of ramblings, these were the threads of thought Adam had picked out over the course of two and a half days, without eating, without sleeping, without so much as bathing. And there was one more.

"Yes, Madame Bellerose. Hiva's Tomb is, as far as we know, the greatest weapon against Hiva. Imagine a machine that can disassemble a man's body into its finest of atoms. . . . Oh, no, Madame—well, it hasn't been tested. . . . I'm not sure if it could destroy the crystal heart. . . . Ah, yes, Madame. We will attempt to retrieve it. And the Moon Skeleton. For the sake of the Ark . . . no, no, you won't be embarrassed. I, on my grandiose honor, fully guarantee—"

The Pompous Fool fell silent. Madame Bellerose was probably screaming at him.

Adam searched his memories, every recollection he had of his father's research and writings that he had been able to get his hands on throughout his lifetime. Every mention of Hiva. Yes, he'd mentioned it before: a way to clip a god's wings. A way to destroy Hiva. Was it the Hiva's Tomb? A machine capable of disassembling man . . . breaking down human flesh . . .

The Naacal would have been able to do so with their technical prowess. But surely they'd known that the Tomb would not be able to destroy the crystal heart. It could be damaged but not destroyed. Seymour Pratt's experiments had proved it.

Adam's own experiments as well.

Adam looked down at the crystal heart on his lap. Pale pink with a faint, dull glow. Round, just bigger than an apple. The gash that Iris had made still throbbing.

He'd tried everything in the days following his sojourn to the South of France, using every resource he could muster, and it seemed Pratt had been correct: It could not be melted or burned. It could not be sliced or broken. And eventually, no matter what damage it had incurred, it would mend itself. And Hiva would form anew.

It had taken Iris's own crystal heart decades to mend. Was this Hiva different? Adam didn't want to take any chances, for on the night he'd been rebuffed by his Hiva, he'd made a decision that defied even the cruelest and most foolish of minds.

Foolish, yes. But in his heart he knew it to be the only course of action he had left. Perhaps this had been his fate all along. A blessed fate. And a cursed one.

Adam left Dr. Heidegger to rot in his basement, dismissing his maids. Without anyone to care for him, he would starve and die soon. Then so too would the Fools. An acceptable loss. He didn't need them to interfere with his schemes. It was a fitting end to the Harlequin Slasher.

So then what should be my father's fitting end?

He readied himself for a hospital visit.

Sitting at his father's bedside silenced his macabre thoughts. A strange irony, for if Adam had ever been seen as a bloodthirsty demon by his friends or by his enemies, then it was his father's actions that were to blame. His father had started everything.

There wasn't any use in hating him now. Not now that his father's body had finally begun to fail, despite the doctor's best efforts. He could no longer eat, not after the parasites had eaten his stomach and intestines. Funny how, despite his medals and accolades, despite his great discoveries and his fame, those tiny creatures had defeated him. They had won the war against science. The laudanum would only keep his emotions steady, at least until the time came.

John Temple was half his usual size underneath the white sheets of his hospital bed. With great effort, he pried open his struggling, milky eyes and looked upon his son. A gentle smile crossed his face. The opium, perhaps. Adam returned it, though his carried no feeling.

"My son," John Temple said, with a voice that more believably belonged to mummified remains. "You've come to see me. That means . . . you've forgiven me."

It wasn't a question. It was a statement. That was how Adam knew that his father had learned nothing. Unable to put himself in the shoes of his son, who had suffered and spiraled without him. It was his own thoughts, his own feelings, his own aspirations, that mattered most. He desired a son who didn't hate him, and so he'd invented one. Adam had only played his part.

"It's been a long time, Father," Adam said. "I'm quite sorry I tried to kill you."

The cough from John Temple's lips was perhaps meant to be a laugh. His pale face looked as if all the fat in his cheeks had disintegrated.

"If only there were a panacea to cure all humans of their misery," he said. "Then there would be no need for apologies. No need for woe."

But you have not once apologized to me. Adam cleared his throat.

"Many things are happening, Father," Adam said. "I need your great mind and wisdom. Hiva's Tomb inside the Coral Temple—"

John Temple's eyes widened. "You know of it?"

"There are many things I've been able to piece together, Father. I know it's a great machine created by the Naacal. I know it's the only way to stop the threat of Hiva, which sadly has befallen our world since your disappearance."

As John Temple's parched lips rubbed against each other, bits of dry skin flaked off. "Yes. Of course you know, Adam. You've always been a smart lad." He fell silent. "So the threat of Hiva hasn't been quelled."

"How can one stop a god that cannot be killed?"

"But Hiva can be killed for good. Only Hiva's own bones can destroy her."

Hiva's own bones? Adam unconsciously placed a hand on top of his jacket pocket. Inside, Hiva's crystal heart was quite heavy. Iris had taken his heart but not killed him. Was Iris unable or unwilling to procure his bones? It didn't matter. Iris's oversight was his boon.

"To my understanding, the female Hiva had been stabbed through the heart with a sword made of her bones. This was what Malakar told me before my voyage back to London. But there's another Hiva. One, perhaps, from another world. I believe he can be killed by *his* bones."

But that was just the thing.

Adam did not want this new Hiva to die.

"Father, what about Hiva's Tomb?" he pressed gently, so his father would not suspect the sudden shift in his questioning. "The Naacal had devised it thinking it would kill Hiva."

"Not kill. No, darling boy, they knew it would not kill her. It would disassemble her body down to her atoms, but only as far as the Tomb draws power. But there is no energy source that lasts forever. Eventually, Hiva's atoms would reassemble inside the glass."

It was as Adam had hypothesized. What the Naacal had created was nothing more than a cage meant to stall the cataclysm until they could truly destroy her.

If that was the case, then Hiva's Tomb would be of use to him.

"Adam, my boy."

Adam waited through the long pause that felt as if it would last forever. He waited as if he were a small child again and hated himself for it. But feelings of sentimental nostalgia were soon wiped away. John Temple suddenly managed a smile. A proud one.

"You've done well."

His father was a fool. But here, at least, he was quite right.

Throughout the several days he'd locked himself in the basement with Heidegger, he'd only once looked at the portrait of himself as a boy in the corner, the one painted after he'd just graduated from Eton. A charming prince from a powerful family.

A weak, pathetic bag of flesh. Just like all humans.

He only once looked at it—not because he was ashamed. Not because he knew that the boy, by that time, had already succumbed to his worship of death. It was because Adam's new schemes had seized him wholly. His goal—his *new* goal, which was not at all different from his first—played out in startlingly vivid fashion in his own mind. A cruel and foolish endeavor. But one that needed to be done.

If only there were a panacea that could clear all human misery. Or the misery that *was* humanity. But if one didn't exist . . .

Then one could be made.

His father was right. Adam *had* done well.

"Tell me everything, Father, about how Hiva's Tomb works."

36

HOW IS JINN?" MAX ASKED UMA, knowing he had absolutely no right to. Saying Jinn's name made him feel superstitious—as if he would never see heaven if he ever dared to utter it. Well, he was going to hell anyway.

The scientist plopped down in her chair, dark shadows beneath her eyes. "The surgery's over, but this is a crucial period. We'll have to wait and see," was all she said.

When the group told Uma of their grand plan, she'd made them all sit down like children being scolded by their mother. Or at least what Max remembered a mother to be like. If they were going to do it, they would explain it to her plainly. And she would decide if she'd let them do it. *Fine,* Max thought. *Isn't she a genius? If anyone can find another way, she can.*

Rin was gone. She hadn't come back since stomping out of the apartment. He couldn't blame her. In fact, he desperately wanted to beg her forgiveness.

"My guards are outside," Uma said, smoking from her pipe, exhausted from the surgery. "If what you say makes sense, I'll let you leave. If it doesn't, they'll shoot you down."

"You sure you can hold us, mate?" Hawkins tilted his head in a cocky way that made Max sigh in irritation.

"Just try me, *mate.*"

Her house. Her rules.

Max sat on the long couch first. The others soon followed. Hawkins sat on the couch with his back pin straight. Hawkins was being unnecessarily stubborn. But they were all just struggling against the inevitable. No one wanted to die.

And Max understood. For as he sat next to his sister, who made sure to link her arm in his, he remembered how desperately he'd wanted to find her. Now that she was here, it felt like a small slice of peace—as if the universe that had taken so much from him had finally decided to give him something back. But when he gave her an encouraging smile, he remembered all the sacrifices he'd made just to find her. All the betrayals.

He'd almost given up on life because of them. But he had a responsibility to see this through. He knew that from the moment he'd woken up on Uma's floor, his sister holding him.

Uma laid out a world map on the floor before swinging around an iron fireplace poker. "You said you wish to use the Titans to destroy Hiva."

From the couch next to Hawkins, Jacob lifted his hand like a boy in school. He seemed to realize it too, because he lowered it quickly, blushing. Max smirked. He didn't know why Jacob would want to hide that adorable side of him. It made Max smile. Maybe he should have told him that more often when they were kids.

"The last time we killed Iris, it was with her own bones," Jacob said.

We. You mean me. Max said nothing. Jacob wasn't a fool; he was just too kind.

"Hiva can only be killed by her own bones—we know that," Jacob continued. "But last time Hiva and Fables took Iris's skeleton from an exhibit inside the British Museum, and now that exhibit's been burned down. Her bones are gone. So if we're going to kill her . . . these Titans may be our only shot."

"That's a contradiction," said Uma. "Nothing can kill her but her bones. That includes the Titans. Why take the risk if it won't get rid of her? As ghoulish as this may sound, why don't we just confront her head-on and try to take another one of her bones?"

"You're right," Max muttered, "it does sound ghoulish." As if Iris could just be disassembled for parts. He glared at Uma. "When we tried that Hail Mary on the other Hiva, one of us died. But heck, why not? Let's give it another go." He looked around. "Right, then. We attack Iris, who's currently on a rampage.

Steal a limb or two somehow without getting burnt to a crisp. Any volunteers?" He waited, but the room was silent as a tomb. "Thought so."

Berta spoke up. "Okay, then why did the Naacal create Hiva's Tomb? Wasn't it to stop her any way they could? Even if you could just slow her down, isn't that better than her razing the earth to the ground?"

For some reason, of all people, it was Berta whose words hurt Max the most. He wouldn't say it. But he wondered why she'd brought it up in the first place. No, that wasn't right. He'd killed Iris for *her*; why wouldn't she for *him*? Max sighed. The pair of siblings they were.

"The Titans are said to be somewhere inside the Atlas Mountains in Northern Africa." Uma pointed to a mountain range close to Morocco with her pointer.

Sitting in a chair with Henry hovering over her, Mary frowned. "Inside the mountains?"

Uma nodded. "I cross-referenced all of John Temple's writings about the Titans with my own research on Naacalian experimentation and warfare. The work I did on the Helios was integral. And you know what I found?"

She waited. They were all silent.

"Each of the two Titans is equipped with an energy weapon that has power, speed, and damage capabilities thousands of times that of the most destructive torpedo other humans have created thus far. Fire this weapon and you won't only take out Hiva. You'll take out the entire Ourika Valley." She tapped the northern tip of the mountain range. "Perhaps even the imperial cities all the way to the Atlantic Coast." She traced a circle, connecting all the dots. "As far as El Jadida, maybe even Casablanca. How many people do you think that is? A million? More?"

A chill descended upon the group.

This time it was Lulu who held up her hand. The little thing sat in an oak chair, swinging her legs because her feet didn't even touch the ground.

"Yes?" Uma answered like a schoolmarm, unironically.

"I don't know much about everything that's going on, but . . ." Lulu rubbed her chin, lifted her gaze to the ceiling, and thought aloud. "I really like this place. You know, my parents always talked about Africa as this 'motherland' for us, you know? Like, we have a history here. It's where our story started, my mom used to say."

That was right. She was an American. Max remembered with a slight chill how casually she'd told him of the demise of her family.

"I like this place, and I don't want to see anything bad happen to it. I don't want to see that anymore. In church, I never really liked it when Jacob went into the Promised Land and just killed everybody, but my mom just said, 'Well, some people gotta be sacrificed for God's people.' But we ain't God. And we're trying to decide who gets sacrificed and who doesn't? And it's always people who look like me—"

By now Lulu must have realized she was babbling, because she sucked in her lips and folded her arms with a sigh. Max wondered if she also realized she was the only one here making any damn sense.

"Someone's got to go," Hawkins whispered, flinching when Jacob, sitting next to him, tossed him a conflicted frown. Gathering himself, he continued. "Look, I'll tell you right now. I don't care about strangers, whether they're in El Jadida, France, or goddamn Japan. I care about the people I can see with my own two eyes. The people I love. *My* folks." Perhaps unconsciously, he gripped Jacob's hand. "I've already lost too many."

Uma inhaled some smoke from her pipe and puffed it out casually. "What a selfish way of thinking," she said. "Perhaps that's why Iris feels we need to die."

"Well, we won't." Henry gripped the back of Mary's chair. "None of us will. This is it. I'm tired of the bloody sword of Damocles dangling over our heads."

Max raised an eyebrow. *Sword of who?*

Uma smirked. "Oh, as educated as he is impetuous," she said, making him turn red.

Lucille laughed and babbled in a language nobody could understand. She knew it and seemed to enjoy it, waving her hands as if giving a grand speech at the opera.

"Have we met before?" Berta scratched her head, her eyebrows furrowed. Lucille stopped.

"*Met?*" Max turned to his sister. "How in the world would you have met this woman?"

But Berta stroked her chin, staring intensely at Lucille's aged mask of a face. "Your voice sounds so familiar. I'm not kidding. You seriously sound . . ."

Berta trailed off, shaking her head, because she wasn't sure. A mischievous grin was all Lucille would give her in response. Max grimaced. This was all a joke to her, wasn't it?

"Well, none of this matters, because if Rin is to be believed, the Titan Control Device is currently charcoal in a furnace." Max crossed his arms. "It's over. Just forget it."

He looked to Uma for support; the scientist's cagey expression didn't bode well. Slowly, Max unfolded his arms.

"I . . . I did see Lulu throw it into the furnace," Berta whispered to Max, though her voice could be clearly heard in the dead-silent room. "You did, kid, didn't you?"

Lulu nodded.

Without looking at her, Uma cried, "Aminadab!"

It took almost a minute for her assistant to hobble up the steps from the basement and into the room where the group was gathered. But the glittering tablet wrapped in hastily folded cloth in his hand was unmistakable. Max felt cold. No bloody way.

"We tried to destroy it," Uma whispered. "Fire didn't do it. Pressure. It's . . . a phenomenally made device. Strong. Too strong for us."

Seeing the tablet, pristine as if untouched by man, made Max's limbs feel numb. He opened his mouth and closed it several times before looking, heartbroken, at Berta. *Oh, Berta, this can of worms . . . You shouldn't have opened your mouth about this one.*

But there was no triumph in Berta's expression. The rose in her cheeks had disappeared from her face, leaving her sickly pale at the sight of it. As if she'd suddenly realized that words had consequences. They really were alike.

"I'll ask one more time." Uma held out her hand. Aminadab placed the tablet in it. "Are you sure you want to do this? Are you sure there is no other choice? This is your last chance."

"I'm not changing my vote." Hawkins kept his gaze on the floor, but he shook his head steadfastly nonetheless. "No way."

"Neither am I," said Henry.

Neither was Max. But Max had voted no. And the "no" votes were in the minority.

The silence that followed was confirmation. The majority still ruled.

Max buried his head in his hands. Cold sweat began forming underneath his hairline. There had to be something he could do. Not sitting here silently, helplessly, paralyzed—like the moment he'd realized his little sister had been whisked away from him in the foreign London streets. He'd hurt Iris enough, hadn't he? He had to do something. But his mind had gone blank.

"In that case, all of you will do your utmost to evacuate the Ourika Valley and surrounding cities. That's not up for debate," Uma added, because Hawkins had already begun to protest. "This is serious, and lives are at stake. I couldn't destroy the device, so I studied it. I won't tell you anything about it unless I know you're not going to half-ass this."

"And how are we supposed to manage evacuating hundreds of thousands of people?" Hawkins grumbled, running his hands through his golden locks.

"You're all men and women of various extraordinary talents. You'll come up with a plan." She waved the device in her hands. "I'll give you seven days. Afterward, we'll lure Iris to Ourika Valley by the river."

"But *how*?" Henry complained. He and Hawkins were the ones pushing this the most. Max hadn't missed it. Then again, all they wanted was to see their friends and family alive and well. And if you wanted something badly enough, you'd do anything for it.

If you wanted something badly enough. Slowly, Max lifted his head out of his hands.

That was it.

"Well . . ." Mary seemed surprised by her own voice. Clearing her throat, she spoke with more force. Might as well, if she were going to help murder someone. Wouldn't be the first time. It was always the quiet ones you had to watch out for. "Is there something that she wants?"

"There is." Max rubbed his cold, sweaty hands together, because it had suddenly come to him. "And when we dangle it in front of her, I'm sure—I *know* that she'll come for it."

"Oh, Morales?" Henry gave Max a skeptical look. "And what's that?"

Max looked at him. "Jinn."

37

IT WAS LIKE HE'D BREATHED IN the first whiff of fresh air after years of being buried. Max had never been surer of anything in his life.

"I don't know how long it'll take for Jinn to wake up or what condition he'll be in once he does. *If* he does," Max corrected himself. "But whether he's sleeping or not, someone's gotta drag the bloke to Ourika Valley, and that someone is gonna be me."

"No!" Berta yelled. "If you're with him, Iris will come straight for you too. You're putting *yourself* in danger!"

"Yep!" Max shrugged with a cheerful grin.

No matter how many times Berta cursed, no matter what she threw at the wall, his mind wasn't changing.

If they were going to do this, they were going to do it his way.

This was the way. It was simple in theory when Uma explained it.

Her apartment was some kind of safe haven from Iris. Why? Because it carried so much of Iris's own body—the white crystals. The anima of those crystals masked their own. The crystals surrounding Jinn, keeping him clinging to life after the surgery.

It was what Max had put him through. *Jinn . . . I'm sorry, mate. I'll make it up to you.*

Hawkins hadn't known, but it had been a boon for Max to recover here after Iris had tried to take his life.

This was the plan:

"Max, once we've evacuated the area, Hawkins will teleport you and Jinn to the valley. Iris will come for Jinn," Jacob said to the group. He seemed calm. Like he'd already acquiesced to Max's cockamamie scheme. Well, there wasn't much choice. "Max and Hawkins will stay with Jinn and wait for Iris in the valley. The rest of us will remain at a safe distance—on the other side of the mountains. Once Iris arrives, Hawkins will let us know, and we'll start operations on the Titans—that is, once Uma tells us how to operate them."

Something about the Titans didn't even feel real. Despite all the impossibilities they'd witnessed with their own eyes, Max didn't think anyone truly felt they existed just yet. Ancient mechanical wonders, scientific death machines from a previous civilization, hiding in the mountains all these thousands of years. Max needed to see them. He needed real proof.

Soon that proof would come.

Max wasn't sure how they'd managed it. He was ordered to stay inside the safe zone of Uma's lab. All the while, the others worked. Bargaining. Begging. And days passed. Hawkins, with his teleportation, was able to move between areas across the northern African region. Uma sent out Bosch's men, loyal as much to her as to him, to move as many people as they could out of the region. The Ourika Valley would be a testing ground for his weapons, she'd told him. And while they worked to evacuate the villagers, Max paced day after day, running his hands through his hair, reminding himself that this was the right choice. That his plan would work.

His plan. Not theirs.

"You really should have gone with them," he told Berta one day, because the girl steadfastly remained at his side. She sat in a chair with her legs crossed, cleaning a shotgun—her favorite type of gun. Max felt a little proud he knew that.

"I'm not gonna let anything go wrong," she said without looking at him. "Not again."

"Love your big brother, don't you?" Max smirked. "You wouldn't if you really knew me. I haven't exactly made the best choices."

"Oh, stop with the self-loathing already." Berta groaned, rolling her eyes, and let her gun rest on her lap. "You think I haven't killed a few people? Neither of us are angels. Some of it wasn't our fault, but some of it was. Either way, it doesn't matter. Just gotta keep on living on our terms. Maybe find a way to make it up. Maybe not. I'm tired of worrying about what's right or wrong. Sometimes surviving's enough. And if the devil snatches us up, then so be it. It's a rough life, so you gotta be rough too."

Max noticed how her gaze lingered along the shining wood of her shotgun. "And who taught you to be so tough?"

Berta scoffed, gripping her cloth and rubbing it back down the gun's shaft. "There was a woman who took me to Nevada from Europe. She taught me a bunch, like how to shoot. Then she went on the run."

"Ran away with a lover?"

"Nah, she shot that cheating bastard."

Max cleared his throat. "Bloody hell. Right, then."

"She always said Nevada was never meant to be her final stop. She took me on a whim, but she always planned on going back to Europe. Singing a little opera. Then maybe traveling down to China, because apparently on top of being a gambling brothel owner and a former opera singer, she was friends with an imperial prince of the Qing Dynasty." Berta laughed. "Never could trust that idiot and her crazy lies. She saved me, then dumped me. That's when I knew I had to do shit on my own."

Berta's hand froze, the dirty cloth still in it. Slowly she narrowed her eyes and lowered her gun.

"Wait a second . . . ," she whispered, and suddenly her eyebrows were knitted tight, her brown eyes widening. "That voice . . ."

Max tilted his head. "What?"

Berta jumped out of her seat. "That voice. That lady's voice—"

Nothing. Max waited. Berta looked as if she could burn a hole in the wall with her wild glare alone. But finally she shook her head and sat down.

"Nah, can't be her. I'm going nuts. Forget it!" And she went back to cleaning her rifle.

Max laughed. Not a bright or strong sound, but the feeling filled him with a sense of relief he hadn't felt in a long time. "I'll say one thing, you've become quite the interesting girl. I definitely look forward to getting to know you better one day. When this is all over, I mean."

When it was all over. Assuming they both survived. Max stopped laughing.

"I didn't vote to kill her, by the way," Berta whispered, brushing a brown curl out of her face. "I voted 'no.' Just so you know. Doesn't matter now, I guess."

"I see." Max considered her words as he rubbed his hands along the couch's seat. The red upholstery gave his palms a slight tickle. After a careful inhale, he gazed at her.

"If this all goes right, there will be a 'one day,' Berta," he told her. "You're right. We just gotta live how we can. And from now on, I'm not living without you. I hope you trust me."

Berta didn't look at him. But she did smile.

One day.

Seeing his sister smile, Max wanted to see that "one day."

38

IT WAS TIME. JINN STILL WASN'T awake, but they couldn't afford to wait any longer.

After seven days had passed, the group met again. Torn clothes and worn faces. Wounded bodies. For Lucille, a face Max had never seen before: an elongated chin and shocking catlike eyes that reminded him of a sculpture of an Egyptian king—or at least a parody of one. The long, twisted black beard was an extra ridiculous touch.

"Pardon me, I wasn't trying to look like an Egyptian king," Lucille answered when Max questioned her. "I was trying to look like I was from the Bible. Not that I've ever read it myself." She scrunched up her nose and shuddered. "But the Berber people seem to believe they're descended from Canaan and Noah and all those Old Testament folks. Pretending to be a mythological figure giving orders from on high isn't easy."

"Did they even believe you?" Henry muttered, slouched over and grabbing his arms, bare because the sleeves were torn off.

Berta glared at Lucille as she laughed. The shape-shifter was no longer using some old woman's voice, nor was she speaking in some gibberish language. Jacob must have relented there. Saving the world made for strange bedfellows. Berta rubbed her chin, listening to her voice, even though the face was all wrong. Wondering.

Beyond Lucille, who seemed extra chatty with her newly regained ability to speak English, none were in the mood to regale him with stories. All that mattered was that the deed was done. Together, Hawkins, Jacob, Henry, Mary, and Lucille had managed it. The valley had been evacuated to the best of their abilities. That was what Hawkins had said, and that was what Max chose to believe. Uma believed it too. And so, in the early morning, Uma gave them a demonstration.

She bit her thumb and pressed the bleeding flesh against the swirling pattern at the top half of the double-sided control device. Ah yes, blood. Berta said it'd taken blood to gain the tablet in the first place. Sacrifice. One had to pay to use such a terrible device.

Uma's blood filled the crevices of the engravings until the tablet absorbed it. Seconds later, a projection of blue light appeared, hovering just above the device.

Good lord, Max thought as Lulu and Berta gasped. *A compass!* Except as Uma twisted her hand above the light, the arrow moved along with it. When she twisted her hand to the left, the arrow followed. To the right. Ninety degrees. It followed its puppet master.

"This controls the direction of the projectile. And I believe the other buttons activate each Titan: The sun symbol." She pointed to one side of the tablet. "The moon symbol." The other side. "They seem to have the exact same capabilities. But take heed. I still don't know everything about this device— only what I can glean from research. But research isn't everything. There's no telling what will happen on the ground." She waved her hand across the blue compass light. It disappeared. "But if you're ready for that . . ."

"We will be," Max told her, just as the door to the apartment opened, and in walked Rin.

The room fell silent. Max's chest tightened, but soon a little gasp escaped his lips when he took in the sight of her. He was used to Rin, the hardened one-eyed warrior, more ferocious than her sixteen years would suggest. He wasn't used to Rin like this.

He stared at her plain, beautiful dress, the hem of which brushed her battle-strengthened calves. A shocking moss-green color, with a white bow for a collar. Her braids had been newly weaved too. The fresh white bandage wrapped around her missing right eye was the one reminder Max even had that she wasn't some dainty young lady.

But the dress style, the color of it . . . it all reminded him of those days during the Tournament of Freaks. The days he'd fought alongside Iris, who had refused to wear anything else but the clothes her Granny Marlow had sewn for her, as if for luck. The way Iris would sometimes grip it like a security blanket. It was all too familiar.

"Where did you get those clothes?" Max asked, wild suspicions starting to bubble up in his mind. "Where have you been?"

"It doesn't matter. I'm here now," Rin said, without so much as a tremor in her voice. "And I'm ready for the mission."

Berta was staring at her, hollowed out, as if she couldn't look away. Nobody seemed completely convinced, but the plan was already in motion. Whatever Rin felt or wanted to do was irrelevant.

It's okay, Rin, Max wanted to say, but there were too many people around. *I've got this.*

"Well, then," Uma said. "If you're all ready . . ."

She gave the Titan Control Device to Jacob. Covering the tablet with his large hands, he closed his eyes, lowered his head, and began whispering in some language Max didn't understand. Who was he praying to? Or was he even praying at all? Neither of them were religious, despite the attempts of some London missionaries who had specialized in bringing orphans to God. Perhaps he was asking Cherice for strength. Or maybe it was an apology to Iris for what they were about to do.

"Hawkins will transport Lucille, Mary, Henry, and Jacob to the southern border of the Atlas Mountains," said Uma. No map was needed. The group had seen enough of the lands with their own eyes.

"What about us?" Berta asked.

"I want you and Lulu to stay with me to help with Jinn's recovery," Uma said. "Don't worry. The others have it covered. After Hawkins transports the others, he'll take Max and our downstairs Sleeping Beauty to Ourika Valley. There they will wait for Iris."

Max squeezed his eyes and slapped his cheeks a few times for good measure. It was do-or-die time. There was no telling what Iris would do when she saw him and Jinn. Would she hug Jinn and kill him? Kill them both? But this was the role he'd chosen for himself. He had his own plan, and he was going to see it through.

"Remember, Max," continued Uma. "Once you leave this apartment, you leave its protection. I don't know how long it'll take for Iris to find Jinn, but once she does . . ." She shook her head. "There's nothing I can do from here."

"That's why I'll be patrolling," said Hawkins. "Going back and forth. Watching Max and the others. When Iris shows up, I'll tell Jacob immediately. Just before the Titans shoot, I'll grab Max and Jinn out of there. I've been working on my teleportation speed. It'll work."

Rin sneered at the sound of their plan. "And you think Jinn is just going to go willingly?"

"He won't be in any shape to refuse," Hawkins retorted.

As Hawkins spoke, it felt to Max like such a hackneyed plan, such a Hail Mary scheme. What if Iris burned both of them alive before they even had a chance to signal Jacob? How long would it even take for the Titans to become operational? Iris could destroy lives in seconds. This plan hinged on Max and Jinn's ability to keep Iris occupied for as long as they needed.

"I'll go with you," Rin offered casually. And yet that casual offer drew everyone's surprised stares.

"What?" Berta narrowed her eyes.

"I'll go with Max. I'll stay with him. With Jinn."

"To do what?" Berta began moving toward the door, but Max lifted a hand to stop her.

"No, that's perfect," he said. And he truly meant it. His plan for Iris needed someone like Rin. Someone else she was connected to. Rin coming along was perfect.

"Max!" Hawkins prodded, but Max didn't repeat himself. He didn't need to. There was a look in Rin's eyes that he quite liked. A tender sense of determination that matched his own.

Hawkins huffed. "I can't guarantee I'll be able to rescue *all* of you."

"Whatever happens, happens," said Rin. "We're all putting our lives on the line. Maybe none of us will survive."

If the room weren't silent before, then what surrounded Max now was the loneliness of a graveyard. It was the kind of silence that seemed unscalable. Berta turned away, her hands squeezed into fists. Jacob bit his lip while Henry, Lucille, and Mary shifted on their feet. Hawkins went stiff but didn't relent. Only Uma seemed to have enough courage to respond.

"I certainly hope you, at least, survive," Uma told her. "You are a phenomenal woman, Olarinde. One of the strongest I've met."

Rin bowed her head ever so slightly. Max looked over to Berta and could tell she wanted to say something. For a time she kept her gaze low. But then, with a loud whimper, she ran to the Dahomey warrior and gripped both of her hands. It was an action that took them both by surprise.

"You are, Rin," Berta said, squeezing Rin's hands so tightly, Max could see her knuckles redden. "You are strong. Stronger than me. I—" She paused. "I'm so sorry. About everything."

She waited, but Rin's gaze stayed on the floor. Her hands were trembling. Or was it Berta who was shaking? Max couldn't tell. Just what had happened between those two while he was gone? Both girls looked so hurt and betrayed. As if they both had so much to confess to the other. Two girls who'd lived broken lives filled with violence.

"We'll begin the preparations," Uma said. "You may be in the valley for some time. Make sure you get what you need beforehand."

Following Uma's orders, the group dispersed, and for one hour they gathered what they needed—all, that is, except Max, who felt he already had what he needed. His body, still miraculously healthy. His mind, thinking more clearly than ever before.

When the apartment was empty but for Uma and her assistant, Max hesitantly descended the steps into the lab. He took in the tools and instruments that Aminadab was cleaning with a washcloth and a bucket, the world map on the wall, and the furnace in the corner. But it was the violet drapes in the center of the room that drew his attention.

And who was inside.

Sitting on the stool at the far table, Uma watched him approach the drapes. He clasped it with his fingers, but his hand wouldn't budge beyond that. That same shame that Berta must have felt earlier: It colonized him. It took him over from the inside out, until he was shivering.

"Can . . . ?" he started, and then stopped. It took him a few more silent beats to steady himself. "Can I see him?"

Uma nodded. His heart was thumping in his ears, his veins pulsating painfully. And finally, after sucking in a breath, he whipped open the curtains.

It really was like a casket. And Jinn looked beautiful in it, Max had to admit. He looked as if he'd been preserved so perfectly. Not a curled black hair on his head had fallen. Not a long eyelash out of place. Max was sure that if Jinn's eyes were open, he'd see those fierce, dark eyes glaring at him—brooding, as per usual, because he wouldn't be Jinn if he weren't brooding.

Iris's white crystal surrounded him: so much of them. Those crystals were responsible for masking his presence from Iris. Berta had once told him that there were flowers there with him, therapeutic herbs. Yew and wolfsbane. Now there was nothing but irises. A fitting touch.

Uma had clothed him, making him ready for battle. "Still," she told him. "I have no idea when he'll wake up. Or if he ever will. Iris will still come for him, though."

Of course she would. She loved him. It was love that Max had seen in her eyes, reflected in Hiva's Tomb, when he'd stabbed them both through.

"What did I do to you, mate? God." Max's eyes filled with tears even as he told himself he didn't have a right to cry. No, he didn't. Not him. Not now, after all he'd done.

Max rubbed his fingers through his brown curls as he let a few rebellious tears drop down his cheeks. He already knew he was responsible for many crimes. He already knew he had to make up for his actions somehow. And that was what was he going to do. Now, more than ever, he knew he had to do everything in his power to bring Iris back.

For Jinn's sake. For her sake.

For the sake of his own soul.

The crew had gathered once more with tools and food they would need for their journey. Max carried Jinn over his shoulders like a lump of potatoes.

Sorry, mate, he apologized silently. If Jinn were conscious, he'd certainly knock Max senseless over this.

Before Uma could send them off, Berta, after slapping her cheeks several times, finally dragged up the courage to speak. "Rin!"

The moment Rin looked at her, Berta's expression became wild, and the toughness in them had given way to the kind of vulnerability Max had only seen reserved for him. She opened her mouth and closed it several times. She tried to speak but failed as Lulu ran over to Rin and gave her a tight hug.

And then so did Berta.

Rin was taken aback. Lulu and Berta squeezed Rin as if they wanted to break her in two. They were both crying.

"Come back alive," Berta said. "No matter what screwed-up things we did to each other, I still want you to come back alive."

"We're family now," Lulu said, her face buried in Rin's stomach. "Family's supposed to be a little screwed up."

At that, tears began to brim in Rin's one good eye. With shaking hands, she enveloped the other two, returning their hug. She was as stiff as one of Henry's toy soldiers, and she kept her face composed, despite the trickle of tears that fell. But she hugged them back. And when she did, a kind of serenity washed over her.

"I'll come back and bring your other sister," Rin whispered to Lulu, making her laugh and nod, and cry a little.

Other sister? Max frowned. What did Rin mean by that?

Iris?

"My dear Berta, you've always been a bit of a softie, haven't you?" Lucille said to Berta with a knowing smile, drawing confused glances from the others. "That's what I've always liked about you."

Berta let go of Rin and whipped around.

"Always liked about you"? What is she on about? Max opened his mouth to protest, but before he could, Berta was already shouting: "You! Moustache!"

"Moustache?" Mary leaned over. "No, she has a beard on today."

"That voice. I *do* know it! You're her!" Berta stuttered, pointing at Lucille's ridiculous form. "Madame Moustache from Nevada! It's you!"

She wasn't making any sense to anyone in the room, though Lucille seemed to find it amusing. Her pharaoh face grinned like the Cheshire Cat as Berta waved her pointed finger at her and turned to Max.

"I swear it's her, Max!" Berta said.

"Who?"

"Madame Moustache! I swear! The woman who took me to Nevada! I'd know that voice anywhere!"

Madame . . . ? Max tilted his head. Nah, it was simply too mad, even for him. With his free hand, Max rubbed his face, and through his fingers peeked at Lucille, who grinned and shrugged.

"The past is important, dear," Lucille said, her voice no less flamboyant than before. "Indeed, I've lived many past lives and enjoyed my frivolous exploits in all of them. But isn't the future more pressing to the living?"

The pharaoh's grin had softened a little. Become genuine, a touch. But Max didn't have time to wrap his head around it. Rin wouldn't give it to them.

"Enough distractions," Rin said, once again the warrior. "Let us begin."

Uma took in the sight of her and let herself draw a deep, steadying breath. "Yes," Uma agreed. "Let's begin." And gazed over them all. "Good luck."

In a move that surprised even him, Mary hugged Henry and kissed him quite assertively on the cheek.

"O-oi!" the boy stuttered, his face turning bright red.

And just as Hawkins drew Jacob into a kiss, Berta wrapped her arms around Max's neck. Max kept his arm firmly around Jinn's back, holding him in place.

"One day, I'll explain everything about me, brother," she whispered in his ear. "Everything you missed. What I've been through. What I plan to do next. Everything."

He nodded, rubbing her hair without saying a word.

"All right," Hawkins said. "Max . . . and Rin." He added her name reluctantly. "Let's go."

Hawkins was right to be hesitant when he grabbed Rin and took her through the portal to Ourika Valley. For once they reached the rolling river that looked over the mountains, once their feet touched the stony path along the rocky hillside, once Hawkins had disappeared from Max's sight to join the other party, Rin drew her white crystal sword from her chest and tried to kill Max.

39

IT HAD HAPPENED SO FAST, MAX had dropped Jinn onto the ground.

"Wait!" Max cried, jumping out of the way fast enough for the edge of Rin's sword to strike the giant rock behind him. "I'm on your side! I'm not going to let Iris die either!"

Rin didn't believe him and didn't hesitate to strike again, this time aiming for his throat. A near miss. Max fell back onto the grassy field, just vaguely registering the roar of a waterfall behind him. She wasn't going to stop. So he held his breath. Her strikes were quick and clean. He hadn't messed with anyone's perception of time for a while, but some things you never unlearn. He managed to tackle Rin to the ground before she could bring her sword down again.

"I'm *on your side*," Max said, pinning her down onto the soil as the babbling river rolled downstream behind them. "I'm not going to let them kill Iris. We'll convince her to come back to her senses. I swear it."

Rin may have stopped struggling with her body, but the struggle was still clear in her eyes. "Why should I believe you?"

Max sighed, lifting himself off Rin. "Right. What reason would you have to believe a traitor like me? Hell, *I* wouldn't trust me."

He walked over to Jinn, placing a hand on his chest. Jinn's breathing was uneven, but as long as he was breathing . . .

Max picked Jinn up and placed him upon what he hoped was a comfortable bed of grass. "Stay here, mate, and wake up quick. We'll need you to bring Iris back." Wiping the sweat from Jinn's forehead, Max stood up. "Know what, Rin? You don't have to believe me. You can strike me down right here. Just promise me you'll do something afterward."

Rin didn't move from the ground as he walked to the river and sat down. "What's that?"

"Save Iris in my place."

He could see the Atakora Mountains in the distance on the other side of the river. In the corner of the valley, the waterfall tumbled down, light from the sun refracting into a rainbow. Green hills, snow covering the highest peaks. Snow. Here? Well, there was plenty he didn't know about this place. Plenty he didn't know about the world. He'd been able to travel it thanks to Iris. He'd been able to learn so much about it, and about himself, about his sister, about life.

All thanks to Iris.

"I owe her everything," Max said, quietly watching the bubbling surface of the river.

He heard footsteps. Whether or not Rin was sneaking up behind him with her sword, he didn't know, and honestly he wouldn't have minded, so long as Rin did as he asked. But to his surprise, she simply sat down next to him, no weapon in sight.

"Where'd you get that dress, love?" Max asked, noticing how expertly made the hem was. It had to have been Granny Marlow. He'd always thought her dresses were better made than the overpriced stuff you could steal from a London store.

"I don't feel like telling you," was Rin's answer. Max laughed. It wouldn't have been Rin otherwise.

"All right, so what do you want to tell me?" he asked, looking at her.

"Nothing."

"Then it's gonna be a long, silent wait. Never know when Iris'll show up to kill me. May be a few days. And in the meantime, that fellow over there might wake up and try to kill me too. Oh!" Max slapped his head. "Damn, I forgot to ask Lulu to pack me some snacks."

"There's enough food here for you to eat without turning Lulu into your maid." Rin gestured to the fruitful trees and shrubs, and the fish swimming in the river.

"You got a little heated there when I mentioned Lulu. Kind of like a big sibling." Max gave her a crooked smile, which only widened when he realized that Rin had also noticed and was squirming because of it. "Well, you're an old softie too, I guess. Like Berta. Tough on the outside, squishy on the inside. Maybe that's why you two are so close now."

Rin drew up her knees and squeezed her chin against it.

"Rin, I just hope you know that Berta voted not to kill Iris. It might not mean anything now, but I don't think she meant any evil. She knows—we *all* know—how dire the situation is."

Rin considered it for a moment before shrugging. "We'll all have to pay for our crimes one day."

Max agreed. When he'd gone to Belgium with Hiva, wanting to die, he was just running away. Now, for the first time in his life, he was standing firm. Everything he'd done to Iris, he would make it up to her here.

They were quiet for hours. Together in silence, they watched the river. The birds chirped as they flocked past. At one point, Hawkins appeared through his blue portal and dumped some cooked potatoes on the ground.

"Potatoes, my favorite!" Max exclaimed, reaching for one. "Aw, you remembered."

"Everyone's started a campfire on the other side of the mountain. I'll stay with you and watch out for Iris."

"Nah," said Max, biting into the potato's soft skin. "We'll be fine here. Wherever she is, Iris won't be able to get here in a hurry. Why don't you come back in the morning?"

Hawkins hesitated, shooting a quick, nervous glance toward Rin.

"Don't worry," Max assured him. "Go be with Jacob. And whatever you do, don't mention Chadwick."

Blushing furiously, Hawkins gave a noncommittal grunt and disappeared back through the blue portal.

"Who is Chadwick?" Rin asked after several beats of silence.

Max was surprised and pleased all at once. "An old friend of mine," he told her eagerly. "Cherice's brother. He's gone now, but back in the day, when we were kids, we all lived together in London. Chadwick, Cherice, Jacob, Hawkins . . ."

Cherice. He dug his fingers into the dirt, feeling the harsh grit between his fingernails. Before he realized it, he'd hurled a rock into the river with a desperate grunt. The rock plopped into the surface, disturbing the water flow.

"Cherice is with her brother now," Max whispered. "At last."

"Did you . . . ?" Rin paused, looking for the right words. "Did you love her?"

A loaded question. He wasn't one to fall for girls easily. Iris had been the exception. She'd just been so dazzling the day he met her in the underground fight club. He'd never seen such a beauty, such a creature that exuded an otherworldly grace and mystery. It'd hit him all at once. Infatuation, probably. Hormones.

What would have happened with Cherice, had the world not gone so terribly wrong? Maybe nothing. But he would have wanted to know. At least now he wanted to know.

"I'm not sure," he answered. "I'm not the brightest lad, you know." He laughed wryly. "Cherice knew that."

"I'm sorry." Rin gazed up at the sky. "Loss seems like a cruel fate forced upon us by the gods. Loss that can drive us to do heinous things. So many of the atrocities that we've both committed in our lifetimes, I'm sure, can be traced back to our losses. That is why I do not hate you, Maximo Morales. As long as you desire to do right by Iris, I will not hate you."

Rin's words felt somehow baptismal. He felt as if he'd been washed in the river. As if her words had taken his sins into the waters and made him clean. He knew it was only wishful thinking. Perhaps a fleeting feeling. But he thanked Rin in his heart nonetheless.

Like that, the days passed between them as they waited. Max regaled her with stories of his childhood: stealing from English gentlemen, evading the police, helping Chadwick write his penny blood, *The Fanciful Freaks of London*. Rin did not say much. She helped him catch and roast fish. She ate with him and listened. That was enough.

"What's that?" he said one day, when he noticed a piece of paper peeking out from the top of her dress.

Quietly Rin shoved the paper back down. "It's nothing. Just a gift from a friend."

"A friend?" Max frowned, confused, but he didn't push her.

After gobbling down a potato, Max peeled the skin off another with a little knife and brought it to Jinn, still sleeping on his pile of grass. Max's heart skipped a beat when he brought some of the white flakes to the young man's mouth—

And his lips twitched open.

"Jinn!" As Jinn began to chew, Max turned to Rin. "He's doing a bit better!"

Rin stood up quickly and ran to his side. They both teared up, watching him slowly eat the potato as Max fed it to him bit by bit. There really was hope yet.

That night, as the owls hooted in the trees close to the hills, Max breathed in the fresh air. He lay on his back with his arms cushioning his head, soaking in the beauty of the earth. Rin sat next to him, using a rough little stick broken from a tree branch to carve spirals in the ground.

"May I ask you another question, Maximo?" Rin asked, tracing her stick back and forth.

"Shoot."

The sound of the wood scratching the dirt joined with the chirping crickets.

"Did you love Iris?"

Max thought for a long time. He remembered her smile. Those heart-shaped lips and that perfectly curved face. No, that was just physical. There had been something deeper in her. A defiance of fate. A love for life. A desire for more.

"No," Max admitted. "But I think . . . I'm thankful to her. Yeah. I'm thankful to her."

"I see." Rin smiled. "You and I have that in common."

The night passed in that quiet understanding that connected them under the stars. But the morning brought sudden dangers that destroyed the momentary peace they'd created. Max had already fed Jinn some berries. His old teammate wasn't quite conscious enough to open his eyes, but he could eat, which meant he would live. Surely he would.

"I'll probably never forgive myself for what I did to you. But I'm doing my best to make things right. I'll reunite you and Iris. I'll give you two your happily ever after. When all this is over, you'll forgive *me*, right, mate?" Max whispered, brushing Jinn's hair from his forehead.

"No . . . you bloody bastard . . ."

Max's heart jumped into his throat. For a moment he couldn't breathe. The harsh whispers that had crawled out of Jinn's throat and through his lips had paralyzed him.

Jinn didn't open his eyes. He didn't move his legs to kick him or his arms to take a swing at him.

He did, however, smile.

As tears began dripping down Max's cheeks, Hawkins appeared through his blue portal, panicking, his face drained of blood.

"The Titan Control Device!" Hawkins nearly tripped over himself stepping out of the blue void, his blond bangs drowned in sweat. "It's not working."

"*What* did you say?" Max wiped his face, his mind muddled and confused. He stepped away from Jinn, his fingers twitching. "It's what?"

"It's gone *wrong*, Max!"

Wrong? That was the last word Max wanted to hear in relation to a mass-destroying weapon of war. The blood drained from his face as his mind raced. "Wrong how?"

Rather than speaking, Hawkins grabbed his wrist and took him back through the blue portal. When Max's feet landed next, the mountain range was on the opposite side. Jacob was calling his name before he'd even gained his bearings.

Over by a shoddy campsite set up on the sand, Henry was using some tools Max had never seen before to prod at the Titan tablet. It lay on one of the few patches of grass in these sandy fields, sparking with a bright blue electricity.

"It just started doing that a few minutes ago," Mary fretted, hovering above Henry. "It hasn't given us any trouble in days—what's going on?"

"It's an ancient device that hasn't been used in thousands of years, if ever." Jacob wiped the sweat from his face, and Max knew it wasn't from the muggy heat or the overbearing sun. "Not even Uma knows everything about this blasted device. Why should we?" And he began to run his hands through his stringy black hair. "This was a bad idea. I should have voted against it."

"Bit too late for that," Henry hissed as he jolted the pointed edge of the thin instrument in his hands, like a little needle, into the side of the tablet, hoping to crack it open. But it simply sparked again. "Damn it!" cried the toymaker in frustration. "I can't get inside this bloody thing. If I can't get inside it, I can't see how it works!"

Hawkins threw his hands up, exasperated. "Uma couldn't destroy it. She couldn't even burn it inside a furnace, and you think you can jolt it a little to take a peek inside?"

"Now, now, let's all just take a breath and figure this out with a little bit of calm and—"

"Shut up, Lucille!" Everyone had said it, save perhaps for Mary, who was still fretting and had just freshly begun to mumble to herself. Max was so preoccupied with the fuss that he hadn't noticed Lucille's face had changed—she looked like some kind of Renaissance princess. It didn't matter. Max shook his head and bent down next to Henry.

"You mean it isn't working? Can you fix it?"

Henry scrunched his face in a pained expression, and Max tried to hide his look of triumph. Henry clearly had no idea what Max's true intentions were. Max didn't want Henry to fix it. That it was malfunctioning at all was a blessing. It would make his and Rin's job easier.

"I may not be some famed scientist, but I'm the grandson of the greatest toymaker on earth," said Henry, and the young boy puffed his chest out with pride. "I'll do it. I'll fix it."

Max feared Henry's confidence more than he did Iris. He patted him on the back anyway, pressing his lips together as he stared up at the other side of the mountain range, hoping they couldn't discern Max's true desire from his insecure expression.

"We'll make sure this all goes right." Jacob nodded steadfastly. Since the day Max had met him in the streets of London, Jacob had always been the gentlest soul he'd ever met. He knew that if Jacob had decided to take this kind of action against Iris, it wasn't in malice or wickedness. Out of their crew of orphan street thieves, Jacob was the only one who understood Max's pain—the acute pain of being lost in a foreign land, all alone, away from your family, away from your people. He didn't take any of this lightly. He'd already lost too much.

Jacob. If Cherice had lived, would you have voted differently?

Max didn't know. But he gave his friend a smile, silently thanking him for years of keeping him sane and making him a little less lonely.

"Hawkins, take me back." Max turned to his other friend, the one who would steal shoes from the rich that were too big for him. But whenever he wore them, he always walked a little taller. Max had noticed and teased him about it relentlessly. But now it made a little more sense. What was wrong with imagining a different life? To live how you wanted to live. To define yourself. Maybe they all understood that to some degree.

So why couldn't they have understood Iris a little? It was all she'd wanted.

The thought lingered in his mind as Hawkins took him back to the other side of the mountains. It remained when his feet touched the grass, when Hawkins's portal disappeared behind him.

When he looked toward the river and saw Iris by the shore, kneeling by Jinn, as a quivering Rin stumbled back.

Why couldn't we have understood you a little? Max thought as he ran toward Iris, calling her name, begging her to come back. *Why couldn't I have understood you?*

Everything was happening so fast. Hawkins dead silent behind him, whimpering helplessly, paralyzed. Rin reaching into her dress with a shaky hand, pulling out a piece of paper. No, a letter. Iris was trembling too. *Trembling.* He hadn't noticed before, but Iris *was* trembling. She was looking from a half-conscious Jinn to a struggling Rin, her lips parting and closing again with nothing but wheezing air slipping through them.

"Iris! I'm begging you! Go back to being you!" Max cried. All the time he'd spent lying around in the valley, thinking of what grand speech he'd tell her once she inevitably tracked him down, and now his mind had gone blank. "Go back to who you used to be. Please! Please, I can't take this anymore!"

Everything slowed down. It was like the moment his sister had been taken from them. The moment he realized he'd lost her. Yes, it was a little like that.

"Iris!"

Iris heard him. She turned. Her eyes widened.

Then she stood and began striding toward him.

Why couldn't we have understood you a little? Before it was too late?

An explosive pressure, like a bomb going off, collided with his chest. He wondered what it was. The pain had been excruciating for maybe a moment, and then he felt nothing—nothing but the wind brushing against his bare skin, against flesh. Blood dripping down his chest. Iris's hot breath brushed the side of his cheek.

This wasn't right. He felt strange. His body felt weak. His chest contracted as cold air entered his body. How had it entered . . . how was that possible?

It was such a strange and funny feeling. He wanted to tell Berta one day.

His body went limp. He saw a beating heart in Iris's bloody hands, smiled a little crooked smile, and felt the grass and the earth and the weeds come up to meet him.

40

HAWKINS WAS SCREAMING, AND RIN COULDN'T tell if she'd joined him or if those desperate howls were only a figment of her imagination. Iris had torn out Max's heart in front of her. The young thief's crooked smile was still on his face, though faded, his eyes open but dull. The frayed edges of the hole in his shirt fluttered in the wind as his corpse lay on the ground.

Rin had done nothing. Fear had gripped her from the moment Iris had slipped out from behind the trees and approached her. Max hadn't been here when it had happened. So had he been the bait? Or had she? It didn't matter now. Not to her. Not to Max.

The sudden realization of Max's death overwhelmed her. Like a great flood, it washed over her—rising to the top of her head and then down again, knocking her off-balance, until she thought she'd collapse on the floor weeping. Rin gasped for air as if she'd run a marathon. She clutched her chest and bent over as panic overrode her senses. All it had taken was a second. A second. A flash, and he was gone. He was *gone.*

She covered her mouth to muffle her whining moans but released it again when she realized she needed more air. But there would never be enough. Iris had murdered Max in front of her.

Hawkins was howling, crying, cradling Max's dead body, hugging him, weeping, cursing. But Iris . . .

Iris . . . why were tears forming in her eyes? Could Hiva cry?

The goddess dropped Max's bloody heart upon the grass and stepped back, confused. But she had been like this before. Back in the Naacalian facility, where they'd stolen the Titan Control Device. Iris could have killed her then. She'd *meant* to kill her then but couldn't.

Iris wasn't a monster. She was trying not to be.

"Oh, Iris," Rin cried, clutching the letter in her right hand so hard, her fingers could have torn through the paper. "Iris . . ."

"You're dead." Hawkins's fiendish whisper interrupted her, harrowed and cruel and filled with hatred. "You're dead, you monster! Your terror ends. *Now!*"

Iris didn't notice him. She was looking at the blood on her own hands. That was good for Hawkins. He was able to whisk Max's corpse away through the blue void, his murderous oath lingering in the air. "You're dead!"

The Titans. Rin couldn't breathe. Suddenly her fear for herself turned into fear for Iris. She ran up to her and grabbed her bloodied hand.

"Iris!" she cried, forgetting how close she was to death when Iris slowly looked up at her, their eyes locking. "Iris, we have to go. Please!"

The Dahomey would be waiting for them to return to Uma's apartment in Lagos, but she needed to get Iris there first. She would, even if by foot. The Ark was her only hope.

But Iris's gaze had turned once again to the blood on her hand. Her face scrunched and twisted as if she was trying to understand what she'd just done. Hawkins was probably giving the others the signal. If she didn't move now . . .

There was another way. The opium bottle in her dress pocket. She'd given one to Sesinu. She had one here. She'd shove it in Iris's mouth now that Iris was distracted. The drug wouldn't hurt Iris. Or, even if it did, even if it killed her, she'd come back to life. They just needed to *leave.*

"Iris . . . ," Rin said, letting go of her and secretively dipping into her dress pocket.

"M-Ma . . . ax . . ."

Rin's hand froze. What was she saying?

"Ma . . . aax. Ma . . . x?"

The word had indeed come from Iris's lips. She didn't look sad. Just surprised. Confused. She turned her bloody hand over and over, rubbed the blood down her face, and then stumbled back, shaking her head, not understanding what she'd just done—not wanting to understand, not *ready* to understand . . .

Iris began screaming. The wind carried her shrieks into the sky.

Rin took in Iris's frantic state, and all at once it hit her: a crushing awareness of her own heartbreak. This was what the world had done to Iris. A world where the powerful crushed the weak. This is what it had reduced her to, this once-unstoppable warrior: unstoppable not because of her magic but because of her will, determination, and compassion.

It was when Iris began scratching her own face that Rin covered her face and cried. They were doomed. Maybe they'd been doomed from the start by this awful world.

"Don't . . . give up . . ."

That voice. Rin lowered her hands. Her breath hitched in her throat. She didn't dare look up, even though she knew that voice, who it belonged to. Even though she heard him clear as day, repeating those words that were directed as much to her as it was to Iris.

"Don't . . . give . . . up . . ."

Jinn. He was holding Iris from behind, his legs barely sturdy but keeping him up as he crushed the screaming Iris against his chest.

"Don't give up." Rin whispered it to herself, wiping her tears. "Don't give up." She said it again, fortifying her own heart as Iris's screams devolved into wild, staccato breaths.

She remembered what Max had told her inside Uma's apartment. About the last time he'd seen Iris. That she'd looked sad.

Hiva had emotions. Of course she did. She was *Iris*. She had always been Iris.

"Rin," Jinn said, and looked up at her. "Don't . . . give up."

Rin touched her trembling lips with a hand and nodded. No tricks. No schemes. Jinn had Iris. She had to do her part too. Rin let go of the opium bottle in her dress and unfolded the letter in her hands instead.

"Iris. This dress. Do you recognize it?"

Rin had asked her slowly, repeating herself when she saw Iris was too pre-occupied with Max's blood to hear her the first time.

"Granny Marlow made it for me. *Your* Granny Marlow."

Iris's arms fell to her sides. She nearly collapsed in Jinn's arms, but Jinn held her firm, just like he always had. She was listening. Listening but unsure. Rin shut her eyes, knowing that the wayward goddess could kill her at any moment, knowing that they were running out of time. But she wanted to remember that day she'd used the Solar Jumps to leap through lands far and wide and ended up trudging, bones weary, into London.

There she'd seen, near Iris's circus camp, an old lady in a tent, shivering in the dark. Afraid and surrounded by fabric that hadn't yet been sewn into clothes. Alone but for a goose with burnt fur, waddling around and pecking at the floor.

"Are you Granny Marlow?" Rin had asked after entering her tent gently, not wanting to frighten the woman. In her rocking chair, Granny Marlow nodded sadly. Her sunken old eyes, dark as coal, had reminded Rin of a deer. "I'm Iris's sister."

The words had simply flown out of Rin's mouth. But at the sound of Iris's name, the old woman had lifted her head. Whimpering and vulnerable, the old woman had reached out to her, gesturing her to come close.

"It's not her fault," she'd said, and Rin was acutely aware that there was not another soul left alive in this camp but the old woman and her goose. "She's lost. She just needs to find herself. You're her sister too. You'll help her, won't you?"

Rin remembered how tightly the old woman had grasped her hands. How the two of them had cried together.

And then Granny Marlow had given her something.

"I wrote this days ago, when I could get my hands on some ink." And she'd shoved the letter into her hands. "It's in my native language because it's easier to write for me than English. Please don't let her think that she's alone."

Standing here in Ourika Valley, with the waterfall ahead of her, the river behind her, and the blood of a friend staining the grass, Rin remembered her promise. She vowed to keep it.

They were sisters.

"Listen to her, Iris . . ." Jinn's whisper was so filled with love that it had paralyzed the god. It must have. Iris took her shaking hand and placed it upon Jinn's arm. She was listening.

Rin took Granny Marlow's letter written in Yoruba. How she had cried that night when she'd realized Granny Marlow's native language was the same as her own. She wondered what kind of impossible fate had bound them all together. Ties of a family that shared no blood, only the promise of a loving future. Rin looked up at Iris, who stared back at her with a helpless, frustrated expression. Then Rin sucked in a breath and began to read, translating it into English for Jinn's benefit as well.

"My dear Iris, my name is not Agnus Marlow. It is Adebisi. My name is Adebisi, and I wish that this were a kinder world.

When you were young, you had aimed to kidnap me and my sister, Adelola. And then someone crueler than you kidnapped all of us, placed us on a slave ship, and took us to England. I remember looking down into the waters and wondering how many ghosts haunted the seas. How many of my people marched along the ocean floors, howling for justice.

The first night I slept inside Gorton Zoo, I remembered thinking that justice didn't exist in this world, because the men who'd made it didn't believe in such things. They believed in only their own power and wealth. Their own comfort and greed. They wanted to satiate their own desires even if it took the blood of children. As long as it was not their children, they would be satisfied. It was those men who had given me the name Agnus, my sister the name Anne, and you the name Iris. They had carved out our identities and forced us to inhabit them.

And as I think about all these things, I wonder if this feeling of the unfairness of it all is what you feel now. I wonder if that is why you gave up your own voice to gain the power of vengeance. But Iris, is this too who you want to be?"

Rin stopped, for Iris was shaking her head. She was trying to speak, but the word was too faint.

"Iris?" Rin whispered, blinking back tears as she watched the girl struggle. "Iris—"

"Read, Rin!" Jinn told her, the desperation and hope clear in his brown eyes. "Read Granny's letter!"

Biting her lip, Rin continued.

"That's the thing, Iris. We have to know who we want to be in this world, and we have to be it without fear, without apology. We have to do it, especially women like us. We have to do it in spite of those who give us fake names and fake lives. Who tell us who we are and tell us where to sleep and what words to speak. We have to choose.

And there are so many terrible, horrible people in this world who will tell you that you have no right to. That there is a script, and you must follow it. That there is a role, and you must play it. But they're wrong. Nobody can decide who you are but you. All you have to do is imagine.

What if we imagined a different world?

What if we imagined a different life?

What if we imagined a different self?

They say a leopard can't change its spots, especially an old one. Maybe it's too late for me. Or maybe my imagination is too limited. But I wonder, Iris. I wonder. Who do you want to be? What kind of world do you want to live in? What kind of life for you, for us, do you imagine?

Imagining something different takes strength. Believing in your own self takes courage. Understanding your own power takes wisdom. And being willing to use it for good—well, that takes kindness, the sort of kindness I've seen in you every day for the past ten years, as you read to me and fed me my medicine and brought me food from the store.

Don't give up on yourself, my dear.

I love you always—Granny."

Tears from Rin's eyes had begun to splash upon the paper. "Don't give up on yourself," Rin repeated, this time in Yoruba, speaking the language that connected the three women, letting the words roll off her tongue as she thought of her parents and the home that had been taken from her. "Don't give up on yourself," she repeated, because though she'd lost one home, the possibility of a new one had opened up for her. And she realized then, so deeply, that where there was life, there was hope. "Don't give up on yourself, Iris."

Rin wiped her tears with one hand, her missing right eye stinging, the letter shaking in her other hand. It was only when her face was dry that she realized that she wasn't crying alone.

Quiet whimpers reached her ears. Rin looked up with a shaky breath.

Iris was crying too.

Tears rolled down her cheeks, one after another, an unstoppable flood. She collapsed into Jinn's arms, squeezing tight the hand that had taken Max's heart.

She shook her head, looked up at Jinn, and whispered, "I'm sorry. I'm sorry! Jinn . . . Rin . . . *Max* . . . I'm so sorry!" Her voice was scratchy with disuse, but it was still her voice. It was *Iris*.

"It's okay, Iris," Jinn whispered back, cradling her head in the crook of his neck. "Everything is going to be okay. There's still hope."

"There's . . . still hope." Iris gazed up at Rin. She stared at the girl, the wind fluttering her braids in the air.

And she smiled.

"There's still hope," Iris repeated with this tearful smile like an oasis in the desert. "Rin . . ." She giggled, half crazed, but then again, hoping was often thought of as insanity in desperate times. "There's still hope. . . ."

Rin's heart stopped. Iris was back.

Dropping her letter, she reached out to her.

And then the Atlas Mountains rumbled. The tremors escalated in a matter of seconds, shaking the earth, knocking Rin to the hard ground. Birds fled from the treetops in droves. Granny Marlow's letter fluttered into the sky with the rush of wind, then fell into the river.

"What the hell is happening?" Rin cried, grasping at the grass.

The end of the world.

The tops of the Atlas Mountains shuttered and then at once crumbled in a massive avalanche that stopped Rin's breath. And two raging beasts, the likes of which Rin had never seen, emerged from inside the rock.

Giant metal machines blotted out the sun. Each spider leg was an iron monstrosity, each bulbous, tanklike head thrice the size of a building. One short and squat, the other tall and lithe, their armor darkening the sky as they blocked the sun from view. The circular glass plates on their heads were sparking. Yellow. Silver. They were worse than the drawings on Bosch's wall could ever have depicted them.

"What are they?" Jinn breathed, his jaw agape in awe.

"The Titans." It was Iris who spoke. But Rin already knew. The Solar Titan and the Shadow Titan. The twin beasts of destruction.

If human beings could make such machines, then did that make them gods too? No. They were devils.

Their glass plates glowed. Their legs were immobile. But their heads were shifting back and forth. Like an octopus spinning in the water, unsure of where to turn.

On the other side of the Atakora Mountains, Hawkins and the others had activated the Titans. Somewhere beyond the blinding fear and awe, that fact registered in Rin's mind. But why were the Titans moving in such a frenzied, uncontrollable way? Was this what they had planned?

"Iris. Jinn." Rin lifted herself to her knees. "We need to go now."

Screech. The piercing sound of metal that hadn't moved in millennia pierced the air. Dark cloud gathered overhead as the Titans' legs began to move—the Shadow Titan down one side of the mountain, the Solar Titan down the other.

"They're coming toward us!" Rin cried when she realized, and blood drained from her face.

Jinn grabbed Iris's wrists. "We have to go, Iris! We have to go now!"

Iris looked at the Titans like she'd seen them before. She was too scared to move.

Rin wasn't. She was a warrior. No matter the enemy, no matter what she faced, she wouldn't fall. She grabbed Iris's hand while Jinn took the other.

"Don't give up, Iris," Rin whispered through gritted teeth as the Shadow Titan made a high-pitched screech that shattered Rin's eardrums.

"Don't give up," Jinn said too, though Rin was no longer able to fully hear him. Blood was leaking from her ears down her neck.

A thunderous blast knocked them all to the ground. Rolling over onto her back, Rin looked behind her. A beam of pure, wondrous light shot from the Shadow Titan like a canon. It was like the waterfall—radiant and beautiful.

"Jinn!"

Iris's shriek called Rin back to her. Iris was kneeling by Jinn. He'd fallen as hard as any of them, but why wasn't he moving? They had to get up. They had to leave before the Titans—

"Jinn! Jinn!" Iris grabbed her hair. *"No!"*

It was then that Rin noticed Jinn's head, twisted and bleeding against a sharp rock. His eyes were open. Lifeless.

No.

No, no, no.

Rin gasped for air, her heart thrashing against her chest as Iris screamed.

This wasn't happening. This wasn't . . . this wasn't the end . . . was it?

The Shadow Titan was firing consecutive blasts. The area behind the Atlas Mountains—the area where Hawkins, Jacob, and the others were—had gone up in flames and smoke.

The Solar Titan began to rumble.

Rin shook her head. "Don't give up," she repeated, because they had been Jinn's last words. She pulled a weeping Iris to her feet and dragged her toward the forest.

"Don't give up!" This time Rin said it to herself too. Iris was the one who'd been honored among the *ahosi*. She Who Does Not Fall. But Rin wouldn't fall either. That was who she decided to be in that moment, as death rained down upon the valley. Another Who Would Not Fall.

I will not fall, Rin thought as the Solar Titan fired at them. *We will not fall.*

Heavenly white light enveloped them, lifting Rin off her feet and into the air. Rin held Iris's hand until the end.

DEATH

TRUTHFULLY, SHE NO LONGER WANTED TO kill. That was what she'd decided once she'd heard Granny Marlow's letter. Once she'd felt Jinn's arms around her. No matter what had happened in the past. She no longer wanted to kill. The Hiva inside her was dead. But so were they.

Half of her crystal heart floated down the Ourika River. The other half had been vaporized, destroyed by the Solar Titan.

With that half of a heart went the valley and the surrounding cities. Humans and animals. Trees and insects. North and south of the mountain range, life had vanished.

Hawkins. Jacob. Mary. Henry. Lucille. Her heart could no longer feel their anima. Their bodies had disappeared, along with Max's corpse, taken with the blast from the Shadow Titan.

And Rin. And Jinn.

Iris's consciousness fluttered as her half-shattered crystal heart floated downstream, letting the river take it into the Atlantic Ocean. And as it drifted, it searched for more anima. Life forces around the Atlas Mountains were disappearing at a furious rate. The Shadow and Solar Titans had not stopped. They *would not* stop. Iris knew from the days of the Naacal. If they were not shut off, they would simply keep killing. And they did. As the days passed, life forces disappeared farther south toward Algeria and north toward Spain. More and more lives, gone.

Like Rin. Like Jinn. Like Max.

Like all life soon. With or without her.

Iris's mind collapsed, leaving something broken in its wake.

Why is this happening? Why?

Iris's crystal heart mended itself quickly, even as it threatened to break all over again.

I'm so sorry. . . .

PART THREE
Imagined Futures

Elegy is a genre that enables fantasies about worlds we cannot yet reach, even as it facilitates investments in a world that will outlast us.

−MAX CAVITCH, "AMERICAN ELEGY"

For rather than be labelled and defined by racist and sexist ideologies, both these [women] chose to shape and invent themselves through the medium of words and the power of the imagination.

−DIANA MAFE, "SELF-MADE WOMEN IN A (RACIST) MAN'S WORLD"

41

THEY FOUND HER ON THE ROCKY coastline of Senegal, crouched upon a rock, letting the waves of the Atlantic Ocean swallow her up once it crashed against the land. The children asked if she was okay. They were speaking the language of the Wolof people. Dakar was close by. She waved them off. They asked her again if she was okay. They asked her why she was jittering so much, what kind of fabric the orange cloth she was wearing was, why she was scratching her arms so roughly that she drew blood from her brown flesh.

"It's because I can't find my friends," she said, speaking to them in their language. She could speak every language.

"We can help you find them if you'd like."

Iris lowered her hands. Find them? Slowly she stood from her crouch, the rock jutting into the soles of her feet.

A smile spread across her lips. "You can help me find them?" she said. "You really can?"

Her white crystal heart thumped excitedly in her chest. Finally. Finally she would see them again!

But the children were not looking at her eyes. It took Iris some time, but she finally realized their fearful gazes were stuck on her arms—on the streaks of painful, bloody gashes she'd made with her nails. At how quickly they closed and healed.

"Demon!"

"Devil!"

"Help!"

The children were scared—of course they were—but they needn't be. She wouldn't hurt them. She just wanted to find her friends.

"Where are you going?" Iris cried over the rush of ocean waves crashing against the rocks, wetting her back.

And as the children ran, a kind of irritation descended upon her that slowly, steadily, turned to anger. Why would they run from her? Did they have fun toying with her?

"Humans," Iris spat, scratching her arms again, turning once more to the ocean and crouching down. "Humans!" She'd killed so many already. Some who hadn't realized they were dying before they'd already disintegrated. *"Humans."* She'd so desperately wanted to be one, once upon a time, but fate had denied her. Her eyes burned with tears.

So hateful and so precious and so vulnerable and so sickening, all at once. Such strange creatures. All she'd met had caused her pain. The pain of hatred and revenge. The agony of love and loss. And this life was somehow more desperate than all the others. This life had been steeped in the very thick messiness of what humanity was, more so than her time with the Naacal. More so than her time with the Atlanteans and the Lemurians. This life had been the most painful by far.

She couldn't kill anyone unless she was close enough. Still, she could feel anima around the world. She could feel thousands dying each day in North Africa as the Titans ran amok. She could feel the aftermath of the anima she'd snuffed out too. Millions and millions through Europe, and then through the Americas and Asia, during the days she'd used the Naacal's Solar Jumps to hop across the world and snuff out lives.

And now she was here, her arms bleeding, her fingernails sticky with blood and skin and flesh, her wild eyes gazing out over the rippling ocean. She'd failed. She'd failed in being human. She'd failed in being Hiva.

She didn't know what she was.

She just wanted to find her friends.

No. There was someone else she needed to find.

She sloppily wiped her tears with the bloody back of her hand. Where was she? The One who'd created her. The One who'd told her, as she'd woven Iris's flesh and bones back together, that she'd bring her back home to the earth's core if she needed. If Iris wanted it enough.

"Anne," Iris whispered, and could almost hear a response calling out from the waves, like the breath of God.

That is not my name.

Her fury exploded. "Anne!" she screamed, baring her teeth. "Anne! Anne!" Her shouts tore through her throat until she tasted her own blood. She screamed until she collapsed upon the rocks and cried.

Are you saying I don't want *it enough?* Iris thought, looking at the seagulls soaring across the clear blue sky. The wind felt chilling. Unwelcoming. The wind fluttered the hairs on her skin and gave her the breath she needed to scream again until she lost her voice. *What else needs to happen?* Iris thought. *What else needs to happen before you think I'd be desperate enough, broken enough, to come home?*

She was sick of this world that never changed. She was sick of these tantalizing humans, with all their potential for goodness, instead creating worlds that caused suffering. She was sick of monstrous contraptions and wars for profit and gold.

Just take me home, Anne. . . .

Iris walked inland from the coast but strayed from the big cities. She traveled south close to the territory of Guinea and found refuge inside a gallery forest. Unlike humans, animals never bothered her. They seemed content with their lives, hunting, sleeping, eating. Along her travels she picked up cannabis and coca plant to chew and let her sorrows drift away with her mind and senses. She followed a group of chimps up a slope covered in vines. She knew nature as well as it knew her. Hiva had been created to destroy mankind for the earth, after all. They were not each other's enemies. It was only man who had never known her.

Underneath the chimps' nests in the branches and tree canopies, Iris made her own by the slope of a sprawling green hill. As night descended, after she'd finished every bit of the mind-addling herbs she'd plucked on her journey, she curled up by a flourishing green bush but didn't sleep. Her eyes were unable to shut for too long, because she could feel it more keenly than ever: Max's heart still beating in her hands. Jinn holding her. Rin crying out her name. Even now she heard Rin crying out her name. She *heard* her.

She should have never asked the One to make her anew. She should have let herself die that day in the Coral Temple. She should have let centuries pass, maybe even millennia, before she rose again to cull humanity.

Now she was neither this nor that. She had lost the will to continue her mission. But the path to humanity, to normalcy, to happiness, was closed. The door would never open again.

Purgatory. It was the only word she could use to describe this burning agony.

Iris looked upon a parrot finding its nest in a tree, and a memory came to mind. Once upon a time, the Atlanteans had gained wings. Using a machine that harnessed the power of dreams, they'd remade themselves in the image that they worshipped. Humans today, if they looked upon them, would call them angels. It was at that moment Iris realized that the Atlanteans had imagined themselves as gods. That, perhaps, was not a problem in and of itself. It was how they defined godhood. To them, their godhood made them superior. Their godhood made them worthy of worship. And those who did not worship them were put to death.

They'd used their imagination and the power of dreams to torture and kill.

Tell me the answer, she thought to herself, hoping the One could hear her too. What was the answer to this endless cycle? This mystery of life's cruelty?

It took all her strength, but Iris finally managed to force her eyes to close. Her mind was weary. She needed rest. *Maybe I'll find them all tomorrow,* she thought, and slept.

In her dreams she saw civilizations fall. She saw a world tree collapse in flames. She saw oceans boil. She saw explosions from nuclear fission wipe away entire kingdoms. She saw herself rising out of the mud and dirt to begin a new lifetime. She spoke languages that sounded like harsh sand and babbling creeks. She saw Hiva, naïve despite his millions of lifetimes, holding Naacalian children in his arms and begging for her help.

"Isn't there a way, sister?"

She wished she could have answered him then. "I don't know, brother. But let us find a solution together."

She saw men, women, and children dragged out with chains around their necks and packed onto ships, bound for the Americas. Or forced to walk across the African continent to work as slaves for centuries to come. She saw cruelty and greed. She saw Doctor Seymour Pratt's beady black eyes hovering above her while she lay immobile on an operating table. She saw war and hatred.

She dreamed of the world of men.

Footsteps crunching on leaves. Iris's eyes snapped open. Someone was coming, but she couldn't feel any human anima. But those were, without a doubt, human footsteps she heard approaching her from deep within the forest. What human had no anima? It didn't make any sense. Or was there something wrong with her?

Iris lifted herself up and waited as the footsteps grew closer. They were light and graceful. This human moved like a dancer. Like a warrior.

Her heart thumped in her chest, nerves and excitement pulsing through her veins. But when the figure revealed himself through the trees, her body went rigid. She was on her feet before she realized it. Her mind rejected it. It was impossible. But as he came closer, as the realization dawned that he was material, as he came close enough for her to touch his strong chest and muscled back, her face flushed.

"It can't be . . . ," she whispered, tears dripping onto her lips.

Jinn smiled at her and welcomed her embrace.

42

B UT HE WAS DEAD. SHE'D SEEN him die! She'd seen the blood from his skull on the stones.

No. He'd clearly survived. She couldn't feel his anima, but she didn't need to. His life force was palpable in his brown skin, his blood pumping against her hot fingers. His high cheekbones and full lips. His large, angular dark eyes that welled up when he embraced her.

"I missed you, Iris." That familiar whisper. His musky smell. Jinn's smell.

How could she not recognize him? They were partners. They would dance together on the tightrope. She would feel his hands supporting her back and her buttocks as he lifted her high in the air, above the roaring crowds. And after he'd toss her, she'd fall back into his arms, linking her leg in his to keep herself steady. She knew his body.

He cupped her chin in his large, rough hands and pressed her against his chest. "I'm never leaving you again."

That was all she needed to hear for her to believe. As the weight of death threatened to swallow her whole, she buried her face in his neck and wept. So much death. So many gone at her hands. And now this. It was too overwhelming. She thought she might break in half from the force of it all.

"It's taken me so long, but I've found you," whispered Jinn. "I needed to tell you—"

But Iris pressed a finger to his lips. She already knew, and she didn't want to speak or cry any longer. The time for both had passed.

Tragedy had a way of destroying inhibitions. Actions she'd been desperate to take for so long but held off on, too frightened to make the first move. Words she'd wanted to say but kept silent for fear of what they could lead to. There was nothing stopping her now.

The cloth the One had given her to cover her nakedness—she gently slid it off her body. The humid air nipped at her stomach, her chest, and her legs. Jinn's clothes were the same as she remembered them in the Coral Temple. Wordlessly he pulled his shirt over his head and let his pants drop against the grass. He laid her down against the forest floor and buried himself in her. A kiss, long and deep. Lips wet, ravenous, relentless. He kissed her deeply, and as she wrapped her arms around his neck, she made sure to feel all of him. His hot tongue against the roof of her mouth. His hips pushing against her. She gasped and moaned in pleasure as he touched every curve of her flesh and filled every crevice with her body with his.

Bring me back to life so that I can kill that man and his human race.

That was what she had told the One who'd created her. But it had been before she'd realized the truth. Her mind had tricked her. Was her mind tricking her now?

But he felt so real, as she grabbed on to his protruding shoulder blades with one hand and his backside with the other. The pressure of his body rocking against hers, her back sliding against the abrasive grass and dirt. When she wrapped her legs around the small of his back, and he whispered her name in her ear. It all felt so real.

So she let it be real.

He hadn't given her time to sleep, so her eyes were a bit blurry as she saw a monkey shake loose an extra coconut from the tree branch above them. Iris was too sluggish to catch it as it fell. No matter—Jinn did, lying on his back and reaching a hand above her head. Sighing, she continued to rest upon his chest.

"Do you want this?" Jinn asked, waving the coconut in her face, and his casual tone slightly irritated her. How could he be so casual with her wrapped around his body like a blanket? With her legs intertwined with his and her hair pooled in the crook of his neck? She was barely holding it together. His body was just so hard, and his muscles sturdy. The little hairs on his chin were so kissable. She'd have a fit if he ever shaved them.

"I don't need to eat," she said with a shrug. "I mean, I do eat. I have to eat or else I'd die, but—"

What was she saying? Her mind was still in knots from last night. Jinn chuckled softly.

"But if you die, you'd just come back to life." He thought about it. "Sounds tedious. Eat."

So bossy, as usual. "Later. *Later.*"

Jinn sighed impatiently, like he always did whenever she acted like a child. But from that she knew he'd given in. Truthfully, Iris didn't want to move. She felt a kind of solace in his arms that she hadn't felt since her body had stitched itself back together on the shores of the Atlantic Ocean. She just wanted to rest here. Rub her hands along his slender, sculpted forearm. Feel the grit of dirt against her behind. Slide her leg up and down his almost absentmindedly.

So that was what she did that morning, breathing in the clean forest air, listening to the parrots chirping above their heads. She never thought to ask if he wanted to eat. Instead, she tilted her chin up and let him swallow her lips with kisses that lasted all the morning.

"You know, I could never once feel your anima when I came back," Iris said at the dawn of the afternoon, when Jinn had finally decided to crack the coconut open on the rock.

"When you came back, eh?" As Jinn looked at the two halves of the coconut and inspected the milk, Iris inspected him. Neither of them had put on their clothes. There was no need to for her. She was more comfortable like this, in nature as she was made and as it was made. But Jinn seemed well suited to braving the elements with his sturdy form, earned through years of difficult training and performances.

"Yes, when I came back." Iris lifted herself into a sitting position.

"You mean, when you came back for revenge because you thought I'd killed you?"

Jinn didn't look at her when he said it. He sat down from his crouch and tasted the coconut milk, letting some dribble down his chin. Iris pressed her lips together, half ashamed, half indignant.

"In the Coral Temple, I saw your reflection in the glass of Hiva's Tomb. I thought you'd killed me."

"No, that was Max," he said rather casually after swallowing the milk.

"I know!" Iris blushed and crossed her arms over her chest. "I only realized later. You were trying to protect me. . . ."

Jinn didn't answer. And when he didn't, Iris got to her feet and threw herself upon his curved back, feeling his spine as she hugged him.

"I'm sorry," she whispered, with her arms around his chest. Sitting down, she wrapped her legs around his back and stomach, hugging him so tightly, not even a sigh of gentle wind could pass between their connected bodies. "I'd gotten everything wrong. I never should have come back." She buried her face in his neck.

His body was as hot as hers. Even with this gentle breeze, the sun was still unforgiving. A bump against her nose gave her a start. The rough surface of the coconut had tickled her skin. When she pulled herself away from him, she realized he was offering one half to her.

Groaning a little, she took it, sat down, and began drinking.

"We all make mistakes," Jinn said. "Though I don't regret what I did at all in that split second. Not even for a moment."

It was only after they'd been drinking in silence that Iris noticed his back was smooth. There was no scar on his brown skin—not even a mark on him. Lowering the coconut from her lips, she inspected it.

"Are you sure you're okay?" she said, only after finishing. "The wound Max gave you was deep enough to pierce through me. And in the valley . . ."

She shut her lips. How exactly had he survived? That was what she wanted to ask, before her heart shook and the words died in her throat. Before she could muster up the courage to try again, Jinn had turned around and embraced her.

"I'm just sorry I couldn't protect you like I'd set out to. I'm sorry, Iris."

His body was so much larger than hers that he enveloped her fully. His long arms crushed her to him.

"It's all right," she said. And it was. Finally it was. Because as he fell on top of her again, as they tangled together upon the grass, as she let him brush his lips upon every part of her body, she realized she could finally let her frantic thoughts disappear into the ether.

"I'm just so tired of worrying," she moaned as Jinn's lips lingered on her chest.

"You've always been far too anxious," Jinn agreed without stopping.

Iris let her arms fall upon her forehead. "I don't want to think anymore."

"Thinking was never your strong suit."

Iris's laughter shook the trees as she let Jinn's wet kisses trail down to her stomach and then to her burning hips, and then her laughter became joyful sighs that continued into the night.

But it was in the night that she heard strange sounds that didn't belong to the forest. The sounds of ghosts calling out to her.

Iris . . .

Iris!

Iris . . . !

The sound of her name, soft in the stagnant air, jolted her awake. She lifted herself off a sleeping Jinn and sat up, startled. The forest was as it had been—trees, shrubs. Nests in the canopy of leaves, vines blocking certain paths from view. Nothing had changed. No human was here but her and Jinn. So where were the voices coming from?

Her body was on alert. She could feel the adrenaline pumping in her arms, electrifying them. She was ready to strike at any movement of the bushes.

Iris . . .

Iris!

Iris . . . !

Three different voices. Words with no masters. They howled in the night along with the chirps of crickets, calling her name, each becoming more distinct, more recognizable, as they grew louder. She covered her ears, her eyes darting around her, looking for the source. But she couldn't block out their screams.

Iris . . . go back to being yourself. Please!

Iris . . . ! Don't give up on yourself!

Don't give up!

"Stop!" Iris pounded her ears with her hands so roughly, she could feel her brain rocking in her skull. "Stop!"

She screamed it over and over again until she couldn't take it anymore. She grabbed Jinn's shoulders, shaking him awake.

"Help me!" she told him, ignoring his surprised expression. "They won't stop talking!"

Iris figured he'd ask her who. There was no one here but them. That was the logical thing to say in this situation for Jinn—for anyone. Instead, he tilted his head to the side.

"If they won't stop talking, then maybe you should listen to them."

Iris drew her hands to her chest and stared at him, confused. "What?"

But Jinn nodded in a comforting way and reached out to touch her face. "It's okay. Try listening to them."

Iris's heart was beating so fast, it was all she could hear. Breathing in and out deeply, she waited for her pulse to even out. Then, closing her eyes, concentrating on Jinn's steady hand on her skin, she listened.

Iris . . . go back to being yourself. Please!

Iris . . . ! Don't give up on yourself!

Don't give up!

It went on like that. Desperate. Loving. Fearful. Iris listened to the ghosts' howls until they went silent.

"Who are they?" Jinn asked, brushing the back of his fingers against her cheeks.

Iris didn't answer, because the answer was too painful. Jinn brushed his lips against her temple and asked her again.

"Who are they?"

And Iris sucked in a breath. "Max," she whispered. "And Rin." And someone else. But she wouldn't say it.

"Max and Rin?" Jinn blinked, confused, and looked around them. "I don't see them here. Where are they?"

"I'm not sure," Iris whispered. As her memories began to whirl, she went to hug Jinn again, but this time he refused her.

"Iris, not now," he said in that serious and hyper-responsible Jinn way. He gripped her shoulders. "Where are they? You should be able to tell. Just feel their anima."

But that was the thing. She couldn't feel their anima. Their life forces were gone.

Jinn wrapped a braid around his finger and tugged it gently. "Can you explain it to me, then? Where they've gone? Go slowly."

There was something too deliciously comforting about Jinn's presence. He shifted her around and let her fall into him. He cradled her like a child, his arms shielding her from the world. She felt foolish and weak, and yet somehow her strength was growing bit by bit all the same. Jinn didn't push her. He waited until she could finally answer.

"When people die," Iris told him, "their bodies return to the earth in some fashion or another. But their souls don't disappear. They travel."

Jinn's chin rubbed the crown of her head. She nestled into his chest more deeply.

"They travel?" He seemed genuinely surprised. Why wouldn't he be? No human would know this. "Where do they go?"

"To the planet's core." Iris's fingers traced a path down his chest. His hairs brushed her skin lightly. "Where they wait for rebirth."

It was the cycle of life and death. Whenever Hiva would destroy humanity, the souls she'd released were sent to the planet's core, the abode of the One who created her. And what an abode it was. The souls were never lonely. In that crystal kingdom, where the sky matched the color of the ground, where soft shades of peach and blue attacked the senses among glittering flora, each soul could live out their happiest fantasies. The souls waited to be reborn for years. And then, once Hiva had finished her mission and returned to the earth's core, they'd be released to live again in new forms. They'd be free to create new societies and civilizations in the hopes that humanity would get it right this time. In the hopes that Hiva would not need to be called again.

And yet, without fail, Hiva was always summoned. Again and again. The same souls in different bodies, living different lives, could not create a different outcome. Corruption, greed, power, and conquest. The story was always the same.

"So," Jinn said calmly, as if he'd heard all this. As if he knew what she was thinking. "Max and Rin are dead."

Each word pounded her like a hammer. The feeling disappeared from her body. Suddenly she felt cold in the humid, still night. Suddenly her pulse had quickened.

Her bloody hand holding Max's heart.

The Titans rising out of the destroyed Atlas Mountains, blasting the earth with energy that seemed equal to the output of the sun. Rin's letter floating and then drowning in the river.

Granny's letter.

Iris pushed Jinn down upon his back and straddled him desperately. She pushed her hands against his chest, sitting upon his hips, trying to feel his flesh. But Jinn gripped her arms.

"No distractions," he said, sitting up, holding her still. "Max and Rin are dead. Say it."

She shook her head, whimpering something. She wasn't sure what.

"Say it!"

She tried to cover her face, but Jinn wouldn't let her. He tugged her hands down and forced her to look at him. Those intense dark eyes, so supernaturally fierce that it had inspired Coolie's nickname for him, "Jinn." She shook her head again in protest but couldn't deny it any longer.

She opened her mouth. "Max and Rin are dead." She said it and went limp.

Jinn rubbed her arms without saying a word. As the night passed, she considered their last moments. Both trying to reach her.

"I did it to them," Iris said with a solemn nod of her head, her eyes unfocused. "I did that to them. That's why I can't find you, Rin. That's why . . ."

The stars were relentlessly bright. She wondered if they agreed with her.

"Didn't I say we all make mistakes?" Jinn crossed his legs. "Max. You. Me. All of us. I think we all just did the best we could."

"My best wasn't good enough."

Millions dead at her hand. All because she'd felt betrayed. She'd found Rin in that valley and had been ready to murder her, all because she was scared of feeling something other than rage. She'd lost friends. She'd taken lives. How could she call that her best?

"I don't think anyone's best is good enough. Not yet," said Jinn. "But even in a terrible, hopeless world, a lot of us try so hard to do good. My father did his best. He became a Young Ottoman and fled to France because he wanted to change things."

He was right. Despite how gruesome this world could be, there were too many across history who hadn't yet given up on it. They hadn't thrown up their hands and opted out of life. They worked for the public good. For the goodness and safety and protection of their communities. Why, in all the lives that Hiva had returned to destroy humanity, had she never noticed them? Why had she only seen the wickedness rather than the potential?

"I've been wondering." Jinn lay back down on the grass, cushioning his head with his arms. "What kind of world do you want to live in? Hiva arises from the earth to destroy civilizations judged as too wicked to continue. So what's your ideal world?"

Iris didn't have to think at all. She answered immediately. "One where humans and the natural world can exist in harmony. Where nobody would hurt each other." She looked at the redness of her palms. "And where people can be who they wish to be."

"Seems so simple."

"It should be."

"So then why don't you make it?"

Surprised, Iris stared at Jinn as he ran one of his hands through his curly hair. "Make it?"

"Why not?" Jinn shrugged. "You can destroy worlds. Surely you can make them too."

A little shaken, Iris shook her head quickly. "Only the One who created me can release souls from the earth's core. Even then, she doesn't guide them in how they re-create their societies, she just . . . waits. And watches."

And then calls Hiva up to judge and destroy them. Such a pointless cycle.

"It frustrates me," Iris admitted finally to herself. "It really frustrates me."

"Then do something about it," Jinn said. "Maybe Hiva can do more than just destroy."

The other Hiva had asked her once before if there was another way. But she couldn't fathom it then. Even now it was frightening to wrap her mind around it. The system had been set in place for millions of years. Who was she to change what was already in etched in stone by a power so much greater than she?

"What's that? You look a little scared." Jinn gave her a sidelong look. "Like the time we were about to perform in Germany, and you stepped out on that stage completely unprepared because you'd knowingly missed practice."

Iris's face flushed. "I didn't knowingly miss practice."

"You did. You were mad at me because I'd called you a blockhead for falling out of your turns. So you kept making excuse after excuse not to practice with me until it was too late." Jinn shook his head. "What a disastrous performance that night."

It had been disastrous. Coolie had let them have it that night. Jinn hadn't said anything. But after they left Coolie's trailer, he'd nudged her in the ribs and told her, "Practice. Every day. No more excuses," before leaving her to sulk in her tent.

"You really thought I didn't know the real reason you kept avoiding me? Surely you didn't think I believed it was because you had really found your long-lost twin in a Munich pub."

"Well, I'm not good at coming up with excuses on the fly, and . . . Ugh! Quiet, you crank. Just leave me alone."

"Ah. That's more like you." Jinn laughed. Such a gorgeous sound.

She was so used to his eyebrows knitted in a brooding scowl. But this time he seemed so at peace. His immaculate chest and curved hips. His strong legs. Perfect without a single blemish. As if he'd never experienced the gruesome death of his father. As if he hadn't hunted the murderer, Gram, across the planet. As if he hadn't lost his life trying to shield her from a killing blow. He looked so at peace. Exactly as Iris wanted to see him. She smiled. Yes, this was how it should be.

It was for this very reason that her eyes began to well up with tears.

"What's wrong?" As she turned away from him, Jinn sat up to rub her arms. "Why are you crying?"

This isn't right, she thought, even as she let the warmth of Jinn against her back wash over her. *I can't feel his anima.*

"If you have something to tell me, then say it," Jinn prodded gently. "You've got my full attention. When haven't you?"

Iris shook her head, because she couldn't say it. If she said it, that would make it real. And nothing real was good. What was real was pain. She couldn't handle any more of it.

"Iris . . ." Jinn kissed her shoulder as she sniffled and wiped her wet face. "Face it."

His words lingered in the hot night.

"No."

"You have to." He gripped her forearm. It was sturdy. Unafraid. Like Jinn was trying to transfer some of that strength into her very body. "You have to face reality."

"But I don't want to," she whimpered, and buried her head in her hands. "It's not fair. I didn't get to say goodbye to anyone. I didn't get to explain myself to Hawkins and Jacob, or Lucille and Mary and Henry. I didn't get to tell Max that I'd forgiven him. And ask him to forgive me. I didn't get to hug Rin. Tell her that it was okay—that her future would be better than her past. That she's my sister and always will be. I didn't get to introduce her to Granny and have lunch. I didn't get to say goodbye to them . . . and . . ."

Her mouth opened and closed. She shivered as the truth crawled up her body, secretly, insidiously, until she couldn't ignore it anymore. Until her body dipped forward, held back only by sheer will.

"I didn't get to say goodbye to you, either," she whispered, and when she inhaled a sharp breath, she dragged her tears into her throat and almost choked. "I didn't get to tell you I loved you."

Jinn kept holding her. "I knew."

"I didn't get to ask you your real name!" Iris whipped around, grabbing his arms, shaking him. "I don't even know your real name, Jinn! Please tell me. Please!"

Jinn didn't answer, and he wouldn't. She knew he wouldn't. He *couldn't*. Jinn wasn't there.

Jinn was dead. This was all in her head.

He cupped her face nonetheless. "Maybe you'll learn it one day," he whispered.

Now Iris's mind had completely collapsed. She coughed and cried, trembled and screamed, at how cruel the world had been to her. To all of them.

"It isn't fair," she yelled as loudly as she could. "How is any of this fair? So many are gone. Struggled and died. And this world doesn't care! Why? I don't want to go back. I don't want anything to do with this world! I don't want to remember any of it! I'm tired of it all!" And she grabbed Jinn's hair because she needed to feel all of him—the rough texture of it against her palms and his familiar musky scent in her nose, but the more she cried, the fainter it all became. As if she were waking up from a dream.

"Don't go," she said desperately. "Let's just stay here."

"Iris . . . ," Jinn said. But she wouldn't let him continue. No, she couldn't.

"There's nothing wrong with it," she went on frantically. "This world will destroy itself soon enough."

Jinn began untangling her fingers from his hair. "Iris . . ."

"Let's just stay here like this forever! Please, Jinn. Please!"

"Face yourself!"

Jinn's shout shook the trees. He grabbed her arms and forced her to look into his eyes. Forced her to realize that they were faded. Hollow. She'd never find such hollowness in the real Jinn's eyes. Everything had been so obvious from the beginning.

"Face yourself," Jinn said again in a whisper. "Face the world."

Iris fell silent, sniffing back her tears, pursing her lips together.

"What did they tell you before they died?"

She closed her eyes. And slowly the resistance in her faded. Gradually she could see them, except in her mind's eye they weren't fearful or desperate. In the darkness they stood in their full glory: Max with his lopsided smile and his hands behind his back; Rin, tall like the warrior she was, the point of her sword buried in the ground.

Iris . . . go back to being yourself.

Iris . . . ! Don't give up on yourself.

Don't give up! Jinn's voice as he'd held her in the valley. His cry before he'd died there.

"They wouldn't want to see you like this, hiding from the world. Hiding from yourself," Jinn said, and he was right. They hadn't died for her to be cowering in the forest, living in a dream. "You have to face reality. Face it with strength and honor, because nobody else is you, Iris."

"And who am I?" Iris asked, because she'd been given so many names by so many people across all her lifetimes that she'd completely lost count.

Jinn leaned in close. His breath, though faint, had a distinct sweet smell. "Whoever you want to be," he said. "This time, decide for yourself. Who you want to be. What you think the world should be. Decide for yourself, Iris."

Iris sat back and let her arms rest upon her knees. He'd won. Jinn had won, as he always would. He leaned back. And suddenly the distance between them seemed insurmountable. She felt lonely. The loneliness crushed her. It wouldn't go away, but it was real. It was real.

"And never forget," he said.

"Forget what?"

"That I've always loved you. And will always love you, no matter where my soul goes next."

She watched him until he faded away.

43

IRIS KNEW ALL THE SOLAR JUMP locations by heart. She'd used them in her past life to destroy the Naacal. Most were still buried in the earth, left over from ancient times. Because of them, a journey that would have taken three weeks took three days. Most were concentrated in this continent. She wondered if Rin knew that. She'd clearly learned about the Jumps somehow. It was how she'd reached the Naacalian facility and taken the Titan Control Device.

Why, Rin? Such a dangerous device . . .

A stupid question. Even the Naacal had believed that only the most horrifically destructive contraptions could get rid of Hiva. Maybe Rin had felt she'd had no choice.

She wanted to know more. So, wearing the slip she'd been given in the earth's core, she followed the anima she could recognize to Lagos. She found the little girl eating roasted plantain by a palm tree in shabby clothes. It looked like one of her arms had been injured but was recovering well. Lulu. Iris beamed at the sight of her before her shoulders slumped. The girl was waiting, but not for her.

Iris walked up to her anyway. And when Lulu saw her approach, she looked shocked for just a moment before grinning and waving her hand wildly. Half the plantain almost fell off.

"Miss Iris! You're back!"

Iris was stunned as the girl jumped to her feet and ran to gave her a hug. "H-how . . . how could you tell?"

"Are you kidding?" Lulu placed her hand on her hip and gave her an incredulous look. "You should have seen yourself before. You looked like a ghost. But you look pretty normal now."

Before. The last time Iris had seen Lulu was in the underground Naacalian facility where they'd taken the Titan Control Device. The girl had clearly seen many adventures. She seemed more confident now. More grown up. And seeing this made Iris feel as if she'd just been born. *She* was the ignorant child who knew nothing about the world, not this girl.

The desire to sit and talk with her was overwhelming. But Lulu dragged her away from the palm trees and through the streets, chattering excitedly.

"Miss Rin knew you'd come back," Lulu said. "She didn't want to kill you. Some others voted for it, but Rin didn't."

Iris blinked, feeling somehow exposed when villagers stared at the two of them as they passed. "Voted?"

"All of us got together in Miss Uma's apartment and voted on whether or not we should—" Lulu suddenly caught herself, looking up at Iris quickly.

"Kill me."

Lulu squirmed. Her hand was little and hot. A different kind of hot than Jinn's had been. It was sticky and uncomfortable. But it was real. The reality of it only made the dream fuzzier.

"Um. I voted no, by the way. So did Max and Berta. Berta told me."

"Well, thank you." Iris smiled down at her. She didn't blame those who voted otherwise. Though using the Titans had been reckless, she had no right to judge, not knowing just how many lives she'd taken while trapped in her Hiva state. But she did feel a little better knowing that Max and Rin had chosen to believe in her until the end.

And now what? she thought as Lulu pulled her to a little square house away from the bustling town core. *What should I do?*

I need to tell them the truth. It was only right.

She opened the door, prepared for the worst, because she'd already felt her anima. And there she was, lying on the couch. At the sight of her, Berta paused, her skin paling by the second, her mouth parted in a frozen gasp. Then Berta reached for her shotgun on the floor.

"She's good!" Lulu stepped in front of Iris and put her hands up.

Berta grabbed the gun and jumped to her feet. "Lulu, out of the way!"

"But Miss Iris is back to normal!"

"Oh yeah?" Berta pointed her gun at Iris's head. "Prove it."

"I've already proven it," said Iris calmly. "You're still alive."

Berta's gun shook in her hand. It hadn't taken much for Berta to remember—a bullet wouldn't have been able to kill her anyway.

"If you're alive, then the plan didn't work," Berta said, her jaw tight. "They didn't use the Titans after all?"

"They used them." Iris knew she had to elaborate further, but seeing Berta's expression become so vulnerable made Iris want to hide in the forest again.

No. No more hiding. She owed them the truth.

"If they used them, then . . ." Berta trailed off, and Iris could see she was trying to work out what had happened while avoiding the most horrific of the possibilities available to her. Iris knew what it meant to want the truth and not want it at the same time.

Face yourself. She thought of Jinn and sucked in a breath.

"They activated the Titans but couldn't control them," Iris said in a neutral tone. "The Titans destroyed everything. Everyone. They're all dead. And only I survived because . . . because I'm me. I can't die. Rin, Jinn . . . Max, they brought me back to myself. But they paid a terrible price. That's the truth, Berta."

She said everything in one breath and let the truth sit in the air between them. She didn't move. No one did. The apartment went painfully silent.

After several minutes, Berta sat on the couch, her hands on her lap, and stayed silent for several more. Gritting her teeth, Iris looked away. Pain brought about sorrow. Loss tore away parts of people's souls. But Iris wanted something different. Even if it was selfish. Even if it was childish, she wanted a different world.

"My brother is dead, then?" Berta said abruptly, giving Iris a start. "And Rin?"

Iris nodded her head silently. "I'm sorry." But there was more to confess. Max had died by Iris's own hands. Even though he would have been killed by the Titans, he'd died minutes earlier than everyone else because she hadn't yet come to her senses. But then, if Max hadn't killed her in the first place, she wouldn't have become Hiva. Where did the cycle of blame end? Why was she even trying to find a person to blame? It was all just nonsensical violence, born from suffering that seemed to simply exist for the sake of existing.

"I see. Okay. Thanks for telling me. Glad you're back." It was all Berta said. She leaned over and propped herself up by her knees. Iris took a hesitant step toward her, but Berta didn't flinch, didn't say a word for another minute. She didn't want to hear anything else.

But this was reality. Neither of them could hide from it. Taking in a deep breath and shaking her head, Iris turned from Berta and looked around. So this is where they'd discussed her fate. The chairs looked newly bought. The bookshelves were filled with tomes, probably everything from the literary to the scientific. This is where they had all sat.

Now they were all dead.

Iris stumbled back and held on to a chair to keep herself steady. She had to be strong. She had to face reality, no matter how painful.

No matter how painful.

"You'll make it, Miss Iris," Lulu said behind her. "If I could make it, I think anyone can."

Iris covered the whining cry that escaped her mouth and let herself shake and cry until her breathing calmed and her chest stilled. *Goodbye, everyone....*

This was Uma's apartment. Uma wasn't around. She couldn't sense the woman's anima here. But she could feel her own. So much white crystal was beneath their feet.

"Where is Uma?" Iris asked.

Because Berta would no longer speak, Lulu hesitated before answering. "That man named Bosch called her back to his big fancy facility inside the

Atakora Mountains," she said, rotating the point of her big toe on the wooden floor. "Don't know what for."

Iris shut her eyes and followed the scent—the trail to the facility. Something had changed. There were far more people there than when she had been in the factory last. It was packed. Tens of thousands. Why? What was going on . . . ?

Because of the throbbing in her head, she'd almost missed it. But when she turned to her right, she saw something she hadn't expected.

Iris narrowed her eyes. Could it be? It was tucked in the corner by the bookcase, placed gingerly against the wall. A weapon, a lance, made of bone.

"This is Hiva's," Iris said, picking it up, feeling the rough surface. It hadn't been fully sanded down. But it'd clearly taken some work to put this together. Hiva's left arm. How had they managed to take it from him?

Iris closed her eyes and tried to sense him. Hiva's anima. It wasn't too far. His crystal heart would soon mend completely, and when it did, he'd be reborn. Good. She wanted a chance to speak with him.

But Hiva's anima was entangled with someone else's.

Someone familiar.

"What?" Her grip hardened around the lance. "It's him. But why does he have Hiva's heart?"

She hadn't thought about Adam Temple in a while. At first, he was the one human she had wanted to kill more than anyone—even more than Jinn, who at the time she'd thought had murdered her. But even if Jinn had murdered her, there was no one who deserved death more than Adam—the one who'd manipulated her. Who'd made her life a living hell.

But then, after seeing him raving and weeping like a madman at the sight of her, after seeing his eyes filled with deranged hope, she'd realized all too clearly that he was nothing more than every other selfish coward who clung to Hiva's power to make up for his own weakness. She didn't need to consider him. He was nothing. That was what she'd decided.

Iris tried to remember. Yes, that night in France. Adam had been desperate for some strange reason, ranting as usual. It had all been such a bother to her that night. She was too preoccupied with her own worries and tired of dealing with that boy's nonsense. Tired of being the receptacle for his baggage when she had plenty of her own. What had happened after she'd left Adam lying there in that bedroom?

He was close now. Too close. He'd taken Hiva's heart to the mining site. The gateway to Heaven's Shrine. Why? She could feel others there too. Barry Bately? And—

Iris's fingers twitched. And Doctor Seymour Pratt. That foul, sick man. They were all together. Gathered like the beasts of Revelation. Why?

This was bad. No matter how badly she wanted to, and no matter how deeply he deserved it, she could no longer afford to ignore the existence of Adam Temple. Between him and the Titans running amok, Iris had to move quickly.

She'd said her goodbyes. It was time to move.

The presence of the white crystal was too strong here. Maybe that was why she couldn't sense the women who'd lain in wait by the open door. Berta hadn't noticed. Why would she? She was preoccupied by her grief, her empty gaze glued to the floor.

The moment Iris turned and saw them, she opened her lips, for she'd recognized Natame's face. But the poisoned darts found her neck quite quickly, too quickly. More found the inside of her elbow and her leg. The drug coursed through her veins and took her so fast, she didn't even feel her body hit the ground.

When next she awoke, Iris's body felt bruised all over, but there wasn't any room to move it. The steel crate was doubly reinforced. Her knees were pressed against her chest, her toes curled awkwardly against the metal. She just barely managed to uncross her arms, but when she placed her palm on the cold surface above and tried to push it, the crate wouldn't open. There wasn't enough room to stretch her arm out fully. Her neck was twisted. Where was she?

The only way she could breathe was through the few holes that brought in chatter with the light.

"So you desire safe passage with your cargo in exchange for the Moon Skeleton? How haughty of you. I'm not a woman who likes to negotiate."

Madame Bellerose. The sound of her voice shocked Iris out of her dull senses. She pounded on the steel cage, only to be met with a fierce kick from the outside.

"Exactly what is in there again?" Madame Bellerose sounded suspicious.

"A baby goat." It was General Sesinu who'd answered. Iris had only met her once, but she recognized her voice, and her life force was unmistakably fierce and proud.

"You really believe you'll need cattle in the New World?" Madame Bellerose snickered. "Well, I'm sure people like you would, what with your silly, unevolved hunter-gatherer ways."

"What did she say?" Iris could hear Aisosa whispering in Fon.

"I don't know. I don't understand French." Natame. So they were here too. "But the general looks annoyed. I don't blame her. That white woman has an irritating face."

"Shh!" Another voice Iris didn't quite recognize. The chatter stopped.

"Well then, fine. I accept your deal," Madame Bellerose said very snottily. "But only two of you can enter the Ark. I have quite too many guests and not enough room."

The Ark. Iris's heart pounded in her chest. *Did she just say the bloody Ark?*

"The Moon Skeleton . . ." Iris could see a tinge of her red smile through one of the air holes in the crate. "Such a little thing, but I can feel its power radiating against my skin. This is it. The missing piece to the puzzle."

The woman's shrieking laughter nearly split Iris's skull in two.

"Cortez. Benini. Temple. Cordiero. And all the others. None of the men managed it. It was me. I am the greatest Enlightener to have ever served on the Committee. And now I will be a queen in two worlds." She giggled. "How very fitting."

Iris closed her eyes and zeroed in on the anima. Sesinu, Natame, and Aisosa were here with Madame Bellerose and some other men, maybe soldiers. Not just them but Izegbe too. Hard to forget a woman who had shot you in the chest. But beneath them, deep in the cavernous mountain, were thousands of strangers lined up, all marching in one row as if boarding a ship.

They *were* boarding a ship. Uma was there too. No wonder she'd been recalled to the mountains.

The Ark was about to take flight.

A YOUNG MAN THINKING

Finale

A DAM HAD FINALLY ARRIVED AT THE site of the Solar Jump in the Oil Rivers region, near the mining site formerly under the British Crown's control. Bosch's men cocked their guns all at once, aiming for him, until they recognized who he was and fell back. The power of the Temple name was one thing he could thank his dead father for.

Don't worry, Father. Soon all will follow you into the bliss of destruction.

Out from behind a soldier walked Doctor Seymour Pratt, his arms behind his hunched back. Even in this relentless heat, the man clung to his long white lab coat as tightly as Civilization clung to her globe and spear at the center of the British Museum's pediment. It was his way of separating him from those he deemed the primordial preman. The savages of the earth. It was what drove Pratt's relentless pursuits toward science and progress. After his many humiliations had shriveled his soul and eaten away his pride, Adam now understood that fully. And that was why he had confidence Pratt would accept his offer.

Barry Bately, still in his working-class rags, stood at Pratt's side, dutiful and silent, his mutilated lips not so much as twitching. The hat upon his bald skull slipped a little as he tilted his head.

"Adam Temple," said Doctor Pratt. "What have you come here to do?"

"I've come to make you an offer." Adam pulled Hiva's heart out of his pocket. The pale pink crystal glittered in Doctor Pratt's ever-widening beady eyes. "Come with me to the Coral Temple. There I will make your greatest dreams come true."

The Solar Jump reacted to Hiva's heart, pulling Adam by the belly button through space and time into Heaven's Shrine. Here in this temple filled with cobwebs, he saw the altar upon which his father had been found half dead and chuckled lightly to himself.

What a life you led, Father. In some ways, I can understand why you abandoned us for this.

Doctor Seymour Pratt already knew the way. A doorway opened in the grand mural, and the glass tube hidden inside took them down, down, down into the Atlantic Ocean.

"And how do you know my dreams, boy?" Doctor Pratt asked as Adam watched the whales and the schools of fish drifting by the glass. Bately stood deathly still in the glass container, uninterested in the sea scenery before him. It was as if he would not so much as breathe unless Doctor Pratt ordered it of him.

"Because I understand you now, Doctor. Though I admit—I didn't before." Adam crossed his arms and looked into the deep waters. All of God's creatures. Subordinate to man. "I wanted to believe that my thinking was far more progressive. That I understood things that an old man like you, like my father, surely couldn't. But by bowing my head to another, I had given up my power. The natural power endowed in me by God himself. My whole life, I have debased myself for an empty vessel of a woman."

"For a creature beneath you?" Doctor Pratt added, his furry eyebrow arched in curiosity.

"That's just the thing, Doctor," Adam said as a dark, domed palace upon the sea floor came into view. "Whether it be written in the books of Darwin or the scrolls of the Old Testament, it has been made clear: all creatures are beneath man. I will not be weaker than her."

As the tube entered through the ceiling of the Coral Temple, Doctor Pratt pressed his old hand against the glass. "I knew it the moment I saw that filthy creature destroy my brother, though trapped in a zoo. Some beings need to be subordinate. It is not an injustice. It is simply progress."

"And progress is exactly what I am here to offer you," said Adam.

The tube dropped them off onto a platform; they were alone in this vast room. Adam's shoes echoed upon the floor. "No," he said as Bately and Doctor Pratt gathered behind him. "What I offer you is something more." He turned and spread out his arms. "Evolution."

Hiva's Tomb loomed overhead. A cube made by the genius hands of the Naacal. A structure built to atomize the body of Hiva.

"On his deathbed, my father told me something about Hiva's Tomb." Adam walked up to it and placed his hand on the glass. There was a little crack in it. *From what?* he wondered. His finger lingered there. "This structure can deconstruct anyone down to their very basic molecules. Not just Hiva. Anyone at all who steps inside. But Hiva's Tomb operates like anything else that requires a power source. If you were to cut the power, you would turn off the machine. With the energy separating the atoms gone, the atoms would come back together, reforming the being." Adam turned to Doctor Pratt. "Shall I teach you how to operate it?"

"And why in the world would you want to do that?" But Doctor Pratt wasn't a fool. He seemed to instinctively know where Adam's line of thinking was heading. As soon as he'd asked the question, the greed in his evil, beady eyes was thirsting for the right answer.

"I read my father's research," Adam said, leaning against the glass. "I read your works as well. Your studies. Every discovery you painstakingly detailed as you destroyed Hiva's body again and again. And I knew as a child: it wasn't just for discovery, nor was it revenge for the brother she killed. It angered you deep inside to think that such a great and powerful being, greater than humankind, greater than the European, could appear in the dark skin of an African woman. It was against all logic. All reason."

Doctor Pratt said nothing. That was how Adam knew he was correct.

"Despite my current ambition, my heart still wavers for her," Adam admitted, crossing his arms against his chest, his bottom lip curled. "Your hatred is pure. It's cold and clinical and wavers for no one. It is the one thing I lack. I will need it to become whole."

Adam's lips twisted in a serene grin as he looked up at the dome ceiling of the Coral Temple. "And you will need *this* to become a being even greater than Hiva."

He pulled out Hiva's crystal heart. It would finish mending soon. Adam did not have another moment to waste.

"Bately will operate the machine. I will teach him how, and you will give him the appropriate commands. You and I will walk into Hiva's Tomb with this." His hand squeezed the crystal heart. "And we will arise as something new. Something greater."

A new Hiva in the place of the one that had failed him.

Doctor Pratt did not need too long to decide.

"It seems you've learned, boy," he said. "We were born of kings."

44

THE CART IRIS WAS TRAPPED IN rocked back and forth so violently, she hit the back of her head multiple times and had to grind her teeth to keep from screaming. How in the hell had the Dahomey gotten their hands on the Moon Skeleton? And why on earth would they give it to the Enlightenment Committee? Something wasn't adding up.

"Then we'll leave it to you," Sesinu said in Fon. "Natame. Aisosa. You know the plan."

"Of course!" Maybe it was because she was so young, but Aisosa sounded all too chipper given the situation. "We'll get Isoke where she needs to go. And you go collect Rin's side of the bargain. We'll be back in Abomey in time for dinner!"

Rin? What bargain?

Iris didn't have much time to consider it before she felt herself lift off the ground. "Wait!" she said, her voice barely croaking out of her lungs because her chin was squished against her chest. The four men carrying her crate wouldn't have heard her anyway, not with all the jostling. She could hear them barking orders at each other in French to coordinate. "Wait . . ."

"Quiet, Isoke," Natame said in Fon. The men wouldn't have known any differently. "Stay still until we get you on board."

On board the Ark. Iris gulped.

The men carried her crate down deep into the mountains. The draft of wind. The mines. All of it smelled familiar. Iris closed her eyes and remembered running with Jinn and Rin, escaping the facility. Rin's serious scowl as she led the way. Jinn feigning irritation with her as they bantered back and forth. His protective hand on the small of her back . . .

No, focus. Iris gritted her teeth as a swell of sorrow began to flow. This wasn't the time for sentimentality. The chattering of thousands grew louder until they had completely overwhelmed her. Laughter. Discussions. So many different languages. As Hiva, she understood them all. But none of it made any sense. Not right away.

"I'm so excited we're finally boarding! Carnegie wasn't invited, was he, dear?"

"I'm surprised you accepted Madame Bellerose's invitation, Your Majesty King Leopold. So you've given up your venture in the Congo?"

Wheels and levers were whirring, along with a giant horn that seemed to blow out a gush of steam. So many sounds clashed against one another. It truly felt like the boarding of some luxury steamship for royals, ready for its maiden voyage.

"What a marvelous ship. The Wonder Ship! The Ship of Dreams! Now that I see it, I can't but call it anything else. It has to be the most amazing contraption I've ever set my eyes on. The history books will call it the Queen of the Skies."

"This way, please! This way! VIP guests, please stay in line. Cargo to the side here!" The officials all repeated the same lines in English, French, German— practically every European language known to man. The Committee had really outdone themselves when it came to preparation, and it was very clear who their clientele were: the rich and powerful. Iris heard names she'd only read in newspapers—or had never heard at all. Henry Stanley. Cecil Rhodes. Lothar Von Trotha. Frederick Sleigh Roberts and Horatio Herbert Kitchener. Queens and kings. Nobles and tsars.

"I told Gladstone it would be magnificent, but the old dodderer chose to stay in England. Doesn't he know the world is ending?"

The musky scent of various colognes slipped into her steel crate as she passed by, along with those of spices, perfumes, and nicotine. Parakeets squawking and dogs barking told her humans weren't the only living creatures allowed on deck. No wonder Bellerose didn't mind a "baby goat."

"They said it'll be another two hours before they're able to take flight. Something about checking the engine."

"How insufferable—do they know how long I've had to wait among those dreaded Africans for this ship to even start boarding? All because I came too early from New York."

A violent bump rattled Iris's crate as the men unceremoniously tossed it onto a platform, which slowly lifted with the sound of clinking chains and grating gears.

"Make sure your name is on all your luggage. Keep all other possessions on your person until the end of the expedition."

The voices were getting farther away.

"Oh, how exciting. We're making history, you know. Next time I'll come back and bring the children!"

Iris couldn't hear the rest of the excitement because the chains had lifted her inside the ship. Several men carried her off the platform and packed her away in some dusty corner. It seemed like they were trying to load as much material as possible.

Iris suddenly thought of Max stowed away on a pirate ship, buried underneath boxes of spices and fabrics. How it had twisted his mind until he could suddenly do terrible things he'd never been capable of before. Would she be buried alone here too? Iris's thigh muscles cramped terribly. She tried to straighten out her legs, stretching out her neck just enough so that she could directly breathe in air from the holes in the steel crate.

After an hour of commotion, she finally heard one of the men say: "All right, Storage Unit 3A is filled. What about the others?"

"Ready. Many of the passengers are inside their palace suites, mingling and whatnot. Someone said Malakar's close to getting the engine up and running. The Ark should take off sooner than expected."

Uma. Iris had to reach her. Get her off this stupid ship and bring her back to her lab, where they could work on what needed to be done—stopping the Titans. Stopping Adam.

"All right, lads, go check that the escape pods are in place."

"Escape pods? Barely got any of those. Guess that wasn't in the budget."

"Just check them, you idiots."

They continued to bicker back and forth until the door shut behind them. The whirring of a chain and the clinking of gears. Several clicks. Whatever hatch her crate had been carried through was shut. And now Iris was alone in stuffy Storage Unit 3A.

She waited until she was sure nobody was around. Then she started kicking. Her legs were too cramped. She couldn't gather the force needed to push the crate open. She tried banging her arm against the top, but it was the same issue. Damn it. She was so much stronger when she was Hiva. She supposed it was the clear focus on destruction. She wasn't nearly as impressive as Iris, but then what else could she do, crouched inside a steel box?

"Damn it," she grunted, jostling her body around, trying to turn over the crate. "Come on, damn you!"

On the other side, a pair of hands tinkered with the steel box deftly. Iris was too shocked to think to check their anima. She didn't have to; she soon heard their voices.

"Use the crowbar," Aisosa said, and after a loud clink: "Quietly, quietly."

Natame sucked her teeth. "It's not easy, you know."

"Natame?" Iris said, pushing the word through her twisted neck. "Aisosa?"

"Quiet, Isoke—we're coming," Aisosa scolded her. "Watch your head now."

After a huge exertion of force, a piece of metal fell from the top of the crate and clattered on the floor. A lock, maybe. Another tug, and the lid flipped open. Iris let out a desperate moan and jumped to her feet, inhaling the biggest breath she'd ever had.

"Holy hell," Iris whispered, taking in the sight. Storage Unit 3A, a vast space where blue carpet stretched from wall to wooden wall. Every inch of the floor was covered in crates, suitcases, bags, and briefcases. Piles of silk in one corner and stacks of gold in another. There was barely any room in which to maneuver.

"You should have seen the other room we thought they took you to," said Aisosa, the red beads around her forearm jingling when she folded her arms over her chest. "There were so many birdcages and dog kennels. So loud and smelly. Imagine being the one to clean up after them."

"What are you two doing here?" Iris said as her bare legs crushed against the inside of her steel crate. "As a matter of fact, what am I doing here?"

"Rin made a bargain with the Dahomey," said Natame.

Rin? A bargain with the Dahomey after what they'd done to her? What could have made her so desperate? She'd left Abomey as a fugitive and knew she could be executed if she were ever caught again. What could have made her expose herself to them?

"It was all about you, Isoke," Natame continued, striking Iris's heart all at once. "She gave us the Moon Skeleton so we'd trade it for your safe passage on the Ark. If we did this for her, she'd give herself up to King Glele."

"What?" Distressed, Iris stared at the blue carpet, gripped with confusion. "Why in the world . . . ?"

"She said it was the only way to rid the world of Hiva," Aisosa said. "But I don't know . . . Rin hadn't been herself since she separated from you. It was as if she'd lost half her limbs. If you ask me, I think it was out of concern for you."

"She certainly doesn't look like she's going to kill everyone, does she?" Natame whispered behind her hand, earning a nudge in the ribs.

To rid the world of Hiva. But when she remembered Rin standing in front of her by the river, wearing a dress clearly sewn by Granny, Iris knew that wasn't true. It had been to save her. The group had voted on killing her. Had decided to use the Titans. Maybe sending her to another dimension, in Rin's mind, was the only way to rescue Iris.

When she thought about that, heat rushed to her face and memories flashed before her eyes. Memories of their first meeting. Their battles. Their adventures. Their victories and struggles. She'd promised to make Rin part of her family. Rin must have held on to that until the very end.

Iris clenched her hands into fists. She wasn't going to cry. Not while the two girls were watching.

"The world is still in trouble—but not from me. I need Uma Malakar—a top scientist who's on this ship. I need to get her off the Ark before it takes flight. Can you help me?"

Aisosa and Natame exchanged hesitant glances before Natame shook her head. "Our job was to deliver you to the Ark," she said. "That job is over."

"But we can still help," Aisosa said.

From her leather breast strap, she pulled out a parchment. After unfolding it, she spread it out in front of Iris's face. Diagrams. Different levels of the ship, with clear symbols and markings.

"The Ark's schematics. This is a map." Iris whipped her head up. "Where did you get this?"

"We're very good at our jobs," said Aisosa, and the young girl grinned wickedly before shoving it in Iris's hands.

"It's yours, Isoke," said Natame. "But take heed—this ship will be launched from the mountains any moment now. If you want to grab your scientist, you must move quickly."

"Good luck." Aisosa gave her a salute by pumping her hand against her chest, and the two skipped over crates to sneak back out of the room.

Any moment now, she says. Any moment now, Uma and Iris would be taken away to some other world, leaving this one to some gruesome fate. Iris had done enough damage to the earth. She couldn't abandon it now. Breathing in and out, she shut her eyes. *Uma, where are you?*

Uma's anima was proud to almost an arrogant degree, but ambivalent—caught between two worlds. Iris hooked onto the warring ideologies and desires and, leaping over the crates and packages, slipped out of Storage Unit 3A.

The Enlightenment Committee truly had done everything they could to make their Ark mimic the look of a luxurious ocean liner. According to the schematics, it was almost two hundred feet longer than the biggest ship Iris had ever heard of. How in the world was this contraption meant to fly?

"Wait a moment—" she heard some valet say in French, as he came out of the arched entrance on the opposite side of the white corridor.

Iris didn't let him finish. She knocked him out swiftly with a punch to the jaw and dragged him into Storage Unit 3A. This wasn't exactly the right ship to walk around without the appropriate attire—or skin color. She could only do something about one of those traits and hope it distracted the Ark's snobbish

patrons from the other. A black suit too big for her and a necktie that choked
her. She really felt as if she were back in England. The oversized black bowler
hat slipped nearly to her eyes. This might work if she kept her head down.

After stuffing the valet inside her steel crate, Iris attempted to match the
"scent" of Uma's life force to the map she was given. Which meant remaining
unseen while she passed by the café, squash courts, the luxury private baths . . .

How thoroughly ridiculous, Iris griped as she started her search through
the labyrinth. There were signs everywhere in various European languages,
directing people to different rooms. This was the passenger area, far busier
and more spacious than the space reserved for storage. Waiters in jackets
stiffer than hers were carrying trays of champagne in and out of suites and
sitting rooms.

It reminded her of Club Uriel—these exclusive spaces locked away from
the prying eyes of "lesser folk," dreamt up by the extravagant imaginations of
those who could only think of themselves. Monet paintings lined one corridor,
hung on flower-patterned wallpaper. Iris couldn't look at them. She instead
kept her gaze down on the shiny mahogany floors and the feet of strangers all
chatting about whose bedroom had a bigger bath.

Following Uma's anima took her past corseted women with giant feathered hats and men in military gear, clinking glasses.

"To discovery!" a few gentlemen cried.

"To riches beyond imagination!" said another before shoving his empty
wineglass in her hand. "Another sherry."

He didn't wait for an answer, nor did he expect one. Iris never broke her
stride but did break the glass when she was far enough away, tossing it into a
potted plant.

"They say this ship is the largest object ever made by man. A flying ship!
Will you stay in the New World?"

"Oh, surely not—at least it'll have to be civilized first. But with this first
voyage, we'll stake claim to the best land."

"Surely the resources we find in the other world will solve whatever's broken in this one. I'm looking forward to it."

This wasn't just an expedition. The schematics made it clear. The hull of the ship was equipped with weapons: the "pacifiers," they were called. What or who were they expecting to pacify? Had Uma come up with that name, or had it been Bosch?

The violins from the musicians playing at every corner almost masked the haunting, whining noise Iris heard in the distance. Almost.

"Oh, is that the mountainside hatch?" said a woman to her military husband.

"It's open," he answered. "The Ark is about to take flight!"

A dark sense of foreboding sunk deep into Iris's immortal bones as she let Uma's anima take her farther and farther away from the passengers, stewards, and porters, past the reception rooms and dining salons. It was when she passed by the ballroom that the double doors opened and she felt a pair of hands throw her inside.

Iris fell hard against the ground, hitting her forehead. As pain split through her skull, she just barely registered the doors closing behind her before staccato giggles began striking the air like the keys of a piano. Iris lifted her head.

"Wait," she said, furrowing her eyebrows. "I know you two."

In front of the grand statue of an angel stood two beautiful little girls, both with black-and-white dresses that fanned out at the skirt. Their curly brown hair was perfectly coiffed, as if they were little dolls. Yes, Iris did remember them, because she'd once fought them in front of the British Museum just before the Tournament of Freaks.

Faith and Virtue. The Sparrow twins.

And they weren't alone.

Sitting along the balustrade that separated the ballroom from the above walkway was a Fool—two Fools. Three. Iris counted them all. Five Fools. Just as they had appeared in Club Uriel's music hall, crouching in the rafters, looking down at her through their harlequin masks.

She was surrounded.

"We caught you, little Hiva," said one Fool, standing prim and proper with his head held high in the air. "Indeed, our system of intelligence gathering is second to none."

"To think those nasty little Dahomey witches would be the ones to bring you in," one Fool spat, but sounded as if he wouldn't have spit on *her* if she were on fire.

"Oh, Miss Iris!" One of the twins waved by the angel statue. She wasn't used to hearing their voices. "Madame Bellerose asked us to watch for any intruders. She's such a nice woman. She took us from that awful facility."

"But then," said the other twin, "it was you who put us inside in the first place. However shall we repay you?"

Iris gritted her teeth and flashed a wry smile. "Let me guess."

And the blizzard fell upon her.

45

THIS IS JUST AN ILLUSION, IRIS told herself, remembering how she, Max, and Jinn had battled the Sparrow twins the first time. The frost forming across her skin. The chill that bit deep into her flesh. The snow and fog blurring her vision. It felt so real, but it wasn't. The Sparrow twins were playing with her mind.

What was real was the strong chop to the neck landed by one Fool. It had almost knocked her out, but she managed to hold on to her senses as she fell to the floor.

"Oh goodness, I'm so sorry." The Fool who'd struck her helped her back to her feet and immediately began begging her forgiveness. "I shouldn't have done that. I shouldn't have done that!"

What? Iris pulled her hand away quickly and rubbed the back of her head in confusion, while the Fool lurched over and clasped his hands together.

"You fool!" cried another, flipping through the snow overhead and landing perfectly behind him. He gave the other Fool a smack. "Grab her and take her to the incinerator. From there, we'll gather her crystal heart and present it to Bellerose."

"Her crystal heart, her crystal heart!" Through the fog, she could just barely see a Fool rolling on the ground and laughing. "Such a fun sight that will be. Don't leave me behind. . . ."

This was chaos. Iris shook her head, but a Fool behind her clasped her wrist.

"You're coming with me, you little wench." And he didn't apologize. She could smell his bloodthirst from beyond his gold-and-white mask.

She didn't have time for this. A shift in the ground told her the Ark was lurching along.

There was an easy way to solve this. She could get rid of them all with just a thought. Just one little thought.

She thought of Max's heart in her hands and bit her lip. No. No more killing. She had to find another way.

"Miss Iris! Oh, Miss Iris!"

She couldn't see the Sparrow twins, but she could hear their voices, carried by the blizzard. "Do you know what they did to us in the Basement?"

"They strapped us up," said the other.

"They poked us."

"They zapped us."

"They made us cry."

"They told us not to cry. And then made us cry again."

"Again and again and again."

She remembered. The experiments. The blood. The human feces. The waste of life. All thanks to the heartless Enlightenment Committee, who had thought they could discover some new scientific revolution inside the bodies of the supernatural.

Iris wrenched herself from one Fool's grip and dodged another. Her warrior training was in full swing as three Fools descended upon her at once. She flipped over one and crashed the second's head into the third's. She jumped upon a fourth Fool's back, striking another as he cursed and promised to tear her to shreds "like all the others."

"We had a mother once, but she died."

"We had a father once, but he abandoned us."

"That old marm at the orphanage hurt us."

"And then you sent us to the Basement."

"Tell me, why did our lives turn out like this?"

The question had come so suddenly that Iris paused, leaving herself open to a swivel kick from one of the Fools. She landed painfully on her back as he stomped on her stomach again and again and again.

Why did our lives turn out like this? It was the very question that Iris had asked since the moment her memories had returned to her.

Why had she been born? Was it only to destroy?

Why had humans been created? Was it only to hurt and be hurt?

Why did the earth exist? Would it one day crumble too?

One day everything would fall apart. Perhaps time was the enemy. But why did things seem to fall apart so quickly when the greed of humans was involved?

As the pain of the Fool's kicks shot up to her head and addled her mind, the shock of each strike felt almost purifying. In the midst of the torment, she understood it clearly. She just wanted a better world. For the Sparrow twins. For the Fanciful Freaks. For herself. For—

"Yeah! Tear off her head, and let's feast upon her brains!" One Fool crouched down next to her, twisting his head here and there, reaching out to grab her hair. He would have too, but another Fool gripped his wrist and grabbed the arm of the Fool stomping her.

"Stop it," he said. He sounded lonely. Somewhere far off in the distance, another Fool was still rolling on the floor, singing, "Don't leave me behind. Don't leave me behind!"

The lonely Fool shoved the other two away from her. "I'm sorry," he told Iris.

"Oh? You're turning traitor, aren't you?" the brain-lusting Fool accused him. "Or is this another order from your true master, Adam Temple?"

Adam? Throwing up saliva on the floor, Iris rolled to a sitting position, gripping her stomach. One of the Fools worked exclusively for Adam?

"Don't think I didn't notice you being so friendly with him," the cruel Fool continued. "Did you think you could betray us?"

"No, no, we should be friends," said the Fool rolling on the ground. "Though I'm Adam's Fool too! Boo-hoo!"

"Treachery!" The snootiest of the Fools clicked his heels together. "I will not stand for this! We are the Committee's greatest tool in the war against all that stands against Enlightenment. Tell me, Fool, why would you stoop so low as to help this creature? Was it Adam's wish that you protect her? Out of *love*?"

The Fool that had saved her from his brother's beating stared at Iris for a moment. "No," he said. "Lord Temple's plans for the girl are quite different now."

Different? Different how? Groaning, Iris stumbled to her feet, dusting off her black valet jacket and holding her head to keep it from spinning. "What do you mean by that?"

"You'll see," answered the Fool. "All I know is that I've been abandoned once again."

There was something so sad and broken about his voice. The moment he mentioned this mysterious abandonment, the other Fools seemed to fly into a range of different explosive emotions.

"Abandoned? Us? Never! We were never abandoned by Mr. and Mrs. Heidegger! *We* abandoned those lowly working-class buffoons and climbed through the medical ranks with our own two hands! Abandoned?" The Fool scoffed. "Us?"

And on he continued.

"I wish I could rip them apart. I wish I could taste the iron in their blood. Everyone else will pay too, I swear it. . . ."

"A mother who couldn't cook and a father who couldn't work. We were better off without them!"

"No . . . no . . . don't leave me . . . Mummy . . . Daddy . . ."

It was too much. Covering her ears, Iris ran past the Fools and through the winter snow to the statue of the angel.

No, don't cover your ears, she scolded herself. *This is just another example of the sorrow of humans. Face it!*

She did. She ran up to the Sparrow twins and ripped their clasped hands from each other, breaking the spell. Then, without even stopping to think first, she swept them into a strong, warm, desperate hug.

"I'm sorry," she whispered. "Faith. Virtue. I'm so sorry about everything."

The snow fell away. The chill disappeared. The frost crawling up her skin was gone. The Sparrow twins fell into her arms and wept.

As warmth returned to the clear ballroom once more, Iris heard a door open behind her. A Fool, the one who'd saved her, opened the door and walked out.

"Heidegger is close to dead," he said. "Lord Temple is allowing him to die. That means he has no more use for me." He looked at his brethren. "Detach your minds from the will of your masters, and for once, search inside yourselves. Then and only then will you come to realize the truth: our time is limited. This is all meaningless."

The moment he spoke this truth, the other Fools seemed to feel it too. After a period of silence, one Fool shut his eyes for a moment, then stumbled back in shock.

"It is true," he said. Iris couldn't recall which Fool he was. "I can feel my life escaping from me, my energy diminishing, my time growing short!" He began clutching at his throat with shaking hands.

"No! It's cruel!" One Fool grabbed another by his jacket. "Heidegger can't die. We can't die. If we die . . . then why were we born?"

Why were we born? What was our purpose? That was, perhaps, the lament of all men.

Once they quieted down, the reality seemed to pin them where they stood.

"Where are you going?" Iris called to Adam's Fool.

"To die in peace. I suggest you all do too," he told the others. "But, Miss Iris, do not think that this is over. For what Lord Temple has in store for you may be the worst to come."

He left her with that warning. The other Fools lingered for a moment before filing out after him. Their circus had ended.

With a sigh of relief, Iris turned to Faith and Virtue Sparrow. "Do you two wish to stay aboard this ship?"

A beat passed as they looked to each other. Then they nodded.

"Perhaps the New World will treat us better than this one did."

As Hiva, she felt responsible. Her culling of the Naacal had begun when she watched Nyeth, the priest, murder a shelterless man in cold blood. Destroying the world because of the pain and suffering of others. There had to be another way to bring about peace.

"Good luck," she told the twins, who smiled at her as she left the ballroom.

Iris ran through the labyrinthine halls to a narrow metal door. Down a flight of stairs.

The clanking of gears and fizzing of steam through pipes grew louder the deeper she descended. With the heavy rumbling in the metal walls, it sounded as if there were something living down here. The entrance opened into a large engine space, crowded with a bustling, shouting crew. Steam gushed out of the metal cylinders and pipes she saw lined in a row beneath the woven metal walkway she stood upon.

"Out of the way," one dirty-faced man in overalls cried, pushing past her, and there was more where that came from. She stuck out like a sore thumb, but at least members of the crew were too busy with their work to notice or care that a "valet" was traipsing around.

Iris checked the schematics. "Exhaust manifolds, fuel pumps, crankcase . . ." And in the northmost direction was a rotunda. That was where Uma was. She could sense it.

The Ark suddenly rumbled. Many in the crew yelped in surprise but stayed steady on their feet.

"We're about to rise, boys!" said one, to the cheers and hoots of the crew. "Keep up the work! Don't stop until we've launched out of the hatch!"

She was running out of time.

A large, rough hand clasped against her shoulder. "Hey, what are you doing here?" said a man behind her with a Cockney accent. "Aren't you supposed to be upstairs sorting the luggage?"

Iris swiveled around but kept her head low. "Yes, I'm here to deliver a package to Uma Malakar," she said with a deepened voice. She didn't know why, it just seemed appropriate.

"I don't see nothing on you."

"I meant a message, sir."

A hesitant snarl and the sniff of a nose. "Fine—quickly! Don't get in our way."

She didn't. As the Ark shook and lumbered forward, she delved deeper into the engine room, sweat pouring from her face as steam and red waves of heat colored the air. She avoided the men shoveling coal into large furnaces and others swiveling around giant wheels. In the center of the room was a rotating black shaft, round and large. The schematics said they generated power for the propellers. And yet Iris couldn't see how any of this had been able to make the Ark perform any differently than a regular ship.

That is, until she finally slipped through a set of heavy iron doors into the rotunda.

The Naacal had once created physical screens made of pure electrical light. Like windows—except with a touch, one could open doors and operate machinery on them. Their research and leftover technology had certainly come in handy here. Discoveries that shouldn't have been possible manifested right before Iris's very eyes. The three screens screwed into the curved front wall were not made of light; they were metal, with a glass surface that displayed a diagram of the entire Ark from the hull to the deck. Uma stood in front of the central screen. On either side of her, facing the other screens, were Boris Bosch and Madame Bellerose.

The loud slam of the iron door behind Iris drew all eyes to her—including the guards'.

"What in the blazes?" Bosch said, tilting his head as he stared at her like the stowaway livestock she was supposed to be.

Uma's eyes widened. "Iris?"

Damn it, Iris thought. If she hadn't been so preoccupied with Uma's anima, she would have realized the scientist wasn't alone.

The Ark's forward speed was quickly increasing. The spacious rotunda, with its simple white curved ceiling and walls, was not nearly as well furnished as the rest of the ship. There was an elevator to her right side within the wall—something that reminded her of the contraption in Heaven's Shrine that had taken them down to the Coral Temple. But everything here, from a decorative perspective, felt drab and uninspired. It didn't suit Bellerose, who wore mink draped around her elaborate gown. The woman appeared satisfied nonetheless. As she looked at Iris, her red smile sharpened.

"And here I was thinking I had been blessed with too much luck!" Madame Bellerose clapped her hands and, turning, tapped her screen with a finger.

The floor vibrated. A square panel shuddered and slid to the side. Out of the newly formed hatch arose a cylinder. A storm seemed to brew inside the glass. Smoke and cracks of electricity mingled, and it seemed as if thunder would soon follow. And in the middle of it, twisting and turning inside an invisible magnetic field, was the Moon Skeleton.

"We have one power source for the Ark, but why stop with one?" Madame Bellerose said, rubbing her hands together. "Let us prepare to take another."

46

*B*URN HER ALIVE, A NASTY VOICE inside Iris's mind snarled.

No. No more of that. She was going to resolve this another way. She had to prove it to herself that she could.

"Iris . . . ," Uma whispered, her trusty long pipe slipping out of her fingers and onto the floor. "Are you really—?"

"Guards, subdue her!" Bosch commanded, and suddenly guns were cocking, firing at her.

"Wait!" Iris heard Uma cry before bullets began piercing Iris's body. Iris lifted her arms to shield her face, but it wouldn't stop the inevitable.

She collapsed to the floor, blacking out. But her death recovery was faster now. She felt their grubby hands picking her up, heard Bellerose's nasty voice crying, "Rip out her heart!" Her hand stopped the small blade against her chest, which had been ready to pierce her flesh, before the guard could thrust it inside.

With her bloodied hand around the blade, her eyes snapped open, terrifying the men. Using the distraction, she elbowed one in the face and kicked one in the knees. Then a huge lurch of the ship launched them back, knocking Iris and the guards off their feet.

"Wait!" Uma cried again, just as Iris climbed to her knees and lifted her hands threateningly. "She's Hiva, you fools! Do you want to be burned alive?"

"A very good question," Iris said, staring at all of them with a smile. "I'm a lot faster these days. Want to see how quickly I can turn an average-sized man to dust?"

The guards stiffened and backed away. Bosch and Bellerose glowered. But Uma stared at Iris curiously. Her sharp words and cocky little smile weren't too Hiva-like. She'd hoped Uma would understand just from that. The woman was a genius, after all.

Apparently she did. Uma hid a little smile of her own behind her fingers before clearing her throat. "What is it you want, Iris?"

Madame Bellerose bared her teeth. "We're not asking this little beast anything—"

"I said," Uma repeated loudly, drowning Madame out, "what is it you want, Iris? Why are you here?"

Giving the guards menacing looks that made them skitter away from her, Iris found her footing. "I came to get you off this ship."

Not exactly the truth, but it was the easiest explanation with what little time they had. The ship was steadily moving. She could see it on each screen, the diagram of the Ark plodding slowly along giant rails toward the hatch that had opened at the side of the mountain. Inside its cylinder tube in front of her, the Moon Skeleton spun like a compass needle in the center of the rotunda.

"Max, Rin, and the rest activated the Titans against me, but they couldn't deactivate it. They're still on, blowing cities to shreds in the north."

While Uma frowned, Bosch grunted as if he'd sniffed game. "The Titans?" he said. "Those contraptions are active? My men are still looking for the device that will control them!"

"Looks like someone beat you to it." Bellerose folded her arms and slid Bosch an arrogant, knowing grin. Uma stiffened as the two Enlighteners on either side of her sized her up.

"Rin and the others. Where are they now?" Uma asked, staying calm despite the accusations on the tips of her employers' lips.

Iris's heart skipped before she could let herself say it. "Dead. They're all dead."

A shuddering gasp came from Uma's lips. It wasn't like the woman to show her emotional hand, but this time she couldn't help it. Her knees buckled and she lurched over, clasping her chest through her shimmering blue sari.

"I'm sorry," Iris said as the familiar pain began to swell inside of her.

"No, I'm sorry," Uma said, quickly collecting herself. "I should have never allowed this to happen." Wiping her face and straightening her sari, she let out an exhale of breath. "What can I do?"

"You can stop what you started," Iris said. "Get off this ship with me. We need to do something about this disaster together."

This disaster, and the ones to come. Iris thought of Adam and shuddered.

"Uma will not leave this ship unless I command her to," said Bosch in his hunter's uniform, his helmet covering the wrinkles on his forehead. "She is my employee. She goes where I tell her."

"She goes where *we* tell her," Madame Bellerose corrected with a haughty *hmph*. "As members of the Enlightenment Committee, our goal from the very beginning has been the launch of the Ark. Now we're on the eve of its maiden voyage, and you want us to throw out our top engineer? You must be as mad as you are dumb, you wicked beast."

As Iris squeezed her fists, Madame Bellerose turned to her monitor. "Find them," she ordered Uma. "These contraptions she calls Titans."

The bitterness of being ordered around like a dog was clear in Uma's expression, but she obeyed, tapping the screen. A line diagram of the planet appeared. All across North Africa, quickly descending south, were glowing splotches of orange outlined in red.

"These are abnormal energy signatures," Uma said before Iris could even ask the question. "This machine is powered by abnormal energy sources. Using Naacalian technology, we made sure it could track other signs of abnormal energy all across the world—those that don't fit into normal categories discovered and used in our civilization. Abnormal. Extraordinary."

Iris nodded. It was very similar to what the Naacal had been able to do in the past. "So the energy pulsating north and south from the Atakora Mountains—"

"Are the Titans," Uma finished. "One has already reached Spain. The other is heading down Algeria. Oh God." Her gear-shaped nose ring shook along with her head. "How did I let this happen?"

"But Uma, this is wondrous news!" Bosch laughed, clapping his hands. "Another weapon has fallen into my hands. When we've finished our maiden voyage into the New World, we will return and take the Titans back into our control."

"And how many people will be dead by then?" Iris waved her hands at the monitor. "Be serious! Have a conscience, goddamn you!"

"The only thing I need more of is what I already have," Bosch said. "Money."

"Hmph." Madame Bellerose dusted off the collar of her shirt. "So crude."

"I can't believe you!" Iris screamed.

"And who are you to judge us?" said Bellerose, looking her up and down. "*You*, the cataclysm known as Hiva. Think of all who've already died at your hands. Think of how many years we in the Enlightenment Committee prepared for you to do the same to us as well. If it were not for your existence and our knowledge of it, the Ark would never have been commissioned."

And if it were not for her existence, the Titans would not have been created either. Max's friends never would have operated it against her. Millions would still be alive. She knew that. She *knew* that. She and Uma shared something profound. And they were both capable of understanding just how profound their connection to each other—and to others—was. That was why Iris no longer bothered with the oafish Enlighteners. Her indignation toward them had transformed into annoyance and indifference. They were fools, and they would one day die fools.

Uma was different. Iris had so much to say and not enough time to say it all. But it was to Uma that she wanted to say it.

It took every bit of willpower Iris had to stay her trembling hands as the quiet anger she still carried toward herself seared her very skin. "So then what do you want, Uma?" she asked the conflicted scientist, who was staring woefully at the screen, watching the destruction in real time. "Do you want to listen to your powerful 'employers,' or listen to me? Do you want to be like the old me and drown in the blood of countless victims you have on your hands? Or do you want to be like the new me and refuse to let there be any more?"

Iris could see Uma's lips mouthing the words, *New me?* as her eyes widened and glistened just a little. But whatever Uma might have been thinking,

Bosch would not let her speak it. He pulled a gun off his waist belt and shot one of the guards in the head.

"Bosch!" Uma screamed. "What the hell are you doing?"

"Miss Hiva may have grown a conscience, but you doing so will affect my pocketbooks, Malakar," he said, his dark eyes boring holes through her. "The Ark is ready. Operate the Helios and launch the ship. Every second you waste, I will kill another man."

The guards didn't look too happy about that, but when one opened his mouth to protest, he was shot in the head.

As Bosch scrunched his nose, his white mustache twitched. "Those who obey me will not die."

He sure knew how to control his men. Because now guns were pointed at everyone—those desperate to show Bosch they were loyal, and those who saw through his empty threats. It was a stalemate. One wrong move and bullets would be flying. They each knew that.

"How ridiculous," Madame Bellerose muttered. "If there's anyone you should shoot, it's that disgusting beast."

"Uma!" Bosch and Iris screamed at the same time.

The room fell silent, but Uma could hear them. The whimpering of some of the guards not knowing when and how their lives would end. Iris knew from Uma's defeated sigh that Bosch had won. Uma pushed the controls. The ceiling began to shudder. A hatch below the Moon Skeleton opened, and down came the Helios, carried by wires. More perfect, more complete than what Iris had seen that day in the Basement of the Crystal Palace.

It still reminded her of a snow globe, though one as tall as her legs. Blue glass with bronze and iron outer frames. Its dome crown pointed toward the floor. And when Uma pressed the screen again, the keyhole inside the Helios began to spark with white energy. An electric current zapped from the dome of the Helios to the Moon Skeleton, whirring around in its glass cylinder below. The current zipped up and down until a continuous energy was looping between the two devices.

Uma had explained it once before. The Moon Skeleton, made of white crystal from Iris's body, moderated and controlled the energy in the Helios's chamber. Once, ten years ago at the South Kensington fair, they had attempted to operate the Helios without the Moon Skeleton, and it had created a terrible reaction that had produced the Fanciful Freaks. Now, through the stabilizing process, the Helios would open a door to other worlds.

It was exactly as the Naacal had imagined it, what they had attempted to do themselves to escape Hiva's wrath. This was the fulfillment of their dreams.

A massive force of energy erupted from the Helios and the Moon Skeleton, knocking everyone down to the ground once again. The Ark propelled itself forward in one large push, causing everyone to roll helplessly across the rotunda. After a minute, everything stilled.

Iris felt suddenly cold. A familiar haze of dread weighed her body down. Getting to her knees, Uma turned and found Iris.

"It's happening," Uma cried. "To the top of the deck!"

While Bosch and Bellerose were still floundering on the floor, the scientist ran to Iris, grabbed her hand, and made for the elevator. The doors opened on their own as she drew near. Pulling Iris inside the cubicle, Uma pressed a button, and the elevator began rising through the hull of the ship.

"This thing is taking us to the top of the ship?" Iris said, turning around inside the metal box.

"To the very top."

The sound of Uma's voice drew out a swell of anger. "Uma." Iris rounded on her, but seeing the dark circles underneath the woman's teary eyes dispelled her fury immediately.

"I'm sorry, Iris," she said, and she sounded as if she truly meant it, the agony clear in her voice. "But I didn't want to see those men die in front of me. Maybe it's easier for me to handle the consequences of my actions when they're far away."

Iris stared at the floor of the elevator, her jaw tight. "It's more than that, though, isn't it? You want to see it," she whispered. "You want to see what's on the other side of the door."

Knowledge for knowledge's sake. Uma had told her once before. She'd wanted to see the impossible. To create the impossible.

"You're not a god," Iris said. "Neither are the Enlighteners. Neither am I?"

She looked at her own palms. Her fingers that had ripped Max's heart from his chest. "None of us have the right."

Uma nodded. "I know, Iris. That I know."

The elevator doors opened to a little room with a short ladder. They climbed up, and once they were outside, a rush of wind greeted them. Iris and Uma stepped out onto the deck of the Ark, the Atakora Mountains behind them.

The Ark had taken flight.

The deck of the ship was like that of any luxury cruise liner, but the smell of the fresh air, the view of the mountains and valleys below—this was unimaginable. Humankind had created a flying ship. The wind jostled Iris's braids. Uma's sari fluttered in the wind. They had been the first two to witness this wonder, before any of the patrons inside the ship. Before the Enlighteners themselves. Uma and Iris stood alone and soaked in the air as the Ark sliced through it, as cleanly as it would have the waves of the ocean. Tears finally fell from Uma's eyes. It was only then that Iris realized how much this had meant to her.

"Look, Iris." Uma pointed at the darkening mass far beyond them. The swirl within them reminded Iris of Hawkins's blue portal, a vortex of sorts. But it was a cloud, dark and sparking with the same white light that Iris had seen pass between the Helios and the Moon Skeleton.

"Look!" Another voice from behind them. Bosch and Bellerose. They'd caught up. Bellerose gathered up her skirt and traipsed down the deck. "The door is opening!"

Not door.

Doors.

For swirls were taking shape within the clouds everywhere, as far as Iris's eyes could see. Dark and terrifying, as if a thunderstorm was coming. They crackled with energy that traveled around the clouds as they formed black rings in the sky.

"I have done it!" Bellerose said. "The Ark. The Helios. I made it happen. *I*, Violet Bellerose. I am the ultimate Enlightener!"

And on the other side of the deck, Bosch was clasping his hands. "The amount of money I'll make from this venture alone . . . Uma! We must pass through the door quickly!"

But Uma didn't answer him. She'd seen something no one else had. And it was because of this that she suddenly grabbed Iris's hand and began running back to the elevator. Confused, Iris looked behind her shoulder.

And saw them.

Ships coming through the dark cloud rings, passing through each door into their skies. Frightening creatures of nightmare, made of pure gold, formed their mastheads. Each vessel was at least three times the size of the Ark. Maybe more.

Warships. Warships from the other side.

An invasion.

Bosch's and Bellerose's laughter was cut short. Uma and Iris jumped into the hatch just as an energy blast from one of the ships tore up the deck, swallowing the two Enlighteners whole.

47

ERTA MORALES AND LULU JONES SAT on a couch together in the Lagos apartment, now empty. The scientist's assistant still had not returned. If the home was haunted by ghosts, then they could hear them even outside, howling in the sky. Crying out with the wind for release.

"Hey, Lulu," Berta whispered, rubbing her hands, because she had not been able to feel them since the moment she'd been told her brother was dead. "Have you ever thought of ending your own life? You know, because it's too hard?"

What an awful question to ask a child, Berta thought—but then again, since when had the laws of civility ever applied to either of them? This was not a civil world, not when the very terms of the world had been created to exclude their happiness.

"Yeah," Lulu admitted. She seemed to approach everything to do with death with the same detached attitude. Maybe it was easier that way. Maybe it was a way to kill part of yourself. The part that wouldn't stop screaming otherwise.

Berta nodded. "But you didn't. How come?"

"I don't know. I guess I like you too much!"

Lulu's smile was the sunshine and the rain that watered the flowers and made them grow. Berta wished they could all be together. Max and Lulu, and Berta's mother too. And the Joneses. All of them together. One happy family.

Maybe it wouldn't happen in this life. Maybe it would happen in another.

Berta pulled her knees up on the couch and hugged Lulu. She hugged her so tightly, she feared she might break the little girl in half.

"Hey, you know what you said earlier on the train? When you, me, and Rin were talking?"

"Miss Rin . . ." Lulu said her name so sadly, it made Berta sigh. Rin, too. Rin had to come along too. One happy family.

"When we were talking about the kind of world we wanted to see," Berta said. "The kind of world we'd want to live in."

"Hmm . . ." Lulu thought for a moment before shaking her head. "I don't really remember."

"I do." When Berta closed her eyes, she could feel the scratchy hat upon her head, smell the train as it sped across the plains to Winnipeg.

A world where nobody hurt each other, Lulu had said in the pretty dress Berta had stolen for her. *A world where you could be who you wanted, or a world where you could eat as much as you like, or a world where who had money and who didn't have money didn't matter. But in the end, it all came down to that: a world where nobody hurt each other.*

"It still sounds like a nice place," Berta whispered, and hugged Lulu tightly. "Max deserved to see it. . . . So did Rin."

Outside, the skies rumbled. Berta and Lulu separated and stared at the door.

"What's that?" Lulu said, turning to Berta.

Without wasting another second, the older girl leaped off the couch and ran out the door. And what she saw above her in the skies, she could not fathom. There were no words to describe the black rings that were forming across the blue but ever-darkening skies, as far as her eye could see. The terrible flying ships appearing out of the rings like spirits carried across the wind. Ships so large, they blotted out the sun. Ships so large, they swallowed the heavens.

Hiva had promised months ago that this would be humanity's final year.

He had been right.

Berta dropped to her knees. She couldn't tear her eyes away from the skies, even as fear mummified her living body. This was it. She smiled. She'd thought that she would see her brother again one day. She'd hoped. *I didn't have to wait too long, after all.*

Behind her, she felt Lulu's hand on her shoulder and heard her singing: a song of rebellion, of rapture, transformed by the innocent chanting of a child.

"'Mine eyes have seen the glory,'" Lulu sang, "'of the coming of the Lord . . .'"

Beams of pure light shot down from the ships to the earth, incinerating all in its path.

The Ark shuddered and whined, hit by another blast from the enemy ships. The elevator rocked, throwing Iris against the wall, but it didn't break. It continued its descent into the lowest parts of the hull.

"The Ark is made of strong stuff," Uma said, even though she flinched from the blast. "It'll hold. I'm just not sure for how long."

Another hit, and the elevator rumbled. Iris could barely gulp in air with each frenzied gasp.

But Uma was laughing. "Ironic!" the woman said, pinning herself against the wall, her arms spread out against the metal. "The Enlightenment Committee believed that they would be invading the New World. Never did any of us think that they would end up invading us!" Uma's laughter sounded crazed—with excitement, with fear. With the knowledge that death was on the horizon. "What a discovery. What a dramatic twist."

"You think this is funny?" Iris yelled, unable to believe her ears.

"A little. It is a little funny." Uma's frightened, nervous giggles seemed to possess her body. "I can't help it."

Iris rushed to the opposite side of the lift and grabbed Uma's sari, pushing her fists against Uma's neck. "Nothing about this is funny, Malakar," Iris hissed. "None of it."

She could feel them disappearing. Bosch and Bellerose had been killed with the first blast, but all over the world, more were dying. Hundreds and thousands at a time, gone in a matter of moments. The Helios was more powerful than any of them could ever imagine, ripping tears through space and time over the entire planet. Too powerful to control. The technology had gotten the better of them. And whoever was on the other side had been waiting. How, Iris didn't know. But she could feel their alien anima throughout the earth. The invasion was global.

So many gone. Even as the elevator descended, so many were evaporating into thin air. The Titans meant nothing anymore. Jacques, the assassin who'd warned her of the end. He'd just died with his family close to the coast of England. Berta and Lulu in Lagos. They were gone. Gone! And—Iris sucked in a breath.

Granny . . . Oh no. Granny!

She fell to her knees, her eyes staring at her hands in unblinking terror, tears dripping down her cheeks in streams. "Everyone is gone. Everyone is dying!"

"But you can't die." Uma lifted her up. "You can't die, Iris. That's your gift. That's your curse. And maybe it'll be our salvation."

The elevator doors opened to the very lowest part of the hull. It was a room Iris had never seen before. Two round silver pods filled the little square white room. They were like eggs, Iris thought, and had she the ability to do so, she would have laughed at the sight of them. Little eggs with shining blue windows. Each egg had only one seat inside.

"Escape pods," Uma said, and as the Ark rattled again, she went to the fuse box next to the elevator door and began pulling levers. The blue window opened. "Get inside!"

"What are you talking about? What can I possibly do?"

"Something," Uma said. She wasn't laughing anymore. Creases appeared across her beautiful brown skin, aging her so suddenly that Iris almost didn't recognize her in that moment. "You're the only one of us who can't die. So do something. Do something for us fools."

Iris was so overwhelmed, she couldn't speak or move. But another blast shook the Ark so deeply, she knew in her heart the ship wouldn't last.

"Go!" Uma ran over to her and shoved her toward the pod.

Iris's mind had gone blank. She stepped inside the pod and sat in the cool leather seat that hugged her body, her neck nestled into the groove. Uma strapped her in and closed the blue door, but somehow Iris could still hear her.

"Bellerose had ordered only two escape pods to be made," Uma said. "For herself and whatever friend she deemed worthy. Now she's nothing more than atoms in the air. Another irony." Uma ran back to the control panel.

Everything was happening too fast. Lives were disappearing in the blink of an eye. With each breath, more died. Death washed over her. "I don't understand what I'm supposed to do!" Iris said, turning around. Through the blue window, she could see Uma behind her, pulling levers.

"You are the cataclysm. You're supposed to destroy humanity so that something new can arise. Do you know what that means, Iris?" Uma punched several buttons. "You were born not just to destroy but to create. In my hubris, I thought that creation was only possible in the hands of someone like me. But I couldn't even properly stand up to those who sought to use my power for their own evil purposes. I couldn't even stand up to my own curiosity. I'm no god, and I was never meant to be."

Uma put her hand on the lever and looked at Iris. "But from the moment I saw you in that train station, I knew you were something special." The scientist's eyes glimmered with sentimentality as Iris remembered that moment in the filthy corner of the station when their eyes had locked for the first time. A seemingly inseparable chasm between them. A strange, wordless bond that connected them. "I'm glad to have met you. Through you, I learned more about this world and myself than I ever could otherwise." And she smiled. "Thank you, Iris."

Uma pulled the lever. A hatch beneath Iris's pod opened. She could feel herself being sucked into the air.

"Uma!"

"Thank you, and live on!"

Uma's cry was the last she heard before the pod dropped from the bottom of the Ark and into the air. Gravity pulled her body against the straps as the pod ripped through the sky. Iris lost her breath as she stared, mouth agape, through the window.

Enemy warships several times bigger than the Ark littered the darkened heavens. Iris held on to Uma's anima like a lifeline, desperately, until one of the warships shot one last blast of energy against the Ark, swallowing it completely, blowing it out of the skies.

"Uma!" Iris's screams ripped through her throat as the scientist's life force disappeared alongside all others on the ill-fated Ark.

And thus it was so. It was not Hiva who destroyed humanity, wiping it from the face of the earth, nor was it a fleet of enemy ships, waiting from across the interdimensional rift to strike. It was a combination of humankind's folly. It was choice after choice that they each made for themselves and for others that had led them down the path of destruction. As Iris's pod fell, she thought of how Granny must have felt when the explosion came.

Was it painful, Granny? Iris's tears fell as pillars of light beamed down from the dark skies. *I hope it didn't hurt too much.*

This was it. This was her limit.

As the last human being on earth perished, she cried out like she never had before. From the depths of her soul, from the depths of her very being, came one name. A name more ancient than any, one she only remembered as she was thrust past the brink of despair. Something had to change. Something new had to spring from this sorrow. Something lasting.

And so Iris cried. She howled for the One who'd created her.

"Necron!"

Somewhere in the deep of the planet's core, a power as old as the earth itself smiled.

And somewhere else, deep within the ocean, another being emerged. A being composed of three intertwined anima. A new being that incinerated the man called Barry Bately the moment it emerged from Hiva's Tomb.

48

I AM THE EARTH, AND THE EARTH is me.

I do not know when I came into existence.

When I was born, so too was the earth.

And I was given the power over life and death.

Three gifts guide the shape and structure of reality: The ability to act. The will to act.

And the greatest of all: imagination.

It is justice that must guide the fate of humanity.

But what is justice? One must choose what is right and what is wrong. And in my heart, I could not.

So I gave my heart to you.

And so you were born of it. You are Hiva. You are justice.

Iris couldn't see. But she could feel her body, weightless in the dark. "Anne, is that you?"

That is not my name.

Iris's fingers and toes twitched. Even in this endless space, her body ached. "Where are you?"

A beat of silence passed.

Find me.

And the darkness leeched away, revealing a wondrous field of crystal as far as her eye could see. Pinks, purples, and blues. Golden butterflies perched upon bulbous red flowers. Every color was a little off, a little too sharp to exist on earth.

But they were not on the earth. They were inside.

They were in the earth's core. A space that existed outside reality.

Necron's core.

Yes, Iris now remembered the name of the One who created her. She was not "Anne."

She was Necron.

Here in the earth's core, Iris was weightless, her body in the slip Necron had made from her out of the sky itself. She drifted in the still, sunset-colored air above a wonderland of crystal trees. She'd been here before. It had been her home whenever her missions had been completed. Whenever humanity had ended. Whenever her body returned to the ground, her soul would come here.

Tulips bigger than beasts of prey. Frosted blue vines twisting around silver trees like serpents. And a sky where she could see endless earths spanning across dimensions.

The other Hiva had come from one of those earths. So too had the invaders.

On one earth, humans have become enslaved by the machines they've built, Necron had told her while weaving her body anew. *On another earth, four warriors battle in an endless cycle against creatures of nightmare that move like phantoms across the lands. On one earth, the diseases of bigotry, capitalist greed, and political strife have brought the planet and its billions of inhabitants to the brink of collapse.*

And on another earth, they plot our destruction. Or rather, the destruction of humans. They heard the distortions of space and time echoing from our earth. And so they waited to strike and conquer. All they needed was for someone to open a door.

The Helios. The distortions of space and time had been produced by the Enlightenment Committee, fiddling with advanced technology they did not understand. What a great irony indeed. On this earth, the Enlighteners had planned their invasion, not knowing that they were another's prey. Not knowing that their hubris would be their own downfall. Of course there were other earths with megalomaniacal conquerors, just as surely as there were other earths with Hivas. Would they still have been able to invade if humanity hadn't been so obsessed with tearing holes in dimensions? If they hadn't let their obsession with progress destroy them?

The worst deaths are brought about by one's own hands.

Twisting out of the ground, the green stems as tall as Iris itself, was a flower she'd seen on earth. There it was called the calla lily. Its pure white spiraling petal folded itself into a single, elegant tube.

Here, there were fields of them. Each lily was a soul. Iris maneuvered around them, her feet so light, she barely felt their crystal edges. This place was a gathering of souls. She brought out her hand and let a blood-red butterfly land upon her finger. Every tension in her body fell away. The knots in her stomach unraveled. This was her home.

And yet she felt sorrow. The souls here, she could sense the anima of each. All of humanity had gathered here.

Where are you? she called out to her friends and family, her words echoing in the permanent sunset sky.

She knew how to find them.

Her feet did not hurt as she crossed the endless fields. Her legs did not grow tired. She followed their anima. One by one, she followed them.

When people die, their bodies return to the earth in some fashion or another. But their souls don't disappear. They travel to the planet's core, where they wait for rebirth.

Iris's own words, during those wondrous and torturous days she had believed she was speaking to someone else.

"Jinn." She let another butterfly rest upon her finger. "I want to see you again." A tear dripped down her cheek.

Here in the earth's core, in Necron's core, souls were never lonely. They lived out their happiest fantasies until they were called back to the earth's surface to live anew.

In that case, she would find them. Before she found Necron, she would find each of them. She came across the first soul. The calla lily trembled and swayed, though there was no wind. She touched it and let her mind wander deep into its dream.

"Brother!" A young woman burst out of the double doors of a grand cathedral, ran down the steps, and crashed through the black iron fence. "Okay, we did the prayer thing. So? Where should we go now?"

She was speaking Spanish, her brown curls flying about her face as she twisted around. Berta. The breeze here in the City of Oranges was fresh against her warm-toned skin.

"I'm not going anywhere until my prayer gets answered." Max sat down upon the steps of the cathedral with an obstinate huff, crossing his arms. "How many times have I prayed and prayed, huh? Mom says if you want something, you pray. Well, I prayed, and now I want what's due." He slapped the back of his hand against his other palm and lay down against the cathedral steps. The other worshippers filing out of the church stepped around him, muttering to one another with irritation.

"Brother, come on, get up!" Berta's cheeks turned a shade of red as she gripped the fence. "You're embarrassing me."

"Nope!" Max said loudly, and began his obnoxious whistling, crossing one leg over the other. "Not until I get what I prayed for. That's how it works, isn't it?"

"Ugh!" Berta groaned, stomping her feet and laying her head against the fence, apologizing quietly as the other churchgoers passed by her. "Okay, so what do you want?"

At this, Max sat up in one straight shot, a goofy grin on his face. "A girlfriend," he said immediately.

Berta made a face. "What?"

"A really, really gorgeous one—you know, luscious dark skin, shiny brown eyes, and—" He waved his hands as if tracing the curves of his ideal body.

"Gross."

"What's gross about it?" Max shrugged. "What's gross about wanting someone to, you know—"

"Cook for you and clean for you and—"

"No, no, trust me, I would do the cooking and the cleaning." Max wagged his finger at her. "Just like I do at home. It's what a man does. Right, Mom?"

The woman who stood on the steps above her son was shorter than all of them but must have seemed tall to Max, as he lay back and looked up into her face. He gave her a mischievous grin.

"Silly boy," she said, and pulled him up from the steps. Max followed his mother dutifully. "You do cook and you do clean, but only because I taught you. I hope you don't forget that when you get your pretty wife."

Max blinked. "Are you jealous? You're not jealous, are you, *mami*?" And he swept her up in a hug from behind, drawing a sweet little gasp from her. "Believe me, no one could ever replace you. Or you, sis."

Berta blushed and turned away. "Ew, as if I care!"

But she did care. This was Berta's dream. To be reunited with her family.

"Hey, you know what?" she said as her brother and mother passed the gate and traveled into the city core. "There are these girls I met in town. They're visiting from other countries, and I kind of think they're great." She was blushing again, because making new friends didn't come so easily to the aloof girl.

"Yeah?" said Max, his eyebrow arched with interest.

"Yeah. You guys should meet them. Their names are Lulu and Rin. . . ."

Smiling sadly, Iris left Berta's soul alone. As Iris continued down the crystal forest, she thought about how Berta would be in this dream for eternity until it was time to be reborn again. It was a kind of mercy given to her by Necron. But something about this mercy felt hollow.

Yards away, she found another soul. The flower bent from side to side. She touched it.

A large haunted house at the center of a mountaintop, isolated from the bustling city nearby. This was not just any house. Inside this gothic manor, a troop of expert hunters had been hired by the Bannerworths to hunt the bane of their lives: Sir Francis Varney. There was but one problem. Varney was not a normal lord. Rightfully so, this troop of hunters were not regular hunters.

They were vampire hunters.

"All right, then. Come on, lads, this vampire's somewhere in this haunted house." In the rotunda, under a grand chandelier, Max placed a wooden crossbow over his shoulder with a cavalier swagger and turned to his group. "Well then, who's got the garlic? Come on, now, we don't have all day."

"I didn't bring it." In her brown buckled trousers, Cherice checked the holes in her belt and shrugged. "Nope. Don't got it. What about you, boys?"

Jacob immediately threw a sack of tools on the Persian rug. "Holy water, stakes, some more penny bloods—hold on, why are these here?"

"Oh, some of those are mine." Max pointed, squeezing his jaw sheepishly. "Must have gotten mixed up in there."

"Some of those are definitely mine too." Chadwick Winterbottom, with his bright ginger hair, slapped his hand against his forehead and leaned over Jacob's shoulder. "Actually, I think I drew some of those."

The door to the manor closed behind them with a creak and a slam. "Varney's lot aren't outside, which means they've definitely escaped into the manor—do you have the garlic?" Hawkins asked.

"We're trying to find it!" Chadwick and Jacob said at the same time, and stared at each other awkwardly.

"I bet Jacob forgot it," Cherice grumbled.

Jacob blushed and pouted. "I did not!"

"You always forget things! How are we supposed to make any good money if you keep forgetting the damn garlic?"

"Hold on, I drew this one too." Chadwick was searching through the penny bloods in the sack of weapons while Hawkins yelled at them all to quiet down.

Max sighed and rubbed the back of his head. But he smiled. This was his crew. He was still deciding on the name. The Phantom Troop, perhaps. The Vampire Hunters. Something cool like that. He didn't want to steal "The Fanciful Freaks" from Chadwick, but he may just have to. Hmm . . . He'd ask Berta and Lily when they got back home. They were always good with that sort of thing.

"All right, Varney, you vampire." Max stroked his crossbow lovingly. "You're not getting the best of us." And he turned to the others. "I'll be off! You guys make sure to find the garlic."

"Just remember, Maxey, there's a pure-hearted maiden trapped in the dungeon," Cherice called out. "Gotta save her first. Those are the rules."

"Of course, of course. Damsels in distress, you think I don't read?" Max ran off through the mansion and down the twisting stairs into the basement.

He took a flaming torch from the wall and let it light his way through the basement until he came to the cellar.

A shadow moved.

"Varney!"

Max could see the vampire from the light that slipped through the little window bars. The monster was skin and bones, his face barely that of a man. A long red bedsheet was draped over his body, and in his arms—

Max gasped. In his arms was the most beautiful woman he'd ever seen. A woman with luscious dark skin and glittering brown eyes, in a fluttering white nightdress. Her braids fell over the arms of the vampire who held her.

"You will never take her from me," Varney the Vampire promised as he moved to begin his feast of blood.

Stirred by the maiden's beauty, Max aimed: one swift blow to the chest. But it missed his heart. Varney twisted in agony. Shrieking, he ripped the bars off the window and slipped through, fleeing into the night.

The battle against Varney would continue. But for now he'd saved an innocent soul. For Max, that was enough.

He scooped the maiden up in his arms, his heart pounding at the sight of her. "You're all right now," he whispered when she struggled a bit in his embrace, a little frightened. He waited for that fear to subside. "My name is Max. Maximo

Morales. I'm the leader of the—" He bit his lip. "Fanciful . . . Phantom Troop." He'd really have to work on the name. "What's your name?"

The girl's smile made his heart skip a beat. "My name is Iris. . . ."

Iris smiled as she left Max's fantasy. Of course a boy who'd spent so much of his childhood indulging in the stories of penny dreadfuls would want to live in one. A silly boy indeed. Iris wiped the wet corners of her eyes and continued down the field.

She met many others like him. Jacob. His dream was a peaceful one, visiting his Inuit family in Labrador. Speaking his native language as he ate and laughed with them. He'd traveled the world and come back to live. But he promised them that he'd let them meet someone special. Someone he'd met. Someone he loved.

In Hawkins's fantasy, he lay on a bed of incense and flower petals— the most expensive room in all of Paris. There he, Jacob, and Chadwick Winterbottom fulfilled their love and carnal passions without restraint, drinking the most expensive champagne the hotel had to offer them.

She saw Henry's too—such a simple dream. He was an adult, running Whittle's toy shop with his grandfather and his forever-fretting wife, Mary. Between the talent of the Whittle men and Mary's business sense, the three of them brought joy to children around the world. And it touched Iris more than she could say when she reached Mary's soul and realized that the two shared the exact same dream.

Lucille would not be bound by the laws of marriage. In her dream she sailed the high seas, standing upon the mast with one woman on each arm, adventuring through the earth, doing as she pleased, singing her operas and fleeing the police while she gathered up the world's wealth.

And Uma. Uma's schools across the earth made geniuses out of women like them, women from the countries men pillaged. Geniuses who moved the evolution of man forward with their intellect and scientific prowess. There was no need for world governments. Politicians around the world had given up their

power to these women of science, for it was they who deserved the power to create policy and infrastructure, to build cities and systems of health and wealth.
The entire British Parliament bowed at her feet, as well as the Queen of England
and her countless children.

Fantasies were so strange, Iris thought as she passed through souls—some
whom she cherished, some she didn't. The deepest desires of humans were
sometimes not so pure. Many desired wealth and power but didn't have the
means to gain it. Others would give anything to destroy the lives of those they
deemed inferior but had no power to achieve it. Everyone wanted happiness,
but what was happiness for some was hell for others. And when they eventually were reborn onto the earth, they would certainly seek to attain it if they
could—some regardless of the cost.

Perhaps that was why Hiva had been created. To sort out these dreams. To
determine what was just and what wasn't.

In her mind, the delineation of right and wrong was already forming.
Indeed, some dreams shouldn't come true. For some, their dreams coming true
meant the pain and murder of others. *Who am I to decide?* Iris thought for a
moment, letting her hands slide along the prickly crystal vines, until another
thought, bold and daring, replaced it.

Why shouldn't *I be the one to decide?*

What kind of world would she want if she could make it? Iris stroked
her chin. She came to two nearby flowers that she thought would tell her the
answer. She sucked in a breath.

Neither were complex dreams. The first was quite simple, really. They
all sat on a tree log eating mangoes. Iris, Granny, and Rin. Rin's parents. Lulu
and Berta. Lulu's brother and parents. In Abeokuta, they sat and talked and
laughed like the family that they were. Iris saw herself laughing, shoving a
piece of melon in Rin's mouth. Rin's two eyes, bright and beautiful, blinked
rapidly as she giggled, pushing the fruit into her mouth and adjusting her wrap.

"There's one story I'd love to tell you," said Granny. "About the time I saw
a witch in the well."

"Not a witch!" Rin covered her mouth before feeling embarrassed at her
outburst of fear.

While Iris gave her a teasing slap on the back, Granny clucked her tongue. "Listen carefully, ọmọ—there are some things you should know before you go out to the well at night. . . ."

That was Rin's dream. Granny's dream was so incredibly similar, it made Iris's heart smile. But this time they were youths. Adelola, the younger sister, and Adebisi, the older sister. They played together in the town streets with Iris carrying a bucket of water upon her head and Rin chopping wood with a machete, while Egg squawked near a gaggle of chickens. The air of tranquility here was unmatched.

Lulu's dream was even simpler. Inside the girl's fantasy, everyone held hands. Everyone. No one was left out. No one was deemed superior to anyone else. It didn't matter who they were or how they were born. Across the beautiful earth, people held hands and were good to each other. Iris liked that dream.

What if some people had the power to create the world they wanted? It was already the case with humankind. The powerful dreamed up a world and brought it to fruition through the tools they had in their possession. But what about worlds like this?

The last flower came close to the end of the field. Iris did not want to touch it. And yet the longing was too strong. She wanted to see him. The real him. And the world he wished for . . .

She touched his flower.

And suddenly she was on a stage. The hall was spacious and luxuriously designed with red curtains stretched around the golden-plated walls. The seats of the audience were empty. The spotlight above was on one man standing upon the tightrope. In the first circus tights Granny had ever made for him, he reached out his hand to her.

"Iris!" he called.

Iris didn't waste any time. She climbed up the ladder to her platform. It was only when her feet touched the surface that she realized her clothes had changed into a light, moss-green dress that brushed her thighs. The first outfit that Granny had ever made her.

With the brightest laugh, she flipped onto the tightrope and let him catch her. The bedazzling young man with brown skin and fierce catlike eyes clutched the rope with his toes, expert precision keeping him in place even as he held her up in the sky. There were feathers in her braids, green to match her dress. Yes, just like back then. Their first performance together.

They wheeled their bodies sideways. He gripped her hands and tossed her up in the air. She flipped, breathing in the freedom of the breeze rushing past her skin. And when he caught her, he twirled her around. It was as if they were dancing across a ballroom.

Forever. She could dance with him forever like this.

Jinn drew her into him, squeezing her tightly, her back against his chest. "Iris," he whispered. "What do you think of me?"

He'd asked her once before. This time she answered without hesitation.

"I love you," she said, touching his face.

"You do?" His voice sounded so youthful and bright, so hopeful and joyful. She'd always thought of Jinn as a cantankerous geezer in a young man's body, but now he really was just like a boy, brimming with love and excitement. He tossed her up in the air, flipping her, catching her with his strong arms before letting her back down onto the rope.

"But I don't know your name," Iris said.

"Didn't I tell you? It's Emin. Emin Ibrahim."

"Emin . . ." With a finger, Iris wiped a tear from her eyes. "Should I still call you Jinn?"

"You can call me whatever you want," Jinn said. "As long as you stay with me."

They kissed. His warm lips felt like home.

Love. Family. Peace. Warmth. Goodness. Health. Togetherness. Equality. Friendship.

Iris didn't care what anyone said. This is how the world should be. This was it.

It was with that conviction that she left the dream of Jinn's soul as she came to the end of the field.

There, "Anne" was waiting for her.

No, not Anne—Necron. As Iris approached, Necron waited for her in Anne's form, a little Black girl who held out a coin in front of her. There, in Necron's core, under the sky of eternal sunset, the two stood in the middle of the flower field of souls and faced each other. A cosmos of memories. After eons of cataclysms, the two faced each other again.

It is time once again, the god said. A familiar phrase.

She already knew the coin without seeing it. She'd seen it so many lifetimes before. On one side of the coin was night, and on the other, day. Life and death. She would make the choice. She would be the one to judge the fate of humankind, because the One who'd created her had been too cowardly to do so herself.

"You took out your own heart and made me from it," Iris said. "I was born from your inability to choose. And yet you ask me to choose. I won't."

Iris slapped Necron's hand. The coin flew from her palm and landed in a patch of twisted green crystal vines.

I have watched humanity die again and again, Necron said. *The power to create a better world resides in me. But what world do I create? What world could I mold that would bring humanity to eternal peace? What is the perfect world? You've walked among them for eons. Should you not know the answer by now, my child?*

Iris felt her blood pumping in her head as she clenched her teeth. Her mind spun with everything but an answer. But she bluffed anyway. "Show me your true face. Then I'll tell you."

Very well.

The body of Anne Marlow, the little girl who had died pointlessly in Gorton Zoo, disappeared into white mist.

And out of the mist grew a figure of white crystal. It gathered and formed many legs, as tall as the skies. A long head bigger than the sun, sharp like the point of a shard of glass. Its hollow blank eyes were an endless void from which life and death danced in endless harmony.

The creature towered above her. A god of white crystal as old as the planet itself.

This was Necron.

What will you do? Necron asked, and as she brought her head close to the ground, the crystal flower field trembled. The shades of pinks and blues, yellows and oranges. The bloodred butterflies that fluttered past Necron's eyes. All in the earth's core, Necron's core, seemed to spring to life at the appearance of her true form.

And suddenly the answer came to Iris, as clear as if it had been there all along.

"I want your job."

Necron twisted her head to the side but waited patiently for Iris's elaboration.

"You said it yourself. You created reality with three gifts: The ability to act. The will to act. And imagination. Well, I hate to say it, but your imagination is truly horrid. Maybe that's why things keep going bad. You never trusted yourself to make real decisions concerning this earth. Of course you wouldn't trust yourself to imagine something *better.*"

Iris closed her eyes and remembered the Atlanteans and the Naacal. The Europeans. The slaves and the destitute. Those pushed to the dregs of society and transformed into the wastes of modernity. It was always the same. In every lifetime, it was always the same.

"I want a different world."

One without pain? But pain is a fact of human life. So is greed. So is oppression.

"Not in my world. And I'm not the only one who thinks so." Iris gritted her teeth and remembered the lovely warmth of Lulu's dream.

Perhaps it isn't possible.

"Stop saying that! It is if we imagine it!" Iris yelled, remembering the goodness in their hearts: Rin, Jinn, Berta, Lulu, Max, Granny, and the others. The love that had moved them in the worst of circumstances.

And you trust yourself to decide this?

"Other people have gotten to decide how the world should be. Now it's my turn." Iris stretched out her hand. "Give me your gifts. Power over life and death. The ability to act. The will to act. I've already decided what my justice is, and with my imagination, I will create a better world—one that never has to be destroyed."

Such an audacious thing to say.

"Yeah." Iris gave her a crooked smile. "It's daring for girls like me to dream, isn't it?"

Necron stretched out her body, becoming so big that she would have put the Titans to shame. After a time, under the eternal sunset, Necron said this:

I will grant you this power. But with this power comes untold responsibility. And there is another who desires this dream. I cannot choose between the two of you. So you will decide among yourselves which of your visions for the world will come to fruition.

"Another?" Iris furrowed her brows. What kind of nonsense was this? She searched Necron's eyes but could find nothing there but the vast eternity of the cosmos.

His footsteps were so quiet. Iris did not hear him approach her. Did not sense his anima until his hand was on her shoulder.

She turned around, and her blood chilled.

Adam Temple's body had become pure bronze. His black hair had grown down to his waist, but there were no flowers there—no. For although Hiva's crystal heart beat inside his chest, this was not Hiva. It was not Adam either. Not truly. The atoms had been mixed together in some sort of terrible experiment, gone horribly wrong.

Or perfectly right.

It was Adam's form, his young and handsome face, his voice that said her name. "Iris." A whisper, with the same obsessive lilt. It was Adam's cruelty and disregard for human life, only this time given Hiva's immortal power.

But inside his blood pumped an emotion that was quite heinous. A hatred Iris knew. One that wanted to tear her skin from her flesh. It belonged to that man. Doctor Seymour Pratt. His hatred took physical form—a single black angel wing that sprang from behind his left shoulder blade. Still, Iris knew the old man himself lay somewhere in Adam's consciousness, spurring him to kill her.

"Adam . . . ," Iris whispered, truly horrified to the greatest depths of her. "What have you done?"

Adam squeezed her shoulder. "Iris. Come see the world I envisioned."

Inside the earth's core, Adam Temple pulled Iris into his dream.

49

THERE WAS NOTHING IN THE BARREN land. It was an earth that had rotted.

The dark skies crackled with lightning. The fractured land crumbled a little as Iris walked upon it, her bare feet picking up bits of dirt. There was no way any flowers could grow from this place. No animal could feed. No human could live.

A dead planet.

But the worst sight was to come. For before Iris's very eyes was a tower so tall it reached into the heavens. A tower made of human corpses and piles of trash. Some men folded inside the tower were still alive. They wailed in eternal agony. She heard John Temple's groans among them. Upon the great tower was a statue made of gray stone. A mother and her cherubic children gripped one another in a desperate hug. A god greater than they embraced them in his arm. A god with Adam Temple's face, his naked back bearing the black wing that symbolized his hatred.

Iris heard an object clatter to the ground. She turned and found Adam in his god form and the bone lance made from Hiva's body on the cracked ground, grazing her feet. In his own hand was the bone sword, made of her skeleton that had hung in the museum.

"Pick it up," Adam ordered. The wicked grin on his bronzed face was gleeful, confident.

"What is that?" Iris asked, gesturing to that horrific pillar with a jerk of her head.

"I call it the Tower of Babel," Adam answered, all to happy to tell her. "Once upon a time, humans built a tower to the skies." He pointed up toward the thunderous cloudy night. "They aimed to show their superiority to God, and he felled them for their arrogance. Such a task was too much for them. But it is not too much for me. Nothing is beyond me."

"I thought you wanted me to destroy the world so you could make something new," Iris whispered, shivering as she heard the wailing. "Something beautiful."

"This is beautiful," Adam answered. "Humanity is weak, and any world of theirs will always be wretched. Only my mother and siblings were perfect. Angels."

This was more than Adam's monument to death. It was a symbol of his endless misery, his selfish grief, and his cowardice. Iris wondered if he realized this.

"So this is what you decided," Iris said, taking in the sight of his twisted form with disgust. "Since the day we met, *this* is what you really wanted, deep down."

"The earth is already destroyed." Adam waved his hands across the land. "The true fate of our earth is not so different from what you see here in my dream. Humanity's been wiped out. By the time Necron brought me to the earth's core, the deed was done."

"So shouldn't you be happy?" Iris stomped on the bone lance, rolling it around underneath the sole of her foot. "You have what you always wanted. For wicked humanity to be punished and all that. What's the point of all this?"

When Adam threw his head back and laughed, the feathers of his black wing twitched. "You really don't get it, love. This is about you. It's always been about you, Iris."

Calm down, Iris told herself as a fit of irritation threatened to crack her.

Adam wasn't just some rich brat anymore. He had somehow taken Hiva's power. He was a Hiva himself. She had to tread carefully.

"I realized it too late. I loved you. Your power. But with that love came envy. You have no idea how frustrated I've been with you, dear Iris. A goddess with the power of life and death at her fingertips. You could do what I've always wanted. You could punish your enemies. Destroy and build as you saw fit."

Iris could only imagine the allure of that power to a little boy who couldn't even keep his family together.

"You never had what it took to decide the fate of men again and again. You don't have what it takes to decide humanity's future. The ideal world where the innocent wouldn't have to lose their lives to rampant, irrational evil."

"The innocent. And in your mind, only those three count?" Iris jerked her head toward the figures of his mother and siblings upon the tower, the only ones who'd passed his judgment.

"You died and came back less than a god. And if you were less than a god, that made me less than a man. You made me remember my own impotence, Iris. And I can't forgive that."

Adam stuck the bone sword into the dead earth. "Necron's incompetence and your weakness are my blessing. I will be the one to create the world based on how I perceive it should be—a world where only the ones I love are happy and everyone else rots."

Iris rolled her eyes. "Well, that isn't selfish at all. But what else can I expect from an arrogant, wealthy, nihilistic white man born into a death cult?"

"That is what Necron has decided," Adam said. "She brought us here. Gave us these weapons. She will have the final say in who will be given her power over life and death."

A flash of lightning. Necron's spiderlike crystal form appeared in the distance. She was watching. Waiting to see who would emerge the victor.

For so long Iris had wondered and worried about why her judgment against humanity had always been the same. What was the purpose of humanity? Why did such brokenness seem to follow them wherever they go? Were suffering and anguish endemic to them? Or was there another way? Hiva had asked her this before, and she'd cut him down. That Hiva inside Adam would never be able to break through the combined hatred of Adam Temple and Doctor Seymour Pratt. But Iris wouldn't let his efforts be in vain. She now had the chance so many people had wished for. A chance to create a better world.

Her vision for the earth. Her vision for humanity.

Her vision for the future.

Or Adam's.

That was the choice before her. And so, with the Tower of Babel wailing in eternal torment in the corner of her eye, Iris picked up her lance.

"I can't let you have your way, Adam," Iris whispered as lightning cracked behind her.

"And I will nonetheless." Adam lifted his sword. "Because my imagination is greater than yours."

He made the first strike, and the impact made the earth shudder. The Tower of Babel wept and howled as Iris slid back, just barely holding off his sword. The soles of her feet were torn, but she ignored the pain. For Adam's next strike had come, this time from above. She held up her lance to protect her head, but he kept pounding at her relentlessly, ruthlessly.

"What's wrong, Iris?" Adam shouted, laughing, as he swung his sword against her lance again and again. Each hit driving her deeper into the earth. "Is this all you have?"

Iris knew she had to find a way to shift from defense to offense. She remembered the training the Dahomey military had given her, sucked in a breath, and lunged for him. *You must have no fear.* No. Iris wouldn't fear. The world she believed in was at stake.

Adam bent back, dodging the jab, slipping underneath her before swiping at her legs. He was fast. Faster than she was.

It was the wing! As he flapped it, it propelled him forward, letting his body cut through the wind. But it was more than that. The hatred it represented was fuel. It blotted out whatever hesitation had come from his or Hiva's intertwined hearts.

"My imagination is greater than yours," Adam repeated through gritted teeth. "My family. My heritage. My wealth. My power. The future I will create. All of it. You never deserved to be the god."

For one split moment, Iris remembered that little body who'd carried her crystal heart to the fair exhibition to bring her back to life. Adam's single black wing took him high into the sky. Hovering there, he looked down at her, the hurt and shame vivid in his blue eyes.

"You *never deserved to be the god!*"

He launched himself down at her. The swing of his sword was disastrous. The tower shook. Debris exploded from beneath Iris's feet. The impact broke Iris's lance in two.

Rasping heavily, Iris stumbled back and leaped away before he could strike again. He'd almost cut her in two, and he wasn't stopping. She held on to both ends of the broken bone lance as he swiped at her again and again. All she could do was dodge. It was only a matter of time. Only a matter of time before Necron's power was his and his sick imagination became reality.

What is the perfect world? You've walked among them for eons. Should you not know the answer by now, my child?

Necron's voice, soft and curious. Was it a memory? Or was it . . . ?

Don't give up on yourself! Iris heard a cry through the cracks of thunder. It'd come from outside of Adam's dream, deep within the earth's core. A battle cry.

"Granny," Iris whispered, and stood her ground. The tranquility of the old woman's dream seeped into her bones. She thought of Max's vampire hunting and Lulu's chain of hands across the world. She thought of herself and Jinn dancing for eternity.

This place was a world of imagination. Human civilization was a world of imagination. Then why not imagine it? Why not dare?

Iris had walked among humanity for eons, and she *had* learned one thing:

To dare takes courage.

Iris took the pieces of the bone lance and imagined it anew. In a haze of mist, the pieces had joined. It had become a weapon Iris had come to trust. A weapon Iris respected from a woman she had loved with all her heart.

Iris held Rin's white crystal sword at the ready and began to attack. She met each of Adam's strikes with her own, her power growing with her confidence, her outrageous determination to dream the wildest of dreams. Adam's black wing flapped, carrying him away from her toward the tower, but Iris followed, allowing her body to lift from the ground, weightless. This was Necron's core, after all. Why couldn't she?

Around Adam's Tower of Babel they clashed swords. From deep within the tower of waste and misery, Iris heard John Temple's voice.

"I'm sorry, Adam. . . . I'm sorry, my boy. . . ."

"Shut up!" Adam hissed, and struck Iris's sword with the greatest blow yet as they whizzed around the pillar. "You never did a damn thing for me, you old fool."

So much pain was in those blue eyes. His sadness. His frailty. And somehow that potential for forgiveness. Was that why Adam had felt he'd needed Doctor Pratt's hatred? To make him stronger?

Iris blocked the clash of his sword, her feet sweeping past something slimy on the surface of the tower. Trash or flesh, she did not know, but Adam pushed her up toward the stone statue as the onslaught continued.

"You endured the kind of tragic loss that no one ever should," Iris told him as she blocked his strikes. "But there is so much good we can do in the wake of tragedy. So much healing if we trust each other. If we help each other!"

"Save your words of wisdom," Adam spat. "I've made up my mind."

Iris watched as his black wing quivered in fury. "I know," she whispered. "So have I."

Ducking his swing, she flew back and kicked him onto the statue. They drew their swords at the same time. And somewhere in the distance, a voice called out to her again, this time also echoing in her mind as if it were a memory. It was Lulu. And she spoke as if she'd been asked a very simple question: *What kind of world do you want to live in?*

A world where nobody hurts each other, Lulu answered.

Adam did not hear it. He would not hear it. He readied his sword.

A world where you could be who you wanted, or a world where you could

eat as much as you like, or a world where who had money and who didn't
have money didn't matter.

Iris readied hers.

They struck.

But in the end, it all came down to that: a world where nobody hurt each
other.

Iris moved at just the right time. She dropped Rin's sword and caught his.
With her hands bleeding, she pulled the blade out of Adam's hand.

And then she pulled him into a hug.

It was more damaging than any blow. Helpless, confused whispers
escaped his mouth like splatters of blood. They remained there, frozen in the
sky, Adam's body twitching in the embrace he'd always so desired but that now
seemed to sap away all his power.

"I'll create a better world for all of us," Iris whispered into his ear. "I
promise."

When she let him go, Adam let his body fall upon his statue, upon the back
of the Adam Temple he wanted to be. He lay upon it, his eyes wide and his
breathing ragged. Tears streamed down his cheeks. He'd been defeated.

And that was what Necron had wanted.

For Iris understood now. The meaning of the coin. The meaning of a
choice. She'd been created not to destroy humanity but to give it another
chance. Necron had never failed to give humanity another chance after Hiva
had brought them to an end. That was because a better world was what
Necron wished for too. And she wanted her Hiva to decide to fight *for* it, not
against it.

The other Hiva's suspicions had been right all along. There *was* another
path for them. Not to destroy humanity but to guide them. To help humanity
live peacefully with the earth—with one another.

She'd already taken the first step in letting Adam live. And now she would
take the next step—the one Necron never could manage, no matter how badly
she desired it. There would be no more war. No sickness. No invaders from
another dimension. Iris would make it so.

Iris landed upon the ground where Rin's sword had fallen and picked it up. Then she faced Necron in the distance and held aloft Rin's sword to the lightning and thunder in the sky.

"Necron!" she cried.

But Necron resisted, hesitant to hand over her power to another. Could it really be? Was it really possible? Necron still couldn't quite imagine it. Still couldn't dare to, despite all she'd done to bring Iris here.

Don't give up on yourself, my dear, Granny said.

Don't give up on yourself! Rin chimed in from behind the clouds.

"Necron!" Iris roared, her hands bloodied from the battle but holding the hilt of the sword nonetheless. There was another way. Her way. She would make her dream come true.

I believe in you, Iris! Max.

We believe in you! Berta.

So many voices joined theirs. So many voices had seen into Iris's heart, seen the kind of world she wanted to create, and agreed. And as they did, flowers began to sprout from the dead earth. Grass began to cover the fields. And Adam's Tower of Babel crumbled to dust.

Yes, there were angry voices among the bunch.

How dare you be the one to dictate all of our lives?

You, who are nothing more than a woman! A beast of burden!

It didn't matter if there were others who weren't happy. Those who thought that the very idea of sharing this world without oppression was a blight upon reason.

Well, damn *reason, then!* Iris decided.

She was tired of apologizing. Tired of compromising. Tired of being given names. Tired of living in the imagination of others.

She believed in herself. Her loved ones believed in her. She would make something new. Something *better.*

Iris! Jinn's scream shattered the earth. *Do it, Iris!*

"Necron!" Iris roared one more time, the word clearing the heavens, sweeping away the lightning and thunder. With all her might, she roared the name of the One who'd created her as the power of her imagination brought love and life to the broken world in Adam's dream.

And at last Necron relented.

It is time, she said.

EPILOGUE

THE YEARS PASSED AS THEY ALWAYS did. And the earth thrived.

With its lush forests and deep hills.

With its beautiful mountains and sparkling oceans.

Animals and all manner of life.

But what about humanity, the ill-fated species that once again populated the earth? What kind of society had they created?

To be honest, it doesn't much matter.

Where people lived and slept.

How they aged and who they loved.

The technology at their fingertips. What they did for fun and pleasure.

The contours of the organization known as "society" aren't so meaningful. By all means, imagine it as you please.

What mattered to Iris was that Lulu's dream had come true: *A world where you could be who you wanted. A world where nobody hurt each other.*

Iris had shrugged her shoulders and said, "Why not?" And so made it happen.

All of humanity was reborn. Her friends and family. Even her enemies. *Let them all have a second chance.* Within the parameters of the world she created, they would be much happier.

Iris was the goddess of this earth. She would watch over it and humanity for eons. That was the pledge she'd made. Humanity would coexist with life forever.

But she did not watch them from inside the earth's core, where dead souls waited to be reborn.

She had another tiny little dream. One born out of selfishness. But one she made come true nonetheless.

A happy little dream she'd had once.

In the West Coast of Africa, Iris ran through the forests, the flowers and grass crunching underneath her feet. He was chasing her again. It was one of his favorite things to do because she would pant happily, giggle, and gasp at even the thought that he'd catch her.

Seagulls flocked over the treetops. Soon the light broke through, and she could see the bright sun and the eternally clear air.

At the rocky edge of a waterfall, she stopped. That was strange. She could hear the leopards and the buzzing of insects. The parrots in the trees. Most of all, she could hear the rushing water plummeting to the earth below. But she couldn't hear him.

Had he stopped chasing her? Had he given up?

How *stupid*.

"That crank. When I said he wouldn't catch me, I didn't actually mean it—" A shriek escaped her lips once she felt arms sweep her off the rocks. The shriek turned to chuckles the moment she looked up and saw his irritated face gazing down at her.

"Would you stop calling me that?"

She couldn't help but smirk at his scowl. Half the time they spent with each other, he'd pretend to be annoyed at the tiniest things she did. Considering they spent every minute with each other, that was quite the feat.

"You said I could call you what I want!" She shrugged. "'Crank' suits you well."

Her partner rolled his eyes. "I told you I don't remember that."

Indeed, none of her friends had retained the memories from when they were in Necron's core. Max, at least, had had fun hearing about his vampire escapades and decided to give it a try, but only Cherice was game. Berta had told her brother that she hated childish games and declared she wanted to visit Lulu and her family, spending time with them first before giving in to her brother's silly comic-strip fantasies.

Rin had finally taken Granny back home to West Africa, newly freed from plunder and colonization. With the help of Rin's friend Abiade, they'd settled in Abeokuta, telling stories of their pasts in the tongue they both shared: Yoruba. Granny had found another daughter to love. But she and Rin would not be alone for long. They had made their friends promise to visit them. Berta and Lulu were already planning their trip across the Atlantic.

Soon they would *all* make that trip. The Fanciful Freaks bonded by fate. Abeokuta would be the place of their reunion. And every year they would celebrate their new beginning. It had been Iris's idea—the new tradition she'd started. One she aimed to continue forever.

Iris looked up at Jinn and sighed. "So then what should I call you? I like 'Emin.'"

He gave her the tiniest grin. "I do too."

She tapped his nose and gave him a kiss. The life she made, she'd made for herself.

She nestled into Emin's chest and screamed with delight as he gripped her tightly and jumped down into the water.

Her laughter and his echoed across the treetops.

ACKNOWLEDGMENTS

This project was a huge undertaking that required the efforts of a number of amazing people. I'd like to thank them now. First, Sarah McCabe, the best editor anyone can ask for, and the entire amazing and hardworking team at Simon & Schuster. Nicole, seeing you geek out in the comments of the copy-edits gave me so much joy. Thank you all so much for giving me the time and space I needed to figure out this huge story and bring it to an epic close. Thank you to my agent, Natalie Lakosil, for selling this project in the first place and always being down for the wild ride of my chaotic ideas.

Sometimes I wonder if my ideas are *too* chaotic! Since childhood, my imagination has always been a little out there. Once I decided to become an author, I started to worry—maybe that out-there-ness of my creativity would hold me back from reaching readers. But eventually, I gained the courage to tell the stories I wanted to tell without apology. It really took people to believe in me, my writing, and my vision to get me to this point. That includes the first editors to ever say "yes" to my projects. But it also includes the fans who continue to geek out with me over this series. Your encouragement is what keeps me writing.

I want to thank Lakehead University and fellow faculty members for celebrating my books, and all the enthusiastic librarians and booksellers who put these books in people's hands. Most importantly, I want to thank God and my family, who are with me every step of the way.

This is starting to sound like an Oscars acceptance speech. But when you finish a trilogy, it does kind of feel like you should be holding a gold statue while crying onstage in a packed auditorium filled with wine-drinking A-listers. It's such an emotional process that it can be easy to just want to give up. I never did because of you guys. And I never will.

I wrote this book during one of the toughest and saddest periods of my life because I wanted to imagine something better. I hope after finishing this series, you can start imagining too.

ABOUT THE AUTHOR

Sarah Raughley grew up in Southern Ontario writing stories about freakish little girls with powers because she secretly wanted to be one. She is a huge fangirl of anything from manga to sci-fi/fantasy TV to Japanese role-playing games and other geeky things, all of which have largely inspired her writing. Sarah has been nominated for the Aurora Award for Best YA Novel and works in the community doing writing workshops for youths and adults. On top of being a YA writer, Sarah has a PhD in English, which makes her a doctor, so it turns out she didn't have to go to medical school after all. As an academic, Sarah has taught undergraduate courses and acted as a postdoctoral fellow. Her research concerns representations of race and gender in popular media culture, youth culture, and postcolonialism. She has written and edited articles in political, cultural, and academic publications. She continues to use her voice for good. You can find her online at SarahRaughley.com.